Felicity Knight is a former teacher who specialized in English and History. She grew up in rural Worcestershire and now lives in South Yorkshire. Felicity is married, with two sons and a granddaughter. She has three novels already published in the genre of historical family sagas.

Website address: http://www.felicityknightauthor.co.uk/

Other books by Felicity Knight:

Carenza's Journey

Carenza's Heirs

The Secrets of Westborough Hall

Dedication

To my granddaughter Amber with love

Felicity Knight

THE DEVINE GIRLS

With best wishes
Felicity Knight.

Austin Macauley Publishers™
LONDON • CAMBRIDGE • NEW YORK • SHARJAH

Copyright Felicity Knight (2017)

The right of Felicity Knight to be identified as author of this work has been asserted by him in accordance with section 77 and 78 of the Copyright, Designs and Patents Act 1988.

All rights reserved. No part of this publication may be reproduced, stored in a retrieval system, or transmitted in any form or by any means, electronic, mechanical, photocopying, recording, or otherwise, without the prior permission of the publishers.

Any person who commits any unauthorised act in relation to this publication may be liable to criminal prosecution and civil claims for damages.

A CIP catalogue record for this title is available from the British Library.

ISBN 9781788235761 (Paperback)
ISBN 9781788235778 (Hardback)
ISBN 9781788235785 (E-Book)
www.austinmacauley.com

First Published (2017)
Austin Macauley Publishers Ltd™
25 Canada Square
Canary Wharf
London
E14 5LQ

Acknowledgements

Thanks to my husband, for his meticulous research for the historical elements of this novel. Also my family, for their IT support, and my sister Judith Milne, for the creation of the novel's front cover.

Prologue

The years after the War had seen the Devine family prosper instead of languishing as many great families and their businesses had done. The Westborough estate was indeed a business and its success was partly down to Thea's running of the land during her years at the helm. She had possessed foresight and an energy which would have reduced others to exhaustion. She had learnt as she went along and had indeed been an apt pupil.

Piers could not have been more proud of her achievements but now that he was home, life had turned out better than they could ever have expected. Piers had decided to put the land in the hands of an old employee, Robert Harper, who had returned from the front badly injured, but his knowledge of the land allowed him to do a desk job on the estate to oversee the running of it. It had always been Piers' intentions to inveigle back as many employees as possible; people he knew and could trust. Many of the men returning home had lost interest in their former lives for their experiences had affected them badly. However, Piers tempted some men by paying better rates than the usual farm worker could expect and as good as the factories in the cities and towns. There was enough credit in the pot to do so. His father had always said that if you looked after the estate workers, the farm would flourish and so it had. It also gave some of the former soldiers' time to heal mentally, but physically was another issue. Piers knew only too well what it was like to suffer mentally and was only just beginning to heal. The land had a way of soothing troubled waters, allowing its yield to bring a purpose to a man's skills coupled with Mother Nature.

Thea had not minded giving up her work on the land although some women found it difficult to return to being a housewife tied to the kitchen sink. But Thea's life had taken a dramatic turn since the end of the War. She had become Piers' Countess and had produced the heir to the Devine inheritance. She had fulfilled her role but it had not quite ended there for along came Harry and Verity. She felt fulfilled having produced the family she had always wanted. It was a house full of children including the three elder girls, two of whom were the daughters of Piers' first wife, Mary, and then there was Scarlett, Thea's daughter by Jack Carson, who had been killed in the War; he was a war hero and had received a medal for gallantry posthumously. It was a lively household when everybody was home but there was also friction which at times spoilt the atmosphere within much to Thea's chagrin. She was the earth mother who wanted everyone's life to be filled with happiness. Although she was blessed with many children of her own, she had taken Mary and Piers' daughters to her heart and loved them as her own. But it was Piers who was lost in his relationship with Jane and Maudie. They had been babies when he had been sent to France with his unit in 1940 and had remained a POW for most of the War. Mary's death after Maudie's birth had left the two little girls like orphans if Thea had not taken them under her wing.

As time went on, the younger Devine children basked in the sunshine of their father's attention while the older girls were left to their own devices, except for Thea's unconditional love. Their father often wondered if other soldiers had fared in the same way with children they had hardly seen during those lost years. He tried to push the problem away, but Thea was his conscience and that troubled him.

Part 1

Chapter 1

Clarissa Devine, Dowager Countess of Westborough, sat erect and dignified on the edge of the Edwardian chaise longue which stood in her parlour having occupied the same position for decades. The walking cane which she had used to aid her mobility for the past few years was in her hands as she began to rise slowly and stiffly to her feet. She was tall of stature and when standing was an imposing sight despite the fact that age and the anxiety of the War years had no doubt taken its heavy toll upon her. But had it not done that for every other family in the land? Her eyes, still sharp and bright, swept around the room which she had made her own ever since her permanent occupation of the Dower House. The valuable ornaments had belonged to previous generations of the Devine family, but she had used her talents to transform the previously drab interior into a luxurious and comfortable home where she entertained at her will. There had once been a time when she had never wished to leave the Hall but now the Dower House had become her refuge, one of peace and tranquillity, away from the wars which were fought ferociously within the walls of her former home and now the threat had reached the threshold of this house. Her face was taut and her lips drawn in a tight line showing her displeasure. The people who had known her in the early days of her marriage and into her early widowhood would say that was her natural demeanour, but that was not the case these days for she had mellowed over the years enjoying the new life that had unravelled over time.

Clarissa took her time to walk to the window to look out onto the splendid gardens which were shared with the big house. Buds were appearing on the trees heralding spring. In the borders surrounding the lawns, daffodils swayed in the gentle breeze under a blue heaven. How she loved this time of year. Bleakly, she wondered how many more springs she would see now that she had entered her ninth decade. Where had all that time gone?

The room was deathly quiet but a figure was hunched miserably on the ancient sofa. It was Lady Jane Devine who did not know how to react to her fearsome grandmother's impending wrath. She regarded the older woman with trepidation. Her grandmother was the only one in her family who made her feel thus. Wishing she had not come to ask the question, Jane also knew that she had no alternative after the unbearable atmosphere which pervaded the Hall, all of which was of her own making. Clarissa turned her stiff body to regard her granddaughter, her facial expression inscrutable.

'You will not come and live here Jane,' the older woman said firmly, never raising her voice but her words specifically chosen had a way of sending shivers of apprehension into the people who were the victims of her wrath. 'You will stay with your family at the Hall and make some kind of recompense for your appalling behaviour. It is time you took full responsibility for your own actions and be prepared to suffer the consequences that your parents will decide upon in due course.'

Jane pulled a face, now knowing that this only grandparent that she possessed and had ever known had turned against her too. Her face had contorted in rage making her look ugly although in reality she had inherited the good looks of the Devines.

'You're as bad as they are,' she spat out her words shrewishly. 'My father does not know me properly even after all this time and that woman, his wife, is not my mother.' The tears now came in a torrent as she sobbed uncontrollably knowing that her words were vicious intending them to reach their mark.

Clarissa looked at her eldest grandchild, concern etching her features but she was not about to give in to emotional blackmail. In some ways Jane was telling the truth. Her son, the Earl, was not an indulgent parent with his eldest daughters. That fact was true enough although she knew that he had tried to make up for his long absence as a POW during the War Years. But there was still a reserve between himself and the older children. The important bonding which comes from the beginning of a child's life to love and protect an infant was not fully there. It would have been wrong to say that he did not care about these children. In fact he had a deep and abiding affection for them but he did not know how to show them the full tide of emotion that they deserved. It was no wonder that all three girls had caused so much trouble over the years. However, the story had been quite different with his three younger children who had been born after the war. They were sweet and compliant and had become the apples of his eye. Clarissa deplored bad behaviour but she had some sympathy for the older children and had decided to have sharp words with her son whether he believed that she was interfering or not. However, Jane's reference to her father's wife, Thea, was etched with a feeling of undeniable contempt and that Clarissa was not going to tolerate. Her daughter-in-law had been instrumental in holding the Devine family together and keeping the Hall and the estate running smoothly when the men were far away during the War years. The debt in Clarissa's mind could never be repaid. Thea had melted the Dowager's iceberg of a heart during the years of the war and they had become firm friends. It was Thea who had become father and mother to Piers' motherless daughters during that time as well as raising her own child. Clarissa regarded her spoilt granddaughter and decided that the problem had to be dealt with now. There was no way that Thea was going to be spoken of in this way by her granddaughter who should by now know her privileged position in this new world which had changed so dramatically since the War. It was a world changed to one of frivolity with the old order of things disappearing before their eyes. Clarissa could understand that those days had been bleak and now the world was turning on its head. She moved to look at Jane whose red, blotchy face was tortured by anger and guilt.

'That woman, Thea Devine, is the only mother you have known. Your own mother was a useless creature who never really wanted children.' Clarissa watched Jane flinch at the cruel words she had inflicted but she knew them to be honest and true. But she knew the truth had to be stated plainly as Jane had lit a candle in her heart for the mother who had deserted her in death at a very early age. Jane was clinging to the one parent whom she believed had loved her truly without an awareness of the full facts. Clarissa only ever told the truth however harsh the words. Cruel to be kind often ran through her mind but there was a fundamental kindness in her heart for the people she loved so much.

Jane had been deep in thought but suddenly she heard her grandmother still talking angrily, 'Thea has brought you and Maudie up as her own children. She has loved you as if you were her own, as if she had given birth to you herself. During the War years she sacrificed her youth to make Westborough work for the whole family and to keep it going until your father returned home. We all owe her a debt of gratitude. Now leave me alone until you have learnt to behave like a young lady and not a shrew. You show no gratitude for what people do for you. The world does not owe you young lady. It is what you can do for others. We are a privileged class and it is our duty to help the less fortunate of society. This great family has always treated the estate workers as if they are part of us. If they hurt we hurt too. That has always been the Devine way of thinking for centuries and will continue while there are still Devines at Westborough.'

Clarissa eased her stiff bones onto the chaise thinking about the Westborough Estate but more particularly about Jane's perception of Thea. The Dowager could honestly say that she loved Thea as if she had been her own daughter and would never hear a bad word said against her daughter-in-law. Thea had proved to be a good wife to her son Piers and it had been a true love match that had been made in Heaven despite all the early problems that had tried their alliance of the heart.

Clarissa still deep in her reverie did not hear Jane rise from the sofa to make an exit from the room. Tears smudged her cheeks as she made her way out of the Dower House into the spring sunshine feeling unloved and unwanted. The lovely weather which should have lifted her spirits had little impact upon her mood. She had thought that her grandmother's home might be a safe harbour away from the battles within Westborough Hall. Her father was full of venom and vitriol at the news that she had been expelled from school for the second time within the past year. She knew that she had been unreasonable about Thea and her grandmother had been quite correct in her defence of her stepmother. Thea had always sprung to the defence of the children however bad their misdemeanours. Now Jane felt that she must have lost her love as well. Unconditional love was not part of her psyche and she had no knowledge that her extreme selfishness was part of her age.

Walking through the gardens, Jane took her time to reflect on her grandmother's words. She knew the dowager was correct in her assessment of the situation. Thea was the nearest she had ever known to a mother. There had been rumours circulating about her mother from time to time but she knew little about her except for the fact that she had died soon after Maudie's birth. Even Thea refused to comment on the matter except to say that Mary had been a true friend to her and her death had caused much grief but there the story ended. She could not ask her father whose temper would flair every time Mary's name was mentioned. Jane knew why she caused trouble. She had analysed her behaviour and realized that it was the only way she could gain attention from her father even if it was for all the wrong reasons. She just wanted his love but instead only gained his wrath.

Piers Devine, Earl of Westborough, was also in a reflective mood. He sat brooding at his desk in his study having made several telephone calls to suitable public schools about placing his eldest daughter in their care. It was not easy to tell educational establishments that Jane was a wild child who flouted convention and the idea of a formal schooling. He was waiting to hear from three schools who had promised to make a decision shortly.

The door to the estate study opened and Thea Devine slipped into the room quietly. She crossed the room placing her hands on her husband's shoulders gently massaging the knot she felt lingering there. Her presence always had a soothing affect upon him. Their love for each other was as strong as it had been before the War. He turned to face her, his eyes showing the love he felt while Thea bent to kiss his lips with passion.

'No news yet?' she asked as she sat on a vacant chair facing him. She looked with concern at the dark shadows under his eyes knowing that he had not slept properly since the news of Jane's second expulsion had been made known to him.

'Not yet, Thea. I just feel that I don't know what to do with her anymore.'

'Then don't do anything. Let her leave school if she doesn't want to be there. Find her something to do on the estate. Idle hands and all that, or send her to finishing school in Switzerland before she is introduced at court. Before you know it she will be married. What you must do is talk to her, Piers. Show her the love you have for her for that is what she is seeking. You have to show that you care for the girls. I know that you do but do they know, Piers?'

'I don't know if they know. I have tried, Thea, but there is always something that holds me back. It is so much easier with our younger children. I was there from the start and it all came so easily then.'

'You have to sort this, Piers, and the longer it goes on the worse it will become. I can't help you on this one even though I try to reassure the girls but they need to hear it from you.'

'I know,' he said placing his head in his hands hoping that all the problems would vanish and he knew that was the cowardly way out. Piers had once more brushed the problem away burying his head in the sand like an ostrich.

Thea left Piers to his troubled thoughts knowing that on this occasion he had to find the solution to the demons that troubled him. Pulling the study door softly closed behind her she crossed the sumptuous, panelled hall of the old house. It never ceased to amaze her about the feeling of pride she felt about belonging to such a building which had been in the hands of the Devines since Elizabethan times. As the Countess she felt responsible for giving her time and energy to the upkeep of the building. Unlike some great houses the Devines did not need to open the doors of their home to the public. Some great families had fallen onto hard times and that was the only way that they could afford to maintain the properties and keep them for the generations to come. Westborough Hall was a genuine home which the entire family hoped to keep that way.

Thea entered the small drawing room which she had claimed as her personal sanctuary. The family only went there when invited; even Piers obeyed these unwritten rules. It was Thea's holy of holies away from family life where she could relax and think. The afternoon was still bright outside. Out in the great hall she heard heavy footsteps, feet dragging wearily on the flagstones as if life was a burden. Knowing that it was Jane, her heart told her to go to the child, to put her arms around her but it was Piers who should be doing that even if the girl was at fault. There were reasons for everything she mused. In the distance a door banged in anger, making Thea sigh and wish for peace. Her thoughts drifted back over the last decade remembering the good times with the man she loved. She hoped that there would be more of those times as the family grew back together in happiness and love.

Chapter 2

Lord Harry Devine had been born in January 1947 just as the bad winter was about to take hold. He had been a lusty baby and the heir to the Devine fortunes. It had been the culmination of Piers' ambitions to have an heir to inherit the estate and his gratitude to the woman he had loved for so long during the long years of the war knew no bounds. In the rare time he had to himself he had often thanked God for his good fortune in being able to marry Thea. The lost hope he had suffered during his incarceration in a POW camp had made him depressed but on his return to Westborough a set of events unbeknown to him had been unravelled allowing the young lovers to marry and move forward with their lives. It was during their time alone together that they would discuss the good fortune that had eventually become theirs but the heartache of all the lies and secrets had also taken their toll. Uncannily, it had been the war that had been their ally in the end when Beatrice Cavendish, Thea's alleged mother, had been killed in the Blitz and all had been revealed about her parentage disproving the fact that Thea and Piers had been half brother and sister. There had been no rush to get married for they required time to get to know each other once more after the long years of the war. But then Thea's revelation of her pregnancy and the possibility of an heir for Westborough had hastened their union much to their joy and that of the dowager countess.

It had taken Piers a considerable time to adjust to the freedoms of civilian life. He knew that he was not alone in this for many servicemen had suffered in a similar fashion. But Thea, he knew had been so patient with him allowing him all the time in the world to make adjustments back into his old life. The old order of things had also changed. Women demanded greater freedom and men did not always want to return to the land when they could get better paid jobs in the factories in the towns and cities. There also had to be changes on the farm. Much of the fields were turned over to arable farming and the newest of machinery was bought to assist in the farming processes. However, there were the older families who still wanted to work the land and some young men who had suffered in various ways during the war years were glad to experience the solitude that working the land gave them.

Piers also took solace from such activities. He rolled up his sleeves and worked hard alongside his employees. There was a satisfaction to being physically tired at the end of the day and when he returned home he could enjoy time with Thea and his family. All these things gladdened his heart as he learned to enjoy his freedom after years in the camp. He knew that in some respects he had had a far easier time during the war than many had experienced but they all had their demons to exorcise. He had thought about returning to his seat in the House of Lords but he still needed time before he was ready for that as well. He had been shocked that his great hero Winston Churchill had lost the election when he had done so much for the country. His valiant speeches had rallied the people into believing that victory would come even if it was at a price taking the lives of young soldiers who had fought for their country subsequently paying the ultimate sacrifice. He could not forgive the voting public for casting such a man aside, a man who returned to the backbenches with dignity and his tremendous wit intact. How could they elect Clement Atlee, the leader of the Labour Party to take the nation back to prosperity after all that had been spent on the war effort? The euphoria of victory did not last forever when the economic problems of the day beckoned to be solved. Piers shook his head in despair when he contemplated these matters.

It was during this time that Clarissa, the Dowager Countess, made her declaration that she would retreat to the Dower House. That time when she had been banished from the Hall had caused her much humiliation all those years ago but now she was ready to go of her own accord.

'You don't have to go Mama,' Piers had said, so grateful for his mother's help to run the Hall during the war years.

She had smiled at him, the son that she loved so much. 'I want to go Piers. I am old now and I value some peace and quiet away from your growing family.'

The house seemed full of children these days and she knew that she would never be lonely. Thea would walk the short distance through the gardens pushing her grandson in his old and battered pram while Nanny Barnes would walk with the girls to see their grandmother. There would be no shortage of company but these days she was happy by herself too. Sometimes solitude could be advantageous, thinking your own thoughts, remembering days gone by whether good or bad. Never had she thought that she could be so content for her youth and young womanhood had brought her only shame and aggravation during her marriage to the old Earl, James Devine. Now, age was a merit that she had never thought she would enjoy.

They had relaxed into her marriage to Piers. His return home in the late summer of 1945 had not been as she imagined. His mood had been distant after the initial euphoria of his return. He had become reclusive and diffident until his mother had finally intervened to reveal the facts about their relationship. There had been no kinship between them. This had opened up their lives and real life possibilities had taken over. They had been happy and fulfilled in their love for each other. After Harry's appearance, there came Charlie and the afterthought but much loved Verity whose sweetness had captured Piers' heart more than he could say. The little Devines as they were often referred to bring a breath of fresh air to the atmosphere of the Hall compared with the arguments of their older siblings, Jane, Maudie and Scarlett.

Scarlett was the quietest of the three older girls; she was Thea's daughter by her short marriage to Jack Carson who had died in North Africa in 1942. Thea had told her daughter about her father on numerous occasions but if she was totally honest she had not known him well having spent more time apart than together during their brief marriage. It had been a marriage on the rebound when Thea believed that there was no hope in her relationship with Piers. She had met Jack in London on leave from his regiment. She had liked him a lot. He had been kind and dependable and loving. The knowledge that she was expecting Scarlett had accelerated their wedding plans. Thea could not have been happier as she wanted a child of her own more than anything. Jack had little or no family and suddenly finding that they would be a family unit had made his departure for war more bearable for there was a reason to want to come home on leave and see them. But none of this reached fruition after he had died a hero on the battlefield saving someone else's life. Thea had never failed in her duty to tell her daughter about Jack's heroism. The child kept his medals as her pride and joy and as the years passed she fantasized about what her relationship with her father would have been like had he lived. She wanted to know his family history but there was little that Thea could tell her. Jack had said his family was dead and as Thea had never met them there was little she could say on the matter. This did not prevent Scarlett's imagination from taking full rein from time to time. Over time Piers had suggested adopting Thea's daughter but Scarlett had resisted this offer, often saying that she had a daddy in Heaven. Thea had always maintained that Scarlet should make the decision on this matter however young she was. But her decision could be reversed at any time. Scarlett had never changed her mind over the years feeling that it made her a little different from the others and this individuality she wore like a badge of pride knowing what a hero her father had been.

As she matured the mysteries of her origins set her adrift from the two older Devine girls giving her a mystique that they envied. Yet in another way they were as close as sisters could be as they were born within eighteen months of each other and had grown up in the nursery together. They had regarded themselves as sisters and referred to each other as such while in the company of people outside their circle. Scarlett had never officially accepted the Devine name but often signed her name Scarlett Devine out of habit. She was an enigma which her own mother could not always solve but love her she did, as she loved all the children in this complex network called family.

Jane Devine, the eldest of the Devine girls, had been the leader of the children in the nursery. She, like her siblings, was highly intelligent: her fertile imagination had led the little girls into endless mischief as they outwitted the nursery staff and their governess. Even Thea who ruled first and foremost through love found her task as mother and father quite daunting as she had to mete out discipline. But it was Clarissa who took the children to task on their misdemeanours. She was an aristocrat who had seen how children of the great houses had been disciplined at the end of the Victorian era. The children had been terrified of her haughty manner, as she demanded respect and good manners. Her tenacity had paid off over time as the children began their lessons to become disciplined members of their class. It had made Thea laugh as she witnessed Clarissa's success but she was full of admiration for the old woman's sagacity. There was also a great love for these children which over time they had come to realize. They never crossed the divide with their grandmother again in their early childhood.

Maudie was a younger version of Jane whom she hero worshipped in those early childhood days. She had been left motherless at just a few weeks old and had been spoilt in the nursery like her sister. But oddly the two girls did not resemble each other physically at all. Jane had inherited the Devine features and those of her grandmother but Maudie took after her mother Mary. She had dark curly hair which hung in ringlets naturally and her dark expressive eyes melted the hearts of the people who met her. She did not possess Jane's wild streak but she could be quietly naughty which made her a good partner in crime for nursery antics. Piers was fascinated by this second daughter trying to find the character that had forged his dead wife but Maudie was her own person from the day that she was born. Somehow there was an alliance between all three girls that could never be broken. There was a divide which school friends could not cross without fear of hurting the three who would always be there for each other. They were called the Three Musketeers, there for one and one for all.

Thea did not want them to go away to school but be educated at home like she had been. If she was honest she did not want them thrust into a world which was tough, hardening them before their time. It had been her first real argument with Piers which had resulted in them not speaking for a week. They had lain back to back in bed in their stubbornness each wishing the other to capitulate but it had not happened. It was one of Clarissa's visits to the Hall which had won the day. Piers had gone up to London to the House and Thea had invited the Dowager to the Hall for afternoon tea which they took sitting in the large sitting room by the log fire. The day outside was blustery and cold.

'What have you and Piers been fighting about? 'The old woman asked anxiously.

'Has Piers been telling tales out of school?' Thea asked churlishly looking with venom at the older woman.

'Of course not,' Clarissa said placidly, 'but it does not require much intelligence to see that things are not well between you.' Clarissa bent and patted Thea's arm. She was now more tactile than she had ever been in her life.

Thea suddenly broke into loud sobs.

'Surely it can't be that bad,' Clarissa said.

'He wants to send the children away to school. He said that it would be the making of them.'

Clarissa chuckled. 'Is this what it is all about? All this hoo-haa over nothing.'

'It is not over nothing,' Thea snapped back. 'You and Piers are plotting this together.'

Suddenly Clarissa's face changed like a cloud passing over the sun. 'Thea pull yourself together,' she said sharply. 'Those girls need the discipline of school. They are naughty and wilful and anyway it is what our class does these days. Do you want them to appear different from their peers?'

'Well the pair of you can do what you want with Jane and Maudie but Scarlett is my daughter.'

'You want Scarlett to be treated differently from the others. You want to make her feel that she is of inferior birth and not worthy of an education. She is a clever girl and might go to university one day. There are so many opportunities for the young now.'

There was a silence while Thea reflected on such matters. She was amazed at Clarissa's forward thinking for an old woman still stuck in a Victorian Age. There was no way that Thea wanted Scarlett to appear different from the older Devine girls for in her heart she knew that Verity would go away to school when the time came. Tradition would demand it.

Clarissa watched her daughter-in-law closely and observed her begin to soften towards the idea. Thea knew that she had no jurisdiction over Jane and Maudie but could she fail to give Scarlett the same opportunities as her siblings. She knew the answer to that question and imagined Scarlett's wrath when she had been denied such opportunities.

'Where would they go to school?' Thea asked.

Clarissa knew that the battle had been won. She smiled. She had discussed this at length with Piers. In fact Piers had asked his mother to intervene on the matter knowing how close her relationship to Thea was. The battle of wills had lasted too long.

'Piers was thinking of sending them to St. Mary's the prep school in Malvern. They could become weekly boarders and have the best of both worlds. And then when the time comes they could go on to be educated in the public schools in Malvern or Cheltenham. They are all very close to us my dear. If I am honest Piers put their names down soon after his return from Germany, even Scarlett's I'm afraid.'

There was silence once more but Clarissa touched Thea's hand in a gesture of conciliation and love. She had noticed the moue that Thea had made with her mouth. Piers had done this without regard to her feelings. She felt that was unforgiveable but....

She rose from her seat and paced the room thinking about the future. It also meant that the younger children would follow suit. She knew that Piers had already put the boys' names down for Eton, his old school. Boys were different though. They coped with the hardships better than the girls. Then she smiled thinking of the three girls and how tough they could be.

Turning to Clarissa she said, 'All right you win. Even Scarlett can go with the others.'

Clarissa was jubilant in her success but she was not prepared to flaunt her victory. She wanted Thea to realize that she had made such a decision herself. It had never been her intention of damaging the close relationship which she shared with the young woman. 'I think you have made the right decision my dear. It is for the best you know. Time will prove it.'

She rose stiffly from her chair taking her walking cane to lean heavily on it for support.

'When is Piers returning from his trip?' She asked.

'I don't know. We haven't been speaking.'

Both women looked at each other momentarily and then laughed. Their humour had been fully restored.

Chapter 3

Clarissa and Piers had been proved correct about sending the girls away to school. Thea acknowledged this some months after they had begun their formal education at St Mary's. They had not suffered at being home tutored for their intelligence and enquiring minds were a testament to that. However, the education they received was broad in every sense of the word. They had areas of the curriculum opened up to them as they were taught by specialists in those subjects; continued education at home would not have allowed this to happen if they had remained in the secure environment of Westborough Hall. They learned to compete and mix with other children of the same age and from a variety of backgrounds. This would set them on the right course for the future. It was not a world any more where aristocracy would just mix with its own class. The two wars had been responsible for that. There was no going back to a bye gone age.

School life proved to be fierce competition in the classroom and on the playing field but it was not unhealthy for it strengthened their characters. The girls loved the great outdoors where they ran for their House or played games at various levels. They played competitive sport against other schools and learned the disappointment that went with failure or the euphoria of success. They learned to share with others. Their manners in public had improved and now when they were home on holiday they spent time with the friends they had made. They were no longer the three Devine girls; each one had their own circle of friends which made them individuals in their own right and yet their allegiance to each other never wavered for it was one which had been forged from the cradle. If one of them was in trouble the others rallied in their support but school had also freed them to become their own person to face what life threw at them.

Thea had to bow to Piers' superior knowledge on this account. It was a success story but Piers did not flaunt this in front of Thea. That was just not his style and the argument that had ensued vanished into the ether, never being mentioned again. There would be no quibbling when it became the turn for the little Devines to follow in the footsteps of the older girls for now it was cast in stone that a formal education was necessary for both girls and boys.

However, the dispute over Piers' relationship with the children had not been addressed. It continued as before much to Thea's chagrin. He seemed to make no attempt to improve the situation and the problem began to grow worse. It would rear its head at weekends and during school holidays when the girls united to bate their father thus spawning his wrath and Thea's bewilderment. She had tried to become the mediator, the go between by lavishing more attention on the girls during this time. She took them places to visit or encouraged them to visit school friends as well as inviting other children to stay on exeat weekends or during the long days of the summer holidays. Piers felt that he could not win because the Hall was constantly filled with noisy children who grew into teenagers. However, he had guessed what Thea was doing and his burden of guilt weighed ever more heavily on his shoulders. The one child he could communicate with on a reasonable level was Scarlett. She was the most amenable of the three but again his conscience would reach new heights when he thought that she was not even his child although he thought of her as such. Deep thinker that he was he wondered if he could not reach Jane and Maudie, his own children, because they had been Mary's children and he knew in all honesty that he had never loved his first wife. She had become tiresome during her two pregnancies and was frightened of the birth process. Subsequently, it had all killed her at the time when Piers had left for France with the Expeditionary Forces in early 1940.

Piers felt that if he visited a psychiatrist to sort out these complex emotions he would only be told the same as his conscience told him. It was easy to blame Mary or the War for these problems but he was the one who ultimately had to find the answers. He knew that Thea and his mother had tried to help him, but he could feel that they too had nearly given up on the situation before they became too worn down by it all.

Chapter 4

Jane had taken to school life more than she had thought possible. She became a natural leader amongst her peers, happy to create mischief at any time of day or night. There were midnight feasts in the dormitory; she was often late for the lessons that she thought were pointless and when the senior girls were allowed into town on their free half day in the week she would sneak out in her own clothes flouting the rules that school uniform was to be worn on such occasions. Sometimes she would need an accomplice to aid and abet her in such matters. She never chose Maudie or Scarlett to help her for she was not prepared to draw them into her ring of mischief. The three girls' loyalty to each other was second to none and they became a closed group when there was trouble looming. On such occasions friends could not penetrate their solidarity and felt left out in the cold, frustrated at their lack of inclusion in this tight knit circle that the Devine girls could suddenly bring to the fore when times and situations dictated it.

However, Jane's leadership skills attracted other miscreants to her circle. Even when they all transferred to their public schools most of their friends followed suit and the old problems continued as before but now there was the extra issue of boys. Jane liked the boys she met when there were events between the different sex public schools. Her Devine good looks attracted attention from the six formers at the neighbouring boys' school. She was fully aware of her effect on others. Her long fair hair worn in braids in school, flowed freely at the upper school dances. She wore the fashion of the time with the tight waists and full skirts which showed off her long, shapely legs to perfection. She attracted the attention of all the boys and became the envy of the wallflowers who sat around the dance floor wondering if their turn would ever come. Jane chose her boyfriends carefully. She was proud of her heritage and her own personal title. She dismissed the snide remarks about her snobbishness; also she failed to remember what her grandmother, Clarissa, said about them being a superior class with a responsibility to the less fortunate. There were many students who attended these schools who were not from titled families but money spoke volumes when privilege could be bought. Thus it was that Jane sought out her titled equals and made secret trysts with them when freedom beckoned but it suddenly became exciting to meet them at other times.

There had been several occasions when Jane had managed to slip out of school after lights out, around ten o'clock for the older girls. There was a sash window, along the corridor from her dormitory, which opened onto a flat roof below. From there she could jump to the ground and run through the school gardens to meet her beau. The one she had fallen in love with was Lord Freddy Soames, the younger son of an Earl but he was not the only one who had captured her heart for there had been many others too.

To allow these secret liaisons to continue required an accomplice. One girl called Emily, plump and jolly, who idolized Jane was the right person for the job. She admired Jane's audacity and daring; but there was one occasion when Jane had argued with Emily calling her spiteful names pertinent to her size. This had been a step too far for the girl decided that the next secret tryst would be the last for Jane. She was going to take revenge although their argument on the surface seemed to have healed. However, Emily's fury had led her one night, near the end of the Christmas term, to close the escape route and not reopen it to allow Jane's return to go unnoticed. It had been a cold night, but Jane had disappeared. A member of staff had noticed Jane's absence when she did her final rounds of checking the dormitories and the alarm was raised. The girls had been questioned on the matter but they did not seem to know anything about the affair. Jane had always been the last to take many girls into her confidence about her misdoings. The fewer people to know the better she believed. Even Emily had the wisdom to deny any knowledge of the proceedings. She did not want to be implicated in Jane's wild actions. It was not her loyalty to Jane that was at stake but just self-preservation. A search had been made of the school. Every part was searched including cupboards, even Science laboratories before finally they claimed defeat on the matter.

'We shall have to call the police,' Miss Dyson, the rather severe headmistress, said speaking to her deputy.

'And her parents. They have a right to know,' replied Miss Tibbs the deputy head, drawing her disapproving mouth into a tight, straight line.

The police arrived ready to begin their investigation just as Jane had returned to the school. There were men shining torches as they searched the school grounds on a cold December night. It did not take her long to ascertain that her absence had been discovered. She remained in the shadows while they continued their business. Jane never went anywhere without her own torch. Shining it up on her route of escape she noticed that the window was firmly closed. There was nothing else to do but brazen out her return. She also knew that she would receive a severe punishment possibly expulsion.

Opening the main doors to the dormitory block she walked through only to be stopped by her gymnastics teacher who had kept a vigil in case Jane did return.

'Well I never,' Miss Grant said rather sarcastically. 'The prodigal daughter has returned.'

Jane said nothing knowing that the game was up.

Miss Grant liked Jane whom she found full of life and energy as well as recognizing her talents on the sports field. In her Miss Grant recognized a kindred spirit. She had often felt and reacted to situations in her youth as Jane did now but facing some of life's adversities and knowing that she had to forge a career for herself had made her grow up very quickly believing that ultimately you were not doing yourself any favours. Experience of life was the greatest educator of all. But Jane was from a privileged and wealthy family which ended the similarities between them.

'And where have you been? 'Miss Grant asked.

Jane jumped at Miss Grant's words.

'Out,' Jane said with a sneer in her voice. She knew she was in the greatest trouble of her life and rudeness added to the situation was going to make the whole affair worse.

Mary Grant looked sadly at the girl. As much as she would have liked to champion Jane amongst the senior members of staff she knew that it was impossible to do so. Justice had to be seen to be done otherwise other girls would follow suit and take advantage.

And so it was that Jane was taken before the Headmistress and a series of actions began to return her to her parental home for good.

Piers was in London when he received a frantic telephone call from Thea urging him to return to Westborough Hall. Thea would not tell him the full story until his return. Piers' imagination, on the other hand, took wing and he had visions of his mother dying. His mind was on overdrive as he travelled on the train to Worcester and on to Westborough. He knew that his mother did not wish to be buried in The Devine Mausoleum next to her husband. They had not got on in life which had made her refuse to spend eternity with him. She had said this on numerous occasions but had not specifically hinted at the alternative. Piers rarely thought about such things but now his mind was a whirl.

Jenkins, the new chauffeur, had met Piers at Worcester railway station. Piers had been almost tempted to ask the man about events at Westborough Hall but it had never been his way to discuss family matters with his employees; and now as they pulled up onto the gravel in front of the Hall he looked around as if there might be evidence of the trauma to come. Suddenly the front door opened and there stood his mother blooming with good health followed by a harassed looking Thea. Piers offered up a prayer of thanks to the Almighty but also felt rather stupid at having such maudlin thoughts on his journey home. As he stepped down from the car with more energy than he had thought possible he decided that he was ready to meet the problem head on whatever it might be because after all it could not be so bad.

The three older Devines sat in Thea's small drawing room as Jane's misdemeanours unfolded. Piers' features were inscrutable as he listened to the story.

'I was summoned to bring her home bag and baggage,' he heard Thea's voice droning on somewhere amongst his own thoughts. 'She is upstairs now awaiting your return.'

Piers looked at his wife and mother, their faces set in stern lines waiting for the explosion of Piers' temper but to their amazement it never came. But his features were deeply saddened by the events.

'It is my fault, isn't it?' He said to them as he self-flagellated.

There was no reply. What was there to say? It had all been said a hundred times before without Piers fully listening to their pleas. Was Jane's behaviour a cri de coeur for attention? Nobody knew until they had talked. Thea had tried her best on the rather strained journey home but Jane had sat mutely; her body language had been one of defiance like a suit of armour protecting her slight frame.

'May I use your sitting room to speak to her?' Piers asked his wife out of respect.

'Of course. Shall I fetch her for you?'

'Please,' he replied, his thoughts in turmoil not knowing how he would approach this unknown daughter.

Thea rose to go. Clarissa rose stiffly to follow.

'Would you stay please Mama?' He asked.

'No,' she said as she walked to the door. 'You have to deal with this alone. You are her father.' That short statement spoke a thousand words. With that the old woman opened the door and closed it behind her softly as she wondered about the outcome of the meeting.

Jane appeared in the doorway observing her father. He had not heard her approach on silent feet. For the first time in her life she felt nervous and uncertain about him. Why? She hardly knew him and felt a little afraid. Usually she saw him when the whole family was together but now they were alone.

Suddenly his gaze rested upon her. He motioned for her to close the door but remained silent gathering his thoughts. His mood appeared to be stern; his demeanour was unbending and unforgiving. Inwardly Jane trembled because she did not know what to expect. The furore at school had passed over her head. She did not want to be there anyway. If she was honest she had had enough of being treated as a child. Had she not proved her intelligence last summer when she had passed her nine 'O' levels without doing a scrap of work? And what was it all about when they would push her into marriage with some foppish idiot, a member of her class when all she wanted was some excitement in her life. The War had been over for years now and women wanted more out of life than they had had in the past. She often thought of her aunts, Diana and Minty, her father's sisters who had married before the war rearing a string of infants and as soon as they left home what was left for them but to while away their lives in doing some charitable deeds. Even Sabine, her stepmother's cousin and her father's half-sister had done much the same. The banality of the situation had driven her to drink along with her husband's very indiscreet affairs. There was new music out there called rock and roll and the dance 'the jive' coming over from America. How she would love to go there to see it all happening particularly Elvis Presley singing, his mood dark and brooding? There was so much for her generation to do. But she knew that her pompous father born in a different era would never agree. Now she sat in trepidation before him awaiting the explosion of his anger.

Clarissa and Thea had retreated to the library both fearful of what would happen. Both women knew that Piers had a temper when goaded and Jane was well capable of that. However, the lack of raised voices from the small sitting room filled them with uncertainty. Clarissa, usually stoic in the face of a crisis found herself in unchartered waters and was regarding the newly filled decanter of brandy with enthusiasm. Her eyes glanced at the hands on the clock on the mantelshelf as it ticked sonorously on. They showed that it was not the right time to be indulging in a tipple. She forced herself into restraint as the two women sat in silence as if they were waiting for the end of the world to come.

Chapter 5

Scarlett was a great observer of people. It had all started in church on Sundays either at school or on exeat weekends at Westborough Hall when she noticed people who kept the same routines and habits and never deviated from the set of rules that they had set from one Sunday to the next. 'Creatures of habit' was the phrase that sprung to mind. There were also people who wore expensive clothes and tried to hob nob with the more affluent of the congregation often engaging them in conversation when the service had finished. Scarlett regarded them as social climbers who could tell their friends that they rubbed shoulders with the aristocracy and landed gentry. She disliked such people with a passion surprising herself at times and would spend her time avoiding them. There were girls at school who could be faux friends too and she learned to avoid them. It was not her fault that she was related to the Devines. She had learned to choose her friends with care after Jane's abrupt departure from school. There were occasions when she emphasized the fact that her name was really Carson but she knew that she could not truly disassociate herself from the Devines until she was totally in charge of her own destiny.

She often remembered the way her mother and the Dowager countess had been waylaid at Church while the younger children grew tired of waiting and began to make a nuisance of themselves. The adults had to be polite to the local community which their position demanded and the young ones had to learn such lessons while they were young. How glad she was that she was not an aristocrat by birth although her life had been one of immense privilege.

There had also been childhood train rides when she had observed people hurrying along station platforms or stood stamping their feet while they waited for their own train. There were others who pushed forward in queues instead of waiting their turn which was the British way. All of this had taught her much about human nature and had made her wise beyond her years but it had opened up other areas of investigation which were beginning to haunt her thoughts and nights when she did not sleep well. She wanted to learn more about the Carson family. Her mother had tried her best to relate the little that she knew about them. Scarlett knew her mother would always be open and honest but her father was an enigma. Her mother's origins had been strange too. She knew that Thea had been brought up as Beatrice's daughter although she was really her niece and Sabine who had been her sister was really her cousin. Did other people have such complex beginnings? And there was also the fact that Sabine was Piers' half-sister. She never mentioned any of this at school for it sounded so farfetched and could have been taken from the pages of fiction. One question Scarlett had never asked was how Thea and Piers had managed to marry in the end. It was better to leave things as they were rather than to delve further into the adult world. But it would be a question to be asked in the future when she was regarded as an adult. She had already promised herself that her life would follow a simple plan unless fate intervened when she was in charge of her own destiny.

Scarlett knew what she wanted out of life and was determined to attain it. Jane's expulsion from school had shown her something else. She missed Jane's presence there; they were close and it might have been easy to be pulled along by her sister's recklessness. But now that they were no longer educated together Scarlett had seen the light about education. It opened doors for you. Success bred success or so the saying went. She could easily fall back on her privileged upbringing although she could not claim a title like her brothers and sisters. There was no jealousy or rancour in her heart for her ambition was to forge her own future, her destiny as she thought of it. She wished to go to Oxford or Cambridge to read law and ultimately to become a barrister in London, maybe a QC when the time came far into the future. She felt there was nothing wrong to have ambitions and to achieve success by your own efforts. This was the one area where she differed from Jane who looked as if she was about to throw all her opportunities away unless she could find another school to accept her. Modern times meant that women particularly intelligent ones could look forward to a career outside the home but every opportunity had to be seized otherwise the moment could pass. Somewhere she had read that it was important to create your own luck and that she would endeavour to do.

Like Jane she had passed her nine 'O' levels but the difference lay in the fact that she had had to work extremely hard for them. Jane had not but her flouting of rules had made her education end abruptly allowing Scarlett to see the waste that defiance and bad behaviour had brought her sister. Also Jane's swift departure from her expensive boarding school had given Scarlett a new edge on life. Her teachers had expected her to behave the same way as her sibling or to react at her leaving but Scarlett remained stalwartly herself. She behaved impeccably winning her the most coveted title of Head girl as she entered the upper sixth with her 'A' levels looming just months ahead.

She met many boys at the Sixth form dances. Like her siblings she was attractive, as was her mother but she had inherited her father's auburn colouring which made her distinctive among the Devines. She had become as popular as Jane amongst the boys at the neighbouring schools but there her interest ended. There was time in the future for relationships. For the moment she had to concentrate on the matter in hand which was to obtain her grades to achieve an Oxbridge education. Sometimes she wondered if her peers thought that she was a blue stocking and had lost her sense of fun.

Thea had felt so proud of her daughter's achievements. After Jane's indiscretions she had expected Scarlett and Maudie to react in a similar manner but their maturity had surprised her and also Piers. Scarlett's exeat weekends and holidays were spent with her mother. Together they had talked endlessly about the future; this was when Scarlett had poured her heart out about her ambitions.

'I thought you might want to be presented at court along with Maudie,' Thea had said one day.

'I don't want that sort of life, Mother,' Scarlett said condemning the idea out right, 'and if you speak to Maudie on the matter she will say the same. We have talked about it a lot over recent months.'

'Oh,' Thea's face looked surprised and dejected about the whole idea. As a Countess she had rather liked the thought of presenting the older girls before the Queen. She had never been given the opportunity during her own girlhood.

Her daughter was surprising her on a regular basis as she grew older. There was much that she did not know about her. Her thoughts returned to her first husband, Scarlett's father, Jack. She had never really known him properly. The war had seen to that. Perhaps some of Jack's characteristics were now appearing in their daughter. She was going to be surprised even more as Scarlett grew older. She relayed this information to Piers.

'I'm glad, you know. The idea of being presented at Court is rather ridiculous these days when young women want different things out of life. Marriage is not always enough for them as soon as they have moved out of the schoolroom. They need to experience more of life before they tie themselves down.'

Thea said nothing but was amused by her husband's more progressive thoughts knowing that really he was still stuck in the early part of the century with his thoughts and ideas although the War years should have taught him something. Even Thea believed that she wanted more independence these days but the responsibilities of the Hall and a growing young family prevented her thoughts becoming a reality. Subtly, though, his relationship with Maudie and Scarlett had moved into calmer waters as he could relate to their more adult role in life. In many ways the two girls had distanced themselves from Jane who was becoming more isolated as time moved on.

Chapter 6

Maudie was enjoying school more than she could say since Jane's abrupt departure. She had developed a talent that she did not know that she possessed. It had begun at the end of her years at Malvern but it had also helped to fill the time after Jane had been banished. She had felt lonely then and had never managed to make the friendships like Jane and Scarlett. Like her siblings she had been taught to play the piano from a very tender age. This had been Thea's idea for she and Sabine had learned to play and although they had not been great pianists they had played for pleasure becoming quite proficient. During the War years Thea had often spent an evening playing for Clarissa. It had calmed their nerves after waiting for information about their loved ones. There had been other evenings when they had listened to music on the wireless, both appreciating the skills that the musicians had taken so long to acquire.

But Maudie had not practiced as she should have done which had annoyed Piers resulting in him refusing to pay for further tuition. This had affected all three girls who were punished accordingly. Thea had told her once long ago that Mary, her mother, had been a talented pianist and if real life had not taken over she could have been a classical pianist of some distinction and might easily have forged a career for herself but circumstances, such as Mary nursing her invalid mother until she died and then her marriage to Piers producing two small children in swift succession had put an end to her ambitions.

Maudie had taken to playing the piano in her spare time. Sometimes she would find her way to the music rooms which were empty at the end of the school day and here she would look through the stack of music sheets and begin to sight read pieces of classical music that she had heard on the wireless or the school orchestra practice before a concert. At first she made many mistakes but determination inspired her to hone her skills until she reached the point where she could move on to harder pieces and she suddenly found such pleasure in her accomplishments that it was beginning to turn into an obsession. One afternoon on a drab winter's day just a few weeks after Jane's expulsion she was at her practice when Joan Masters, one of the music teachers, returned to fetch her violin which had been forgotten in her haste to supervise junior prep. She stood transfixed outside the music room door, swept away by the beautiful sounds that emanated from within. She was desperate to collect her instrument and quietly entered the room. Maudie had not heard her enter and so the flow of music continued. Joan sat down on a hard backed chair blown away by the musical talent.

As the piece of music reached its conclusion Joan Masters could not contain herself. Rising to her feet she applauded enthusiastically surprising Maudie in the process.

'I didn't know anybody was here,' Maudie said feeling foolish to have been discovered.

'Maudie, you have a great talent. Why did you not tell us before?'

Maudie blushed to the roots of her hair at such grand praise. 'I was not aware that I had any talent,' she said modestly. 'I just enjoy the music so much. It releases the stress that I sometimes feel.'

'I can understand that. The music takes you to another place when you are feeling down. Who is your teacher?' Joan asked. She had not heard any of the music teachers mention such talent within the school. There were some girls who played in the school orchestra but they could not be called gifted.

'I don't have a teacher,' Maudie answered truthfully.

'You have a teacher when you go home for the holidays?'

'I have nobody. My father will not pay for one because I would not practice when I was younger,' she said.

'But he would surely now if he knew the kind of talent that you have.'

Maudie shook her head. 'I don't think that he would. I don't get on well with him, nor do my sisters. It has always been difficult for us since we were little girls.' She did not say any more for loyalty to her family had always been in the Devines' psyche.

Joan suddenly remembered Jane Devine and her escapades. She frowned slightly wondering what sort of father could deny such talent in his daughter; that was if he realized her true potential. He should be proud that this child had turned out so well. How could he believe that all the girls would be the same? She had heard conversations in the staffroom about Scarlett and her academic achievements and how she might become an Oxbridge student. That would be a feather in the cap for the school the Head mistress had said.

She looked seriously at Maudie. 'Do you want lessons?' She asked.

'Oh yes,' she said even surprising herself. 'I can't learn any more without help. But I don't want to lose the fun element of it, the true enjoyment.'

Joan looked at her for a moment knowing exactly what she meant and then she smiled. 'I know just what you mean and we won't allow that to happen. Well, I will teach you,' the young woman said meaning every word.

Such talent should not pass unnoticed. 'We will do it after supper during our free time. I believe that you could really make something of yourself with such talent.'

Maudie was not sure about becoming a star but she felt that it would be lovely to play better. 'I don't know what to say,' Maudie said puzzled that somebody wanted to do something for her without some form of recompense.

'You don't need to thank me, Maudie. I can see a great talent in you but you must continue to work hard. There will be exams to take and believe me you could do something with this talent. You could go far but only if you continue to work hard.'

Now Maudie like Scarlett had something to aim for. As time moved on she became ambitious allowing the music to take control of her life. There was academia beckoning her too. Like Jane she was a gifted pupil and found learning easy but it was the music which ruled her. As she began to take her music exams she found that distinctions were easy to achieve. Joan also became her closest friend outside her family. Joan, a great talent in her own right encouraged her to learn the violin and clarinet. She discovered that Maudie also had a great singing voice enjoying jazz and other forms of music. Again her voice could be trained professionally, which could open the musical world to her. Suddenly nothing seemed impossible as long as she worked hard to nurture her talent.

During her return to Westborough Hall she hid much of what she had been doing under a veil of secrecy. It was in Clarissa she confided about what had been happening at school and she spent much of her time at the Dower House practicing and honing her talent on the old grand piano which stood in the drawing room. The Dowager Countess could not have been happier to be a confidante to her granddaughter feeling huge delight in the subterfuge which followed. She felt annoyed at her son who again had not witnessed such success believing that the older girls still followed in the same footsteps as Jane. Their school reports told a different story.

Thea, though, had some inkling of what was going on. She realized that great changes had been taking place in Maudie's life. Clarissa had dropped odd clues into their conversations but annoyingly withdrawing further information. This had annoyed Thea who had taken it upon herself to investigate further to see what her mother-in-law was alluding to.

However, much of Thea's time was taken up with the younger Devine children and the issues which had to be dealt with in her role as Countess. There was another problem to deal with as if there were not enough already. In previous days although she had had suspicions for a while she had also discovered that she was pregnant once more and at her age this had shocked her more than she would admit. This was not a situation that she relished for she felt that she did not have the time to give to another baby. She was already mother to four and stepmother to two and she would have to put aside her own desires for quite some time to lavish love and attention on a new baby. She knew Piers would be thrilled but at forty-two she was too old she believed for child bearing. Then there was the issue of the three older girls and their feelings on the matter. They would be embarrassed in front of their friends to admit such a thing. She dared not allow her thoughts to wander that far. It was not worth the angst. As it was the nursery was empty, as the children had drifted off to school. Nanny was getting too old to deal with a new born, Thea thought, and she might give in her notice once she heard the news. Now everything would be starting all over again. Her personal independence seemed further away than ever. And Piers would laugh and wonder what all the fuss was about.

Chapter 7

Piers was home for the time being now that the House was on summer recess. It had seemed so long, Thea felt, since they had had much time together to be a couple or a family. There had seemed to be too many problems to keep them from enjoying life but for now he was hers. The older girls were not at home for the moment. They had gone to stay with different school friends but Jane had travelled to London to stay with Sabine. Over the past few years they had become close. Thea was not happy about the deepening relationship between the two women. Sabine had changed so much over the years. Their closeness as young women had begun to evaporate at the end of the war years when Sabine had kept Thea's true identity from her. Thea had never quite forgiven her for that although she had made an effort at the beginning but Sabine's marriage had begun to disintegrate when Peter started having affairs. They had not divorced but their life together was painful leading Peter to live most of the time in London, sometimes with his mistress of the moment. Occasionally he would return to their country house in Essex to see their children but they were almost grown up now, about to flee the nest.

Sabine was lonely finding solace in alcohol more than in the company of others. She had lost friends through her attachment to the bottle but with help Thea felt that she could be weaned away from it but it was also up to Sabine to say no and to have the strength of character to help herself. Thea had discussed the issue at length with Piers who had agreed that something should be done about it. Consequently, he had written a strongly worded letter to Peter regarding the matter. The reply was short and to the point. He had agreed that he should be a more attentive husband and would do his best to help Sabine along the way. Without interfering further they felt that they had gone as far as they could in the matter. However, Thea wondered if Sabine's battle with alcohol had produced any effect on Jane. She was forever vigilant but had not witnessed any problems so far.

One morning at breakfast, Thea had decided it was time to disclose her secret. The younger Devines had been arguing over whose turn it was to clear the table. Westborough Hall no longer had the staff that had been available before the war and as the children at their prep schools had to do jobs for themselves Piers had indicated that it was what they would do when they came home for holidays and weekends. They might be a privileged class but their feet were to be firmly anchored to terra firma.

'It is not my turn,' Harry said vociferously, 'anyway all this is women's work.'

Thea's face turned purple as she spluttered into her teacup. Where had that idea come from she wondered.

Piers was used to noisy mealtimes since the arrival of the younger children. He enjoyed their banter and the rumbustious nature of the boys. It was so different from his own childhood when he had been surrounded by female company. Even Verity gave as good as she got. Her hand was reaching out to tug the rather shaggy locks of her oldest brother.

'Enough,' Piers shouted out as he watched their initial good behaviour begin to disintegrate. 'Harry you will not say such things. You will all clear the table and then go and make your beds.'

'But we have servants to do that,' Harry continued along the same lines although he knew that such reference to the staff would annoy his mother. Thea had adopted the Devines' attitude of treating the family's workers with respect and they loved her for it. She was caring and this attitude kept the turnover of staff to a minimum for they felt valued and cared for. This was not always the case in other large establishments.

Piers' face darkened and Thea could see the storm clouds gathering on her husband's features.

'Hurry all of you. Go and do your chores and then you will all be free to go and do what you want to do. There will be a surprise for you later,' Thea intervened to dispel Piers' dramatic mood swing.

Verity responded immediately. She, at eight years old, was sweet and compliant unlike her older siblings had been at a similar age. She began to clatter the dishes onto a large, old-fashioned wooden tray which had graced the Westborough kitchens for several decades. Thea felt on edge feeling that the dishes would go crashing to the floor at any moment. Just then Jenny, the young maid, entered the dining room and rushed to Verity's assistance.

'Here let me do this Miss Verity,' she said rescuing the situation.

Harry and Charlie looked at each other for a long moment and smirked. They held their faces away from the vision of their parents; Piers had already returned his attention to the Financial Times, but Thea had caught the edge of the look and her glacial facial expression took the edge off their mischief. Their mother was rarely out of humour but when she was angry she was a force to be reckoned with.

'May we leave the table?' They asked in unison. Thea nodded, watching them scamper from the room. Verity lingered longer. She came and leaned against her mother whom she adored. The emotion was reciprocated. Thea had believed Verity to be her last child and the bond between then was tangible. At the end of the summer this daughter would begin at her prep school and the thought of her being away from home saddened Thea. She touched the secret place where the new baby grew and wondered what life would be like to begin parenting all over again. It would have most of her attention that was for sure. She remembered the years when the little Devines came along in a rush. Three children in three years. They had been exciting times but she had been so much younger then and she had the nursery staff to help. Nanny Barnes was thinking of retiring now that Verity was going away. Would she stay on when she heard the news? It was all too exhausting to think about.

Thea whispered in Verity's ear making the little girl smile and skip happily from the room. Turning to regard Piers she wondered how she could divulge the news but she took courage for it was partly Piers' fault anyway. She smiled at this thought as she turned to speak to him before there were any more interruptions.

***

Clarissa was enjoying a glass of sherry before dinner. She had declined an invitation from the Hall earlier in the day feeling the need of a quiet evening to herself. She had plans to enjoy an hour of television with a tray on her lap before she went to bed with a good book. She had dined at the Hall twice already that week and on both occasions there had been guests to help entertain. However, she found some of Piers' political friends tiresome and pompous. Her mind often wondered if her son was beginning to turn out that way too. It also occurred to her that Thea had had much to put up with since her marriage to Piers. She was a saint she thought but their deep and abiding love for each other made her smile too. Thea had made such a difference to all their lives ever since her arrival at James Devine's funeral. Those had been really dark days when Clarissa became an outcast from her family for her meddling in family affairs. The lessons that she had learnt had been humiliating like her marriage had been to Piers' father but Thea's presence had helped in her return to grace. She would have nothing wrong said against the young woman who had gladdened her heart and their friendship was still as strong today as it had been for the past twenty years.

Clarissa believed that her memories of more recent times were the happiest moments of her life even defying the births of her three children.

A knock on the door, followed by her maid, Peggy, entering the room ended her reverie.

'Sorry to disturb you your ladyship, but his lordship is here to see you.'

Inwardly, she cursed that her solitude had been interrupted. 'Please, send him in.'

She wondered at the formality. Usually Piers would stride into her parlour and make himself at home. Fixing her smile in place to greet her son she wondered what had sent him at this hour. He surely should be readying himself for the evening ahead. Thea had mentioned that they were expecting more guests for dinner. Piers was appropriately dressed for the evening. She felt that he looked rather debonair in his evening attire. His blond hair neat and expertly cut hid the traces of grey that had started to appear in recent months and there was a distinguished air about him, rather resembling his father in middle age. A tear lingered at the back of her eye. 'You sentimental fool,' she scolded herself but outwardly nothing looked amiss as she smiled a welcome.

'Mama,' he bent to kiss her wrinkled cheek. 'How are you today?'

'As usual,' she said wondering where all this was leading.

'Can I refresh your glass of sherry?' He asked as he moved to the drinks table and poured himself a generous measure of whisky. Clarissa noted a rather youthful spring in her son's step.

'I have only had a sip out of this one,' she rebuked. 'Anyway what are you doing here when you have guests tonight?'

'I have come to give you some news. Thea is coming to see you tomorrow and when she tells you I want you to act surprised.'

Clarissa was not in the mood for games. As it was Piers had interrupted her solitude. 'Well what is it? 'She sounded tetchy, her sentiment of earlier beginning to evaporate.

It must be good news for Piers was smiling. 'It's Thea. She is pregnant again. I think it is wonderful, one last chance before middle age really sets in and we don't have to worry about an heir. Remember all that anxiety when Mary was pregnant?'

Clarissa was silent for a moment mulling over this piece of intelligence. She could have wiped the smile from her son's handsome features. What did men know about such matters? They had none of the discomfort of childbirth to experience and had Thea not had enough children in this modern age.

'Are you pleased, Mama?' He asked knowing that he required his mother's assistance in order to placate Thea.

'It is not a question of being pleased Piers,' she said pragmatically. 'It is always lovely to have a baby in the nursery but child birth does not become any easier as you enter your forties. I know Thea is a fit woman but there are other issues. She would have had her freedom back this autumn with Verity starting at prep school and that is important to all women. Now she will have to start all over again. She has had enough to do with those silly girls.'

Piers pondered his mother's words. 'There will be more help in the nursery to give her more freedom,' he said not totally understanding his mother's words.

'That is all very well to say that if you can find the staff. The old ways have gone when a big house provided so much work for the estate. And another baby is another one to worry about.'

Piers was perplexed by the outburst. Thea's news that morning had filled his world with happiness and pride. He felt quite proud that he could father another child and its arrival would block the feelings of guilt he felt about his older daughters.

'So you won't support me then,' his face had taken on a serious expression, disappointed at his mother's reaction.

'I love all my grandchildren, Piers, you know that and I will do everything to support Thea. Please make this the last one.' Clarissa had turned her face away to take a fortifying sip of her sherry. Secretly she was pleased to know that another Devine was on the way. She loved all her grandchildren whatever their misdemeanours. She was loyal to her family but she felt sorry for Thea. Another baby as a woman entered middle age was not easy.

Piers smiled ruefully. 'I promise that it will be the last one, Mama. I have already told Thea that there will be no more. She is also worried what the girls will say. They don't like to think of parents....' His words dried in his mouth not wishing to discuss what was in his head. His cheeks had already taken on a reddish hue.

Clarissa had noticed and tried to make a special effort not to smile. She was not easily shocked by real life.

'Leave them to me if anything is said,' she said, 'and I should use some of the new devices that are out for stopping babies. I have read the newspapers about such things.' Her face still expressed no emotion.

Piers looked at his mother wondering how a woman of her advancing years could have entered a more enlightened way of thinking. They smiled knowingly at each other as her son rose to his feet to leave.

'I think that you might be right,' he said wishing that he had left this visit to Thea in the first place. 'Well as you said I should go back to welcome our guests.' He bent to kiss his mother's cheek and was gone leaving Clarissa with much to think about. How different these modern times were she thought hoping that Thea would come through this new ordeal unscathed.

Chapter 8

Jane had been left to her own devices after her second expulsion from her new school. Piers was not prepared to go through another debacle in case it happened again. Jane could enjoy the feeling of isolation at the Hall away from her friends and sisters who were getting on with their lives rather marvellously Piers felt. They had their own ambitions and both parents felt deeply proud of them. Jane felt she had nothing to do, feeling rather like a loose cannon. She knew deep down that her life had no structure and purpose. Everybody had tried to help but received no positive response from the girl. In her heart Jane knew that much of her problem was self-inflicted. All she had hoped to do was to receive a little attention from the father she had to admit she loved very much. But the attention had not been the right kind. She angered and frustrated him in equal measure and he followed his usual course of action by burying his head in the sand, hoping that the problems would go away or wishing that Thea could find the magic solution.

Thea heavily pregnant with the new baby had tried to take Jane aside to talk to her. But it was all to no avail. Jane had remained wilful and unrelenting about her behaviour. She had repeated the same misdemeanour by being caught red-handed entering school property after a secret tryst with a boy she had to admit she felt nothing for. He, in his turn, had been expelled from his own school, his parents blaming Jane for her bad influence on him. Piers had bristled at such implications taking it upon himself to write a cryptic letter to the boy's parents who never bothered to reply. But if he was honest Piers had suspected that Jane was at fault once more.

As Piers and Thea discussed the matter they failed to find a solution to the problem. Jane had not sat her 'A' levels which meant that she could not move on to university.

'It is just a waste of a good brain,' Thea had moaned as she moved her unwieldy bulk into a more comfortable position on the sofa in her sitting room.

'University would have solved some of the immediate future but even then she does not have the ambitions of her siblings,' Thea continued with a sigh.

'She is a complete waste of space,' Piers said, worry etching his brow. 'I could cut off her allowance which would mean that she would have to work. That might make her see sense.'

'She would just use her legacy from her mother,' Thea said equally worried, 'and she would spend it all and have nothing left. '

Piers regarded Thea thoughtfully, 'I thought you knew. She can't spend it until she is twenty-five. After I came home when the war had ended I went to see Fellowes and he drew up the legal documents for Jane and Maudie. They were both young children and I had the legal right to protect the interest of both my daughters.'

Thea looked thoughtfully at her husband wondering why he had never told her. It was not their way to keep secrets from each other.

'Why did you never tell me?' She asked rather peevishly.

Piers 'face coloured to a bright red. 'It was during the days when we were not speaking very much.' He coughed to hide his embarrassment of the memory of that time. 'It was before you revealed your true parentage.'

'Oh,' she said a little taken aback for those days were long behind them now.

'Once it was done there was nothing to reveal.'

'But I told you what I had done for Scarlett. Whatever I inherited from Jack and my mother was put in Scarlett's name and I told you about it.' She was beginning to feel annoyed.

'And if I am correct you had done it without discussion with me. You told me after the event.'

They regarded each other with hostility and voices were raised as each began to score points over the other. Suddenly the library door opened and Clarissa stood regarding them, an eyebrow raised to question a scene that she had never witnessed before. Leaning heavily on her cane she made her way slowly further into the room.

'Mama, please come and sit down,' Piers said as he tried to help his mother to a chair.

'You can do that when I no longer have capability of independence,' she said churlishly as she shrugged him off.

'What is all this shrieking about sounding as if you were a couple of fish wives?' She asked, her face looking like thunder. 'What would the children say and the staff think? As you know there is always gossip below stairs even in this more enlightened age.'

Both Thea and Piers regarded each other shame faced before Thea began to cry. She sat on her chair and howled her eyes out.

'I don't think that I can cope with all this much more. All we seem to have are arguments about the children and what they are doing wrong.'

Piers looked on bewildered by the tears but he knew that what she said was correct. Her condition did not help the matter either.

'My dear, this all needs to be sorted out, but at the moment you are feeling at a low point because of the baby. As soon as the baby comes…?' Clarissa moved closer to her daughter-in-law putting a comforting hand on her shoulder.

Thea's own hand moved to the huge arc of her stomach which she caressed comfortably. Suddenly she gasped and bent over in pain, not able to move. The spasm returned for a second time. She remained in the same position for several moments.

'Get her to bed, Piers. It looks as if the baby is coming and I will telephone Doctor Johnson.' Clarissa was the best person in a crisis. 'And tell Nanny Barnes to help you. Send Jenny to fetch her.'

'The baby is not due for another three or four weeks.' Piers stood rooted to the spot.

'Well this one is on its way. So hurry.'

Piers ran to the door and opened it. 'Jenny, come quickly,' he shouted, his voice echoed through the great hall before he returned to pick up Thea as if she was no weight at all. He carried her to the bottom of the great staircase turning as he heard the maid approaching.

She had bounded up the basement stairs wondering what all the fuss was about. 'Don't just stand there girl. Run and fetch Nanny Barnes at once.'

'Yes,' she said running ahead of him as if her life depended on it.

Clarissa had telephoned the doctor who was out on a call but would be with them before too long or so his wife informed them. Jane had heard the panic and raised voices wondering what was going on. She watched in the shadows as her father carried her stepmother upstairs to Thea's bedroom. Pulling a face, she had thought that it was disgusting to be having a baby at their age. Were there not enough Devine children as it was? Papa had his heir and there was Charlie as well if anything should happen to Harry. There were many aristocratic families unable to produce a male. Jane even surprised herself at the depth of her contempt at this late baby. However, for once she had kept her own council, not even bothering to mention the situation to Scarlett or Maudie. They knew of course but were so involved in their own activities now that 'A' levels were rapidly advancing and their school life reaching its conclusion. If she was honest she knew that she had spoiled her future and now had very little to look forward to except for marriage to some boring husband. That was like being shackled to someone for a lifetime ending up like her parents having a large family. There would be nothing worse she had thought. But what else was there?

After asking her grandmother if she could live at the Dower house, Jane had felt shunned and isolated for many months. Several schools had refused to educate her feeling that she would besmirch their reputation so she had remained at home trying to occupy herself the best she could. Thea had tried to talk to her about her future and what she might want to do. This had made her feel guilt ridden after how she had spoken to her grandmother about her stepmother.

'Jane, we really must discuss your future, darling,' Thea had found Jane alone in the library as she flicked through old classics bound in leather.

'Do we have to, Thea?' Jane said sighing deeply, closing a copy of 'Jane Eyre' with a loud noise showing her displeasure at the idea.

'Well, actually I think we must. There are several options available to you and you cannot go on living here with nothing to do. It is so frightfully boring for you. Everyone needs a focus or purpose and if I don't talk to you Daddy will but I'm afraid that he will get quite cross about the whole business.'

'When is he not cross,' Jane said sulkily looking at her stepmother.

'Well, Jane, there are several options for you to think about. You could take a job as a nanny. That might be interesting,' Thea said hopefully.

Jane shrugged her shoulders in despair, 'You know I don't like children.'

'But you get on so well with the little ones.'

'Only because I have to,' Jane retorted.

'You could take on a cordon bleu cooking course or go to a Swiss finishing school. There is also the debutante season. That might be fun.'

Jane continued to regard Thea with contempt. 'They are all boring,' she said picking up another classic novel trying to indicate that the conversation was at an end.

'Well, you have rather brought it on yourself. If you had behaved you could have been going to university like the others.' Thea had lost her temper as much as she had tried to stay calm. Jane threw her book across the library and walked away knowing that for now she had won the argument, but soon her father would show his displeasure at the way she had treated Thea. For once she would have his full and undivided attention.

Jane knew that Thea had always been there for her and the others over time and it was only lately that she had learned the true nature of her parents' relationship. It was quite romantic how it had all worked out for them. During the War Thea could have walked away from Westborough Hall with Scarlett but instead she had made unbelievable sacrifices. Her grandmother had been correct on that account. Jane had tried to build bridges with her grandmother after their argument allowing the thaw to set in over the following months but Clarissa was adamant that Jane remain at the Hall. They had eventually discussed her future. It was the same ideas being paraded out all the time with Jane being tired of hearing about it. If she was honest she was envious of her sisters going to university but she had burnt her boats well and truly in that department.

'I think that you should go to finishing school in Switzerland for a year before being presented at Court. It is what our kind of girls do,' Clarissa said.

'But I don't want to do that, Granny,' Jane protested. 'You know what I think about being displayed like that. It is so awful to be looking for a husband, humiliating really and I would make a terrible wife.'

Clarissa remained silent knowing that the family had run out of ideas. Piers had said that the discipline would be good for Jane. Thea had remained unsure about the whole matter feeling that if Jane caused another scandal it would reach the newspapers. She could see the headlines in her mind's eye screeching out at them. Piers again refused to discuss his daughter's future with her but used family members to deliver his thoughts and feelings. They had reached an impasse which was not getting any better. And so it continued.

Chapter 9

You lay back on the pillows feeling exhausted but also triumphant. In her arms she held the new infant, another girl but that did not matter for there were sons aplenty for their dynasty. Piers had kissed his wife with gratitude particularly for the safe delivery of the child and his prayers had been answered for Thea to come through the ordeal unscathed. Plenty of women produced late babies but he had promised himself and his wife that this would be the very last little Devine that they would have; there was also the fact that he had promised his mother and there was no way that he was going to incur her wrath but deep in his heart he knew that common sense had to prevail. Seven children were enough for any family, even if you were the richest people on the planet.

Thea, a good mother at the best of times, felt that this last baby was special. Although she had felt that Verity was to be the last child before the new baby had been conceived, she had taken this infant to her heart. She had been born several weeks early and had weighed far less than her lusty siblings. Doctor Johnson had only just arrived to see the infant enter the world but the whole process was in the capable hands of the new midwife, Sarah Lind, who had joined his practice only recently. However, little Amelia, had come into the world like many new and premature babies suffering from a case of jaundice. Her frail, little body looked yellowish in the light of day. There had been a new treatment for the condition in recent years placing the baby under lights. The hospital would have all the paraphernalia to treat the baby but the doctor knew from reading his medical journals that natural light might make a considerable difference to the child's symptoms.

Thea was confident in Doctor Johnson's skills and watched as the days passed to see the changes in her small daughter as the jaundice receded. Now little Amelia was gaining weight rapidly and was at last thriving. This birth had taken much out of Thea and she had been told to rest, to take her time to recover. And so she did luxuriating in the time spent with this new child, bonding with her without feeling the pressures of previous times when she had known that her other children needed her. They were away at school except for Jane who had only visited her stepmother once after the birth, giving only a cursory glance at her new sibling as she slept in her crib. All the older children were to be given an exeat weekend to see their new sister but Thea had been instructed to stay in bed by Clarissa who had agreed to return to the Hall for the few days of her grandchildren's return to oversee the situation while the small staff took their orders from the Dowager Countess whom they found terrifying. Even Mrs Tubbs the new housekeeper felt in awe of Clarissa and only wished for the swift recovery of Thea who was relaxed in her approach to servants and family life. However, the plus side of Thea's in disposal was the fact that the Devines would not be entertaining for quite some time. Piers had decreed this under strict instructions from his mother who did not have much faith in the male of the species as it was.

Piers had remained at home during this time fussing over Thea until she could not take any more. It was Clarissa who told her son to return to the House before he drove everybody demented by his behaviour. Sheepishly, he did his mother's bidding leaving his wife and child in her capable hands. Little Lady Amelia Devine was like an only child to Thea. There was all the time in the world to devote to the child although Nanny had insisted that Thea should not tire herself too much. But the truth lay in the fact that Nanny felt useful again. There had certainly been a shock to the system to learn there was to be a new baby in the nursery. Nanny remembered Thea sheepishly visiting the nursery one dreary afternoon when the rain streamed down the windowpanes. There was a fire lit in the grate of the day nursery where Nanny sat by the fire doing some repairs to some of Verity's outfits. She was rather poor at looking after her clothes particularly when she was out and about with her daredevil brothers. Thea had sat down opposite Nanny enjoying the domestic scene but fear nibbled at her heart as she contemplated the response of the older woman who by now must be well beyond her sixtieth birthday.

'Nanny I want you to be perfectly frank with me....' Thea began.

Nanny looked up at the young Countess as she tended to think of Thea. She looked quite serious because she was not quite sure what to expect but she said nothing and waited for Thea to continue.

'I want to say that if it is all too much you must say.' Thea knew that she was handling this very badly. She observed Nanny's eyes brim with tears. Both women did not know how to respond to each other.

'When do you want me to leave?' Nanny asked.

Thea at last understood. Taking Nanny's hand she stroked it feeling the raised veins and the roughness of her skin. Laughing she said, 'We don't want you to leave. I have come to tell you that I am having another baby and wondered how you would feel about it. We don't want you to be overworked. You might not want another baby here.'

Thea looked around remembering other times when she visited the nursery when the younger Devine children were boisterous and noisy. They had been happy days. She turned her attention back towards the old woman whose face looked animated like a beacon in the dark.

'I could not think of anything better,' was all she said.

Thea beamed in response. Rising from her chair she went into the nursery kitchen where she lit the gas under the kettle to make a celebratory cup of tea.

It had been quite a shock for Nanny when young Verity had begun her first year at prep school only returning home for some weekends and the school holidays. Even the governess had been dispatched with a good reference and had found other employment in the home of another aristocratic family. Now at eight years old Verity had moved out of the Nursery into the children's wing of the house. Nanny had felt redundant.

Verity had found her feet now that she was no longer the youngest child. Her time away at school had been a make or break time and it had been the making of her. She had grown in stature as well as confidence, making Piers and Thea smile indulgently upon her. But her move into a grown up room of her own was just the icing on the cake. She relished her independence away from Nanny's watchful eye and had flourished as a result.

The exeat weekend was a true family one. The younger Devine children came in a rush into the Hall calling for their mother. The chauffeur had picked them up at school and had been very happy to deliver them safely to the Hall. They were a lively bunch at the best of times but as they travelled home he felt his responsibility deeply. Normally Thea would have accompanied him, but her being indisposed had complicated the matter. Thea was resting in her room when she heard the noisy arrival and she could not help but smile for every return home was always joyous. It was good to have them there. The Hall was not a proper home until their return for the old place was made for a lot of people to inhabit its interior. A sobering thought entered her mind. It would be so quiet when they had all grown and left. The alternative would be that the Hall would be filled with weekend shooting parties which happened occasionally but Thea was not really interested in the snobbery that entered such occasions. Sometimes it was good to entertain and dress up in her finery but it was mainly family occasions which she enjoyed like Christmas and Easter. The summer brought different activities like picnics with the younger Devines out in the fields and in the woods. Sometimes they would climb the Malvern Hills when the House was in recess for the summer. Piers enjoyed these occasions en famille as well. Thea felt that was Piers at his best as a family man except for the occasions when the older girls were at home.

The children did not seem to want to go away anywhere but preferred the attractions of home life as they grew older. They also enjoyed using the boating lake. Thea had taught them to row during previous summers and to have a great respect for the dangers of water. Piers had bought two ponies for the children. They were stabled at the Home Farm which was the nearest Westborough land to the Hall. The farm was rented out to the Potter family who were responsible for the stabling of the horses and their welfare. They were always on hand when the children wanted to go riding. It was no good stabling the ponies in the old stables near the Hall for the Westborough car was kept within its walls when not in use. Piers had often thought about demolishing the stables but it was just one of those jobs which always seemed to be put off until another day.

School friends would often come to visit and stay with the young Devines for days on end. Thea loved the buzz of family life so much and always looked forward to the holidays when the Hall was full. Occasionally she and Piers would take the children to London to stay in the Devine Town House in Fenton Street. It was the home where Thea had grown up with Sabine and every time she visited it, feelings of nostalgia surfaced of her childhood there. It was the place where she had discovered the secrets of her family. It evoked thoughts of Beatrice who was not her natural mother but she had cared for Thea as if she had given birth to her. There was also the closeness that she had shared with Sabine but these days there was very little that they had in common which saddened her more than she dared to admit even to herself. Even Clarissa would travel to Fenton Street these days. It had been a place in the past which had been forbidden to her but now she enjoyed seeing old friends and visiting the theatre in the West End. But home was always Westborough Hall and the solitude she enjoyed on her return. It was strange how all their lives had changed and moved on over the years and for the better the Dowager countess often thought. She tried not to think about her life when her husband was alive. She felt a well of despair if she ever cast her mind back. The Devine children whom she loved so much kept her focused in the present with a small thought cast to the future as the children took charge of their own destiny.

Thea lay in bed listening to the young Devines as they clattered up the stairs.

'Quiet,' Piers hushed them believing Thea to be asleep but he was amused by their antics. Thea had to smile, too, as she listened to them trying to be quiet. It was an impossibility.

'Papa, where is Mummy and the baby?' Verity asked. She was close to her mother and perhaps a little jealous that her new sister might take away the special bond that they shared.

'She is asleep upstairs. You can see her later.'

Verity took no notice of her father and dashed up to her mother's bedroom, opening the door to reveal her mother nursing the new baby. Thea smiled at her daughter's entrance.

'Shh,' she said, putting a finger to her lips. 'Come and see your new sister.'

Verity shut the bedroom door quietly and tiptoed across the room where she sat on the bed leaning heavily against her mother looking at the new arrival.

'Did I look like that when I was born?' She asked looking at the small face which could just be seen emerging from the whiteness of the shawl.

Thea smiled and kissed her daughter's apple red cheeks. 'You were just like that,' she said remembering Verity's arrival into the world quite vividly and believing that she would be the last child in their nursery. Sadly she knew that the latest arrival was going to be definitely the last. The baby that she had not wanted had filled her heart with love and joy just as she had known deep down that she would.

* * *

The summer was beginning to run its course. The August days were hot and stifling but the days were shortening heralding the nearing of autumn. Even some of the leaves on the trees in the woods were beginning to change their hues. The young Devines knew that it would be time to return to school and for Scarlett and Maudie life was going to change beyond recognition. Only days previously they had received the dreaded envelopes containing their results that would determine their futures. Having risen late that day they found envelopes addressed to each of them lying on the great hall table next to the telephone. Giving the other a knowing look they snatched up their mail and departed for the privacy of their bedrooms to assimilate the contents of the envelopes. Thea had been busy in the library during the course of the morning wondering what would happen. Usually calm in a crisis Thea had hoped that the girls would open their post in front of her divulging their euphoria and excitement but nothing happened. There was just quiet which unnerved her even more. Piers was not at home for her to confide her angst and so she waited while her blood pressure seemed to soar and pound in her ears. She could not stand the tension that was growing out of her control and then suddenly two bedroom doors opened almost simultaneously and banged closed, followed by two pairs of feet running along the long landing and down the curved staircase.

Thea opened the library door and waited, expectation etched on her pretty features. Both girls looked at each other and then in jubilation jumped up and down as they demonstrated the triumph that had been richly deserved. They all hugged each other, as the journey into the unknown was now a reality.

'I have managed to get into Oxford,' Scarlett said. Thea moved to her to give her a hug feeling so proud of her. 'Your father would have been so pleased and proud of you.'

'You think so?' Scarlett's cheeks flushed with the pleasure of her mother's words.

'Oh yes, my darling. Never doubt that.' Thea held tightly onto her daughter remembering her first husband quite vividly after all these years. She released her daughter and turned to Maudie wanting to value her success too.

Maudie smiled joyously. She had no doubt in her mind that Thea loved her too.

'My results are not as illustrious as Scarlett's,' she said modestly.

'Don't be so ridiculous, Maudie,' Scarlett said quite angrily knowing how hard Maudie had worked particularly on the practical side of her music where she had passed her Grade 8 examination with distinction. It had been difficult to make up for all those years when her talent had lain hidden.

Maudie smiled knowing how hard Scarlett had championed her over her talent. They had grown closer since Jane's departure from school.

'Come on tell us,' Thea said.

'I've got into the Royal College of music,' Maudie smiled in triumph.

'Oh, Maudie, how wonderful.' Thea wrapped her arms around her stepdaughter as tears of joy reached her eyes. She was so proud of them both to have reached this part of the long journey ahead to fulfil their ambitions.

'I think you need to ring your father,' Thea said to them both. She glanced at the long case clock, 'I think that he should be in Fenton Street by now. He wanted to know how you had got on. He will be anxious too.'

Somehow both girls remained reluctant to telephone their father and not for the first time Thea cursed Piers' refusal to have reached out to the girls that she knew he really loved.

Chapter 10

Jane was desperately unhappy about life in general but the worst thing of all was the fact that it was her own fault. Witnessing the success of her siblings made her realize how stupid she had been over her time at school. If she was even more honest she knew how intelligent she was, probably more so than either Maudie or Scarlett but that should not take away from their success story. However, her pride played a major part in the aftermath of her downfall. She did not wish to acknowledge the fact to herself or any other senior member of her family. Now was the time to organize her future, give herself some kind of purpose instead of wasting her time at the hall with little or nothing to do. She did not want to admit to Thea how she was feeling and there was no point explaining how she felt to her father who was permanently enraged with her. Then she thought about her grandmother who would be pleased at the thought that she was willing to do something constructive with her time. Clarissa was not of the generation who thought that young women had to go to university to achieve something with their lives, particularly her class. A good and suitable marriage and a family had always been the way forward for such girls of noble birth. Although Clarissa acknowledged the changes in the modern world she was still heavily steeped in the traditions of the aristocracy.

It was a warm morning in late August when Jane slipped out of the hall to walk through the gardens to the Dower House. Her mood was sombre wondering how her grandmother would react to the news she was about to impart. She entered the building through the French windows which led into her grandmother's sitting room. The room was cool as the morning air breezed in and the flutter of the curtains bore testament to this. The day was going to be stifling in an hour or two. Jane continued her journey through the hallway until she reached the morning room where grandmother usually breakfasted alone surrounded by the daily papers, the *Times* and the *Observer*. She did have the courtesy to knock but walked straight in without a summons. Clarissa looked up in surprise at the intrusion to the peace that was usually hers so early in the day.

'So sorry to disturb you, Grandmamma,' Jane said. She smiled sheepishly at her elderly relative. Since the stern lecture that Clarissa had given her, Jane had been wary of her grandmother, but Clarissa bore no resentment to this tiresome grandchild. It had taken her half a lifetime to learn the lesson that resentment only hurt oneself most of all.

'Come and sit with me, Jane, dear,' Clarissa said, 'Have you had breakfast yet?'

Jane shook her head, 'I'm not really hungry.'

'Nonsense,' Clarissa exclaimed, 'It's the most important meal of the day. It sets you up.'

Jane took a seat opposite her grandmother. She did not wish to invite criticism for she required this old woman's support. 'I'll just have a slice of toast then.'

Clarissa stood up stiffly to ring the bell for the maid. 'Please don't, I can use this plate and knife,' Jane said indicating the ones which had been placed on the table as extras.

Clarissa promptly sat down again, her eyebrows raised to question the situation but failed to say anything. She waited in silence for an explanation of the impromptu visit. Jane took a half slice of toast from the toast rack and buttered it with precision before spreading a generous layer of marmalade on top. She bit into the toast and crunched noisily much to her grandmother's dislike but she knew better not to mention this, as she somehow knew that Jane had come to say something important. Over her long life Clarissa had learned to read body language and human behaviour. She knew Jane's character inside out and only wished that the girl's father did too. Perhaps if he could put his selfishness aside none of the nonsense of previous months would have happened. The morning room door opened suddenly and Betty the new young maid entered the room.

'Is there anything I can get your highness?' The girl asked.

'Yes please, Betty. Could you bring Lady Jane a cup and saucer and a fresh pot of tea please?'

The girl scuttled off and Clarissa muttered under her breath. 'Stupid girl, calling me your highness. She never knows how to address me.'

Jane, despite how she was feeling, allowed a chuckle to escape her lips. 'It's not like it was before the War you know. Thea keeps saying that.'

'And she is right,' Clarissa said with an acid expression on her face. The world was not getting any better she believed.

'Now then tell me about the purpose of this visit. It is most unusual to see you at this unearthly hour.'

Jane grimaced knowing that the time had come. 'You won't be cross with me Granny but I feel I need to do something constructive with my time. Scarlett and Maudie are moving on with their lives but I—'

Jane saw Clarissa's mouth tighten into a line, her demeanour forbidding. She waited for the onslaught of temper to break like a dam opening its floodgates but nothing happened. This gave her some measure of courage to go on. 'I feel it might be useful to go to finishing school in Switzerland and then go to a crammer to take my 'A' levels like the others and eventually go to university.' Now it was all out in the open. 'I just wondered what you thought. I wanted your advice on the matter.'

Clarissa raised an eyebrow on the matter. Since when did Jane listen to advice?

She was silent for a few moments as she regarded the girl. She had steepled her hands in front of her almost as if she was praying for patience.

'I am glad you have come to your senses, Jane. You have caused a lot of heartache up until now.' Clarissa's features were set sternly as she weighed up the situation. 'Why have you not talked this through with Thea? She would have sorted it with your father although he is as stubborn as a mule. No doubt that is where you get it from.'

'I never seem to see Thea by herself these days. She is always doing things with Amelia. Nanny gets ever so cross about it.'

The Dowager Countess looked at Jane sharply. 'I hope that you have not been talking to Nanny behind Thea's back young lady.'

Jane's cheeks flushed red, 'Of course not, but it is plainly obvious.'

Clarissa was not so certain about that. She hated tittle tattle at the best of times. It had never happened under her regime at the Hall and it should not be happening now. 'Very well. I know that Thea is busy with Amelia.' Here Clarissa's face softened as she thought about the newest addition to the family who had melted everybody's heart. The little girl was the dearest thing she thought and relished the days when Thea pushed her in her pram through the gardens to the Dower house.

'I shall walk over to the Hall after luncheon to see Thea and then we shall see what we can do for you.'

'Thank you, Granny. I knew that I could depend on you.' Jane rose and moved to kiss her grandmother on her wrinkled cheek.

As Jane disappeared through the morning room door still nibbling on a piece of toast Clarissa was rising stiffly from her chair in readiness to telephone the Hall to forewarn Thea of her impending visit and her reason for it.

***

'Well that is a turn up for the book,' Piers beamed broadly at Thea as he untied the cord of his dressing gown to get into bed beside his wife. 'Why does she want to go now?'

'Oh Piers don't be so slow on the uptake,' Thea laughed happy that Piers had taken it all so well. 'Maudie and Scarlett are moving on with their lives, which leaves Jane at home without their company. If she could spend six months in Switzerland and then return to cram for her exams she would have only lost a little time and she could go to university next year. All this has made her grow up a lot in recent months and she had seen the error of her ways. Surely you must see that.'

Piers pulled a face. 'I hope that you are right Thea. But we must be tactful over the situation of course.'

Thea had to smile about Piers being tactful; since when was he tactful with anyone these days except perhaps for his mother she thought. He was not known for his tact and as he headed into his middle years he could be grumpy if things did not suit him. He did not dare do this with Thea either, for she could hold her corner and usually make him laugh. But she saw James Devine in his son and his aristocratic ways had become enhanced as he grew older. What would life be like when Piers entered old age she thought as she watched him getting ready for sleep? She pushed the thoughts away and thought of her baby daughter who was developing very quickly now. How she loved that child. She turned over and fell into a somnolent state, a smile on her face.

Chapter 11

Jane had mellowed in the last few months feeling that she owed it to herself to forge a life away from Westborough Hall and the suffocating family that lay within its walls. Even at this moment in time she had not made her peace with her father but life had become easier and less complicated. The olive branch that she had offered her grandmother had been the beginning of forging her future and the turning of the tide in her relationship with her stepmother. She had an easy alliance now with Thea who had set in motion with Piers' blessing the visit to the finishing school in Switzerland where Jane was to master her expected role of becoming the wife of an aristocrat or somebody equally distinguished. She would learn how to run a large house and to socialize to full advantage with her equals something Jane had never wanted to do. This should have been easy for her considering her aristocratic background but it still remained a task to be mastered.

And so it was that Jane left England in the September of 1958 to travel to her finishing school at Berghausen on the shores of Lake Geneva. She was to remain there until March when she would return home to make decisions about her future. She had chosen to stay for six months instead of a year fearing that she would become bored and this should lead to trouble as in her school years. Piers had also insisted that she should continue with the languages that she had passed so easily in her school exams hoping that they might lead her down the path to taking them for university entrance. Jane for once had not protested but she was beginning to think that she did not wish to follow the road of academia like her sisters. It all seemed like hard work. Freedom beckoned her and here she could follow her heart. But for now she would fulfil what was expected of her before she steered her ship safely into the future.

'Don't cross your father,' Thea had advised sagely.

'No,' Jane said realizing the wisdom of her stepmother's words.

'You never know you might change your mind on many issues,' Thea had counselled feeling that maturity quite often ended disputes and acts of rebellion. But she witnessed the stubborn tilt of Jane's head and expected a retort but none came.

Thea had smiled at this new Jane who was willing to take advice. Their alliance had led to a new era of peace and contentment at the Hall. Even Piers was beginning to mellow to this daughter who had caused so much trouble but the drawbridge had not been fully lowered yet to allow them to be totally easy in each other's company.

The days before Jane's departure were passed in a blur and frenzy of activity. Cases and trunks were humped from the attics to be filled with the new array of clothes that Piers had generously paid for, as part of the unspoken truce that was in the air. The trunks were to be sent ahead by boat and train but Jane was to fly from Birmingham's Elmdon Airport on this new adventure. The Hall was in turmoil as all the children were home for the holidays and Amelia was constantly crying as she demanded her mother's attention. Nanny just would not do. It was almost as if the young child could sense that everybody else was demanding and receiving her mother's attention. Thea was too busy and stressed to notice what was happening and fell into bed exhausted every night.

As the stuffy August days drifted into September the full impact of what was to happen had struck Jane like a coup de foudre. She had never been so far from home and for so long. She began to see the Hall and her family through sentimental eyes. This volte-face had made her treat everyone in a much better fashion and as a result the family had said that they would miss her but her absence was only for a few months. She would be home for Christmas and then it would not be long until the spring.

Jim the chauffeur drove her to Birmingham; they were accompanied by Thea who took Jane's hand in the airport and told this prickly natured daughter of Mary Devine that she must telephone the Hall regularly and write too.

'It won't be long until Christmas and if you want a visit home sooner we can make the arrangements. You only have to ask, darling,' Thea said taking Jane in her arms for a last minute hug.

Jane looked over Thea's shoulder as she stood stiffly in the embrace looking into the middle distance and seeing nothing. She felt tears prick the back of her eyes but she blinked them away. 'I don't think there will be time to come home before Christmas,' she said trying to make her voice light and bright. 'I was told that it was not so easy to settle if you had thoughts of going home again soon.'

'Well you can always change your mind or I could fly over to see you,' Thea said kindly having guessed at Jane's stiff upper lip. She felt sorry for the girl.

Jane felt guilt ridden for treating Thea so badly over more recent years and knew now what a decent person her stepmother had been. Her grandmother had been right that Thea had been the only mother she had known and her love for her had been unconditional as if she had given birth to her. She had come to see her off while her father had not. That had upset her more than she was prepared to admit even to herself. Piers had been in London at the House of Lords when Jane had been due to leave. Thea had asked him to return home to be present at Jane's departure but Piers had buried his head in the sand once more declaring that there were pressing affairs to attend to in London and he would not be able to make it home in time.

'Give her my love,' he had said gruffly down the telephone.

Thea felt impatience as she listened to her husband's words. 'You should be doing that yourself, Piers,' she said pointedly but he was not listening to her. He had deflected her words very skilfully as he found another topic of conversation.

'I shall be back on Saturday,' he informed her with bonhomie before replacing the telephone in its cradle.

Thea stood for several moments thinking about this non-existent relationship between father and daughter. She had complete sympathy for Jane as every child wanted the affection and support of their parents at whatever age. She decided that she would speak to Piers again but doubted that he could truly cross the divide.

Thea had felt thwarted and angry at his reaction and had tried to soften the blow to Jane's pride the best she could.

'Your father said to wish you a lovely stay in Switzerland and he will be thinking of you. He sent his love and is very sorry not to go to the airport with you. The House is sitting and there is a very important debate about to take place.' Thea reached for Jane's hand and squeezed it. She knew that she was bluffing her way through the situation but hoped Jane would accept the excuse.

Jane had taken her father's absence well on the surface but inside it was another rejection in the series she had suffered over the years since her father's return from the war. The barricades had been lowered once more so that her mood became inscrutable. Both mother and daughter felt a sense of relief when the time of departure finally arrived. Perhaps Jane's return at Christmas would tell a more hopeful story.

＊

The first few days, after Jane's arrival at Berghausen, were busy with settling into her new life. She found that she was too busy to dwell on events at home or even to feel a pang of homesickness. Each arrival shared a brightly decorated room with another new girl and there was an older girl who was always there to lend a sympathetic ear and help calm any troubled water.

Jane's room overlooked the Lake; its breathtaking views were at their best in the late summer light and Jane could have spent hours drinking in the beauty of the scene. But there was much to be done as the young women signed up for the courses that would be useful to them in the future. But as the first flurry of activity began to calm down Jane surprised herself by feeling homesick for Westborough and her family. She thought about her father wondering if he felt remorse by dismissing her departure so easily. Thea had glossed over Piers' refusal to return home as best as she could but Jane had no doubt that her stepmother was trying to protect her from her father. The person she missed the most was her grandmother which surprised her more than anything.

However, Jane knew that she had been away to school like many of her class but here she could not return home for a weekend exeat easily like she had done before. She also knew that she had to stay until Christmas otherwise she would show a weakness that had never manifested itself before. Her pride was always an issue that kept her apart from others. She had always been the one to show a sense of defiance against her father and the establishment and little would change that.

However, the scenery and the warmth of the September weather began to raise her spirits as the days progressed and as time moved on she came to know many of the girls, some aristocratic while others were the daughters of the nouveau riche. And so the time passed and to her surprise she began to enjoy the experience. For the first time she felt that she was treated as an adult and with respect. Her opinions were asked and she developed a new confidence. Her misdemeanours of the past were not known here and a clean slate had been established. Her friendships were carefree, frivolous and fun. Their free time was spent in shopping in Geneva and as the weeks passed Jane had acquired a wardrobe full of clothes, some fashionable while others were classical in their style, to be worn at events where the girls were able to shine in their own right when they met the young, rich men of the area. For the first time Jane was grateful for her father's generous allowance to her. She knew he could have been spiteful for she had proved to be a nuisance in his eyes but now she began to see another side of him, a side that softened her heart a little as the weeks passed. The saying that absence and distance made the heart grow fonder was correct in this instance. Thea wrote regularly about the family sending little anecdotes about each member including her father. Verity had gone down with a nasty attack of measles and had come home to convalesce. Harry and Charlie had been chosen to play rugby for their House at school and had written home with enthusiasm. Piers had been thrilled about that for rugby had been his game when he had been a boy at Eton. Amelia was walking now and was finding her way into all kinds of mischief. Thea continued her saga omitting any details about Scarlett and Maudie believing that the older girls would correspond with each other. But that had not been the case as the older girls had quickly become involved in their new lives.

Clarissa wrote to her too in her old-fashioned handwriting and filled in the gaps that Thea had missed. So a complete picture emerged of life at Westborough Hall. There was even a letter from Piers; slightly unbending in its attitude but it was a beginning. Jane suspected that Thea had instigated its arrival but nevertheless it was a start. Jane's roommate Stella had become a good friend over the weeks following their arrival and it was to her that Jane could unburden her soul about her family and her eternal conflict with her father. Stella was pragmatic about such issues.

'You have left childhood behind,' she said. 'Forge your own life and try and be happy. We all have to make a life of our own at some point. Take responsibility for yourself and try not to have regrets. If your father is such a fool, let him get on and have his own regrets.'

Jane looked at her friend in surprise wondering where such wisdom came from in somebody so young.

'How do you come to think like that?' Jane asked.

Stella smiled. 'Experience I suppose. My father rejected my mother and me when I was ten. We were abandoned to our own fate without a penny to our name.' She laughed mirthlessly as she remembered. 'One day you feel loved and secure and the next it has all gone.'

'But how are you here then? This place costs a fortune?'

'I am here, my dear Jane, because my mother met my stepfather who is worth a tidy fortune. He is titled and wishes to do the very best for me. I can't argue with that and next year I'm going to do the season to find a husband. My life will be my own then to do as I wish.'

For days Jane could not get Stella's story from her mind. She knew that her friend was right in the fact that each person had to forge a life and with the inheritance from her mother she would eventually be able to do that. But she would not inherit that for a few years. However, this had to be the buffer to protect her from Piers' negligence.

Some of the other girls were making decisions for their future which included doing the Season on their return to England. Jane had never wanted this but hearing them talk and Stella's words made her think again. This might be the key to her future. She could write to Thea to say that this was what she wanted to do. She knew Thea and her grandmother would support her against her father's condemnation of such events. He wanted the world of academia for his children but Jane was discovering her true identity which was one of a free spirit and a life of fun. Who knew what the future held? Live for the day became her motto and one day she hoped to become mistress of her own home wherever it may be.

Chapter 12

Life had taken a new turn for all of the older girls. Thea was subdued about the whole proceedings realizing that everything was changing at such a fast pace but was it for the better? She knew that she was being rather selfish about these new events. She had been so thrilled and proud by the results that had been achieved by Scarlett and Maudie that she had lived off it for days but as time went on she realized that the three oldest girls were moving on with their lives and were in a fizz of eternal excitement. Their lives were opening up beyond measure. Thea did not resent this but she felt that life at the Hall would never be the same again. Feelings of nostalgia hit her like a tidal wave as she thought deeply about their lives. It made her look at her own life and how she had made the family into her life's work. Did not other mothers do that?

Of course the young Devines were not moving on yet nor would they for several years but it was the onset of new beginnings when the fledglings would fly the nest and their lives would change dramatically. She had tried talking to Piers about the situation but he just laughed saying she would have her own life back so that she could do what she wanted. It was all right for Piers; he had his life mapped out. Home was where his heart lay but he had another life in London at the Lords and when he was at home he spent much of his time on the estate or huddled in his study with the estate manager while she ran the Hall and oversaw family occasions often doing the arranging of events all by herself. This was how she had spent most of her life, even during the War years. When the children went she did not know what she would do with herself. Even Amelia would grow and leave in time. A depression had descended upon her which she found difficult to shrug off. But nobody seemed to notice as they were engaged with their own lives. Suddenly Thea felt that she had not really achieved anything in her own right except be there for other people. The future would be a shock she thought but self-pity was not usually her way and so she tried her best to be involved with the young women and their future.

Maudie was the next one to leave now that Jane was at finishing school. It was the middle of September and summer was waning and the chillier days of autumn were just around the corner. She had spent much of her time at the Dower House practicing the piano and her clarinet. Clarissa had not minded the interruption to her solitude but there were times when she felt the intrusion. However, she did not want to discourage Maudie and the two of them had formed a friendship of a kind. She thought about these difficult granddaughters who were now turning into fine young women. What a foolish man her son had been to keep them at bay for all these years. What had he missed she wondered? Perhaps she would never know the answer.

Maudie had turned into a beautiful young woman, elegant and unassuming about her talent. The day had arrived for her to travel to London to settle herself into student life. Thea had suggested that she should live at the Devine Town House in Belgravia where she would be well looked after by the small staff that ran it for the family; she would also be company for her father when he was in London at Westminster. Maudie had other ideas though. Firstly, she did not want to be restrained by her father's lifestyle as an aristocrat. She was a wealthy young woman in her own right but she wanted to be regarded as an ordinary person who did not have the privileges of the rich and famous. She was not prepared to use her own title either but wanted to make her own way through her own efforts and her talent. She had so much to fall back on should she fail but she had no intention of doing that. Tenacity was her middle name she had decided but to placate Thea she had agreed to stay at the Town House until she had found a place of her own.

Her early arrival in the capital allowed her to look for an apartment. She had found one quite quickly above a small boutique not far from the Royal College of Music where she was to study. It was homely and just what she wanted. She had decided from the outset that she did not want to share with anybody else for it was to be her domain and she wished to furnish it in her own way. There was a bedroom and a sitting room with a small galley kitchen and a bathroom. It was perfect too for here she could practice her clarinet without disturbing any neighbours. She also wished to learn the violin and knew that the squeakiness of the early days of learning the new instrument would be upsetting for anyone who might have the misfortune to listen. Maudie was delighted with the potential of her own private space. She had brought much of her personal possessions from Westborough Hall and as soon as she had moved in set about making the place like home. Piers had been generous once more with her allowance which enabled her to scour the local markets for items that would enhance her home. However, he was not so pleased to find that she had left the Town House. As usual he had not confronted Maudie about his doubts about her desire for independence but had complained to Thea whom he hoped would persuade Maudie to give up such silly ideas. Although, Thea hated the girls leaving home she was not prepared to spoil their desire for freedom in a changing world. The lives of the young were vastly different from the days of her youth; there were opportunities for them to move away from the drudgery of being chained to the kitchen sink or an early marriage. She would support the girls as much as she could in that although she had been hit hard by their absences; and so it was that Piers had to accept the changing world whether he liked it or not.

Maudie knew London well having spent much time there during her childhood. The time before she started at the Conservatoire she spent shopping for clothes, ones that she thought a student would wear. There was to be nothing stylish from the fashion houses that members of her family had used. For the first time in her life she was to be ordinary, to mix with people who had extraordinary talents but who had had to fight for the privileges that they hoped to have in the future earned by their own hands.

So, it was that Maudie began her new life as she walked to South Kensington to her new place of learning which was situated near the Royal Albert Hall on Prince Consort Road. The interior of the building was not huge but there were many practice rooms where she could work at the piano or the clarinet and begin to learn the violin. But what surprised her was the fact that there was no concert hall but no doubt she would find out more as time went by.

At the beginning of this new adventure Maudie had feelings of self-doubt about her own talents. Would they be good enough compared with the new influx of students? Had she aimed too high? What would she achieve by the end of her course? All this fed her thoughts but she had received such encouragement from her teachers who had praised her talent; but she had heard the exquisite music which emanated from the music rooms as the new students practiced. However, she tried to calm the doubts that circled endlessly through her mind. She would have to work harder than ever she told herself. Only time would tell where her future lay.

It had not been difficult to make friends for the students were like minded, overawed to have reached such lofty heights because of their talents. They came from many backgrounds but not once did Maudie let slip about her aristocratic and privileged background and she felt that she melded into the background as well as she could.

The day that Thea had dreaded most of all had arrived. It was now the end of September and Scarlett was packed and ready to leave for Oxford. She was excited to be going but she had one pang which caused her much angst. It was leaving her mother. She knew she was being foolish for she would be home for the holidays and university holidays were notoriously long and she might return for a weekend here and there. The two women were close; Scarlett had only ever had her mother as a parent which had forged this unbreakable bond between them.

Piers was civil but she had never regarded him as a surrogate father. Her mother had always been both to her. At the same time Scarlett had to be pragmatic. The umbilical cord had to be severed as hard as it might be so that they could all move forward with their lives. She was also very aware that her mother had been keeping her emotions tightly in check, trying not to upset either of them. Once Maudie had left for London, they had shared some quality time together going on shopping trips to Worcester, Birmingham and even Hereford. They had eaten lunch in some lovely restaurants and talked about the past and what might lie ahead in the future. It was during this time that Scarlett raised the subject of her own father, Jack Carson. Again Thea had repeated the little that she knew about the Carson Family and Scarlett told her mother that there would be a time when she would decide to discover that side of her family. Thea had said nothing knowing that a child wanted to know more about an absent parent but it pained her that she could not help fill the void that Jack's death had left behind for their daughter. It was also Scarlett's intention to be known as a Carson, her Devine years were now over.

Thea kept her silence once more, only listening and wondering how serious her daughter was in these ideas about her unknown heritage or would university life take over allowing her long dead father to lie in peace in his North African grave. Thea doubted that Scarlett would find anything new in her quest for knowledge about her father for had she not been on this journey before all those years ago?

Scarlett had wanted to leave for Oxford on her own. She knew this would upset her mother but this was her journey and she wanted to experience every facet of it for herself. Thea had been brave and had travelled as far as Worcester to see Scarlett onto the train. This farewell was reminiscent of the times when she had witnessed the departures of Jack and Piers during the war years. They were filled with dread about whether they would return and there the comparisons ended so Thea admonished herself for her foolishness. Scarlett was to be gone weeks not months or forever. Possessiveness was not usually Thea's way and it was there on the station platform with the trains hissing their welcome or farewells where she witnessed Scarlett take control of her own destiny. One last hug and then windows were opened to wave and shout last messages leaving Thea standing alone to look through the mist of tears which had been controlled for so long and left to fall now that the train vanished like a speck into the distance. Scarlett had not been unaffected by the separation from her mother but the excitement of a new life amongst the dreaming spires beckoned and that was what she had worked towards for a long time.

For days after Scarlett's departure, Thea was left with a feeling of despondency and loneliness which even little Amelia's presence could not erase. She wondered if other mothers felt the void after their children had flown the nest and guessed that she was not alone in that respect. She returned to Westborough Hall with intense feelings of abandonment and telephoned Piers at the Town House to just tell him that she missed him.

'Oh Thea,' he had laughed at her down the telephone, 'Scarlett has only been gone a few hours and she will be home again before too long. She won't be able to stay away. You know how close you two are. Any way I shall be home in a few days and I will stay for as long as I can.'

'Thank you Piers. That will be lovely,' Thea said as tears filled her eyes.

This time they were not tears of happiness but a gratitude that he understood her so well and his actions reflected the love he still felt for her. And he was right that Scarlett would be home, but not yet for she had to forge a life of her own. However there was the possibility that Thea could visit her in Oxford, a place she had never been to in her entire life. The distraction of the young Devines would have been wonderful but they had returned to school weeks ago and were not allowed a weekend at home for a while. Only Amelia offered comfort to her mother but it was adult company that she sought. She wished to pour out her feelings and tell the world why she felt so bereft but she also felt foolish that she was needy and decided to keep her inner angst to herself.

A few days later it was Clarissa with her intuitive nature who came to the rescue. She had not seen or heard from Thea since Scarlett's departure. This was unusual for the two women had forged such a close bond over the years and little time passed without them lunching in each other's homes or meeting for family events. Instead of telephoning the Hall as she usually did, she set out after breakfast one morning to make the walk through the gardens which were dressed in their best autumn finery. She took the walk steadily stopping to lean heavily on her cane from time to time, to look around her and to observe what was going on and mostly to drink in the beauty of the morning. In the distance she could see the Malvern Hills rising, their hue a faded blue as the sun sparkled upon them. The world was a beautiful place if your mind was open and uncluttered by melancholy thoughts and fears she mused. Somehow she felt that Thea was troubled and that worried her. There was a gentle warmth to the day, not the searing heat that summer brought with it but still a feeling that there was an Indian summer just around the corner before the chill of autumn took hold.

She walked on and as she approached the terrace behind the Hall she saw that the French windows were open as if to welcome her. Passing through them into the sitting room where she had once reigned supreme she found Thea drinking a late morning cup of tea and sifting through the newspapers. She glanced up when she heard footsteps and smiled a welcome.

'Am I intruding?' Clarissa asked as she settled herself breathlessly into a wing backed chair near the stone fireplace.

'Of course not,' Thea said. 'You know that you are always welcome.'

Clarissa observed the younger woman's demeanour. It was not like Thea to be quiet and lifeless. She was always the one who took control of a situation and looked life straight in the eye. Clarissa knew that she had been right to come.

'Oh, my dear, is it really that bad?' She asked.

Thea suddenly burst into tears, her resolve of tackling life now completely exploded by the kindness in her mother-in-law's voice.

'Yes,' she said, 'it is really that bad.'

'You are the only one who can help yourself through this until the world becomes less bleak,' came the words of wisdom. 'You have always been so busy doing for others but now it's the time to do something for yourself when the family is away.'

'I know,' Thea said through the tears. 'I just don't seem to know how to go about it.'

'Well,' Clarissa paused, 'you do have a husband who has a responsibility to his family. Go and stay in the Town House. Go out to dinner or to the theatre with him. Meet old friends. Piers is selfish and has left you too much on your own and I'm afraid that I must say this but he has also taken you for granted. He is becoming too much like his father.'

'But I have Amelia to think about,' Thea protested.

'You have yourself to attend to as well. Women always put the needs of others before themselves denying their own rights. Amelia is a well looked after child, much loved by us all. She will not suffer. If you are not happy at leaving her behind take her with you to London. Nanny will cope in there. But this is the beginning of your new life my dear. If you don't heed the warnings of your heart you might rue the day.'

Thea was silent for a few moments as Clarissa watched her closely. The older woman was determined that Thea should not sink into a great abyss, a slough of despond she thought with a rueful smile wondering where that had come from.

'Yes you are right as always, Clarissa,' Thea said looking into the pair of kindly eyes so much like Piers' own. 'You have such a wise head on your shoulders. I should not have allowed myself time to feel so down. It is rather selfish of me. The young are entitled to spread their wings as they think fit and not have to feel guilty about a moping mother. Anyway Piers will be home by the weekend for a few days and then I will return to London with him and do what you have suggested. Thank you for being so kind.'

Thea rose from her seat on the sofa to sit on the arm of her mother-in-law's chair. She leaned closely and kissed the old woman's soft but craggy cheek.

'Don't thank me, Thea. I have lived a long time and I must have learnt something along the way. But I'm afraid it has taken me a life time to learn.' Her face took on a rueful expression as memories came flooding back.

She took Thea's hands into her own gnarled, wrinkly ones, holding them tightly and then she patted them. Even she had wondered what all the fuss was about. Life should be taken by the horns she thought; her eyes misted over as she recalled much humiliation from her husband James Devine but she had risen above it to move into calmer waters after his death.

Suddenly she looked up from her reverie and glanced at Thea. 'What's for lunch, my dear?' She asked as if she had been purposely invited.

Thea smiled and burst into laughter. 'You'll just have to wait and see,' she said as she rose from her chair to investigate in the kitchen below stairs. Clarissa always had a way of lightening her mood.

Chapter 13

Jane had found life in Switzerland exciting, partly because she felt like a different person. Nobody apart from Stella knew about her previous misdemeanours and she was the last person who was going to explain her past to others. It was a pleasure to be herself. The physical distance that lay between Switzerland and Westborough Hall had given her clarity of mind and she could think more rationally about everything including her father. She saw him in a different light at times, neglectful certainly in some ways with his absences from home but not always unloving. But he took Thea for granted considering how much she had done for the Devine family before her marriage. Perhaps that was true love for you. Her brothers and sisters were loved but she and Maudie were products of his disastrous marriage to their mother Mary. She now believed that he did love them but was undemonstrative as a parent. In fact since her long absence from home he had written to her three times in stiff unemotional language but he had shown some care in his words despite everything. He had not bonded with the three older ones despite Thea's warnings. He just did not know how to do it. Maudie and Scarlett had their own ways of coping with the situation. Maudie had wrapped herself in her music and Scarlett had her mother who loved everyone regardless of their misdeeds. Thea's love was always unconditional. Jane had learned this from her grandmother who had been so right.

Jane had replied to Piers' letters with care. She wrote about her daily life in Switzerland; about the day to day events and the new skills that she had learnt. There were anecdotes she wrote in German partly to show how her knowledge of the language had improved and partly because her father had learnt to speak it during his time as a prisoner of war. This she hoped would go some way to making them closer. Such thoughts seemed to haunt her during nights when she could not sleep. In the daytime she was occupied and engrossed in her activities and her new friendships.

The first term of Jane's sojourn in Geneva had resulted in her not returning home for a long weekend which the girls were allowed to do. Consequently, she chose to stay with Stella and their friendship was based on loyalty and mutual trust. Stella was a confident girl who had grown up quickly. She had learnt about life the hard way, learning from her mistakes but never looking back only forwards with an optimism which was mature for her young age. In Jane she had found somebody who was desperately needy for love and affection. Instead of this pushing them apart it had somehow strengthened their friendship, each fulfilling whatever they saw and liked in the other. During the weekends when they could have returned home they had taken trips around Geneva, shopping and sightseeing and practicing their language skills. They laughed at the same things and for once Jane could relax away from critical eyes and throw aside the role of errant daughter which she had formulated for herself. They were not the only girls who had remained at the finishing school which allowed them to make other friendships. In the evening they frequented café life where there was a buzz among the people enjoying après ski but they were careful never to flout the curfew of returning at the correct hour. The freedom they experienced was like an aphrodisiac. They just could not get enough of it.

However, Westborough Hall beckoned for Christmas. Jane was to be pulled back into the arms of her all-consuming family. Surprising herself she felt a tug of excitement to be going home. Before the Christmas vacation arrived she had taken time to shop in Geneva for presents which she thought about with care. The shops offered a far different perspective on the festive season than the British ones and she enjoyed buying presents which definitely had a continental theme to them. Each present was gift wrapped by the shop and she felt proud and very adult in the decisions that she made. This was a far different Jane from the one who had left England just three months earlier.

The young Devines had missed Jane during their exeat weekends and once the Christmas vacation had commenced they made a tremendous fuss of their eldest sister. Thea showed her happiness at having the family together despite the angst she had felt in previous months but Jane found Maudie and Scarlett filled with their world in academia. This had sapped her confidence feeling that what she was doing in a finishing school was frivolous compared to Oxford and the Conservatoire.

Piers was jovial too. His mood had lightened in previous months. Thea had credited this change to her time spent in London. They had enjoyed time to themselves interspersed with Amelia's presence. She had become the light of their lives. They were like a little family with the other children so far away.

Now they sat down to Christmas lunch in the large dining room which had been decorated to perfection by Thea and Verity. The lights on the Christmas tree flickered in the already gathering dusk and the log fire flared in the large fireplace which seemed to dominate the room. Thea was in a jovial mood which reflected her delight to have the whole family back under Westborough Hall's roof. They had been joined this year by Piers' sister Minty and her new husband Matthew. She had been a widow for several years and so it was that Piers and Thea had had pleasure in welcoming a new family member. Clarissa had as usual become firmly entrenched at the Hall where she stayed for the duration of the festive season. Her mood was mellow and reflective as she observed the family around the huge table. She remembered Christmases past, both good and bad, but today's gathering showed a family who was comfortable to be together. How long that would remain she could not guess but all families had times when they could tear themselves apart. 'Live in the moment' her inner voice said and she settled down to do just that.

After the traditional meal had been consumed Piers rose to make the speech he made every year. His face was flushed partly from the heat of the room where a cheerful log fire still blazed in the old Elizabethan fireplace, a hiss or spit emanating from it but he had also imbibed well of the expensive wines which filled the Westborough cellars, long ago restocked after its depletion during the War. There was a slight slur to his words which Thea could detect but she kept her own council as she smiled indulgently through his heart-felt words.

'It is wonderful that we are here as a family once more. Christmas does that for us. It grounds us making us realize what we have missed or taken for granted throughout the year. Where did this last year fly to? But we are all here which tells us much about ourselves.' Here he paused and looked around indulgently at all the family members. There was only Amelia absent for she was taking her nap in the nursery. 'Here is to you all, my family. God bless you all.' He finished his speech with those words and lifted his glass of claret to toast them. There was a murmur of voices as glasses were raised and 'here, here,' could be heard followed by laughter and happy chatter.

He found Thea's hand which he brought to his lips to kiss. She blushed at this old-fashioned display of love and her heart flipped over as it had during their forbidden romance.

Clarissa had sat and listened. Her eyes glistened with sentimental tears as she brought her rather full brandy bloom to her lips to sip the rich dark contents. Her Christmas hat sat slightly askew on her head as it had done so many times over the years. The ever-thoughtful Thea put out a hand to squeeze that of her mother-in-law and saw a very different woman from the one that she had met all those years ago. Happier times had made the dowager what she was now and Thea thought about James Devine whom she had loved as a father. The two facets of the man were still hard to believe.

But now was not the time for regrets or recriminations as a new year would shortly be upon them.

The young Devines had left the table happy and sated to watch the television in Thea's sitting room while the adults continued their celebrations. The wine had made them all mellow in their affection for each other. The afternoon light now faded to dark blues, the colours of twilight. Lamps had been lit casting long shadows and making the lights on the Christmas tree seemed brighter still. The magic of the moment still lingered and the older Devines felt reluctant to break the spell that had been cast upon them.

The large Christmas tree in the Great Hall had been brought in from the estate only days before and had been set up by the gardeners as was the tradition. It had been dressed in its finery by the older girls. A fire also blazed in the great hearth at one end of the hall lending the dark interior with its wood panelling a cosy feel.

'Shall we move into the Great Hall,' Thea said aware that the family would be reluctant to move but knowing that the staff would wish to clear the detritus from the table before they enjoyed their own Christmas meal. She stood up to encourage her family to follow her lead but it was with regret that they did so.

A cold buffet would then be laid out in the small dining room if anybody wanted it later but it was unusual if they did. The long case clock struck the hour. Piers glanced in its direction.

'We've missed the Queen's speech,' he said jovially. He was forever the patriot but the lunch had passed in such happiness and harmony that it had quite escaped him. 'We will catch it later on the news.'

Nobody seemed to hear but he was not worried by that.

The family sat around the fire in the great hall talking and laughing, the older girls feeling like adults for the first time in their lives. They were no longer fearful of their father and in relaxed fashion began to relate anecdotes about their experiences over the past term. Maudie was full of her musical life and could not wait to return but for the moment they were all content to be together. Clarissa had fallen asleep tucked into the arm of the sofa; her brandy glass safely rescued by Piers and was now standing empty on the occasional table at the side of her. Thea sat silent in her observation of her family, her heart gladdened by what she saw. It was her belief that they had individually been on a long journey to reach this point but now it looked as if life had turned the corner. Her heart flipped with happiness believing that life was going to get better.

Thea had listened to Clarissa's wise words and had embraced the absence of her family to move her own life forward. Amelia would always be her number one priority but she had taken to visiting London more often. Her time alone with Piers had rejuvenated their marriage. They had found that little je ne sais quoi which had driven their love in the early years of their relationship and it was plain for all to see.

The extra time that Piers had spent with Thea over the previous few months had relaxed him more than he could believe and it had made his relationship with his children easier. He had time for them now and wanted to know what the older girls planned to do with their futures. His attention turned to Jane whose face had reddened under his close scrutiny. This is what she had cried out for over the years, his love and his interest in her. The constant flow of wine had mellowed them all.

'What will you do, Jane, once you finish in Switzerland?' He had asked with care, a look of tenderness on his face.

Thea had looked on, her face glowing with happiness that at last Piers was making the effort that he should have done years ago. She smiled encouragingly at Jane whose eyes had momentarily rested on her stepmother's face before they returned to her father who still waited patiently for the answer to his question.

'Well,' she began hesitantly, 'I had thought of doing the London season. I no longer wish to go to university like the others.'

'Oh, Jane, you would love university,' Scarlett protested. It had become her world which she had embraced so completely.

Thea said nothing but her face told a story like no other. Scarlett understood what was written there and suddenly had nothing more to say on the matter.

Jane laughed as she said, 'you know my track record of working hard is not very good so I thought I would try something different.'

They had all laughed trying to lighten the mood once more.

'I think doing the season is a wonderful idea,' Thea said offering encouragement. 'We could have such fun, Jane.'

Jane flashed Thea a grateful smile. 'Yes,' she said, 'I think that it will be fun.'

'There will be no presentation before the Queen; that all finished last year. Apparently she found it outdated and some say that the Duke found it a bit of an insult to women in general, a bit like a cattle market,' Thea said.

'I know,' Jane continued, 'but all the same it would help me get to know people. I have decided that I would like to marry and have my own home one day.'

Piers sat back in his chair, lost in thought. He felt that it was not what he wanted for his daughter who had a sharp brain which needed to be nourished. However, if he said anything the chasm that divided him from Jane would ever widen. It was his turn to support what his children decided for their futures. After all it was their happiness which mattered the most. Perhaps he was beginning to learn lessons this late in life he mused. It had all taken a very long time to reach this point in the relationships with his oldest daughters. He wondered if his mother and Thea had noticed how hard he was trying. Glancing at his mother he noticed that the brandy bloom had been drained but she sat with her head thrown back gently snoring, her mouth open with a dribble beginning to escape from the corner. He had to smile for years ago such a scene would have been his mother's worst nightmare to lose such dignity before others. Around him the conversation continued as he began to listen once more sipping at his own rather splendid glass of claret.

Thea was glowing in her enthusiasm about the forthcoming season. This would give her another project for the summer months to chaperone Jane and to plan for her own ball at Westborough Hall.

'Jane we must discuss this in more detail before you return to Switzerland,' Thea's voice sounded almost high pitched in her excitement. 'It will be exciting, won't it, Piers.' She touched her husband's hand to draw him into the conversation. She had a feeling that he was no longer listening.

'Of course,' he replied without much enthusiasm. Jane noticed the closed expression on her father's face making her feel that she had disappointed him once again.

After the Christmas holidays had ended and life had returned to normal Thea had felt very optimistic about forthcoming events. Even Piers despite Jane's unspoken fears had not made any adverse comment on Jane's decision to take part in the Season. Thea had visited Clarissa at the Dower House to discuss the matter as Piers' sisters Diana and Minty had 'done' the season in their day. They had been presented to their majesties King George V and Queen Mary.

'I don't think that it will be too different from the girls' day except that there will be no visit to the Palace. It will do Jane good to dress in her finery and to feel confident. She would be a much more attractive girl if she was happy and smiled more. All this sullenness does her no favours,' Clarissa said sagely.

Thea looked at the older woman and knew what she meant. Clarissa never failed to surprise her with her observations and wisdom about life. 'Yes,' Thea said, 'I do believe Jane is moving forward with her life.'

'And when she leaves Westborough it will be for good. I don't see her wishing to return too often in the future. She has been such an unhappy young woman and I'm afraid that I blame Piers for that. He has been a bitter disappointment in that direction.'

'Yes,' said Thea. What else was there to say? Clarissa was correct again on that issue. Thea could not defend her husband as she knew the truth had been spoken.

Chapter 14

Jane had indeed returned to Geneva happier than she had been in a long time. She was facing one last term in Switzerland with mixed emotions. On the one hand she felt homesick for the family she loved deeply but Switzerland had given her the freedom she craved where she could make her own decisions and be herself.

On the afternoon of her return to Geneva she discovered Stella in their room. 'You look relaxed and happy,' Stella had said as they unpacked their suitcases.

'Yes I am. Christmas was good and I have made some decisions,' Jane smiled.

Stella raised an enquiring eyebrow. 'What decisions?' she asked rather surprised as she had found Jane very indecisive over the past few months of their friendship.

'Oh you know. I want to do the season and then if I marry someone that will be just perfect.'

Stella raised an eyebrow again to this piece of intelligence but she said nothing. She was not somebody to make sarcastic comments to hurt another's fragile confidence. She genuinely liked Jane; it was a shame that the girl did not really like herself. Making decisions on her future was good for this very mixed up girl with the complicated family. Stella offered up a prayer for her own good fortune before continuing her chores.

Christmas had been the most special of her life Jane felt. The younger Devines had been full of joie de vivre and had livened up the whole proceedings. But it was not just that for she had witnessed the deep and abiding love which endured between her parents. There was a freshness to their banter and happiness oozed through them as they laughed and joked with the younger children but most of all her relationship had turned a corner with her father. He had spoken to her at length on several occasions during her time at Westborough. Piers appeared to be interested in what she was doing and thinking and he also felt better in himself by taking an interest. Her gratitude to Thea knew no bounds for it was her stepmother to whom she attributed this turn of events.

***

There was no hope of returning to Westborough as the half term holiday advanced rapidly. Jane had assignments to do and she also wanted to make the most of her last few weeks in Switzerland. It was truly a winter wonderland with the mountains covered in snow and the towns buzzed with the après-ski. She had not been tempted onto the ski slopes as some of the girls from her school had been. She felt a diffidence about it but she loved the atmosphere that pervaded through the towns making her wish that she was more confident.

As the month of March advanced Geneva was still shrouded in snow and it was with regret that Jane was ready to go home. Everything had been accomplished that she had set out to do and with this success story came an element of pride. Her German both in the written and spoken forms were near perfect and her French passably good. It was this success story which had made Jane feel that she could make her way as a translator if her other plans did not come to fruition. Her parting from Stella was emotionally charged; they had become close, best friends in the full sense of the word and had sworn to keep in touch particularly now that their paths would inevitably cross as they took part in the Season. They had become kindred spirits over the months making Jane feel closer to her than her sisters who were entirely wrapped up in their own lives.

'You're the sister I never had,' Stella said on the morning of their departure looking at Jane whose eyes were brimming with tears. 'Don't worry we will see each other soon.' They hugged each other with genuine warmth before collecting their possessions which were to be placed in the same taxi that would transport them to the airport.

They were catching the same aeroplane out of Geneva to Heathrow. Those last hours together would be precious to them before they went their separate ways. Landing and going through passport control took a while but reclaiming their luggage was not a major issue for most of it returned to England in the same manner as it had been sent.

Standing waiting for their individual pickups they hugged one last time and then they were gone, once more returning to their separate lives.

***

For Maudie the Conservatoire had fulfilled a dream. She was making great strides in learning the violin and honing her skills in the other instruments that she was learning. Her personal tutor Mr Ravenscroft had asked her what she wanted to do once she had finished her course.

'I haven't thought that far ahead yet. It all seems too far away at the moment.'

He had looked at her quite seriously making her believe that any ambitions that she possessed might be a step too far. 'Might you consider being a concert pianist?' He asked.

Maudie laughed at this thought. 'You're not serious,' she asked looking at him expecting him to break into laughter and say that he was joking.

The contours of his face did not change as he spoke. 'Of course I am serious. I have never been more serious in my life. You have a rare talent and I believe that you could go far.'

At the end of the day Maudie did not know what to do with herself through sheer excitement. She wanted the world to know and then wondered who she could really tell. If she told her friends they would think that she was boasting and then she thought about her grandmother who had encouraged her all along.

She telephoned the Dower House. A message had been brought to Clarissa in her sitting room as she was about to take a sip of a very large sherry. It was her pre-dinner tipple which she imbibed most nights when she was dining alone.

'There's a young woman on the telephone who wishes to speak to you your ladyship,' Polly the young girl said.

'Who is it?' Clarissa asked rather crossly not wishing to be disturbed now that she was beginning her nightly routine.

'I didn't catch her name my lady,' the girl said.

'Haven't I trained you to always ask for the caller's name?' Clarissa was annoyed.

Polly said nothing as her mistress began to rise stiffly and unsteadily to her feet reaching for her cane in the process. Maudie waited patiently at the other end of the telephone knowing that Clarissa was not swift of foot and she wondered now whether she had chosen the right person to whom to divulge her news. Perhaps she should have telephoned Thea who was always so supportive of everyone's achievements. But now it was too late for she heard Clarissa's heaving breathing from all her efforts to reach the telephone.

'Who is this?' Her grandmother's voice spiralled shrilly down the wire.

Maudie gritted her teeth. 'It's Maudie, Grandma. I have some news for you.'

'I hope you are not pregnant Maudie for if you are you should be telephoning Thea,' she said wondering why the girl was ringing at this hour.

Maudie giggled at the thought. 'Of course not,' she said still amused by the comment. 'I have been told today that I am a very talented musician and I could become a concert pianist. That could take me all over the world.'

There was silence at Clarissa's end of the telephone. She was digesting this piece of news very carefully. She still inhabited a world where she wondered why rich young women wanted a career.

'Granny, are you there?' Maudie wondered if there was something wrong with her grandmother. She was becoming old and infirm now.

Clarissa's voice now mellow as she found her answer said, 'that is wonderful, my dear. Well done. Have you told your parents?'

'No, I wanted you to be the first to know. You have encouraged me so much.'

Suddenly Clarissa felt so emotional that she did not know what to say. These strange daughters of Piers were not so bad after all thanks to Thea.

'I will tell your parents and Maudie thank you for telling me first.'

Without making further conversation Clarissa put the telephone back in its cradle and returned to her sitting room to sip her sherry and to mull over this piece of intelligence. It was so good to have something positive to celebrate she thought. Maudie had put the telephone down with a feeling of warmth stirring inside her. She had been right to telephone her grandmother but she also knew that she should also tell her parents.

Maudie had continued to practice hard but she was also enjoying life to the full. She now had a circle of friends who were an eclectic mix from all kinds of backgrounds and talents. She still had not divulged her heritage but knew that she was accepted for herself, Maudie Devine the musician. The Conservatoire knew about her background when she applied to study there but she had made it known that she wanted no privileges which had been honoured by the staff who worked there. As the time wore on Maudie would go out for dinner with her friends. They frequented low budget cafes and restaurants and then they spread their wings to attend clubs where there was music played by people of diverse talents and musical taste.

There was the jazz scene which had drifted across the Atlantic to open up new horizons of music and then there was rock 'n roll which set the foot tapping and young people danced the jive between the tables to the lively beat. There were the young singers who parodied the likes of Elvis Presley with his slicked back hair style or Eddie Cochran who sang 'Summer time blues.' It was all heady stuff and the young could not get enough of it but the older generation was bewildered by this changing world. Their youth had been spent fighting wars across the world to keep peace and stem the tide of changing frontiers in Europe. The older generation could not throw off the mantle which had been placed around their shoulders. Now, though, it seemed that frivolity was the order of the day. Some could not understand which was better but the young could tell them. Freedom was an aphrodisiac which should be enjoyed to the full.

There were times when Maudie would stay a night or two at the Town House in Belgravia when Thea was in residence. She could not deny the fact that occasionally she enjoyed being spoilt and the trappings that went with her class. Thea was good company and the two women would lunch together in the most expensive of places like the Ritz. But to her friends it would appear at these times that she had disappeared off the face of the Earth when they wished to contact her. However, she never divulged her whereabouts to anyone for here she had returned to her roots where she once more became Lady Maud Devine. That was still part of who she really was in her family's world and this she was never going to deny to herself or her family.

'I'd love to see your flat,' Thea had said several times on her now frequent visits to London.

Maudie had made a range of excuses to keep her stepmother at bay but she knew that time was running out when she would have to accept a visit. Her flat was her personal space where she could be herself. Even her friends were not invited there. Her nightly social life had left its mark on her. She was tired and knew that she looked it. But returning to Westborough Hall for the long Easter vacation would give her the opportunity to rest. But hawkeyed Thea, the eternal Earth mother, had noticed.

'I think that you are working too hard, darling,' she had said on one of her visits to the capital.

'Don't fuss, Thea,' Maudie had said using the familiarity of her name. This had stopped Thea in her tracks wondering not for the first time in her life who was the mother or the child. Were their roles reversing?

Piers had heard this and was not happy but Thea laughed it off not wanting an argument to ensue, after all she was not their mother and times were rapidly changing.

At the Conservatoire it was part of their training that the students could use their voice as an instrument. The only time that Maudie had sung was in the bath or when she listened to the wireless and sang along to songs that she loved. Her training gave her breathing a different strength and her voice a different range. It was not a voice suited to classical opera but it was still a good voice which could vary between ballads and jazz; it had a gravelly and sometimes haunting quality to it. And so on her nights out in the clubs with friends she would sing out in confidence along with the professional singers. But one night the singers called for somebody from the audience to join them on stage. Maudie's friends pushed her forward and there she was looking down into the mass of faces below her. The music began again and she felt the thrill of singing with a band. Suddenly she realized that she was the only one singing for the others had given her centre stage while they listened to her musical talent. As the lights dimmed and the music came to the end the audience stood up and gave her a standing ovation and shouted for more. Flushed from her triumph she sang again receiving the same accolade. After that night the manager of the club called her over to ask if she would like a regular slot during the week and she would be paid. Maudie accepted feeling excited about her future. The money in some ways was irrelevant but it was the first money she ever earned in the whole of her life and in that there was a measure of self-respect. Perhaps there was a career to surface from her talents after all.

Chapter 15

Scarlett was enjoying Oxford. She loved the whole atmosphere of the place with the wonderful architecture and the buzz of academia. She knew that she had chosen the right subject; law had always been what she wanted to do. It had not taken her long to settle into this new life although the wrench of leaving her mother had been unbelievably hard. During the Christmas term she had returned home for a long weekend as she had promised. Seeing her mother looking ill had prompted feelings of guilt but she also knew that it was only natural that the young should fly the nest. On her return to Oxford she telephoned Thea more regularly either at Westborough or at the Town House where her mother was often to be found. But it was the Christmas holidays where Scarlett saw her mother through different eyes. She was vivacious and the haunted look of desperation had disappeared. This she had attributed to the extra time that Thea spent with Piers. It was as if their love had been rejuvenated over recent months. Thea was not as consumed with family problems as they dealt with them together. Scarlett was happy about that but there was still the deep-seated feeling that her mother had had to take on too much responsibility while Piers thought about his career and the estate. Here she could not quite forgive his selfishness and her mother for being so compliant. That was certainly Thea's Achilles heel. But for now there was a glow about her which gladdened Scarlett's heart and allowed her to move on with her own life.

As the time approached to return to Oxford Scarlett no longer had any qualms about leaving her mother and they had said their farewells only with talk of what they would do together when they saw each other next. This was her time now and Scarlett was determined to concentrate on her own life. It was her intention to gain a first class degree. She had no illusions about her ability to do it but she also knew that she had no choice but to work hard to achieve her goal. She allowed no distractions to get in the way so she kept the idea of a boyfriend low on her horizons. There were plenty of friends to help lighten her life and perhaps an odd date but that was all she was interested in for the foreseeable future. Few distractions meant that she could accomplish her goals. She was an attractive girl with her reddish hair which she had had cut during her first term to sit nicely on her shoulders and it curled naturally in an enviable way. Its wildness during her childhood years did not enhance her looks now that she would embark on a professional career sometime in the future. She was no longer that child who could wear it in plaits to combat the life that it had of its own.

Some male students thought her to be a blue stocking because her nose was always in her books but Scarlett knew otherwise. There would be a time when life would be sweet when she finally called it her own. But the other purpose in her life was to find out about her father. She accepted that he was dead but were there members of his family still alive? Her mother's family was dead apart from her cousin Sabine but there was little contact with them these days. The two adults had drifted apart over the years much to Thea's disappointment but all the Devine children kept Thea occupied.

But it was her father who haunted her. He had been a War hero and the medal which endorsed this fact was securely hidden in her room at Westborough. It was only as she grew older that she had recognized her mother's generosity of spirit when she had passed the medal to her daughter. It could have remained in Thea's possession but it was the last remaining tangible possession of her father's life and heroism. However, that was not quite correct for the house that had been her father's was still in the family possession. It had passed to Thea on his death. Thea had never lived there with Jack for whenever he was on leave he had stayed at the Town House. After that when Thea returned to Westborough Hall Jack would come to find Thea there. Thea never mentioned Jack's London home for it had been placed in the hands of the Devine family solicitors to run for the benefit of his family. The one piece of information that Thea had given her was the fact that the house belonged to Thea but the rent received from the property over the years had been placed in another trust fund for Scarlett to inherit when she was twenty-one. The other trust fund would be inherited when she was twenty-five. She was going to be a wealthy young woman one day.

During the long weeks of the Easter term Scarlett had made up her mind to visit London before she returned to Westborough Hall for Easter but she was not prepared to stay at the Town House where her actions would be under close scrutiny from Piers. She had made up her mind that she would stay with Maudie in her Holy of Holies whether her sister liked it or not.

Chapter 16

Scarlett had written to Maudie not to ask for permission to stay but wrote as if it was a fait accompli. She required somewhere to stay away from the prying eyes of their family. Maudie had replied unexpectedly by return of post curtly saying that she did not usually have visitors staying but on this occasion she would make allowances. It had made Scarlett smile knowing that she had forced Maudie's hand but she would not dwell on it for she might need to repeat the experience at some point. The evening before she should have been returning to Westborough Hall she telephoned Thea.

'Hello, Mama,' she said addressing her mother by her childhood name. 'There is a slight change of plan.'

'Oh,' Thea said disappointment filling her voice. 'What's that about?'

'I thought that I would go and stay with Maudie for two or three days before I come home,' she said.

'Oh,' was all Thea seemed capable of saying before pulling herself together. 'I thought you might have wanted to stay in Belgravia. I could catch the train down to London and we could have some girls' outings.'

Scarlett had not missed the barb in Thea's words but on this occasion she did not want her mother around for she had things to do. 'I will only be staying with Maudie a couple of nights so I don't think that it is worth you coming. I wondered whether we could go to Birmingham to look for evening dresses when I come home. Jane might like to go as the London Season will soon be upon us.'

She heard the smile back in Thea's voice as she said, 'what a lovely idea and Maudie might want to come as well.'

Scarlett had deflected her mother's idea well. It was something she had learned to do over the years when she had been in trouble.

'I think Maudie will need to go. Have you seen those terrible clothes she wears these days? She is trying to hide her true identity but when she becomes a concert pianist she will have to wear beautiful clothes.'

Thea laughed, 'don't tell her that darling. Pretend that you don't know otherwise she will think that Clarissa has been telling tales. Poor Clarissa does not understand Maudie's way of dressing.'

They both laughed as they said their 'goodbyes' for the time being.

Scarlett thought about her mother. Thea had certainly been in a happier mood as the conversation ended but she did not want her mother to become possessive making Scarlett feel guilt ridden about not returning home immediately the term had finished. There was nobody she loved more in the world than Thea. That would never change but Scarlett was also enjoying her freedom in Oxford where she could make her own decisions. It was heady stuff after years spent at boarding school following petty rules.

Scarlett had decided to take a small suitcase to London for her short stay and then she would travel straight to Westborough where her wardrobes were stuffed to capacity with the clothes that she wore there.

Her journey to London was quick. It was exciting to be back in the capital again because it had been months since her last visit. Her letter to Maudie had stated that she would meet her at her flat at six-ish. She did not know where it was but she had planned to take a taxi which would solve the problem. But first of all she had an appointment to keep. This was with the firm of lawyers who had worked for the Devines for decades. It had been Ernest Fellowes who had dealt with the family for the last thirty years or more but he had retired recently due to ill health. In his place was a much younger man, Scarlett assumed although she was not totally sure. The appointment was for eleven o'clock. As usual Scarlett took a taxi. She usually had plenty of money for she was always frugal with her allowance and never wished to be accused of extravagance by Piers. She had to admit he had never been mean in that way and quite often her mother would buy extra clothes for her. But she wished for the days when she controlled her own purse strings. She knew that she was not totally free. Patience had never been her greatest asset.

The taxi had taken her to West London where the offices were. They were lodged in an elegant building with steps leading up to the front door. There was a notice which stated 'Please ring' placed next to a rather ostentatious brass bell. Scarlett did as she was bidden and the ring of the bell could be heard reverberating through the inner hallows. Footsteps could be heard swiftly approaching and the great, heavy door swung open followed by a sharp voice, 'have you an appointment?'

'Yes,' Scarlett said taken by surprise at the woman's tone and also feeling her youth and inexperience in such matters.

'Who might that be with?' The voice came again and the owner suddenly revealed herself as someone who was hardly older than Scarlett.

Scarlett regained her composure once she realized that she was not speaking to a harridan. 'I have an appointment with Mr Arbuthnot,' she said in an assertive fashion using her received pronunciation.

'If you will come this way please,' the officious young woman said opening the heavy door wider to admit Scarlett into the spacious oak panelled hallway.

Scarlett walked in noting that the interior could not have changed much over the decades. In the distance she heard the clatter of typewriters but was led to a large door with the name of the lawyer emblazoned on the front. The young woman knocked and opened the door on command saying rather rudely, 'she's here.'

'Mary how often have I told you how to announce a client?' Mr Arbuthnot's voice was rather irate. He had spoken to his colleagues before about her rudeness but they had come to the conclusion that girls were more like that these days. Manners and intonation were no longer BBC worthy. How times were changing and not always for the better the older generation of solicitors thought.

'Come in Miss Carson,' Antony Arbuthnot said opening his office door wider. 'Please take a seat.'

He glared at Mary who skipped away back to her desk wondering if she would suffer a further reprimand. Scarlett took a seat that had been indicated to her. Perching on the edge of the chair like an exotic bird she looked around her. She saw a panelled room with bookcases covering one wall where leather bound law books stood behind a glass frontage. She thought this could be herself in years to come with her own law books which would contain the area of law that she would specialize in when the time came. Antony Arbuthnot had inherited the collection from his uncle Ernest Fellowes so it was only fitting that he should also inherit his rather magnificent office.

'Well, Miss Carson, your letter stated that you wished to know something about your late father's estate,' he said looking her straight in the eye, wondering how old she was.

'Yes,' Scarlett said as confidently as she could.

'And have you asked your mother questions about her former husband's affairs?' He asked treating her as a child.

'Yes, but she knows very little and so I thought I would come and ask questions here.'

'And does your mother know that you are here?'

Scarlett was beginning to see the game that the lawyer was playing and suddenly her temper exploded. 'Please don't treat me like a child, Mr Arbuthnot. I have every right to find out more about my father. My mother was not married to him for long before he was sent overseas in the war.'

Antony Arbuthnot was taken rather by surprise at Scarlett's fit of temper and his supercilious attitude disappeared. 'Quite so,' he said. 'How can I help you?'

'What can you tell me about my father?'

'Not a lot really. I never met him personally. He was killed in North Africa in 1942 performing an act of gallantry. He saved the lives of two men by shielding them with his body. He was killed outright. I do believe that these men lived, but they were seriously injured. Your father was very brave and that is why he received his medal.'

Scarlett's eyes were brimming with tears as she imagined her father's act of valour. 'One day I would like to visit his grave.'

'Of course. I am sure that will be the case. His estate was left in its entirety to your mother but it was not large. There is a house of course which will be transferred to you when you are twenty five but until then it remains in your mother's possession but the property is let out and your mother instructed my uncle Ernest Fellowes to set up a deed whereby the rent from the property is paid into a trust fund which again you will inherit on your twenty first birthday. This means that you will receive a staggered inheritance. You could well be a wealthy young lady.' He smiled superciliously at her but she ignored him.

'Do you know anything about my father's family?' Scarlett asked.

'I do not know what happened to your father's parents. I know they were alive at the end of the War but as time passes people die or their lives change. It is a long time ago now.'

'My father told my mother that he did not have parents still alive and he was an only child my mother said.'

'No that is not the case. Your father had an identical twin brother and a younger sister but again it is a long time ago. I don't know where they are now. As a law firm we did not deal with their affairs. Apparently your father transferred his business to this firm after he had met and married your mother.'

Scarlett remained silent mulling over these facts which had come as a great surprise until she said, 'could I have the address of the house please and I would like the names of my family and any information you might have?'

Antony Arbuthnot looked at the file which lay on the desk before him. He turned each page looking for the information. 'Ah it is here,' he said before taking a piece of paper from a pad and writing it down. Passing it across to Scarlett he looked at her quizzically.

'Are you going to tell your mother of your visit here?' He asked.

'No are you?'

'No,' he said smiling at her, 'client confidentiality is the name of the game. I assume you wish to become one.' He was observing this tough talking young woman in a new light despite the fact that she was still under age.

'Yes,' she said and then looking directly at him asked. 'How did you become a lawyer?'

This time he regarded her more seriously. 'Is that what you want to do?'

'Yes, I am studying law at Oxford.'

Anthony Arbuthnot looked suitably impressed. He had managed to gain a place at Leeds to read Law but Oxford was top of the tree as far as he was concerned.

'Come back to me when you have your degree and we will discuss it then and see if we can be of assistance to you.'

He stood up holding out his hand to shake hers but this time there was a look of respect in his eyes as he opened the office door for her to pass through before she crossed the reception area to exit the building into the spring sunshine.

Chapter 17

Scarlett had left the lawyers' chambers with much on her mind. The one piece of information that Antony Arbuthnot had divulged was the fact that her father had a twin brother and a sister and parents who had been alive at the end of the War. Her mother had stated that Jack had told her that all his family was dead. She did not know why he would have said that but she just knew her mother would not lie to her. That was not in her nature. However, Scarlett felt that she needed to know why this had happened and more than anything she wanted to meet this family, Jack's legacy to her. She walked for a long time along the busy London streets mulling over the exciting facts that she now possessed and reached the conclusion that she did not wish to share them with anyone particularly her mother who would be shocked at the possible resurrection of a family that she had never known had existed. But why did Jack say that when it was obviously untrue. Was he estranged from his family for whatever reason? It was a mystery which required answers.

The light was beginning to fade on this late April afternoon. It was cloudy and looked as if it might turn to rain. She was already late in reaching Maudie's flat so she hailed a taxi to travel the rest of the way. She was excited on two levels now but at this moment in time she wanted to see Maudie's flat and then go and paint the town red as a celebration of a new journey into the unknown that she would shortly undertake.

Maudie was pacing her living room floor and then stopping every so often to look out of her window into the busy street below. Although she loved Scarlett as if she had been a true sister this visit had gone against the grain. But now that it was happening she felt a pride in her precious flat and wished to show it off. She had scrubbed and polished for days and the whole ambiance was one of perfection. The whole place gleamed. Maudie had changed the sheets on her bed in readiness for the visit and had placed a pile of bedding in the lounge for her use when she slept on the sofa that night. However, she was upset by Scarlett's tardiness. Scarlett was not usually like that for she often complained about her mother on that account. On her next advance to the window she saw a taxi draw up and a figure get out only to stick her head in through the driver's window to pay for her fare. Maudie overcome by excitement at seeing Scarlett, whom she had not seen since that blissful Christmas at Westborough, ran down the stairs that led to the street entrance to her flat.

'You are late,' she said, arms akimbo looking stern but her face dissolved into smiles and giggles.

They hugged warmly realizing how much they had missed each other over the intervening months.

'What on earth are you wearing, Maudie?' Scarlett asked as she pulled away from her sister and looked at the uniform that Maudie wore in her role as an ordinary mortal, a student at that.

'I'm a student so I can look like whatever I want,' she pretended to pout but there were giggles emanating from both of them. 'Anyway come on up and leave your luggage. We are going out on the town. I know some wonderful clubs and places to eat.'

'I'm starving,' Scarlett declared not remembering when she had last eaten as they clattered up the stairs.

Inside the flat Scarlett explored every nook and cranny before declaring, 'It's wonderful Maudie. It is so homely but it's got your style stamped all over it.'

Maudie stood back regarding this precious space in a critical fashion. She was proud of what she had accomplished over the past few months and Scarlett was right; it did look homely

'Thank you,' she said suddenly very pleased that she could share her triumph with somebody after all. 'Time to go,' she said shrugging on her jacket. 'Let's go and party.'

They locked the downstairs front door and set off down the street to the tube station both of them enjoying the freedom of their lives. This was not the London of the family Town House in Belgravia but more like living the life of ordinary Londoners. It was so exciting to be normal and yet at the same time they enjoyed the privilege of their class. To have the best of both worlds was wonderful. What Piers would have thought they dared not think? But at the same time there was no need for him to know.

The girls had eaten a feast at an Italian restaurant which Maudie often frequented with her student friends. The food was cheap but tasty and nourishing and they had ordered a cheap Italian red wine which was not the best quality but was full of flavour which complemented the food. Scarlett was enjoying Maudie's company in this adult environment and school days seemed so far behind them now. This was an adventure but it was a legitimate one unlike school days when they flouted the rules gaining excitement from so doing but now they made their own decisions and that felt like a freedom that only those who had attended boarding school could possibly understand.

The evening had grown dark before they left the restaurant. They had decided to move on to one of Maudie's night clubs that she visited with her conservatoire friends. The friends she had made enjoyed an eclectic range of music and often could be found in the clubs as well as the concert halls listening to classical music. This was all so different from Scarlett's life at Oxford where she spent most of her time working in pursuit of her first class degree but for the first time she realized what she was missing. University was about achievement but the balance lay in the other side of the coin too. It was there to be enjoyed in order to make you a well, rounded person. Scarlett wondered if she could have both. She was too young to have regrets she thought. When she returned after the Easter vacation she would rethink her life at Oxford.

They arrived at the Jazz Club which was nearly full but having managed to find a last table they sat down in anticipation of the evening ahead. There was the buzz of conversation. Waiters walked past holding trays aloft to squeeze through the melee of bodies. The singers were beginning to assemble on the small stage and instruments were readied and tuned for the evening performance. Scarlett was not sure how she felt about jazz music but the atmosphere was electric which sent a tingle down her spine. Maudie looked happy for this had become her world over recent months. She waved at people she knew and then she turned to Scarlett.

'You'll be all right on your own for a few minutes.' It was a statement not a question.

'Of course,' Scarlett said slightly puzzled, not realizing where Maudie was going. Maudie squeezed her arm in reassurance before she made her own way through the audience to the stage.

The room went quiet; you could hear a pin drop. The music started and Scarlett watched her sister start to sing 'Ol' Man River' in her low husky voice. Scarlet was mesmerized by the music and the singing but most of all it was the talent that emanated from Maudie, herself, which she could not believe. It was no wonder that her sister was happy in this new life that she had formulated for herself and did not wish the family to know about. Scarlett knew for a fact that Piers would not understand Maudie's desire to be normal. She was from a different class from the people who frequented the Clubs. At home at Westborough Hall she could play her role as Lady Maudie Devine but here she was really herself. Scarlett suddenly thought of Jane and her problems. If the older girl had had more sense to complete her school career her life would be so much better for she could have found her own niche in society.

The music faded as the session came to its conclusion and the audience clapped and cheered. Maudie had a quick word with the band and then returned to her table. She looked a little sheepish as she regarded Scarlett.

'Wow, Maudie how wonderful you were. You are a dark horse and what a talent.'

'Thank you. You won't tell them at home will you Scarlett. I don't want them to know until I am ready to tell them. I have ambitions about my future but it is difficult to know which route to take. I still have a long time at the Conservatoire before I have to decide.'

'I won't spill the beans, I promise but I do want to come again. It is wonderful. I didn't know you had such talent. You should be so proud of yourself.'

Maudie looked at Scarlett, smiling shyly. 'Thank you,' was all she could say.

Scarlett had enjoyed her time with Maudie. She was not prepared to break her promise to her sister but she was not ready to divulge her own secret thoughts either. It would seem that they all had places inside them where their secrets were deeply hidden. Two days later Scarlett was off on a quest of her own before returning to Westborough Hall.

She had left Maudie's during the early morning rush hour and had hailed a taxi to take her across the city to Forman Street to look for the house which had been her father's before his marriage to Thea. She was sure that it would not give her any information about the past but it was just the fact that she would feel nearer to him even just for a few moments.

The taxi dropped her at the end of the street so that she could walk the rest of the way to have a feel of the place. It was number 17 which she had to look out for so she had been told by Arbuthnot. The fact that Jack Carson had walked these streets made Scarlett feel that she was walking in dead man's shoes. She walked slowly gazing up at the Victorian facades. They were terraced houses just like many others in the capital and once they would have been quite grand. She wondered why Jack had bought such a large property when he lived on his own. She had found it and stood staring at it wondering why she and her mother had never lived there. But she knew the answer to that for Thea had had to live at the Hall to keep it safe for the Devines. Her mother had never mentioned coming to look at the house in those far away days. That thought had remained with her in recent years but perhaps that was the way people were in the War. It had been a far different time then. She lingered wishing that she could see inside but it would be wrong to knock the brass knocker and be intrusive. Suddenly the front door opened and a young woman holding a baby in arms stood at the top of the steps looking down on her.

'Can I help you?' She asked pleasantly. 'You appear to be lost.'

Scarlett felt lost for words. Was there a way to explain that you just wanted to satisfy your curiosity? 'I was looking to see the house where my father had lived during the early part of the War. I am so rarely in London these days.'

The young woman seemed satisfied enough by the explanation. 'You can come in and see it if you like if you don't mind the untidiness that a baby causes.'

Scarlett laughed. 'We have a baby at home so that doesn't bother me.'

She climbed the steps into the house and followed the young woman into the front sitting room where a fire blazed in the hearth surrounded by a protective guard. Nappies dried on top reminding Scarlett how privileged they were to have nanny and the staff to do the laundry. The young woman put the baby to sit on the floor amongst his toys. He banged the little drum and laughed while the two young women smiled at his antics.

Scarlett looked around her and found the room beautifully proportioned. It still perplexed her that her father had bought such a large house when he was supposed to have possessed little money. There was so much that she wished to learn about the Carsons and all the secrets shrouding their lives. The young woman returned from the kitchen carrying two mugs of steaming coffee placing them as far away from the baby as possible.

'By the way I'm Francesca, Francesca Somerville.' She held out her hand.

'Scarlett Devine,' she said wondering suddenly why she had said that. She used the name Carson nearly all the time now. Perhaps it was easier to not arouse suspicion if the name Carson appeared familiar. Scarlett was not sure why she was using cloak and dagger tactics but it just seemed the most sensible thing to do.

Chapter 18

It was strange how the Devine family as a whole were looking forward to being en famille for a while despite the fact that some of them had been at loggerheads for years. But the Christmas festivities had helped them turn a corner into better times.

'I shall be at Westborough for a few weeks over Easter,' Piers had said to Thea over breakfast one morning after his return from the House. He had peered at her over the top of his morning newspaper at breakfast. Then he smiled to emphasize the point before returning to read the financial news.

'Oh, how lovely, darling. It will be so good to have you home for a while,' Thea enthused.

Inwardly she had to smile because knowing her husband so well she knew that he was feeling rather pleased with himself about the burgeoning relationship with the older girls. She would have called it smugness if she was honest but she was desperately trying to be charitable. What Piers did not know was the fact that it had been almost a lifetime's work on her own part to make him reconciled with his daughters. His eyes had returned to his newspaper as he continued to read, deeply engrossed in the fiscal affairs of the moment. Thea's eyes were riveted on him suddenly thinking how like his father he was becoming in looks and mannerisms. Was that because age made such a difference? She blinked tears away wondering if she might look like her natural mother whom she had never known. What had brought all these nonsense ideas into her head she wondered? She had not thought of Ruth, her birth mother, or Beatrice for quite some time. It was not always healthy to dwell on the past. However, life was far too busy she had to admit to herself now that she no longer let time rule her. How foolish she had been when the older girls had moved on with their lives. She vowed that she was not going to do that again when the next wave of Devines reached a similar age. And then there was Amelia. It was going to be a long time before she flew the nest. Piers said that his youngest child was going to be spoilt beyond measure and who was guilty of that she thought looking once more at her husband, his face creased into a series of lines as he read on. The child was hardly out of his sight when he was home from London. He even wheeled the dilapidated pram which had been occupied by all the Devine children at some time or another around the Westborough gardens pointing out flowers and landmarks of the family property as if the baby truly understood. But he was bonding with this last precious child and Thea did not have the heart to complain; she just smiled indulgently and got on with life.

Jane had returned to Westborough in a whirl of excitement. Geneva had been great she felt and now with the season looming she felt that she would have plenty to think about and enjoy. The dreadful years of academia seemed to be a whole lifetime away. Now was the time to look forward and forget about the past.

'Thea, when are we going to buy my dresses for the Season?' She had asked on her first night home.

Jane had barged into Thea's small sitting room uninvited. The door had been slightly ajar. Thea looked up from what she was doing and smiled. It would have been easy to admonish her stepdaughter for her unsolicited invasion but the change in Jane had been so remarkable that there was no going back to the young woman who had caused so much anxiety in the past.

'Sit down, Jane,' Thea said beaming broadly. 'Please don't panic. It is all in hand. I have asked a good dressmaker from London to come and stay for a few days during the holiday. I had thought we would go and buy your dresses but this way you can choose your own distinct style which will fit you properly as long as you don't lose weight. You must keep a tight grip on what you eat in the next few months.'

Thea had noticed that Jane's waistline had slightly thickened during her time in Switzerland; undoubtedly it was the good living and Thea had suspected that alcohol had been consumed quite liberally too. She was just going to have to keep an eye on Jane's diet. Jane giggled and jumped up from the chair where she had been sitting. She twirled this way and that and tossed her long blonde hair about.

'You have a lovely figure Jane which you need to look after but your hair will be the problem though.'

Jane stopped moving and stared at her stepmother. 'Why?' She asked.

Thea laughed. 'Darling you do rather look as if you have been pulled through a hedge backwards.'

Jane ran her hands through her hair, 'I don't want it short Thea.'

'Of course not. Stop panicking. We must find a hairdresser who will be able to do the elegant upswept chignons that will complement your evening dresses. Maudie and Scarlett will have to do the same for your coming out dance when we have it here at the end of June. We have decided that was the best time to do it because they will have finished university for the summer.'

Jane sat down again as if all the fizz had been taken out of her. 'Thea it is only just over two and a half months away. Will we get it all ready in time?' She was all of a panic.

'Of course,' Thea said partly wondering the same thing. 'The dress maker assures me that she has a team of workers who will be able to do it for us in time but you must be available to go to the fittings when you can. That will mean living in London for most of the Season which should coincide with the major balls unless they are the ones you are invited to in the country.'

'Does Papa know all about this?' Jane asked.

'Of course. I have discussed everything at length with him. He is happy about it. Scarlett is home today and Maudie by the weekend. We will be ready to go, go, go.'

'Is there anybody home?' came a familiar voice. The sitting room door opened and Scarlett stood there grinning at her mother and Jane in joyous expectation of a reunion and three glorious weeks of freedom.

Her visit to her father's house had fuelled her thoughts on her journey home. She had found Francesca Somerville friendly and they planned to meet again at some point when Scarlett next visited London. Scarlett for reasons only known to herself had been vague about her father when Francesca asked questions. She was not ready to divulge details to someone who was a stranger. Scarlett could not quite understand her own reasons to be so reticent but Jack Carson was her possession. She did not even want to share him with her mother. Thea had moved forward with her life nearly two decades after her father had died and her world was that of the Devines. She was a Devine by marriage whereas Scarlett hoped to take a walk into the future to discover her father's legacy. She really hoped there would be one otherwise she was not sure that she could stand the disappointment. However, she had tried to ready herself for such eventualities.

Chapter 19

Easter had come and gone in a flurry of activity and impending excitement. Piers had taken refuge in the estate office for much of the time or had tramped through the grounds in the lovely spring weather to visit his mother at the Dower House. It was the most time he had spent with her in a very long time and they had both enjoyed the new rapport that was surfacing between them. They had grown closer again but he had noted one or two changes in Clarissa. She did not appear as robust as before. Of course she was getting older but were they not all ageing? However, there was a fragile air about her which worried him. He remembered Thea saying that there were changes in his mother, subtle changes that she could not quite put her finger on but as usual Piers had buried his head in the sand spending so much time in London and leaving most of the care to Thea. That was another guilt trip too. He knew that he had left far too much to rest on his wife's shoulders over the past twenty years starting with the War years. Perhaps it was time to be home more to share the burden. He thought about Thea allowing his heart to fill with the deep love that he still felt for her. She had never complained about how much she had to shoulder but he also knew that it had taken its toll too. She had been there for everybody including his eldest daughters and they had not been easy to handle. What would he do without Thea if anything untoward happened to her? That thought he brushed aside swiftly not wishing to dwell on any negative possibilities.

He had walked through the gardens to reach the Dower House acknowledging gardeners at work. He greeted Timms the senior gardener who had appeared quite old in the last War. Now he had a definite stoop but he was fit with his ruddy cheeks shining like polished apples in the spring sunshine. As Piers approached the old man touched his brown flat cap which remained on his head night or day whatever the weather allowing nobody to see what lay beneath. He might have been as bald as a coot but nobody was any the wiser. Perhaps the old man slept in it Piers mused. It was a distinct possibility for Mrs Timms had passed on years ago.

''Morning, milord,' Timms said.

'Good morning, Timms. The gardens are looking rather splendid,' Piers said looking around showing the pleasure that he felt. 'Winter has lost its hold at last and look at the blossom on the trees. There could be a bumper crop of apples in the autumn.'

'Indeed yes. Are you on your way to see your mother, milord? I heard she was taken poorly in the night.' Timms not normally one to gossip had heard the news on the rumour mill which seemed to operate with extreme efficiency upon the estate.

This was news to Piers but he did not comment. He continued his conversation briefly but after excusing himself he walked with speed and purpose towards the Dower House feeling anxiety rising within him. His mother was old and Thea's words seemed to ring in his ears. He wondered why he never seemed to be in the right place when things began to go wrong.

Letting himself in through the garden door of the boot room, he then entered the main hallway before taking a turn towards his mother's sitting room.

'Oh, milord,' a voice called out to him in relief, 'I'm so glad you have come. We have been trying to get hold of you at the Hall but nobody was answering. Her ladyship is ill.'

Piers turned around to confront the worried maid Jenny. He wondered momentarily why the telephone had not been answered in the main house but then pictured the scene that had sent him scurrying out of the way of its female occupants. The whole place seemed to be shrouded under piles of material for Jane's forthcoming Season. The easiest decision was to find the nearest exit as soon as possible for his escape to a saner world.

'How ill?' He asked surprising himself by the panic he could hear in his voice.

'Quite poorly, I do believe, milord. The Doctor is with her now.'

Piers' instincts were to rush up the stairs to his mother's bedroom but if the Doctor was there he knew that he could not do so.

Looking at the maid he said, 'why did nobody run up to the Hall to tell me?' His voice was angry but without allowing the girl to reply he said, 'as soon as the doctor comes down tell him to come and see me in my mother's sitting room.'

'Yes, m'lord.'

Piers walked into the sitting room and strode straight to the brandy decanter and poured a generous measure into his glass. It was not usual for him to drink so early in the day but he was worried about his mother and rather angry that the estate workers knew before he did. The rumour mill had been at work again. Seating himself in his chair he glanced around the room looking at the family portraits that lined the walls. On the grand piano in front of the French windows he noted the photographs of his sisters and himself as children. There were also photographs of his children happily posing in front of the camera. There was Harry, his own heir, smiling broadly and a feeling of pride overtook him. His dynasty was safe for the time being. But suddenly a thought engulfed him that there was no photograph of James Devine, Clarissa's husband and his own father. It was a painful thought for once again he registered how terrible his parents' marriage had been and that in death there were no happy memories to mask what had happened in real life. He wondered what his marriage would have been like if Mary had lived. They would have been divorced no doubt which made him ever more thankful to have Thea in his life. Just at that moment there was a knock at the door and the doctor entered the room extending a hand to shake but his face remained grave.

'Hello, Piers,' Doctor Brownlow said. There was no ceremony between these two men. They treated each other as equals.

'How is my mother?' Piers asked. 'I didn't even know that she was ill.'

'She is quite ill. It is pneumonia. She did not want any fuss but I sent Jenny to ring the Hall. She should go into hospital for she requires specialist nursing but she won't.'

'Stubborn as a mule as ever,' Piers said, pouring the Doctor a brandy which was his normal tipple.

Doctor Brownlow put his medical bag onto the floor before taking his brandy. Sinking into a winged back armchair he said, 'she is being stubborn I'm afraid but I do believe it goes deeper than that. She mumbled that she did not want to die in hospital. I don't know where she got that notion from.'

'Nor do I but she has been rather gloomy in her outlook lately, whether it is a premonition....' Piers broke off mid-sentence and looked at the Doctor. 'You don't think that she is going to die do you?'

Doctor Brownlow looked very grave. 'The trouble is, Piers, your mother is not very strong. She has a weak heart and her condition has been deteriorating over the last few months. I had tried to persuade her to tell you about her health but she would not hear of it. "They are all so busy and I don't want to be a burden to them," she would say. I tried to make her listen but... I hope she will be strong enough to pull through. I have taken it upon myself to employ two nurses to provide round the clock care. I did not wish to upset her by sending her into hospital. I hope you don't mind.'

'No you did the right thing. Thea has been saying for a while that my mother looked frail. I'm surprised that she did not tell me or Thea about this.'

Doctor Brownlow gave a rueful smile, 'You know your mother better than anyone, Piers. She is stoical in the full sense of the word. She would not want to bother you or your family more than she need. I believe that has always been her way.'

'Yes,' Piers said, 'she was always feisty. May I see her?'

'She is asleep now, but it would not hurt to just go in. Jenny is with her but the nurses will be here this afternoon. I will be back later to check up on her.'

'Thank you, Thomas.'

The two men shook hands before the Doctor drained his glass of brandy and picked up his bag in readiness to leave the Dower House.

Piers left his mother's home with feelings of foreboding. The sight that met his eyes on entering his mother's bedroom was enough to cause him great consternation. She lay in a foetal position, heavily sedated and her breathing came in short rasping breaths as she tried courageously to fight the pneumonia which had taken hold. Jenny sat by the bedside holding the hand of the old Countess. The maid had great affection for her employer who had been generous towards her over the years. She rose to go in order to leave Piers alone with his mother.

'Stay, Jenny, please. I won't be here long but I shall be back later.' He gently caressed his mother's cheek with the back of his finger but she did not stir and continued to breathe with difficulty. He had never expected to see the day when his indomitable mother would not be there with the family and tears blurred his vision. It was true that they had had their difficult times over the years particularly when his father had passed away but they had come through and their relationship had been the stronger for it. Suddenly he felt he needed Thea so badly that he turned to leave the room then he half turned back to take one last look. Tears filled his eyes hoping that she would pull through but his heart was full of foreboding.

'Telephone me if there is any change,' he said to the girl who merely nodded.

Thea was in her sitting room writing letters when Piers returned. He entered the room making her look up sharply to see who had barged in so abruptly. Sometimes the younger Devines would do so when they were home. They were no great respecters of their mother's privacy feeling that she was their possession. She regarded Piers closely and noted his demeanour.

'What is it?' She said rising to go to him seeing that he was so troubled.

'Mama is ill. Brownlow says that it is pneumonia.'

Thea looked shocked by what she had heard. There had been no warning about her illness. She took Piers in her arms and held him momentarily before releasing him.

'I will go and sit with her. She will need to be with her family.'

'Thank you,' he said, the shock still registering on his face. It was Thea again who was there for anyone who was troubled.

It did not take Thea long to cross the gardens to the Dower House. She had run most of the way and when she entered the house she was out of breath. Stopping for a moment she leaned against the newel post of the stairs gasping but recovering, she slowly ascended to the upper floor. Clarissa's bedroom door was a jar and Thea pushed it open wider wondering what to expect.

She was shocked at Clarissa's appearance. It was only a few days since Thea had seen Piers' mother but the deterioration in her condition was unbelievable. Jenny still sat there but was relieved to see Thea.

'I'll stay with the Countess, Jenny. You go and have a break and thank you.'

They smiled at each other before the young maid exited the room.

Thea sat and held the old woman's hand as she gazed at her grey pallor. During the two hours that she spent with her, Clarissa slept, emanating rasping short breaths in her uneasy sleep. Later that afternoon Doctor Brownlow returned to see his patient and he was accompanied by two nurses who with great efficiency made the large bedroom into a sick room. Doctor Brownlow said there was no change from the previous visit.

'Isn't that good news,' Thea said, her voice full of hope for the woman she loved like a mother.

Doctor Brownlow looked at her. 'Possibly. I hope so. I think you should go home and get some rest yourself, Thea. This could go on for some time. Let the nurses do their job. Come and see her regularly but visitors are exhausting for the ill. We will keep you updated about the Dowager Countess' condition.'

'All right, if I must.'

Thea rose reluctantly but knew there was nothing she could do for her mother-in-law. She was in the best possible hands. She left the room with a single backward glance accompanied by the Doctor.

'Is there hope for her to make a full recovery?' Thea asked as they descended the stairs. Her voice sounded doubtful after what she had witnessed.

'I can't answer that honestly Thea. It is not just the pneumonia that is making her ill but also her heart. But fundamentally she has got to have the will to pull through. Many old people eventually give up. Sometimes they feel that they have lived their life and there is nothing more to strive for.'

'But surely not, Clarissa. She has so much in her life and she is a fighter. She always has been,' Thea looked aghast. She was remembering the time during the War when Piers had been declared missing. Clarissa had been so strong then.

Doctor Brownlow patted her shoulder. 'We all change over time but don't give up hope. We will do the best for her.'

With those words he left the Dower House still seeing the devastation in Thea's face. What a wonderful woman she had been in the Devine family. They were lucky to have her he mused as he placed his medical bag on the leather upholstery of his car before he drove off. Thea waved as he drove off before walking slowly back through the Westborough gardens. She needed time to think and remember the old woman she had always loved as a mother. Her thoughts were maudlin as she walked. She was almost sure that life this time would be too much for the Dowager Countess. The whole family would miss her but Thea suspected that she would most of all for had Clarissa not been her greatest support and friend when she had needed it most of all. The old woman was not yet dead but tears of sorrow ran down her cheeks. She stopped momentarily and sat on a bench in the spring sunshine trying to compose herself before her return to the Hall and Piers. The last thing she wanted was for him to see her this way.

Chapter 20

Life still had to go on despite Clarissa's illness. Piers did not return to the House of Lords giving the excuse that his mother was ill and he was needed at home. Scarlett and Maudie returned to their other lives reluctantly but Thea had explained that there was nothing that they could do. They would be informed if there were any changes. Jane had said that she was happy to miss the start of the Season. It was too frivolous to be participating in that way of life while her grandmother lay so ill. Jane knew how good her grandmother had been to her during those years when life had been so difficult. Even Piers could see how Jane had changed in the last year.

'She has suddenly grown up,' he said to Thea one day.

'Yes,' Thea replied but she failed to utter what lay in her heart. She felt that the change of circumstances was no thanks to Piers. However, the great thaw had begun to set in between father and daughter in more recent times was mostly due to their joint feelings over Clarissa's health. Jane often walked to the Dower house to keep her grandmother company but it also helped Thea who had much to do with life at the Hall but she never failed in her task to see as much of Clarissa as she could. Piers often went to see his mother too. She was beginning to rally. Her cheeks gained more colour and she began to walk very stiffly to sit for a short time in a bedroom chair and as the warmer days of May approached she could descend the stairs to sit in her drawing room to receive members of her family. But the visits were short for she became tired once more and would fall asleep to recover her strength. However, this prolonged illness had taken its toll. Her appetite was poor and she lost weight making her appear wizened.

Everyone now expected her to recover eventually; even Thea was more hopeful and relieved. Her mother-in-law had proved once more how stoic she could be. And as the days progressed, thoughts returned to Jane's season. She had an ample supply of evening dresses which had been purchased or made on her return from Switzerland. However, she had missed the presentation ball at the Old Bailey Law Courts but nevertheless invitations to balls in the social season began to arrive through the post. The Devines were a well-respected family within the aristocratic world and news of

Clarissa's illness at such a time had brought about a feeling of sympathy for the old countess and feelings too that Jane could not quite fulfil her destiny in social circles on account of her grandmother's illness. Conventions had to be followed. It was a double-edged sword.

Thea who had expected to chaperone Jane to all the events found it difficult to leave Clarissa. She was uncertain how to tackle the problem without Jane taking extreme umbrage at such neglect. Jane, though, had grown up as Piers had declared and took the situation well under the circumstances. But as if a coup de foudre had been sent from the Heavens, Piers' sister Minty arrived to see her mother. She had decided to stay for a few days at the Dower House to relieve the situation at the Hall.

'Oh Minty, how good of you,' Thea had said warmly when Minty had telephoned to announce her imminent arrival.

'Nonsense, Thea, you cannot do everything yourself. You will run yourself into an early grave if you are not careful.'

Thea did not comment but had begun to think that herself. Piers was burying his head in the sand during another crisis. Sometimes Thea in a slightly disloyal moment wondered how her husband had coped with his part in the war. There could not have been anything more stressful than that.

Minty arrived just a day later laden down with more luggage than Thea felt she had hanging in her own wardrobe. How long this sister-in-law was staying was a question that Thea wished to ask but it would appear churlish at such a time when Clarissa had been so ill. Her daughter's company would surely raise the old countess's spirits and relieve some of the pressure on other members of the family. Thea felt a modicum of guilt as she always did when she found it difficult not to be there for all of them but that had always been her nature and possible undoing.

The chauffeur had taken Minty the long way round to the Dower House, through the leafy lanes and along the long driveway which in the past had been the sole access to the property. He carried Minty's luggage into the house and awaited further instructions. The Dower House was entirely a female domain without anybody to heft anything heavy unless there was a special request to the big house. Minty having spent a few moments with her mother reappeared giving instructions to carry her luggage to the room which she had once used when her mother had first moved there a very long time ago after her father's death.

Thea had skipped through the gardens in the May sunshine to meet Minty. The two women had not been close over the years for Minty had rarely returned to her childhood home but there was still some affection which lingered there and made them hug. Clarissa had stayed in bed that day declaring that she was feeling tired and any meals that she might tackle could be taken to her on a tray. The sudden arrival of her daughter had done little to raise her spirits. She was at a stage where she wanted peace and not have to pay lip service to anybody and particularly to this selfish daughter who only visited to suit her own ends.

'Come to the hall for dinner tonight Minty. It will be like old times,' Thea said knowing Clarissa's state of health. Minty could be demanding at the best of times but when somebody was ill it could be draining at the very least to have to keep a conversation flowing.

'Clarissa will be asleep by then. She does tend to sleep rather a lot these days but it is only to be expected after illness,' Thea continued hoping that she had been direct enough without causing offence.

'That will be lovely, Thea. Thank you. It would be a little lonely here if Mama is not well and in bed.' She bent to kiss Thea's cheek. 'I had better unpack now, so I will see you later.'

She turned and left Clarissa's sitting room. Thea's eyes followed her departure. There was just a little unease in her mind that she could not quite put her finger on although somehow it was to do with all those clothes that Minty had brought with her.

At precisely seven thirty Minty entered the large sitting room where the family was waiting. Piers rose to embrace her. She had been his favourite sister over the years and family occasions these days were rare and made him feel sentimental. Thea observed her husband without saying anything but she knew that deep down he was upset by his mother's state of health. Thea was more pragmatic. Although she was upset by Clarissa's health issues she also felt that at her advancing age ill health was not unusual. Nobody would live forever. She had come to this conclusion after the onset of Clarissa's health problem. To her it was a safety valve for when the inevitable would surely happen.

Piers offered Minty a sherry just as the dinner was announced.

'I will wait until we eat, Piers dear,' Minty said sweetly as they made their way into the small dining room. She put an affectionate arm around Jane's shoulders uttering sympathy about the timing of Clarissa's illness and the beginning of the season.

As the meal was half way through the main course Minty put down her knife and fork and looked at her brother, a serious expression on her face.

'Piers, dear, I must say that I have not been totally truthful with you.' If Minty had wanted their attention she certainly had it now. They regarded her with perplexion. She gave a thin lipped smile. Thea felt that her concerns might be vindicated as she waited for her sister-in-law to continue

'I might just come out and say it. Alexander and I have separated. He has had a mistress for quite some time and now he wants a divorce so that he can marry her. I have agreed so as I have nowhere else to go I thought that I would come and live with Mother. She must be lonely. And I thought, Thea dear, that perhaps I could help out by chaperoning Jane to some of her balls because you are so frightfully busy and need a break. You are looking frightfully peaky.'

Knives and forks clattered on to unfinished plates of food. Thea's face remained expressionless as she regarded her sister-in-law. There was silence as everybody was rendered speechless. What Thea never voiced was the fact that if Clarissa did pull through she would not want anybody living with her. Clarissa was mistress of her own destiny and enjoyed her own solitude. What a state of affairs this was going to be. Thea could hear Piers through the whirlwind of her thoughts.

'Of course you must come home Minty old thing. It will always be your home here and Mama will be so pleased to have you. But do you want me to speak to Alex to see what I can do?' Piers' voice was full of concern. He did not have the intuition to read other people's situation or thoughts. It had always been thus. Thea, however much she loved Piers, knew that there was always going to be the spoiled element about him. He had grown up as the only boy in the family. He had been the heir and had been pampered as a result.

Minty extracted a lacy handkerchief from her insubstantial evening bag. Dabbing her eyes she looked at her brother before shaking her head. 'It is too late for that. I don't wish to return to him or be humiliated any more. As it is the divorce is going through. Even our children are reconciled to the fact. Anyway we don't see them too often. They have their own lives to lead.'

Thea just sat and stared at Piers' sister remembering all the suitcases that had been unloaded from the Bentley. Her intuition of earlier in the day had been totally vindicated. All this was a fait accompli. She had not come to see her mother after all. Thea's lips turned downward showing her disapproval. And the other fact was that Minty was ready to take over the role that should be hers alone to chaperone Jane for the Season. Thea had worked so hard to make Jane's life so much better. She had wanted the girl to have self-respect after all the problems that had lain at their door. And as for Jane they were only now starting to win her back into the bosom of the family. There was a new harmony between them all which had brought much pleasure to Piers who had lived under a cloud all these years wondering how the problems could be resolved. The buzz of conversation continued without Thea participating as she looked from face to face of the people who sat around the table trying to assess their mood and thoughts.

The telephone ringing in the hallway interrupted the conversation. Johnson, who doubled as a footman and butler, knocked on the door of the small dining room before entering the room.

'A telephone call for you my lord,' he said putting his head around the door, his demeanour grave, as Piers rose from his seat at the table to take the call. All eyes followed him, wondering what was the matter. Johnson's grave face had not gone unnoticed.

Chapter 21

Piers returned to the small dining room; his face was ashen as he resumed his place at the table.

'That was Doctor Brownlow. He is at the Dower House. Mama has had a heart attack. The prognosis is not good, I'm afraid.'

'Are you going over there now, Piers? I will come with you,' Thea said.

'No. Minty and I will go,' he said. His churlish attitude hid the anguish he felt and he only had thoughts for his mother, not able to hear the sensitivity in his wife's voice.

Thea looked as if he had struck her. He had not reasoned how close the two women had been. He had closed ranks with his sister and shut her out. The hurt registered on her face but nobody saw it as the blood relatives took over. Even Jane said that she was going with them, and the in-law remained at home waiting to hear the news whenever that might be and whatever it might be, but the outcome seemed almost to be written in stone. Thea felt bitter towards them all, an alien sensation to her normally tranquil persona, as she watched them leave the room without a backward glance. Suddenly, she placed her hand over her mouth as a sob emanated from her. Clarissa meant everything to her.

Thea rose unsteadily from her chair and fled from the dining room, leaving the remnants of the meal behind. Rushing up the stairs to her room, she tried to control her emotions, but as soon as the door was closed behind her, she threw herself onto the bed and cried her heart out for Clarissa, herself and the cruelty which she believed that Piers had meted out to her, whether he meant it or not. She was not in the right frame of mind to think logically. Eventually, she lay within the covers of her bed, allowing the soothing calmness of sleep to envelope her and take her away from the problems which littered her mind.

It must have been during the early hours of the morning when Thea began to surface from her disturbed slumbers. The troubles came flooding back, but at the same time, she heard the bedroom door click shut and then she felt her body enveloped in Piers' soothing embrace, but she began to start pushing him away as her anguish resurfaced.

'Please don't, Thea. I know you are upset and angry with me for what I did. Hear me out first,' he begged. His arms were now wrapped firmly around her, not allowing her to resist him and his voice was full of the emotion which dwelt inside him.

'That call during dinner was from Brownlow. He had been telephoned by Mama's nurse and told that she had slipped away in her sleep. She had not suffered but her heart was so weak by the end that it took only a minor heart attack to take her away from us. Brownlow told me that she was dead but I didn't want to upset you more than need be. I did not want you to see her like that. I'm sorry if I did not handle it very well. Please forgive me.'

Thea lay peacefully in Piers' arms, the hurt she had felt slowly evaporating. She tried to register that Clarissa was not there anymore. Her heart ached for the old woman that she had loved so much, who could be a tremendous source of wisdom and love. But, perhaps, she was being selfish for now; she would not suffer any more but they would all miss her so much. It was her wit and wisdom which had helped all the Devines at some point in their lives. She had been stoic all of her life simply because she had to be, she had once told Thea. Then there was the guilt that Thea felt for blaming Piers about his thoughtlessness. That gave her feelings of shame to be able to think in such a way. She moved closer into his arms to help compensate for the terrible loss that he must be feeling.

'I'm so very sorry,' she said. 'I know that you are hurting too. Words fail me.'

Piers kissed her gently on her brow, 'Ssh,' he tried to calm her before saying, 'please don't ever doubt how much I love you, Thea. I haven't always been the best husband and father I know but I am getting better now. I have made a decision that I will only go to the House when there is a big debate. My time is here now with my family. It is not just Mama passing but I have been thinking about it for quite some time.'

Thea did not acknowledge this statement for her thoughts were for others. 'How are Minty and Jane?' She suddenly asked.

'They have taken it quite well considering. They did not go and see Mama. I thought it best that they remembered her as she had been. Brownlow went with me. He is such a good chap, thoughtful and caring but I suppose that is the calling of his profession. Mama looked very peaceful, really just asleep. I told Minty to come back to stay at the Hall for the time being. She can't stay there under the present circumstances. I hope you don't mind, Thea.'

Thea knew that she did mind but said, 'of course she must come to the hall.' Sobs wracked her slight body, 'Oh, Piers, I am so dreadfully sorry.'

'Hush,' he said as he kissed her again, then sleep gently began to engulf them and numb their troubled minds.

Chapter 22

The next morning Piers and Thea woke early as the late spring sunshine shone brightly through the chinks in the curtains. They still lay entwined in each other's arms and were reluctant to move as this moment of closeness was precious to both of them. As they opened their eyes the real world came flooding back bringing with it all the troubles and tribulations of the previous day and there were things to do and people to contact. The children needed to be informed about their grandmother's death, friends and relations contacted and articles placed in the national and society papers as well. There was the vicar to inform and decisions to be made on the service. The family solicitor would advise them about instructions that had been placed in Clarissa's will about the service. It all seemed too much to bear but it had to be done and there was nobody else to do it. Thea began to cry again as she thought of Clarissa's cold body lying all alone at the Dower house. Although in sombre mood Piers pulled his wife close once more to give her comfort before he rose to start the errands of the day.

After breakfast, Piers had telephoned the Reverend Dunwoody regarding Clarissa's demise. The clergyman had cycled to the Hall straight away for his meeting with the Earl. He was a man in his early fifties with an erect physique of military bearing. During the war he had been a padre in the forces but had returned to civilian life a little shaken by experiences he had witnessed close to the front but a rural parish had calmed his nerves and as the years had rolled away his sympathetic manner had often helped his parishioners when they called for advice on a number of issues. Piers received him in the library. Both men held a grudging admiration for the other and over the years of their friendship they had discussed the war and the nightmares which had invaded their sleep after the war had ended.

'I'm so sorry, Piers, about the loss of your mother. She went downhill so quickly at the end I believe.'

'Yes she did,' Piers said shaking the extended hand that had been proffered.

'Can I offer you anything, tea, coffee? It is a little early for anything stronger.'

'No I have just had my breakfast, thank you. You wanted to speak of the service?'

'Yes. It is a little too soon to make all the....'

'Quite so. I have already spoken to your mother on that score.'

Piers looked at Dunwoody quizzically. 'When?' Came the question.

'It must have been a little over a year ago. Clarissa asked me to go and see her. She said that she wanted to sort out her place of burial. She seemed very determined on the matter and very preoccupied with death if I may say so. In fact I felt a little concerned about it but she laughed off my concerns saying that she was getting old.'

'She did talk about dying quite a lot recently but I just put it down to old age. However she will be buried with my father in the mausoleum like all the Devines.'

Piers stopped speaking momentarily and looked closely at Dunwoody. Suddenly he said, 'I remember now. She doesn't want to be buried with my father. She said something odd when my father died about not wanting to be buried with him but I thought she was joking. I know that they did not get along but it is a tradition for the Earl and his Countess to be buried in the mausoleum. It will look strange to the rest of society if this does not happen.'

'It might look strange to some but there are locals with long memories who remember the state of your parents' marriage. However, she was adamant that she wanted a plot to herself in the corner of the churchyard away from the riff raff. I am quoting her verbatim,' the vicar half smiled at the recollection. 'She loved this county with a passion and wanted a personal view of the Malvern Hills. She was quite a character your mother.'

'Yes,' Piers said half heartily. He felt that all these idiosyncrasies of his mother's were going to make the Devines a laughing stock in society once it became public knowledge. 'I suppose we could not forget that this little discourse between you and my mother took place.'

Dunwoody looked serious and shook his head. 'I'm afraid not Piers. I would not renege on my word but even more I believe it is written in her will.'

'Damnation!' Piers swore and then apologized to the vicar. 'So I have to abide by her instructions. 'I suppose she was in sound mind when she decided this.'

'Your mother was always in sound mind,' Dunwoody laughed. Piers smiled too for the first time since the news of his mother's death.

After the Reverend Dunwoody had taken his leave Piers entered the estate office which he found empty. Lifting the telephone receiver he dialled the solicitor's number in London and asked for Antony Arbuthnot.

'Arbuthnot speaking.'

'Ah Antony it is Piers Devine here. I need to tell you that my mother passed away yesterday. I have also a question to ask you.'

'My condolences, your Lordship. I am very sorry to hear that. What do you wish to ask me?'

'Well I must know whether my mother updated her will in recent times.'

'Yes she did. I believe without looking it up that it was about a year ago now.'

'She seems to have been very busy a year ago,' Piers muttered to himself before addressing his next comment to the solicitor.

'And did she specify anything about her place of burial?' Piers asked fervently hoping that she had not.

'I believe she did but the exact details escape me. I would have to look it up but I will be reading the will soon by all accounts anyway.'

'The funeral has to be arranged so could you find out for me and ring me back.' Without further niceties Piers slammed down the receiver in a fit of temper waiting to hear the information that he did not want to know.

Behind him Piers heard footsteps and he turned to see who was there.

'Whatever is the matter Piers?' Thea said advancing towards him her arms outstretched to continue the closeness they had felt during their intimacies of the night.

Piers began to calm down as he enfolded Thea in his embrace. 'It is mother. She wants to be buried in the churchyard and not the mausoleum.'

Thea pulled away from Piers and laughed. 'Do you blame her? Who would want to be incarcerated in that dank, gloomy place forever? I won't be buried there ever.'

Piers pulled away from her looking deep into her eyes. 'Have I got you to contend with too?' He said as they both laughed again pulling close once more each taking much comfort from the other's presence.'

Chapter 23

Clarissa, Dowager Countess of Westborough lay in state in her sitting room in the Dower House. Her body had initially been removed but had been returned the morning before the funeral for anyone who wished to pay their last respects to do so. There had been a steady stream of people from the village who had worked for the estate during Clarissa's time as Countess and then members of the Devine family were to attend during a private time in the early evening. Thea had gone alone to see her mother-in-law for she wanted to remember times they had shared in the past, good and bad when they had been there for each other over the years. She remembered the time when Clarissa had finally been instrumental in bringing Piers to his senses after his return from the War. These had all been times when Clarissa's stoical nature had been to the fore. Now looking into the face of her mother-in-law Thea felt saddened at the toll her last illness had taken of the old woman. She had suffered more than they had known for Doctor Dunwoody had finally said that the old Countess had suffered from cancer and she had been in much pain but she had not wanted to bother her family. This they had assumed had been the cause of her preoccupation with death for many months.

'Why did you not tell us? I was always there for you,' Thea thought as tears streamed down her face. She bent forward to kiss the cold forehead which felt smooth to the touch. Death had removed the wrinkles and the look of pain which had obviously touched the old woman's features.

The door to the sitting room opened and Piers looked in. 'There you are,' he said as concern etched his brow.

He walked into the room followed by Minty and Diana. Their eyes brimmed with tears too. Thea looked sideways at them wondering why they were so upset for they had rarely visited the Hall in recent years and now Minty had returned when it suited her. Thea tried to admonish her vitriolic thoughts but somehow she could not for she knew them to be true. She felt Piers take her hand which he gripped tightly. They had grown closer since his mother's passing. She looked into his face and he smiled that secret smile which had been theirs all those years ago when they believed that their love had been forbidden. Suddenly the sitting room door opened and Jane and Maudie entered to pay their last respects. Jane suddenly howled in anguish and it was Thea who moved to give comfort to the young woman who had believed that her grandmother had always been the support she needed over the years even though she often disapproved of her behaviour. Somehow everyone assumed the old countess to be invincible. How foolish they had been.

The young Devines had returned home the previous evening but Thea and Piers had felt that it was not appropriate for them to view their grandmother.

'Why not?' Young Henry demanded. 'I am the heir.'

'You might be the heir, my son, but you will do as you are told,' Piers said, his voice firm and Henry realized that his father could not be swayed.

Both Piers and Thea had recognized the fact that their son was often boastful of his aristocratic heritage and this might also enter into the macabre viewing of his dead grandmother which might fill the corridors of Eton on his return. They were taking no chances.

Now on the morning of Clarissa's funeral the undertakers sealed her coffin for the last time and her casket was placed inside the horse drawn hearse ready to take her on her last journey. Antony Arbuthnot had returned Piers' call to say that it was written into Clarissa's will that she was to be buried exactly where the Reverend Dunwoody had stated. Piers had had no choice but to accept the inevitable but he was far from happy.

The family followed the hearse on foot towards the church of Saint Peters, on the edge of Durston village. Piers, erect and dignified, held the hand of his tearful Countess followed by the Devine children including Scarlett on this last journey. Behind them came Minty and Diana clad in black veils and any other relation there might be. As was the usual custom estate workers, now fewer in number than in previous decades bent their heads as a mark of respect as the hearse passed by. Inside the ancient church members of the aristocracy were sitting like sardines in pews that were to seat fewer people and others stood in the side aisles for the duration of the service. The Reverend Dunwoody gave a moving farewell for the woman he had known for many years. Again the funeral party returned to the churchyard while a depressing drizzle descended upon them as the coffin was borne to its final resting place. Only family were present at the internment where Clarissa was buried in the place that she had chosen within view of the Malvern Hills in her adopted county of Worcestershire.

Antony Arbuthnot had attended the service and was to return to the Hall to read the will. Clarissa had specified that there was to be no wake but a family dinner to celebrate her life. Piers by now realized that he had lost control of his mother's departure and had just had to come to terms with it. The family waited at the church to say their farewells to mourners who had come from different parts of the county and beyond and then slowly they returned to the Hall where Antony Arbuthnot was waiting in the library. Dispensing of their outer garments for the day was chill with a cold wind blowing, the family stood in the great hall for Piers to rally the troops.

Piers turned to his family as they lingered in the great hall. 'I would like Scarlett, Jane and Maudie to attend the reading of the will. The rest of you will be told if it is appropriate for you to know.' Harry Devine looked vexed feeling that as the heir to the Earldom it was his duty to be there. He was just about to say something for the second time in two days when he caught sight of the expression on his father's face. Sensibly he turned his back herding his brother and sister towards the large sitting room where they were expected to stay for the duration of the reading of the will.

Thea glanced at Scarlett and noted the look of mutiny on her face. She turned to her mother and sotto voce she said, 'I don't like being told what to do. Clarissa was not my grandmother and Piers has no right to tell me what to do. He is not my father.'

'But I am your mother,' Thea said sternly for the first time in Scarlett's adult life. 'This once you will do what I say because you are part of this family whether you like it or not.'

Scarlett was stung by her mother's words. She had never spoken to her in that way before. Without another word she flounced into the library tossing her mane of red hair and taking a seat the furthest away from anybody else. Piers who had witnessed the altercation between mother and daughter was not sure what it had been about. He hung back to enter the library with Thea.

'What was that all about?' He asked.

'Nothing to worry about,' Thea said truly unhappy at the drama which had been played out in front of the others. She knew she would take her errant daughter to task later but she was perplexed by her attitude.

Antony Arbuthnot had spread his papers across the highly polished library table. To his right hand stood a glass of water from which he had imbibed even before he had started his diatribe. He looked around at the faces of the family who were waiting for him to begin. Minty and Diana sat shoulder to shoulder wondering how long the proceedings would go on. Diana knew that she had a train to catch and would not be staying to the family dinner. Piers thought it could not go on long because his mother had few personal possessions of value and she had no money of her own as his father had left her nothing in her will. She had been reliant on Piers' generosity since he had inherited the Earldom.

Arbuthnot coughed to gain the attention of his audience. 'This is the last will and testament of Clarissa Augusta, Dowager Countess of Westborough. There was a slight snigger from the back row of the library. The girls had not known their grandmother's other name. Piers turned around with a face like thunder and quelled the hilarity behind him. Arbuthnot continued with small items which had been bequeathed to her grandchildren. It was mostly jewellery for the girls and a small gift of money to the boys.

Thea looked across at Scarlett and noticed a look of remorse on the girl's face. The point had been proved to her daughter. There would be no need for words later. However, it still puzzled Thea that Scarlett was still wondering about the father she had never met. Her attention returned to the will not quite believing her ears.

'There is nothing left to my two daughters Araminta Spencer and Diana Martin Jenkins for they deserted me after their marriages.' Arbuthnot's voice intoned.

Diana had left the room in shock ready to leave the Hall for London at once. Minty shell shocked that this revelation had been made public within the family sat looking straight ahead, ashen white as she tried to assemble some dignity but also knowing that she too had thrown herself on her brother's charity as her mother had had to do all those years ago. Piers wondered what else was to come because he knew that his mother had a reputation for her vitriol particularly in her younger years. Thea placed her hand in her husband's knowing that he was feeling this upset acutely.

'To my son Piers Devine I leave half of the residue of my estate equally with his wife Thea who has been more of a daughter to me than my own flesh and blood.'

Arbuthnot looked up registering that the will reading had reached its conclusion. The girls made a swift exit wanting to discuss their inheritance. Minty still in a daze stood up unsteady on her feet and walked to the door wanting to be alone with her thoughts. She knew that she had to talk to her brother later in the day. Thea sat and wondered at it all. She knew that her mother-in-law could be shrewish but except for her early meetings with the woman Clarissa had been warm and wonderful with her.

'Thank you,' Piers said shaking the solicitor's hand. 'How much money did my mother leave. A few hundred?'

Arbuthnot smiled and shook his head. 'It was a quarter of a million pounds.'

'Where did she get that kind of money from?' He asked aghast.

Arbuthnot could not keep his face straight. When he smiled he looked rather handsome Thea thought as she observed the proceedings.

'She began to save some money from her allowance and then she began to play the stock market. I believe that she became rather good at it.'

'Well, I'll be damned. Wily old bird,' Piers said bemused as he looked from Arbuthnot to his wife. Thea smiled broadly at the prospect that Clarissa had as usual confounded them all. How she would miss her.

'It will only be worth that providing the stock market does not plummet, your Lordship,' Arbuthnot said having collected his papers together before going to shake Thea's hand on departure.

And within minutes he was on his way home relieved that the reading of the will was over. He remembered his uncle telling him that the Devine wills always came as a shock to the family and how right he was.

Chapter 24

The family was missing Clarissa more than they would admit. She had been a fixture in their lives ready to give advice if it was wanted but not interfering if there was no call for it. She had often walked up to the Hall to talk to Thea on matters to do with the family that she cared so passionately about, like the great matriarch that she had become. She had also been company for Thea during the long periods of time Piers spent at the House. Like many people of her age experience of life had given her a wisdom which younger people had to learn through good and bad times. She had been nurtured on the knocks that life had thrown at her particularly after her marriage. Happiness had passed her by for years and it was the death of her husband which had released her from the tomb of unhappiness in which she had been incarcerated. It was no wonder that she would never lie by his side in death through eternity.

It was probably Thea who missed her the most. During those early summer days Thea went to visit the grave taking flowers and arranging them in the urns which had been provided for just that purpose. How Clarissa had loved the flowers of the different seasons. But life was moving on a pace and Thea had to move forwards too and as the old adage said life was for the living. And there was still much of that to do.

Piers had considered that the Dower House could be closed up after Clarissa's passing but Minty still lingered at the Hall simply because she had nowhere else to go after the break down of her marriage and had very little money to move her life forward. She had to be catered for in some way. It had become clear over the intervening weeks since her arrival on their doorstep that her substantial inheritance from her father had been eroded over the years. How and why this had happened she did not reveal nor would she Piers thought acerbically. But Minty could not stay at the Hall because her presence was making Thea ill. Minty often made reference to Thea's inheritance from Clarissa and with her sister Diana there was mischief afoot. This had never happened in the old days, Piers thought, as he remembered how fond his sisters had become of Thea but along life's journey everything had changed and not for the better. Thea had not complained; she rarely did to Piers but his more constant presence at the Hall had made him observe the goings on around him. Minty's conversations with Thea were insidious. She never actually gave full vent to her anger and jealousy which made it difficult for Thea to properly put her finger on it. But the undercurrents were there all the same. Piers was not going to allow his sister to make Thea's life a misery. Thea had always been the peacemaker and he was certainly not going to allow others to make her life a misery. He loved her too much to allow that to happen and as it was the hall was her home. It was her refuge as it was for all the Devines and Minty was here on sufferance.

One day Piers had found Thea taking refuge in her small sitting room in a flood of tears. It was her only place of safety away from the demands of the family. He had knocked and walked into the room; she tried to cover her tears under a brave smile but Piers was not deceived. Sitting next to her on the sofa he did not mince his words.

'It's Minty again isn't it,' he said placing a comforting arm around her shoulders. 'You really must not allow her to make you feel so bad. She is being spiteful and jealous and she will have to go.'

'No Piers you can't do that when she has nowhere to go. Her husband is unkind to her and also her children: she has such little money to find somewhere else to live. She is your sister after all.'

'And you are my wife. She will not stay a moment longer in our home to upset you further.' He kissed Thea on the cheek and left the room in search of his errant sister.

As he entered the great hall at Westborough he noticed that the library door was ajar. He pushed it open further and looked inside. Minty with her spectacles perched at the end of her nose looking uncannily like their mother glanced up from the letters she was writing and smiled at her brother. Piers did not reciprocate. Minty frowned and then glanced down once more at her correspondence. Piers closed the library door with a sharpness that made his sister look up again, this time removing her glasses in readiness to listen to whatever was on his mind.

'You look upset, Piers,' she cooed sweetly. 'Is there anything I can help you with?'

'Yes I believe you can Minty. You see Thea is continually upset and I don't like seeing my wife that way.'

Suddenly lines furrowed Minty's brow. 'Is she still missing Mama?' She asked rather innocently.

'I think she will miss our mother for quite some considerable time. Thea was like a daughter to her. They were very close.'

'Of course they were.' A rather bitter half smile played around his sister's lips.

Piers continued regardless. 'You see Minty you have stuck your claws into Thea. You are jealous that mother had a good relationship with her and Thea was left money in her will. Thea had no knowledge that mother had any money at all. Mama was a closed book on the subject. As it was none of us knew. Mama was shrewd on such matters and she liked us to know that she was grateful for how she was helped while all along she was making her own. So if you must continue to treat Thea as you have been doing I will have no alternative but to send you away.'

Minty bristled with temper and emotion trying to bluff her way out of this straight talking accusation. 'I don't know what you mean Piers.' There was alarm etched on her features at Piers' attitude. She had nowhere else to go. Nobody wanted her; this place, the home of her childhood, was her only sanctuary.

'Oh yes you do know what I mean, Minty, and I won't have it. You have thrown yourself on our mercy pleading poverty and a broken marriage. Why did your marriage break up?'

'That's none of your business,' she said waspishly.

'Oh but it is if you want to return to Westborough.'

'He went off with another woman. He called me shrewish and bad tempered. Plus we had nearly run out of money.'

'Well you are shrewish if you deal with Thea in this way. And what happened to your inheritance from Papa? That was to last you a lifetime if it was invested properly.'

'Oh, Piers, please don't talk to me this way. You treated Mama like this after Papa died. If you don't want me then I am lost.'

Piers rose from his seat and walked to the window looking out onto the garden which was a riot of colour. How his mother would have loved this. Tears stuck behind his eyes, sheer determination not allowing them to fall. How long would this sensation of loss continue he wondered? Remaining silent for a few minutes, his thoughts turning cartwheels in response to the problems which would not be settled any time soon, he then turned back to look at his sister who was waiting expectantly for him to say something. Her face was a picture of misery. Piers' expression softened slightly and Minty exhaled as if she had been holding her breath.

'Minty if you wish to stay here you must live at the Dower house and wait to be invited to the Hall. I won't have Thea upset like this. She has been good to this family, far better than you have been over the last few years. I will give you a sum of money which will have to last you but you will have to do your bit to see that everything runs smoothly from now on. If there are more upsets I will ask you to leave. I hope this will be a temporary measure for I wish you to move your life forward. I only want the happiness of this family and not the turmoil which dogged our parents' marriage. Do you understand, Araminta?'

Minty regarded Piers thoughtfully. She knew the look which masked his still handsome features. It was an expression from their childhood and he had only ever called her Araminta when he was displeased with her.

Having stated what was on his mind Piers left the room, leaving Minty to look after him feeling frightened and helpless in this ever changing world. With great bitterness she knew she was at his mercy regarding her future. It was not a feeling that she enjoyed. Independence was her goal in life but she was not sure how to achieve that. Some people would say find a job but that was an anathema to Minty. She had not been brought up to expect to work for her living and if she did it would intimate to the world that she was impoverished. Her pride would never let her do that and so she had to grit her teeth to take the handouts that her brother proffered with the greatest humility that she could muster. It all went against the grain. What was the saying? Pride went before a fall but she had had the fall so now she had to pick herself up and eat humble pie.

Chapter 25

The summer was passing at a frightening speed. Although Clarissa was not forgotten by her family and Thea still visited the Dowager's grave on a regular basis life was moving on. Jane's Season as a Debutante had hardly taken off with all that had been happening at Westborough Hall. Piers had stipulated that they had to show some respect at his mother's passing otherwise there could be gossip in the society papers as well as on the Estate. Even in the second half of the twentieth century estate workers of the old school albeit they were few and far between these days were still steeped in the traditions of their forebears. Clarissa had been revered for what she had done over the decades for the local workers. This had been something she and her husband had in accord. It was a tradition to look after the welfare of the estate workers which Piers had continued since his inheritance of the title. This was also something that he wished Harry to continue and it would not be long before his heir would be working alongside him despite his time at school and no doubt university.

Jane had been disappointed that her Season had been shortened but since her time at school she had grown up considerably and had become closer to her father despite everything that had gone on over the years and as a result she was reconciled to the situation. She missed her grandmother too and had understood her father's rigid observance of the old ways. But as the appointed time of mourning came to its conclusion she had received invitations to some balls in London. Minty had spoken to Piers about becoming Jane's chaperone to release Thea who was busy organizing Jane's ball which was to take place in the middle of July at Westborough Hall when all the family would be home for the holidays. Thea was full of nervous energy rushing hither and thither to make all the arrangements. Piers had not been of great help to her for mostly he believed that it was a woman's job although he could see that the stress of the whole business was beginning to take its toll on Thea's wellbeing.

Minty had invited herself to see Piers at the Hall where they had entrenched themselves in the estate office one afternoon at the end of June. Since his mother's death Piers had been monitoring Minty's behaviour in many ways. Occasionally he had visited her unannounced at the Dower House. Their relationship had improved over the weeks. Certainly Minty had made subtle changes to the house, of which he approved. She had kept her promise to visit the Hall when invited and as the weeks progressed she received more and more invitations to dine with the family. Her relationship with Thea was never going to form a solid friendship but over time they became tolerant of each other and the episode of the inheritance appeared to have been dusted under the carpet.

So Minty sat opposite her brother as she outlined the purpose of her visit.

'I can see how busy Thea is with Jane's ball so swiftly approaching and I wondered if I could be of use to help chaperone Jane on the two balls she has in London.'

Piers steepled his hands and raised his eyes to his sister's face. 'It would be a great help to all of us but you must allow Thea to decide. I would not wish to decide for her. She would not thank me if I did. But thank you for the offer,' he said politely wondering if there was anything ominous behind his sister's words.

'Oh don't thank me. It was Jane's idea. We have become firm friends in recent weeks. She comes to see me most days in the Dower House.'

Piers regarded his sister warily seeing her in a new light. He had been completely unaware of the clandestine visits.

'Well, Minty, I shall ask Thea and let you know what she says.'

Minty stood up feeling that she was being dismissed like a naughty child.

'Well all right,' she said rising from her chair, anger rising within her. She noted that Piers' attention had once more returned to the accounts book that he had been studying on her arrival. Without saying anything else she left the office and pulled the door sharply to making Piers glance up taking note of his sister's anger at not receiving her own way.

Piers knew that he had not treated her very well but he did not want even family meddling in his and Thea's affairs and why had Jane forged this unusual alliance. He banged the table hard with his fist before rising to go in search of his wife to sort out the situation.

He found Thea in her small sitting room in the middle of a telephone call. From the drift of it she was making more arrangements for Jane's ball. Uninvited he sat in a wing backed chair which stood in front of the open French windows allowing a pleasant breeze to waft the curtains and to fan the temper that had risen inside him after his previous conversation. He listened to the end of Thea's conversation as he watched the afternoon sunshine dapple the carpet in the centre of the room. Thea replaced the telephone receiver in its cradle. A telephone extension had only recently been put into the little sitting room but already it offered privacy from ears that wanted to know other people's business. Thea's features were arranged in an expression of perplexity.

'Problems?' Piers asked.

'Probably not,' she said not wishing to expand on the possibility.

'I've just had a visit from Minty.'

Thea raised an eyebrow knowing that her sister-in-law was expected to visit through invitation.

'Did you know that Jane goes to visit her on a regular basis?' He said.

The proportions of Thea's face appeared to rearrange themselves as she expressed surprise. 'No I didn't but perhaps I should not be surprised because Jane often went to visit Clarissa at the Dower. It became a kind of sanctuary for her. Besides she has been rather at a loose end lately with the mourning.'

Piers listened to this piece of information quietly for a moment before saying, 'Minty wondered whether she could chaperone Jane to some of the balls. It seems as if it was Jane's idea.'

'Well it would be a help I suppose. It has been rather busy lately with all that has been happening.'

'I don't want you to feel that Jane does not want you or that Minty has been interfering. It has to be your decision, darling.'

'Well after Jane's ball I can start again. I do feel sorry for her because she has missed out so much and she is being very good about it.'

'Yes I believe she is,' Piers agreed. 'I will go and telephone Minty and give her the news.'

'You can telephone from here, Piers.'

'I think I will do it from the estate office. I have disturbed you long enough.'

And he walked from the room feeling a little mollified that Thea had taken the news so well.

Thea became quite grateful to Minty for the assistance she had received. There appeared to be a truce between the two warring factions and responsibility had been lifted from Thea's shoulders giving her a breathing space to organize Jane's ball.

Jane and Minty had gone to stay at the Devine Town House in London for there were two balls in quick succession. They had had a lovely time enjoying the dressing up as much as the ball itself. Minty had had great pleasure in using her title among the well-heeled of society. During her marriage to Alexander she had rarely had the opportunity to mix with her own class but here she met people from long ago, people whom she had met in her young adulthood and people who might have been candidates for marriage had she taken the opportunity to be properly courted. Now she was meeting their children. They were around Jane's age doing the Season to find a 'catch' in order to marry well. Some had already found a suitor and at all costs were determined to hold onto him. Jane was new to the Season and her sudden appearance had caused a stir amongst the young beaux. Her time in Switzerland had stood her in good stead. She was young, beautiful and sophisticated and the daughter of an Earl. She danced all the dances and by the end of the evenings was exhausted but happy. The honourable Douglas Severton had asked to see her again. He was older than Jane by a few years and was the heir to Lord Severton, the son and heir of the Earl of Foray whose estate was on the Scottish borders. There had been news in the society papers that Douglas had been engaged for six months to a young woman who had aspirations to be an actress but his grandfather had not approved although the ruling Prince of Monaco had already married the beautiful Grace Kelly only a few years before. However, the Earl of Foray was not progressive in his attitude and the engagement had been terminated. Douglas believed that there could be no complaint about Jane's heritage and now that she had entered his life he felt that she could be a candidate for his heart although he did not properly know her but that could be easily put right. As for Jane she was unaware of what was going on but was just enjoying all the attention she was receiving. This fussing around her in adulthood seemed to be suddenly making up for the neglect she had received from her father during her childhood and it was all beginning to go to her head. Minty had noticed but was happy for her niece to be the centre of attention. But there was something, perhaps a twinge of regret that she had missed out on this all those years ago. Now she was living every moment through her niece's experiences.

Time was passing quickly and the July ball was just a week away. Thea was consumed by nerves wondering if they had thought of everything. There was much activity going on at the Hall. A dais had been erected in the corner of the great hall where a quartet was to play the night away. Chairs were found from all parts of the house and the Dower House to line the walls where those not dancing could watch all the goings on. The hall floor had been resurfaced and then a temporary dance floor had been put down in the centre. The large dining room had been taken over by the catering company as they brought in a range of glasses and china especially for the night. It was to be a finger buffet and no expense was to be spared. Tables had also been placed at one end of the hall and on the night there would be candles glowing as darkness began to fall. Again the Hall and the Dower House had been searched for large antique vases which would be filled on the night with fresh flowers giving off a scent that would fill the air. Thea was hoping that it would be a night to remember.

The younger Devines were home from school excited by what would be the high light of their school vacation. They, too, were to be decked out in their finery and for this once did not mind. Verity had had a new dress made especially for the evening. She had tried it on so many times that it had begun to look like a piece of old rag. Thea, in her exasperation, had taken the garment away from her daughter and had asked the dressmaker to deal with the dress and keep it until the day of the ball.

Usually the young Devines spent their free time running wild on the estate but this time Piers had other ideas for his heir. It was now time that he learned the seriousness of his future inheritance just as Piers had to do before his own father died.

Thea was experiencing a guilt trip. She had neglected little Amelia lately. The child who was nearly two had been left to the devices of Nanny and the nursery staff. Of course she was well looked after and Nanny was delighted to have the little girl under her wing more. She was old fashioned and did not agree with a hands on mother amongst the aristocracy. But Thea was different in those respects and had always wanted more access to her children than the previous family that Nanny had worked for. Although Thea and Sabine had had a nanny of their own their mother had always done much with her children.

Scarlett had arrived home from university for her vacation flushed with success. She had received a first for her end of year exams. Although she had worked hard she had taken her own advice to have fun too. She had made a new set of friends and as a result was feeling happier with her lot. Although the term had passed very quickly she had not managed to visit Maudie again but in the autumn she would do so and return to see her new friend in her father's London House. Maudie had come to a decision that she was not going to spend the summer at Westborough Hall. She would come and go so that she could see her family and was feeling a sense of anticipation about Jane's ball but she wanted to continue her musical nights which filled her world with the thrill of the music she loved. By chance she had also come across a small orchestra which was beginning to make its name as it toured some of the larger cities. She had been invited to play the clarinet with them on tour and this would give her an insight into what life might be like when she finished her course at the conservatoire. Perhaps one day she might even become a concert pianist. The world was her oyster with so much choice. She had a master card up her sleeve which she would play on the night of Jane's ball. She so wanted her family to share her secrets and the success that was coming her way. She shivered with anticipation every time she thought about what she was about to do.

Chapter 26

The day of the ball had everyone in a spin. Thea watched intently as the allotted people went about their tasks with efficiency and professionalism. She was beginning to breathe a sigh of relief that everything would come together to be a success. During the afternoon two local hairdressers had arrived to twist and tease the women's hair into elegant chignons which would complement the dresses which had been made by the dressmaker. Verity, a tomboy at heart, had succumbed to her new upswept hairstyle with a quiet dignity and had received her father's teasing with aloofness and forbearance which had made him tease her more.

'Piers leave her alone,' Thea said laughing at his light heartedness considering how much the whole proceedings were going to cost. At one point over the previous weeks he had said to Thea how glad he was to have only one daughter go through this experience, as the other girls did not wish to participate in a Season.

'But you have another two daughters waiting in the wings,' Thea said sweetly.

'Oh that will be years away yet. Perhaps the whole ridiculous ritual will have been put an end to by then.'

Thea had silently agreed but it was not the expense which bothered her. She knew that they could afford it but it was the organization which had fallen on her shoulders. It had gone on for weeks and it had not been helped by Clarissa's illness and subsequent death. Who knew whether Verity would want to go through it in a few years' time when she would shed her tomboyishness like shedding a chrysalis and turn into a butterfly. She had the potential like all the Devine girls who had turned out to be beautiful. Even Scarlett was lovely with her red hair and delicate features.

Then there had been the invitations to send out and there were the guests who would have to stay if they were travelling a distance. All the guest bedrooms at the Hall and the Dower House were filled to capacity. She had left much of that organization to their housekeeper, Mrs Jeffries, who had only worked for the Devines for a few years. She was like gold dust Thea thought warmly of the woman. She had drafted in more help and a chef to produce the food for the breakfasts at the Dower House. The guests who were staying at the Hall were joining the family for a formal dinner at seven thirty promptly followed by the ball at nine thirty which was expected to last until the early hours or even dawn. Thea wondered how she would last the night but she could catch up on sleep afterwards she laughed at herself.

The great hall was looking splendid by late afternoon. The perfume from the flowers filled the air and by evening with the low lights and the candles flickering in their medieval sconces would lend a romantic ambiance to the Elizabethan Hall. The family came to view the great hall late in the afternoon with shouts of delight at what had been achieved.

'You have done so well, Thea,' Piers said full of admiration for what his wife had achieved.

'Thank you kind sir,' she said dipping a curtsey and laughing. 'The fire will be lit just before our guests arrive. You know how cold it can be when it is quite dark in here.'

'But it will be warm when everybody has arrived.'

'Yes I know but the women will be in such flimsy dresses and when it warms up the fire can go out.'

'You've thought of everything,' he said as he put his arm around her shoulder to pull her close. Thea snuggled closer to bask in her little bit of glory. Piers did not give accolades lightly.

Jane had also arrived to give her seal of approval to her stepmother. The two women had become close in recent weeks despite Jane's time in London with Minty for Thea had included her stepdaughter in all the arrangements for the ball.

'You have done wonders Thea,' she said to her and spontaneously hugged the older woman.

'I'm glad you approve,' Thea said giving the girl a warm hug in response. They had turned a corner in recent months and it warmed Thea's heart to have the closeness that existed with Piers' rather prickly daughter.

By late afternoon the guests who were staying began to arrive and were shown to their rooms with strict instructions to appear for cocktails in the library by six thirty. The small dining room was to be used for the dinner and the seating capacity had been stretched to the limit to achieve the near impossible. By the set time everyone had assembled. The men were wearing the deemed uniform of evening dress and the women were wearing colourful cocktail dresses until they changed into their ball gowns before the main event of the evening took place. It was a lively affair with Piers at his best as the genial host. After the dinner was over he gave an impromptu speech making his guests laugh and Jane blush. She was not always happy to be the centre of attention these days and it felt strange for her father to be making out that their relationship was close. That had never been the case but they had turned a corner quite some time ago. When the women disappeared to change their attire the select group of men retired to the library to drink a brandy or a whisky and smoke their cigars. It was going to be an evening to remember. The Hall had not witnessed such an event for decades.

As the women began to make their appearance, cars of all descriptions driven by the rich and famous began to crunch the gravel in front of the Hall allowing their occupants to walk into the great hall to an amazing spectacle. Then the chauffeurs drove away to park the cars and receive a much welcome dinner of their own in the basement kitchen.

Piers, Thea and Jane stood in a line to meet their guests while the quartet began to play a variety of tunes including the Glen Miller big band sound setting feet tapping. The dancing started and the ball had begun. Jane danced with her father. She thought how smart and attractive he looked in his evening dress and how attentive he was to her. She had longed to see this side of him during her childhood as all the older Devine girls had done but now her siblings had their own lives mapped out for them while on this balmy July night she was just beginning on her journey into the future.

Thea danced with Harry who was looking like a much younger version of his father. For the first time in his life he was wearing evening dress which made him look older than his thirteen years. Thea could not have been more proud of him or his younger siblings. They knew that they had to be mature and respectful to the guests but they were still children after all.

Jane had danced the night away with young men she had met at previous balls but there was a lingering feeling of doubt and disappointment as she watched for the arrival of Douglas Severton. He had asked to be invited to her ball as her partner for the evening but his intention was to continue the burgeoning courtship and to be introduced to her family. He wanted to ingratiate himself with them and to win their approval. He had heard much of the Devines and was well aware that Piers Devine did not suffer fools gladly as well as being a true blue aristocrat who was snobbish to his very core but at the same time could be very charming. Douglas knew that he had the right aristocratic background knowing that his family could rub shoulders with the Devines as true equals in all but riches.

The dalliances Jane had experienced during her school days now felt remote and childish by comparison to the world she now inhabited. She knew that she was a woman now, ripe for a far deeper and meaningful relationship and she felt that it was wonderful that she had put the immaturities of her past behind her. She took a glass of champagne from a passing waiter and sipped at it, watching as the waiters and waitresses dressed in uniform and supplied by the agency approached the guests with small trays carrying a range of drinks as the guests talked during an interval in the music while the quartet took a well-earned break. She had placed herself near the fireplace where she could survey the guests. She was not in a mood to make small talk for the moment as her anxiety began to flair. And then she saw him immaculate in his evening dress looking handsome. He had accepted a glass of champagne as he looked around him. All her anxiety had dissipated as she watched what he would do next and there he was striding towards her with a smile on his face. They stood face to face smiling, even beaming and then he kissed her cheek. They dismissed the world around them as they only had eyes for each other until the music began to play again. They found somewhere for their glasses as he then took her in his arms to whirl her around the floor, holding her closely as he whispered in her ear and making Jane giggle with happiness. She did not care who saw her for this evening belonged to them alone.

Piers and Thea stood watching the proceedings. They had danced together but had also danced with some of their guests but now they were taking time to observe and judge how the evening was progressing. They had seen Jane and this new young man together, each wondering who he could be. Looking at each other they had smiled remembering their own early love and wondering if this was a relationship which might make Jane happy but only time would tell. As Piers took Thea in his arms again to dance the waltz she took one more cursory glance around the floor noting there was now no sight of Jane and her beau. It was as if they had vanished off the face of the earth.

As the long case clock in the great hall struck 12 the music began to slow and the quartet began to play a haunting folk song. On cue a familiar figure stepped onto the stage and began to sing. The dancing slowed as the timbre of her voice was enjoyed; dancers stood and watched as the haunting song filled their ears and souls. Thea and Piers joined the rest of the dancers equally enthralled and stood and listened. Then he turned to Thea who had made the same realization.

'My God,' Piers said, having found Thea's ear, 'it's Maudie. Did you know that she could sing like that?'

'No,' Thea replied enraptured by what she was hearing, 'but isn't she talented?'

As the song reached its conclusion there was thunderous applause which Maudie acknowledged before slipping from the stage back into the other world that she inhabited.

In another part of the hall nanny as instructed came to collect the younger Devine children. They were reluctant to go with her but Piers had made it clear that midnight was their curfew. The evening had been magical to them as well.

Jane suddenly reappeared alone looking for Thea. She had hunted everywhere but nobody had seen her and then a thought struck her. Thea was found having taken refuge in her sitting room. This room was out of bounds for guests. She had needed a breathing space away from all the music and noise. There were dark shadows smudged under her eyes and the lateness of the hour was taking its toll. But Jane was effervescent in her sparkle and humour.

'Thea,' she said, 'why on earth are you hiding away in here?'

Thea smiled wearily. 'Just taking a moment out. What can I do for you Jane?'

'I have a request Thea.' She could not see that Thea had had enough of demands on her time even though exhaustion oozed from every bone in her body.

'My boyfriend, Douglas,' she continued, 'has just arrived and I wondered if he could stay the night.'

Thea made a face which Jane mistook for displeasure.

'It is only a small request, not a lot to ask really,' her mood was now churlish.

Thea laughed. 'Jane all the rooms are taken. Why did you not tell me before?'

'I wasn't sure that he was coming. It was a last minute decision.'

Thea ran a hand across her forehead as the tiredness began to take hold. Jane put an arm around her stepmother's shoulders suddenly realizing that she was taking too much for granted after all that Thea had done for her.

'I'll go and ask nanny. She will think of something. I'm sorry to have bothered you.' She placed an affectionate kiss on her cheek before making for the door but turned back as Thea said,

'Tell nanny to put Charlie in with Harry for tonight.'

'Thanks,' she said blowing a kiss at Thea.

Thea sighed remembering that she had been young once and had demanded the earth. That seemed such a long time ago now. She rose to return to the guests and fixed her face into a smile ready to confront anybody who wished to speak to her.

Jane disappeared as quickly as she had arrived. She was not convinced that Douglas would stay in Harry's room but that was another matter. She felt desire stirring within her as she hurried to find him.

Chapter 27

The ball had lasted until nearly dawn. There was much banging of car doors as guests began their weary way home full of the night's activities; reporters would be interviewing them quite soon undoubtedly about their opinions on the evening and the comparisons they would obviously make with other balls of the Season. Also that next morning the clearing up process began. Staying guests had departed at all times leaving a trail of detritus in the rooms where there had been food and drink. Others climbed the stairs to their bedrooms having made full use of the accommodation on hand having danced the night away. That morning breakfast was served in the small dining room for anyone who could face it before their journey home began. Thea rolled over in bed towards Piers who slept the sleep of the dead. She lay there willing herself to wake up properly to face the day trying to be hostess to the remaining guests. Her mind was sluggish but then it cleared as she thought back to the end of the evening. She had been talking to Minty at the front door of the Hall to watch departing guests leave and also to say a few words of pleasantry. But there had been a strange moment when a mother and daughter had come up to them and had turned to Minty to thank her for their invitation to the Ball. They had not cast a look in Thea's direction as the Countess. It was all a bit blurred but she could have sworn that Minty had said that it was her pleasure to invite them. Thea knew that she could have words privately with her sister-in-law but she would not put it above Minty to say that she had imagined it. She could tell Piers but he would be angry at Minty again and she could not bear the atmosphere this created between brother and sister or the distress that the Devines caused within their family. Life was too short for such aggression. So she would leave it but all these funny little things that were happening had made Thea resolved to be watchful. She knew that she could not let Minty get away with these things but she would deal with it in her own way making sure that for once her sister-in-law was aware of who was the true Countess. Thea knew that if Clarissa had been alive she would have stepped in to end such a situation and Minty would have been sent away in disgrace. Clarissa had been loyal to

Thea to the very end of her days. How she missed the older woman more than she could say and anyone else could understand, even Piers.

Douglas Severton had spent the night in Jane's room but they had not slept very much. But when Jane eventually awoke she found Douglas slumped across her bed in a dishevelled heap. This amused her as she remembered back just a few hours. He had crept into her room just as she knew he would as the Hall fell silent, everyone dead to the world with exhaustion, except themselves, as they found renewed energy to discover much about each other wondering if they would share a future together each with their own reasons for such conjecture. Now as she lay sated and at ease with herself at this quiet early hour she could hear distant noises in the rest of the house as the clean-up operation began. As she tried to shake Douglas awake she found that he was reluctant to stir but eventually he surfaced from a deep slumber.

'Dougie, you have to go back to your own room, 'she said anxiously.

He yawned loudly. 'Do I really?' He said as exhaustion overtook him and he settled down once more.

'Ssh,' she whispered, 'you have to go back to your own room. She could not cope with her father's anger should he find out about their night of love making. Piers was Victorian in his attitude to such matters and when her life was just turning a corner for the better she could not go and spoil it now. She prodded him in his side as he began to snore softly once more.

'Go,' she said anxiously rising from the bed to seek abandoned attire from the floor.

He rose begrudgingly as she pushed the clothes at him. Smiling at his dishevelled state and comparing him with the debonair young man of the previous evening she opened her bedroom door to find the coast clear before anyone stirred.

Dougie disappeared into Charlie's room and fell onto the bed instantly falling asleep. She knew that her father would be angry if he knew about their sleeping arrangements. Slipping across the landing she was going to try and rumple the bedclothes in order for it to look as if it had been slept in.

Hours later when the guests were finally leaving, Douglas was reluctant to depart the Hall. He had enjoyed meeting Jane's family including her very aristocratic father. Piers had been charming to the young man reminding him that he had met his grandfather, the Earl of Foray, many years before at the House when Piers had first inherited his title. They were of the same political persuasion and had spoken before the House on subjects that were dear to them both. But now the old Earl rarely left his fine home on the Scottish borders as his age and health had rendered him infirm.

'With your permission, sir, I would like to take Jane to meet my grandfather and father in Scotland if you don't mind?'

'I am sure that is possible at some point,' Piers said wondering if there might be a future between the young couple. However, in his mind they had only just met and he did not want to push Jane into a liaison too soon. His attention was suddenly claimed by another visitor.

'Excuse me please,' he said to Douglas before hurrying away. Douglas looked around to see if Jane was nearby. He knew that it was time to leave. He obviously had not made such a huge impression on the person he was beginning to think of as his future father-in-law.

***

The Devine Ball had been regarded as a huge success. There was a report in the Society Papers about the lovely Lady Jane Devine who had looked wonderful on the night along with her siblings and her mother the Countess. Piers had lowered the paper for he had been reading aloud to Thea. It was a week since the Ball and Westborough Hall was back to normal after the clearing up had been completed. Thea was still tired but happy that it had been such a success.

'You did look wonderful, Thea,' Piers said lowering his paper and looking at his wife across the breakfast table before bursting out laughing.

'What is it?' She said rather crossly for all the activity had sapped her energy.

'Cinders is back,' Piers continued to tease.

Thea knew what he meant. She was in old slacks and jumper and her hair which she had allowed to grow for the ball fell in untidy but charming ringlets around her attractive face.

'I'm going to do some digging in the kitchen garden,' she snapped at him; she was not in a mood to be the victim of Piers' ridicule. 'Would you rather that I wore my ball gown in the garden?'

Suddenly Piers looked serious. 'Don't you think that you would be better having a rest rather than working so hard? One of the gardeners can do that job until you are feeling better.'

Suddenly Thea burst into tears as the past weeks caught up with her. She looked suddenly how she felt, exhausted.

'I shall send for Dunwoody if you don't do as you are told and he will make you rest,' Piers said regarding his wife with concern, the humour of previous minutes had suddenly evaporated. 'You are worn out by everything, darling. This isn't just about the dance but there was mother's death too. It all takes its toll.'

Thea knew that Piers was right. It had all taken its toll on her. She did not wish for Brownlow to come and preach at her for neglecting her own health so she allowed Piers to dictate to her.

Thea spent the next week sleeping off her exhaustion. Piers saw that she had the peace and quiet she needed. The usually noisy household seemed to tiptoe around. Even little Amelia, somewhat perplexed by her mother's absence, was kept at a distance and any household decisions were left in the capable hands of the housekeeper.

A few days after the Ball Jane had returned to London to stay in the Town House. She had just packed a small bag and travelled by train to the capital. She had left with the flimsy excuse that she wanted time with her friends but she knew that she wanted to see Douglas who had his own apartment in London and they wanted to spend some time together as a couple. There were just two balls left that would end the season and then she would have a little time to herself before she knew her father would make demands about what she wished to do with her life. He was a person who did not like the idea of idle hands. Unless she married there was little that she could do with herself. Her education had been a disaster left far behind by now but could she return to it? Could she use the languages that had been honed and polished during her time in Switzerland? These were questions to which she had few answers.

Chapter 28

Thea had had two weeks sleeping and relaxing under Piers' strict instructions. He had told the staff at Westborough Hall that his wife required pampering because she was exhausted. Gossip which tended to run wild in the lower region of the house had never disputed the fact that the Countess was suffering from exhaustion. She seemed to be at everybody's beck and call was the general consensus of opinion and all the work for the ball had been the catalyst that had made her ill. The staff loved Thea. She had time for them all and would stop and have a word when she knew that anyone had a problem. She was not regarded to be high and mighty like her stepdaughter Lady Jane who made extra demands on staff and flaunted her title as if she owned the place. And so it was that they pampered Thea with breakfast in bed and cook made special delicacies to tempt her dwindling appetite. For the first time in a long time Thea felt pampered and dare she admit it cherished by everybody but at the same time she felt guilty at being a nuisance to them all when they had had so much extra work with the ball.

'You have no reason to feel guilty, Thea,' Piers said on one of his regular visits to see how she was. 'You run a good home here and the family doesn't always appreciate you including myself.'

Thea had looked at Piers in surprise at this comment. Deep down she agreed with him but for him to admit such a thing was truly out of character. She made no comment but snuggled down in the bed feeling the luxury that only laziness could provide.

During her second week when she was feeling so much better she had learned a lesson. Although she was not selfish by nature she had made the decision that she was going to delegate more to others. She had once remembered Clarissa saying that to her during the war years. As usual, how right the old dowager had been.

'You will burn yourself out, my dear,' she would say when Thea tried to juggle so many things during Piers' absence, 'what you can't do today can be done tomorrow.'

How she missed the wisdom of the old Countess who had become a second mother to her over the years and her confidante. If she could aspire to be half as wise over the coming years she felt that she would achieve something quite special. But Clarissa was no more and still she mourned the old woman's passing.

Towards the end of the second week Thea spent some of the time in the nursery playing with Amelia. She was an affectionate child and the constant presence of her mother after the enforced absence had been a great joy to her. Occasionally Piers ventured up to the nursery to see his youngest child also feeling that she was special. But the satisfaction that he felt at this contact with her was partly based on the extra time that he spent at home. In many ways he missed the House of Lords but he also relished the time he could spend with Thea and the rest of the family when they were around.

Into the third week of her recuperation Piers took a long hard look at his wife. He had been quite worried about her and guilt played a huge part in the thoughts that engulfed him knowing how much she did for the family and little for herself. He had taken her for granted for far too long. But at his suggestion Thea had point blankly refused to see Doctor Dunwoody. He knew that he could not make her but he felt that her decision was regrettable. Now he had to admit she had been correct. The smudges of tiredness beneath her eyes had vanished and her hair shone with the health and vitality that had returned to her. Even in her middle years there was no hint of grey in her hair. On this bright late summer morning she looked breathtakingly beautiful with her hair curling around her face in a natural way. She reminded him of the time when he had first seen her more than two decades before. His heart seemed to summersault in his chest as he watched her pour a breakfast cup of tea totally unaware that his gaze was upon her. As she looked up she saw him watching her. He smiled but felt embarrassed to have been caught in the act. She smiled back before taking a sip of her tea.

Piers continued to stare and as she found him still regarding her she laughed and blushed like a teenager. 'Why are you staring at me, Piers?' She said.

'Because you look so lovely, Thea. You know how much I love you don't you. I'm afraid that I don't tell you enough,' he said.

'Ssh, of course we both love each other very much;' she said and impulsively rose from her chair to hug and kiss him. They kissed a long lingering kiss until they heard a noise at the door. Reluctantly, they pulled away from each other as Rose, one of the maids, entered the room carrying a tray. Rose was renowned for her gossiping in the kitchen. As Thea sat down she could not prevent a giggle escaping from her while Piers smiled and then winked at her knowingly.

After a few minutes Piers' attention returned to his newspaper while Thea's thoughts had turned elsewhere. Jane had telephoned her the night before to say that she required a chaperone for the last two balls of the Season and wondered if Thea was well enough to attend.

'Of course, darling. I would love to,' she had trilled. It had made Thea happy that Jane had asked her to do it instead of Minty. The Season had not worked out too well for Jane with all the problems that had occurred in the family but if she could make the ending pass without a hitch she was only too happy. It also forestalled Minty's interference which had become rather a worry.

'Piers I have to be in London next week. Jane has her last two balls to attend and I want to be there for her.'

Piers put down his newspaper and looked intently at her once more. 'Are you sure you are well enough to go? Minty won't mind doing it.'

'I have not felt so well for a long time so don't fuss. I will be away a week and then I shall be at home for the rest of the summer. I owe this to Jane.' There she was again being the doormat everyone expected her to be. It had now become the habit of a life time she thought cynically. She knew Piers meant well by his suggestion but this was going to make a point to Minty who was gradually worming her way back into life at Westborough Hall. Minty was still living at the Hall three weeks after Jane's ball. She had made no attempt to move back to the Dower House. She knew that the staff at the Hall were making comments for the housekeeper had actually spoken to Thea about it. She was the uninvited guest for Minty demanded much of the staff like breakfast in bed and she did not get up until late which made the routine of household duties run much later into the day. Thea looked at Piers who was still engrossed in his newspaper. Should she mention the situation to him? Their relationship was in such a good place at the moment that it might be the best time to act.

'Piers,' she said diffidently.

He lowered his newspaper; a frown creased his brow as he recognized the worried look upon her face. 'Are you all right darling?'

'Yes of course. I was just wondering about Minty. Is she returning to the Dower House any time soon?'

The thought had obviously never crossed Piers' mind. 'I suppose so. Why?'

'Well I think that the staff have been a little overrun lately what with the Ball and me playing the invalid and then Minty does not get up in time for breakfast which makes the running of the house quite difficult. It is rather trying to find good staff as it is.'

Piers had received the message loud and clear. Minty was being difficult once more and he had not noticed. He chided himself on his selfishness.

'I will sort it,' he said and by the tone of his voice Thea knew that she had won another round in the battle of wills with her sister-in-law.

***

The week in London had been wonderful for Thea and Jane. They became closer than ever before and the Balls had been the best of the Season except for Jane's own Ball at Westborough Hall. Douglas Severton had been attentive Thea noticed and it did cross her mind that the young couple seemed very emotionally involved. However, Jane was reluctant to expand on any details so Thea kept her own council and allowed love to take its course. Douglas came to dine most evenings at the Town House when they had not attended a ball. The Town House held so many memories for Thea from her life there before the War that after dinner she was quite happy to retire to her room with a good book or the television which she had very little time to watch while she was at the Hall. But regularly her mind would drift into the past. This allowed Douglas and Jane the freedom that they desperately wanted to pursue their own lives.

After the last ball was over Thea had her plans to return home hoping that Jane would join her to think about her future but it was not to be. Jane had made the decision that she would stay in the capital a while longer for there was something that she wanted to do without the hindrance of her parents or Douglas who had been called home to the Scottish borders for his grandfather had become ill and not expected to last much longer. She also wanted to spend some time with Maudie whose life style had intrigued Jane since the night of the Ball. Maudie, after Scarlett's visit back in the spring, had come to terms with the fact that her siblings would venture forth to her little domain from time to time and in some respect she was proud of the independence that she had achieved through her own efforts. This did not mean that her homesickness for her other life did not rear its head from time to time. If that occurred she only had to catch the train to Worcester and then venture forth to the Hall. When she arrived it was almost as if time had stood still and she could pick up the threads of her old life to become Lady Maud Devine once more.

The whole family had been so supportive about her singing debut for Jane's Ball but apart from Scarlett nobody realized that this had become a way of life now that the world was changing with rock 'n' roll and the other kinds of music entering the pop charts and so easily available through the media of television, records and film. She could lend her voice to a range of music and had received high praise in the musical papers. It was strange how a classical voice had eluded her when she could play classical pieces on the piano and the violin. She was also thinking about playing in a small orchestra which might lead to another career change. The world had opened up to her through her unique talents but in contrast to Jane she had seized every opportunity that had been thrown in her path to her full advantage.

Autumn had arrived early showing off its rich hues to perfection. There were cool mornings followed by warm afternoons which spoke of an Indian summer. Thea was happy to return to a normal uneventful life after the stress of the summer months. She and Piers enjoyed walks on the estate taking Amelia with them. This last child of their own was the only one who had their undivided attention. The others for a variety of reasons had had to share one parent or two with the others. Perhaps a late child was the product of so much indulgence but older children had the camaraderie of their siblings Thea often thought in times of guilt when she recognized signs of precociousness in her younger daughter. But the child had brought them such happiness that Thea often dismissed such thoughts as they entered her head.

It was only Myra the nursery maid who listened to Nanny's constant moan about her charge. 'She's becoming a precocious little madam,' she would say. 'They give her far too much attention. Those were the days when the little ones were seen and not heard. They would see their parents for half an hour before bedtime.'

Myra never commented on such talk. As a young woman she knew that the times were changing and it was the older people like Nanny who could not cope with the situation when they were so used to the old ways. It was turning into a far better world the girl thought.

***

Scarlett and Thea had spent part of the summer avoiding each other after the girl's uncharacteristic outburst at the reading of Clarissa's will. Thea hoped that her daughter had learned a lesson but the obvious tension between them had taken its toll on both. But the thaw had begun to set in as the time approached for Scarlett to return to Oxford. A truce was finally declared when they knew that it would be months before Scarlett would be home for the Christmas vacation. Now both had learned lessons; Thea recognized the fact that she should let her daughter fly in order for her to return happily to the nest of her childhood. Their 'goodbyes' had been filled with talk of love and apologies for bad behaviour and the promise of Thea visiting Oxford before too long. Both women had heaved a sigh of relief to know that everything seemed to have improved but time and space away from each other would be the greatest healer of all.

The Hall seemed quiet once more with the young Devines returning to their schools as a new academic year began. It gave Thea and Piers a sense of freedom to indulge themselves for the first time in a long time. But as usual Thea felt her heart strings tug as her children disappeared to their academic worlds. But the summer had also taught Thea a few lessons and the greatest of all was to allow time for herself. With the family growing up she would take this time like a gift to be cherished she had decided but a niggling voice in her head wondered if she would ever change at all.

Chapter 29

Thea and Piers were indulging themselves in afternoon tea which had become a habit of late. This had been the aristocratic way of life but in more recent years it had died a death but Thea had been keen to resurrect the habit. It was especially comforting on winter days when the fire roared and the elements were battering against the windows. But that was not such a day although there was a fire in the grate and the early October light was beginning to fade as dusk came early. Amelia was sitting on Thea's knee nibbling away at a dainty chocolate cake that cook had made for this express purpose. Piers was enjoying the domestic scene too. He had decided that he would go to the House at the beginning of the next week as there was a Bill passing through Parliament which he felt required his presence. He knew Thea would not mind because she was still enjoying the solitude that the life at the Hall was giving her. There was a tranquillity about the place after the whirlwind of a summer which had demanded so much of them all.

Piers had been true to his word and had approached Minty about returning to the Dower House. He could tell by her manner that she had been less than pleased but she had complied and had not set foot in the Hall since. Thea had been happy to have Piers and her home to herself once more. Neither of them felt inclined to invite Minty to the Hall for dinner and it was certainly one of Minty's priorities to invite them to the Dower House; thus a stalemate existed between them. It was a kind of froideur Thea thought and for once her kind heart did not melt. She was learning a lesson which others regarded as a rite of passage to put themselves first but it all went against Thea's true nature.

As they sat in companionable silence listening to the chatter of their daughter who now played with great contentment on the carpet with an old doll which had been the possession of an older sibling Piers suddenly said.

'I read in the *Times* this morning that the old Earl of Foray passed away yesterday. He had been quite ill for some time but his passing was quite peaceful.'

'The Earl of Foray?' Thea repeated the name not quite sure where she had heard the title before.

'It is Douglas' grandfather so he will now be Lord Douglas Severton and his father has inherited the title.'

The connection had now dawned on Thea.

'Is Jane still seeing him?' She asked.

'I don't know. When did we last hear from Jane?' Piers said feeling guilty once more that this was another area where Thea kept the family together.

'I last saw her at the last ball. She said that she had things to do.' Thea said wondering why such a time elapse had passed her by without her even noticing.

'When I leave on Sunday I should see her at the Belgravia House,' Piers said expecting his daughter to comply with unwritten family rules that the Town House was used whenever the Devines were in London. 'She must be staying there.'

Thea said nothing but she was worried. It must have been six weeks since they had last heard from her and she surely could not be with Douglas because he would be in the Scottish borders awaiting his grandfather's funeral. The peace of mind she had so enjoyed of late had suddenly evaporated.

Jane was not at the Town house but she had persuaded Maudie to allow her to stay at her London apartment. With very few close friends of her own Jane had desperately needed someone to confide in for she was desperate for help and she felt that she could not turn to her father. These days she felt that she was close enough to confide in Thea but she knew what would happen if she did. Thea would go straight to her father not because she wished to tell tales but because she would believe that he would be the one to sort out the situation. Jane knew otherwise. This time she would incur her father's ire more than at any time in the past. Deep down she knew she had to sort her life out on her own but a little sibling support would not go amiss.

'What's the matter?' Maudie asked slightly perplexed by her sister's manner. She was like a walking wreck she thought. What had she been up to in recent weeks to leave her in such a state of turmoil?

'I'm in big trouble, Maudie.' She began to sob.

Maudie looked at her sister wondering if she was in financial trouble but that could not be so because their father was generous with their allowances and they had not come into any of their inheritances.

'Well tell me, then I might be able to help you.'

'Not this time, you can't.'

'Well it can't be so bad,' Maudie said but a light suddenly switched on in her mind. 'Are you pregnant Jane?' She said voicing her thoughts.

Jane nodded and then sobbed uncontrollably.

'Oh dear, Jane, that was a bit careless.' She said unkindly and nearly laughed. She then remembered what their father would be like. It was a sobering thought. 'Do you know whose it is?' she added, all trace of ridicule having vanished.

'Yes of course,' Jane said indignantly. 'What do you think I am?'

'Pregnant and a bit careless if you ask me. So who is the father?'

'Douglas,' she said.

'Do you mean the one you slept with on the night of the Ball?'

Jane's jaw dropped. 'How did you know?'

'Well you are hardly subtle, Jane. He knew where to put his hands on that night from what I saw of the pair of you. Does he know?'

'No.'

'Don't you think he should? Would he marry you?'

'I don't know. Our relationship has not gone that far.'

'Well it looks as if it has gone far enough.' Maudie laughed unsympathetically.

'A lot of help you are,' Jane complained.

'Well what about an abortion then. There will always be someone with a knitting needle.'

'You are no help, Maudie, and you are being unkind. I wish I hadn't come to you.'

'Yes I suppose that I am being unkind but these days there are things that you can use so you do not to have babies if you don't want them. Do you want this child?' Maudie was feeling rather moralistic. If Jane had to learn a lesson it would have to be the hard way.

Suddenly she felt sorry for her sister. She had been cruel enough.

'I think that you need to telephone Douglas, Jane, very soon. He is responsible too. There is too much these days of shifting the blame onto women. You cannot trip up the aisle with a huge stomach. You would be a laughing stock in all the society papers. I can just see the headlines saying—'

Jane had covered her ears. 'I don't want to hear any more. Stop it at once.'

Maudie stopped mid-sentence watching her sister as she became hysterical. This certainly was not the Jane she knew. They were silent momentarily both lost in their thoughts.

The tears still cascaded down Jane's cheeks as she broke the silence first. 'Douglas' grandfather has just died and there is so much for his family to do. This is not something that he would want to hear while they are in mourning.'

Maudie regarded her sister's tear ravaged face with concern. 'Well ask him if you can go to the funeral and tell him face to face. Don't let him slip away from you. Take control of your life, Jane.'

'You won't tell Thea and Papa will you, Maudie?' Jane had received the advice from her sister that she had given herself but it was difficult to choose the right path while her emotions tumbled down around her.

'I won't tell them; you know me better than that, Jane, but you must sort this out.' There was still loyalty in the sisterhood Maudie thought but something told her that Jane might not be able to sort the problems alone.

'Don't tell them that you have seen me either. I need time to figure out what I will do.'

'I can't promise that, for Thea will worry because that is her nature and I could not bear to be unfair to her. She has been a mother to us both. So go and sort this out but let me know what you decide.'

Jane had decided to return to the Town House. The autumnal sky was leaden showing that rain was in the air. It only reflected Jane's mood. The day that the doctor had confirmed her pregnancy had left her feeling bereft, that her life was over and with it her freedom. Although Maudie had not been sympathetic she had also given her some backbone. The words 'take control of your life' echoed through her mind. The thought of a back street abortionist also made her shudder. What it could do to her body and of course the child did not bear contemplating. And as she travelled across the capital she had come to some decisions. There was never going to be a way that she would give up her child. Douglas had to share the responsibility for the new life growing inside her and if he could not be adult about it she would bring it up as a single parent. She had the money to provide for them and then at twenty-five she would inherit her money from her mother. But first she had to see Douglas. So it was decided she was on her way to Scotland. She was going to do just what Maudie had suggested and take control of her own life. Whatever the outcome, it was going to be the most momentous decision of her life and a very grown up one as well.

Chapter 30

Piers arrived in Belgravia by taxi. He very rarely used the car for long distances these days and now that he spent longer at Westborough Hall he could drive himself around and had dispensed with the chauffeur's services. If he required to be driven there was Forbes in the village, now retired, who would be more than willing to take on such duties at short notice. As for Thea, she often liked to drive herself. Paying a chauffeur seemed an awful waste of money he felt but there were still occasions when the need arose. He turned his key in the front door. As he entered the house looked neat and tidy but then that was what they paid the small retaining staff for. It was Jane who left a trail of detritus after herself. He could hear Thea in his head saying to Jane to clear up her mess. A smile etched his rather anxious features as he thought of the young Thea who had been exactly the same. Time and a large family had taught her differently. Although servants were paid to do a job Thea was not one to treat staff like slaves. Respect was an important issue in her world and that had to be passed onto the young Devines to treat people from all walks of life with the courtesy that they deserved.

Piers took off his trilby and placed it on the hall table. He looked around expecting somebody to appear but it was as quiet as the grave.

'Is anybody home?' He called into the inner void expecting to hear a voice. Jane was not an early riser either which was another irritation that rankled him. There was no reply but footsteps could be heard rushing up the stairs from the basement kitchen.

Jenna the young maid appeared in the doorway of the sitting room where Piers was helping himself to brandy. He made a note that he was becoming like his mother and it was a habit that he had to give up.

'Can I get you anything, my lord? We were not expecting you until later.' The girl asked.

'No, Jenna, thank you,' he smiled at her anxious face, 'but tell me is Lady Jane still here?'

'No, my Lord. She was but you have just missed her. She said she was going away for a few days but I don't know where for she never said. She had a suitcase with her and a taxi called for her at about nine o'clock.'

Piers glanced at the ornate carriage clock on the mantelpiece which stated that it was nearly one o'clock. Perhaps she was returning to Westborough Hall. He dismissed the maid feeling a little less anxious about his daughter's whereabouts. He would ring Thea later with the information.

There was a pile of post on the study desk which he must peruse before he went to the House. He sat down placing his glass of refilled brandy on his desk top despite his good intentions of earlier to reduce his normal intake of the amber liquid. Later he would dine at his club before returning to Westborough Hall the following afternoon. Then another idea overtook him. Curious about Maudie and her life in London which had been fuelled by her revealing her multiple talents on the night of Jane's ball he wondered whether he would go and surprise her and take her out to dinner. She kept her life in the capital an undisclosed secret unless she talked about her music which she was more than willing to do now that it was out in the open. His decision had been made. Life with his daughters was slowly improving, a fact for which he was thankful.

* * *

Jane had made a reservation for the train which was to take her to Scotland. Her decision was to stay in a hotel before presenting herself at Foray House. She knew that Douglas was there because he had sent her a letter explaining that he did not know how long he would be away from London. His father wanted his presence for some time now that he had inherited the title and there was much for Douglas to learn in the meantime now that he was the direct heir. Jane had been quite content with this explanation knowing how her father was involving her brother little by little in readiness for taking over Westborough. But it remained imperative that she saw Douglas as soon as possible. The thought of telling him the news made her anxious but a little nugget of hope also rose in her mind that another possible heir for the Severtons might not go amiss.

Jane was used to travelling alone now that she stayed so frequently at the Town House but this journey to the Scottish borders was long and protracted. Her life so far had rarely taken her north. It seemed strange that as a wealthy family they were not well travelled in their own country or abroad for that matter. All roads seemed to lead to London which filled the other part of their year. She had heard her father telling Thea more than once that he was not interested in going overseas because he had spent so long abroad during the war fighting or as a POW. Jane knew that when she came of age and had inherited the legacy from her mother she would travel through Europe and beyond. There was a big world out there to explore. She watched with interest as the train stopped at the large cities on route. There were great screeches of breaks while steam hissed from the engine as the train came to a halt. People rushed for their seats before doors slammed, a whistle blown and the train moved forward again. The cities looked grimy but the smaller towns and villages appeared more picturesque. As the train journeyed north she saw how the multi-hued autumn leaves had turned to sludgy browns while others had fallen from the trees leaving a wintry landscape and it was feeling much colder. If this was taking her destiny in her own hands she was beginning to falter, unsure how Douglas would react or even his father at this intrusion into their well-ordered lives. Now she realized that her feelings of bravado during her rebelliousness during her school days were pathetic. This was the real world making adult decisions and accepting the consequences of those actions. She had been cushioned from the real world by her parents and all she had done was to cause them angst. Now that she had made the decision to keep the baby she wondered if her role as a mother would be adequate enough for her to love it and keep it safe. It was only now on the brink of becoming a parent that she appreciated for the first time Thea being a role model. She was not Thea's natural daughter but her stepmother had never treated her differently from her own children. Childhood blinkered one from such thoughts but adulthood showed another perspective on such issues.

Jane placed her head against the seat and closed her eyes hoping to sleep but her solitude only increased the volume of her thoughts. She remembered Douglas had once hinted not long after he had met her that he would have to marry to produce an heir. He had hinted of her understanding of such matters as the daughter of an Earl but had not mentioned to Jane that she might be the one and the four years difference in their ages had made her appear young and gauche. Her confidence began to wane.

**

Piers looking very dapper in his London attire had ordered a taxi to take him across London to find Maudie's flat. The taxi stopped outside a shop and Piers wrinkled his nose in distaste.

'Is this the right place?' He asked the taxi driver as he heard the meter ticking at the front of the cab.

'It is, gov'nor,' the taxi driver said wanting his fare and wishing to be gone. It had been a long shift and he wanted his tea and a pint or two down at the pub to play a game of darts.

Piers paid the driver and then stood contemplating what he would do next before spying a bell on a side door next to the shop entrance. He pressed hard three times and waited. Inside Maudie had changed her attire to go out for the evening. As she rarely had unexpected visitors curiosity made her look through the window. She did not always answer her door if she had something special to do; however she gasped when she saw the figure standing there. Looking around at the flat she noticed how untidy it was. Perhaps she need not answer the door she thought but thinking better of it she ran down the stairs to confront her father wondering if something might be amiss at Westborough. Anxiety crossed her features momentarily.

'This is an unexpected surprise, Papa,' she said smiling as she answered the door to her father. He leaned forward to kiss her cheek with a look and feel of bonhomie.

'Can I come in?' He asked as Maudie still gazed at him in partial disbelief.

'Of course,' she said stepping aside as she indicated for him to climb the stairs hoping the visit would be short lived.

He entered the apartment, taking note of the lack of space and the untidiness.

'Please sit down, Papa. Can I make you a pot of tea?'

'No thank you,' he said as he made himself comfortable on the sofa smiling at her but wondering how she could live in such a place when there was the house in Belgravia where she could live in comfort. It had always made him wonder why modern young people were happy to live in such conditions particularly when they had grown up used to wealth and comfort. Piers was a man of his time not realizing the protest that the young made against such things. His youth had been one of conformity followed by fighting for King and country. Why were the youth not happy with their lot when so many people had lost their lives to fight for freedom? It was a great enigma to him.

'I thought that I would surprise you Maudie.'

'You have certainly done that,' she said with a hint of sarcasm which passed her father by.

'Have you seen Jane by any chance?' He asked without any preamble. Alarm bells rang in Maudie's head. Did he know Jane's circumstances?

'Yes as a matter of fact I have. She was here a few days ago. She stayed for a few nights.'

Piers took another look around the room wondering where on earth Jane would have slept.

'She left Belgravia with a suitcase early this morning. Jenna does not know where she was going and Thea says that she had not arrived at the Hall. Do you know where she might have gone?'

So this was it, Maudie thought, playing for time. Had Jane gone to Scotland? Whatever happened she was not going to tell her father. This was Jane's war to fight.

'She didn't confide in me, Papa. You know what Jane is like; she is a law unto herself.'

'Yes, indeed,' he said.

Both of them sat in silence for a few minutes contemplating those words. Piers felt that she might have gone to stay with unknown friends but Maudie had other ideas

'Yes she is rather a law unto herself. I expect that she will turn up soon rather like a bad penny,' Piers said, his face inscrutable but suddenly it brightened. 'Anyway the reason that I came was to take you out to supper so go and change quickly.'

Maudie looked down at her outfit suddenly wishing to laugh. She was wearing her 'going out' clothes for her London life while her father was wearing what he wore for an evening on the Town.

'I won't be a minute,' she said jumping up. She could not refuse him after he had made such an effort to find her. On entering her bedroom she closed the door. Opening the wardrobe she took out the only dress she possessed that her father would deem presentable. It was a little black number that had graced her wardrobe for quite some time but had not been worn. As she looked at her reflection in the cheval mirror she smiled. She looked sophisticated with her hair tied on top of her head and wispy tendrils curling about her face softening her features. On her feet she wore black stilettos and took a black clutch bag from a drawer to complete the ensemble. Her greatest wish was that she would not meet anybody she knew for tonight she would become Lady Maud Devine, daughter of the Earl of Westborough. And somehow it was the most glorious of feelings.

* * *

Jane stepped down from the train at a small station called Gretna which was not too far from Foray House. She placed her suitcase on the platform to look around and give herself chance to think. She felt bemused having not booked a hotel room in advance. It was strange to be somewhere but with nowhere to go. Watching as a small number of passengers disembarked she saw them walk into the arms of loved ones or stride purposely to the exit and then on with their lives.

She turned around as someone tapped her on the shoulder. 'Are you lost bonnie wee lassie?' A kindly voice said to her. It was the stationmaster who had watched her for a few minutes wondering why she was lingering when the platform had rapidly emptied.

'I suppose I am,' she said smiling at him. 'I need to find a hotel for the night and I don't know where to go.'

'Well I can find you a taxi. You canna hump yon case very far. There will be room at the Foray Arms at this time of year. The tourists will have gone.'

The old stationmaster picked up Jane's suitcase and walked with her out of the station where a battered old taxi stood waiting expectantly for a passenger. Opening the back door to allow Jane inside, the taxi driver took the suitcase to place in the boot of the car.

'To the Foray Arms, Hamish.'

'Righto.'

The journey did not take long. The taxi driver drew up outside an old building, but Jane had not taken note for she was looking in her purse to find her fare. The rather taciturn driver had retrieved her case and placed it noisily on the pavement waiting for his fare and hopefully a tip. Jane provided both and the driver touched his cap in readiness to return to the railway station to find his next fare.

But Jane with all the authority of her class expected more from the man.

'Can you carry my suitcase into the hotel?' There was a delay before she added 'please' to her request. The taxi driver grumbling to himself, hefted the case into the bowels of the building before disappearing into the darkness.

The Foray Arms was a quaint old building built during the fifteenth century, probably at the same time as Foray House. However, Jane could not see too much because it was now dark but as she entered the hotel following in the footsteps of her driver she found a welcoming log fire burning in an old-fashioned grate. Probably Tudor she thought thinking about Westborough Hall. It gave an air of homeliness. At this very moment she could do with that thinking nostalgically of Westborough Hall. There was a touch of homesickness churning inside her but she pushed such thoughts away.

'You need a room?' The man on the reception desk asked in a bored fashion. His shift had been long and tedious.

'Yes a single if you have one please.'

'We do indeed,' came the gruff reply. 'Sign here please,' he said in his strong Scottish accent indicating the place with his index finger.

He pressed a bell and a teenage boy appeared from behind the reception area.

'Number 16,' the man said.

The boy picked up the suitcase and with a curt, 'Follow me,' he led Jane through swing doors into the inner bowels of the hotel and up some twisting stairs until they arrived at the room. Unlocking the door he turned on lights and placed the suitcase on its rack before saying, 'Dinner is at 7.30 if you want.' And without ceremony he had gone pulling the door noisily behind him.

Jane looked around at the shabby interior. This was not Westborough Hall or the Ritz with its comforts but it would have to do.

'I'm spoilt,' she thought as another wave of homesickness wafted over her. She was not hungry, just tired. Tomorrow she hoped that she would be able to find Douglas and her baby's future would be assured. But fear still lurked in her heart.

***

Piers and Maudie had found themselves enjoying each other's company. Her father had taken her to Claridges to dine. He had booked his habitual table in a corner of the large dining room where he usually brought Thea when they were in town. This was not a novelty for Maudie but it was still a treat after the usual places that she frequented when in London. There would be nobody here to recognize her from her London set; this made her relax and enjoy her father's company even more. She regarded him almost for the first time in months or perhaps years at least since her adulthood. She saw a man of genteel bearing who despite his advancing years was still handsome. His sense of humour had made her laugh. There had been people who had looked at them curiously making Maudie wonder if they thought that they were lovers. This tickled her sense of humour and so she reported this to her father. He roared with laughter too. This must be what Thea saw in him although through her childhood he had been this stern and distant figure. She wondered if she could ask him about this before deciding against it; there was the possibility that it might spoil the evening.

'When do you go home, papa?' She said.

'I was going home to Westborough tomorrow but I rang Thea to tell her the day after tomorrow. I have to be at the House a little longer than I thought. Would you like to do this again tomorrow night? Perhaps we could go to the Ritz for a change.'

Maudie burst out laughing, 'We rich folks,' she said.

Piers laughed too. He looked at this daughter through new eyes wondering how he could have been frightened of the three older girls over the years since his return home. But he was a different man from the one who had returned from a POW camp. The painful years of incarceration had receded but would never be forgotten. Life experiences could scar the mind. He had been luckier than most. What would it have been like to have lost limbs or been burnt? It had been difficult enough to sustain family relationships without feeling beholden to others. He had known soldiers who could not return to family situations. How lucky he had been with Thea who had loved him enough to keep faith with him. She could never really understand how much he loved her and how much he still wanted her in every sense of the word despite telling her frequently.

His hand crept across the table and covered his daughter's small one. He then squeezed it in affection before saying, 'Maudie, I wish to apologise for all the hurt I have caused you girls. I should have been a better father to you all, but I did not listen to Thea's pleadings and your grandmother's advice. They were right and I was wrong, so wrong.'

Maudie's eyes filled with tears at her father's confession. She did not know what to say to this man who at last was becoming human and she knew that she loved him despite everything that had gone before.

'Ssh,' she said, 'this is a new beginning for us all so let's keep it that way.'

'I do love you,' he reiterated, his own eyes glistening too.

'I know now and that is all that really matters. But Jane and Scarlett should be told too. Jane has been struggling more than any of us. It was one of the reasons that she was so wilful at school. It was her way of making you notice her. She is very clever, Papa, and her silliness made her miss out on university. I don't know where her future lies.' Maudie stopped before she said too much. She did not want to spoil this new and fragile relationship. She regarded him noticing his thoughtful demeanour. The humour had vanished from his face, hardening the contours once more.

But suddenly his humour was restored and he said, 'I know and I intend to make it up to her too. But Scarlett is in pursuit of her own father in some form.'

'And why do you think that would be?' Maudie asked more sharply than she intended, her face having taken on a sombre look.

Piers looked at her closely not wishing to lose what they had gained during their evening together. 'He is dead and was a hero. There is a touch of mystery about him. There is glamour in such a combination. I wish her well.' He thought about Scarlett and her pursuit of Jack Carson's history. If he was honest, Scarlett was as much a daughter to him as any of his other children and her determination to find out more of her natural father hurt him more than he could say.

Maudie still nodded in agreement hoping that her stepsister Scarlett would not be too disappointed when she finally found what she was looking for.

Chapter 31

Jane woke the next morning feeling refreshed but famished. She had been bone weary the previous evening after travelling for most of the day so bed beckoned rather than food. Stretching and then luxuriating in the comfort of the old bed, her thoughts turned to the baby and how she would contact Douglas. She could telephone or she could take a taxi to Foray House and chance her luck. Neither situation was appealing but remembering Maudie's words she decided that she would go to Foray House and find out how other aristocrats lived. The Devines rarely socialized with their peers. Country house parties were not their style. Piers had thought about this often over the years and had blamed his parents for the situation. Their loveless marriage and his father's liaison with Beatrice had not encouraged entertaining on a lavish scale. It had been weddings and funerals which had dictated an integration into the company of other aristocrats on a certain level to keep up appearances.

Jane had remembered that Douglas had said that his ancestral home needed money spending on it. The interiors were shabby and structural work was required in some areas of the old building. That raised alarm bells within her head for there was no way that she would share her inheritance with anyone except her child. Piers had always warned his older children about gold-diggers. The Devines were renowned for their wealth even though they did not splash it about. Some aristocratic families were poor by comparison and had to find ways to increase their incomes to keep their homes and life styles together.

The decision to seek Douglas on his home territory made Jane feel better about the situation. She did not need Douglas' money just his name if her child was to be legitimate. She ran her hand over where her child lay feeling the slight swell of her stomach as her body began to change shape. If the marriage did not work out it did not matter she felt. She would have done the right thing for her child. Divorce was commonplace nowadays. She would be financially secure to live her own life if need be. But if the child was a boy could it be taken away from her to live on the Scottish borders, to learn about its heritage if it did not work out between herself and Douglas. Fear gripped her but she tried to stay calm for the sake of the child. She was in control of her own destiny.

After a huge breakfast which had fortified her, Jane went in search of Hamish's taxi. It was parked outside the railway station awaiting the next train but he was more than happy to deviate from his plan and drive the few miles to Foray House.

'Foray House indeed,' he said in his soft Scottish accent. 'Are you going for a job there?'

'No just to visit,' Jane said mysteriously. 'Do you know the Severtons?'

'Oh aye. They are friendly folk and can often be seen around. They are good to the locals and the people who work for them. The old Earl favoured the local community as does his son. They are good people.'

Part of this reassured Jane, but she remained quiet wondering how the present Earl would accept a pregnant woman calling on the family. The thought almost made her laugh. Looking at the passing countryside she felt as if she was in a foreign land. Again the absurdness of her thoughts made her wonder if it was her condition which made her so fanciful.

'Do you want me to drive up to the House or are you going to walk?' Hamish said.

Looking through the taxi window Jane could see the House from the drive. It was inevitable that she would make comparisons with Westborough Hall. The house was quite old in grey, granite stone but it could have been older than her home by a hundred years. It was quite imposing from this distance she thought but the question that haunted her was if she could live so far away from all that she knew and loved. Her hand touched the secret place where her child grew and suddenly she smiled. There was London where the Severtons had a home. She could live there for part of the year and visit Westborough for long stretches so life would not be quite so bad after all. The thought had given her confidence but whatever her feelings she had to do this for her child.

'I'll walk, Hamish, thank you. It does not look too far to walk.' It was inevitable that she would compare it with Westborough which had the long drive.

Hamish, the taciturn man of the previous evening, opened the door of the taxi to allow her to step down. If nothing else he had been brought up to be respectful to women.

'Will you be all right from here, lassie?' he asked, his face etched in genuine concern.

Jane laughed, 'I will be fine, Hamish. Thank you.'

Hamish's face told another story, but he touched his cap out of respect. 'I'll see you again,' he said hopefully turning towards his taxi and stiffly sitting in the driver's seat before driving off.

This was it; time to find out where her future lay. Hamish had been correct in a way for nerves were beginning to gnaw at her stomach but she continued her walk and as she reached the House the beautiful façade looked in poor repair, crumbling in places and now she knew that it would take a lot of money to put it right. Her stomach turned over at the thought but there was nothing that she could do about it. The thought of living in what she termed poverty genuinely alarmed her. Again the thought that she was being selfish, a poor little rich girl, entered her mind. Piers had always been generous with the allowance he granted each of his older daughters. It was common knowledge that some members of the aristocracy lived in penury compared to the Devines. But James Devine had instilled into his son that family inheritance had to be looked after despite death duties which came as a punishing burden generation after generation. Piers had followed his father's instructions to the letter having invested his wealth wisely and made the estate pay its way. He wished his heir to do the same when his day came to take the helm.

Suddenly around the corner of the building, a tall man puffing on a pipe strode purposely followed by two Labradors. He sounded English rather than Scottish as he called to the dogs; his accent was upper class but Jane noticed that he was wearing old clothes which were threadbare and had seen better days.

'Hello,' he said quietly, 'can I help you?

'I was looking for Douglas, Lord Douglas Severton,' she felt nervous and young, puzzled by whom the man could be.

'Douglas is on the estate, but he should be back in time for lunch. Back in about half an hour. And you are?'

Jane straightened to her full height suddenly wanting to sound rather grand. 'I'm Lady Jane Devine.'

The man smiled and stretched out his hand. 'I am pleased to meet you, Jane. I have heard all about you from Douglas. By the way I'm his father. It is a long journey to have made to just come and see him. But come away in and you must stay to lunch.'

Jane was rendered speechless.

The grand entrance hall of Foray House was dark, but it was lit by artificial light even in the daytime. She surveyed the scene; she noticed the deer heads which lined one wall, undoubtedly hunting trophies in a bygone era. A display of fire arms were exhibited on another wall in precise rows and on another pistols and guns, probably from as far back as the seventeenth century, were ordered in a regular formation giving credence to the long history of the House and the family who had no doubt fought in border skirmishes over the centuries. Jane's knowledge of history was not great but there was a thread of memory from her school days telling her about marauding Scots crossing the border into England.

There were also portraits of generations of Severtons which looked down upon the activities of younger members of their family. The eyes seemed to follow you wherever you walked. Jane shivered; the darkness of the house made her feel the cold on a dull autumnal morning. At Westborough Hall the large fire would be lit and the central heating that Piers had insisted on installing would lend warmth to such a large house. They must be hardy Scots Jane thought as she wrapped her coat more closely around her.

Archie Severton, Earl of Foray, led his guest into a drawing room which was small but cosy. Here the roaring log fire warmed the room. Each side of the fireplace, roughly hewn logs were untidily stacked. Jane had noted the faded grandeur of the furnishings which would have been sumptuous in their day but even so it was not lost on her that money did not come as easily to this family as it did to her own. Somehow, though, the threadbare chairs and sofa made her feel comfortable and at home. The dogs followed them into the drawing room and lay by the fire to sleep after their activities. Thea would not allow dogs anywhere near the main rooms of Westborough Hall. She had always regarded them as working animals and Piers had never made an issue on this subject respecting Thea's authority in the home.

Something at the back of Jane's mind registered that there were no women here at Foray House. Douglas' mother had died when he was born and he had told her that his father had never wished to marry again having felt that he could never replace the great love he had shared with Douglas' mother. When Jane thought more deeply she felt that she had much in common with Douglas Severton. They had both lost a parent at a tender age. Again her hand touched the secret place where her baby grew making her wonder if she would make a good mother. The Earl returned to the drawing room having informed his kitchen staff that they had a guest for lunch. Dining was informal at Foray House whereas at Westborough, life was quite different. Jane had decided that there would always be comparisons between each house.

The gong sounded for lunch.

'Come along,' the Earl said taking her hand and linking it through his arm.

He led her into the dining room which was smaller than the drawing room but equally as grand in a very old-fashioned way. Pulling out a chair from the table for Jane to sit down he found his own place, but there was still no sign of Douglas. Jane noticed that three places had already been laid.

'Douglas should not be long,' he said. 'Would you like a glass of wine?'

'Yes please,' said Jane feeling ill at ease, but hoping the wine would calm her down. She knew that she should not drink alcohol but one glass would not hurt her. The Earl moved to the drinks cabinet to pour her a glass.

It had not escaped him that Jane had arrived unannounced. Douglas had not mentioned that she was visiting. Although he did not show it he was quite bemused by her arrival and wondered if there was a significant reason for her visit.

Just at that moment the door of the dining room opened. Douglas, dressed in farming type clothes, entered the room. A sound emanated from his mouth as if he was about to start a conversation with his father but he stopped mid-sentence noticing another presence in the room.

'Jane,' he said, the look of surprise and pleasure uniting on his face.

Jane had turned round to greet him, 'Hello, Douglas,' she said feeling better at his welcome.

'Jane my goodness what are you doing here?'

Before she could answer Archie broke into a smile of amusement which etched his weather beaten features. 'I found her wandering the grounds wanting to see you, Dougie.'

Jane went red.

'Well it is a surprise. Are you staying?'

Jane went red again. 'Of course she is staying. But I don't know where she put her suitcase.' Archie laughed uproariously at Jane's discomfort

'I, I....'

'We'll sort that afterwards Father,' Douglas intervened taking his seat at the table and unfolding a napkin as the first course of their meal was brought in on a tray. Jane could not but compare the houses of Foray and Westborough appreciating how well Thea ran her ancestral home. Perhaps everything was different north of the border or was it because there was no woman at the helm. A thought had occurred to Jane that if everything worked out and she had to live in this back of beyond place she would work her magic on it to make it more comfortable. But did she want to live here while the hustle and bustle of London always beckoned? Life at Westborough Hall beckoned too. She felt so confused and uncertain about everything. As she looked around the table she found two pairs of eyes regarding her. Douglas laughed.

'You were lost in your own little world for a moment,' Douglas teased.

Once again Jane blushed. Archie wondered what was going on but he knew that he would find out soon enough. Douglas was not one to hold secrets. Father and son had always been close. But on this occasion he had a feeling that Douglas did not know what Jane was concealing and he had an inkling about what it might be.

Chapter 32

Scarlett had enjoyed her return to Oxford. Her relationship with her mother had improved since the reading of the will but it was still tinged with unease. A break from each other would perhaps improve the situation and if she could prevent Thea from visiting Oxford during the term everything might return to normal when she went home for the Christmas vacation. There still lingered in her mind the fact that she wanted to find out more about her father but there was always the fear there would be little to tell for he had been quite a young man when he had been killed in North Africa and she was not sure that she could take the disappointment. She knew that she had built him up in her mind to be someone special. There was a great expectation when he had been proclaimed a war hero. She supposed that his medal for valour had done that. Without the war he would have been somebody ordinary. It was exceptional circumstances which brought out the best in people. There was Winston Churchill who was a hero in the War years but after it was all over he was rejected by the voting public. Piers had often spoken of this with regret. He knew the great man well and had been only too pleased when he had again been made Prime Minister in the last decade.

But there was her father's ancestry which might have been interesting. Perhaps there were cousins who were still alive. That thought was a little reassuring. Her life was so entwined with the Devines even though they were not her blood relatives except for the younger ones that there was a yearning within her to have something unique of her own, to carve out an identity of her own. In the not too distant future she wished to pursue this dream but her present life was too full of her ambitions and dreams.

As she returned to her hall of residence one afternoon after lectures Scarlett stopped in the entrance hall at the letter rack for incoming mail. She did not usually receive many letters. Occasionally there would be one from her mother or school friends who only wrote infrequently but she knew she could not complain, as she was not very good at corresponding either. The here and now had inevitably taken over. However, as she went into her pigeonhole she looked through the thick wad of mail only to discover three letters for herself. Two were from school friends and the third was from

Maudie; she would recognize her sloping, distinctive hand anywhere. Maudie did not write many letters so this must be something special or important. Taking the letters to her room she threw her books onto a chair and sat on the bed anxious to know what Maudie wanted. It was not like her to write at all.

As she took out the single sheet of paper from the envelope it contained an invitation to visit Maudie as soon as possible for she had news to impart. Scarlett was puzzled. Why could she not have told her in a letter? Why did she have to travel to London and upset her routine? It all seemed top secret. However, if she went up to London there was something that she wanted to do.

Scarlett had replied by return of post. She had decided that she would travel on Friday afternoon and return on Monday evening. Monday was a day free from lectures. This day she usually spent in the university library catching up on assignments but it was not the end of the world should she miss one. Quietly she was beginning to relish the fact that she and Maudie would visit the clubs again. That had been a turning point in her life. At Oxford, life had taken off for her once she had decided to start enjoying herself. Greater relaxation had made her hard work more palatable and her ambitions were as bright as ever. And then there was Toby Price who was showing interest since her return from the summer vacation. He was a member of her law classes. He had been there during her first year but had believed Scarlett to be rather a blue stocking. Suddenly all that had changed when, the new Scarlett emerged from her chrysalis. However, Scarlett in her usual way was giving him little encouragement which made him more ardent in his pursuit of her. Somehow it made her feel warm inside that somebody was showing interest in her at last. Her self-esteem had risen dramatically but the two things that meant the most to her were her university degree and the pursuit of her father's history. On these two issues she was totally single minded. A demanding relationship was not on the cards.

The week seemed endless until she travelled to London and heard Maudie's news. She could not wait but the wisest scenario was that she should keep herself busy until the hour of her departure to the capital arrived. There were assignments pending as well as an evening out with Toby. At last she had relented and they had agreed to visit a jazz club in the city. Toby not so interested in such music had readily agreed if it meant an evening with the enigmatic Scarlett.

On Friday afternoon Scarlett took the train to Paddington and then the underground to Maudie's flat. Maudie was waiting eagerly for her arrival. The little apartment had been scrubbed until it shone. This was not purely on Scarlett's account but she had a premonition that her father might call unannounced on his next visit to London as the first one had gone surprisingly well.

On Scarlett's appearance Maudie had opened a bottle of white wine which had been chilling in the rather small refrigerator; this had been bought second hand from an advert she had seen in an evening newspaper.

'Well tell me, Maudie,' Scarlett could not contain her curiosity as she settled herself into one of the ancient armchairs which were covered in colourful throws and began to sip with relish the first glass of the evening.

Maudie exploded into gales of laughter. 'Jane is pregnant,' she said. There was no point prevaricating.

Scarlett nearly dropped her overflowing glass of wine. 'You're joking.'

'No I'm not. I told her that she had to get her life together and then she left and I haven't heard from her since. She had thought about an abortion. I feel so guilty now. I should have done more to help her.'

At this thought Maudie had become serious and Scarlett pensive. Both knew that Jane could get herself into tight corners and this time Piers would be furious, angrier than he had ever been with Jane. They surmised that she would be sent away to have it and it would be adopted. Piers was very Victorian about such things.

'I think I know who the father is. It is that Douglas who was with her on the night of her ball. I saw them going into her bedroom. I was just about to go downstairs and they did not see me. Their hands were all over each other.'

Silence!

Suddenly Maudie smiled. 'I had a visit from Papa. We had dinner together twice. He was witty and funny but most of all caring. It was the best I have seen him. I am beginning to change my opinion of him. However he wanted to know if I had seen Jane. I told him I had but omitted to give him all the details.'

Again silence!

It was no wonder that Maudie had wanted to see Scarlett face to face.

'What do you think Jane will do?' Scarlett asked feeling quite sorry for her stepsister.

'I don't know but I had a feeling that she wanted to keep it. But it is not something one does in our class.' Maudie did her best impression of her father. Scarlett smiled but there was concern etched on her face. 'If we don't know where she is we can't help her. You don't think she would do anything silly do you? It is quite hard to be on your own. She needs somebody to turn to. Thea would help her. She has a way with defusing a situation particularly with Papa.'

Maudie was serious. She had not totally empathised with Jane's solitary state but had felt that her sister had brought this on herself without much thought.

'Jane can be such a drama queen when she wants to,' Maudie said unkindly.

'Well what can we do?' Scarlett stood up and moved to the window gazing into the darkness watching the pace of London life continue in the street below. She turned back to look at Maudie, 'it is not as if she has many friends who could help her out. She had obviously come to you....' Her voice stopped mid-sentence as she began to accuse Maudie of not helping her sister.

Maudie had grasped the meaning and she sank into silence with a feeling of tremendous guilt. Scarlett had turned back to look out of the window. She did not want to fall out with Maudie. Returning to her seat she sipped at her wine then looked up with a smile on her face. 'Shall we go out on the town?'

Maudie looked up and smiled only too relieved that the moment of criticism had passed. 'Of course,' abandoning her unfinished glass of wine in order to make readiness for the evening.

***

Although the sisters had enjoyed the company of each other, Scarlett was pleased to leave on the Monday morning. She was going to visit her father's house before catching the train back to Oxford. But Jane's silence had hung like a cloud over them for the few days of her visit. Scarlett wanted to tell her mother; Thea with her great common sense would know what to do. Maudie wanted to leave it longer believing Jane would be in touch at some point. However neither was convinced of the fact.

Scarlett stood on the pavement outside her father's house looking upwards with a puzzled expression. On a board outside were written the two words 'to let' with the name of the company who dealt with such procedures. It had been a rather puzzling weekend leaving Scarlett anxious about both situations. She wondered where the girl with the baby had gone. It was all very puzzling.

Now as she looked out of the train windows not really seeing the passing countryside another thought had struck her. She was really worried about Jane, more than she believed possible. Jane was her own worst enemy at times getting into scrapes and not always finding the best route out of them. It had happened time and again despite Thea and Piers feeling happier that Jane had begun to grow up. The news of her pregnancy demonstrated that she had not grown up enough Scarlett thought. There was little excuse these days with the new pill that was there to prevent mishaps. This was a form of emancipation for young women as a new decade approached. Scarlett, a deep thinker at the best of times, was allowing her imagination to run away with her. What was happening to her sister? Had she already had an abortion? What if she was ill from having one? The nightmare raged on and on.

By the time she had reached Oxford, Scarlett had decided that she should tell her mother for Thea was the only one who could handle Piers' wrath. There had been plenty of evidence of that in the past. Somehow it would seem disloyal to Jane but anxiety had a funny way of making you act in the most inappropriate of ways. This was all rather a nightmare. But somehow she had to act before disaster struck.

Chapter 33

Jane quite unaware of the furore she had caused between her sisters was now feeling better than she had done for days. When she and Douglas had returned to the hotel to collect her luggage they had a serious conversation.

'Dougie I'm pregnant,' she declared sitting on the edge of the bed in the hotel bedroom; there was little need to prevaricate.

Sitting facing her in the only chair in the room he remained silent looking at her quizzically. This fact of becoming a father he found difficult to assimilate. The protracted silence made Jane feel nervous until he suddenly beamed. Rising from the chair he moved towards her, suddenly taking her in his arms holding her in a tight bear hug until she laughed with him.

'What wonderful news, Jane,' he said enthusiastically. He now felt euphoric although the news had greatly stunned him. He knew that he had to marry and produce an heir at some point and why not now. He was very fond of Jane. She was beautiful and had the right pedigree for such an old aristocratic family as his.

Suddenly she grew serious again. 'My father will kill me for bringing shame on our family name. He still lives in the dark ages as far as things like that are concerned. Dougie what can I do?'

Douglas looked serious once more before kneeling before her and taking her hand. 'Lady Jane Devine will you do me the honour of marrying me?'

His hand strayed to the small bump that lay below her ribcage and remained there protectively, gently caressing it.

'Oh, Dougie, do you mean it? I am not trying to trap you into marriage but I have been at my wits end trying to find a solution.' Her face clouded once more as doubt began to set in. 'You do mean it, Dougie, not just for the baby's sake but for us, too.'

Douglas kissed her to quieten her protests. 'Yes I mean it. It has been on my mind for quite some time. I feared that you were a little too young but this has speeded everything up Jane. It was my grandfather dying which prevented me from asking you and my father needed me here as I am the heir now. But he will be thrilled to know that there is a new life growing. He has wanted me to marry and produce an heir for quite some time. The Severtons for several generations have only produced one child in a generation and it has been quite an anxiety for an Earl. It makes us a bit like King Henry VIII.' He laughed uproariously at his own joke.

'I know all about that with my brother Harry. Papa is trying to train him but he is still very young.' Jane went silent as she watched Dougie's face. He was still smiling like the cat that had got the cream.

'A society wedding will take a long time to plan and then everyone will see why we are getting married.' Her beautiful face was etched with concern. She had not fully grasped the fact that the solutions to her problems had been solved so easily. Neither had it crossed her mind that her family would be out of their minds with worry over her disappearance.

Douglas smiled. 'Don't worry. There is a perfectly good way round it but we will have to tell my father. He is already aware that I wish to get married. However, my grandfather's death has up scuttled everything. There is so much to do here at Foray House and on the estate which is why I'm needed here.'

'Yes, of course,' she said knowing only too well.

'Do your parents know where you are?'

'No,' she said, 'I don't want them to know until everything is settled.'

Later that evening, when Jane had retired to bed exhausted by the emotional upheaval of previous days, Douglas found his father in the library smoking his pipe deep in thought. He looked up as his son appeared and smiled enigmatically.

'Whisky, father?'

'Aye.' Archie was still looking at his son. Douglas felt uneasy under such intense scrutiny. 'Is the lass all right?'

'Yes. Just tired. Everything has been a bit too much for her. I have something to tell you, Father.'

'I thought you might,' he said and then he waited.

'Jane and I are getting married.'

'And she is pregnant?'

'Yes. I want to do the decent thing but I do love her and it would have happened at some point.'

'Do her parents know about the bairn?'

'No and neither does she want them to before the deed is done.'

'I know her father and he won't be pleased. He is much of the old school about such matters. I would feel the same if I had a daughter.'

'Perhaps so, but there is nothing to be done when it is all sorted,' Douglas said.

'No,' Archie said, his face inscrutable. He was thinking of Piers and what he might say about the matter. But if the girl was already married by the time that he knew there was not a lot he could do about it except vent his venom but at least the girl would be marrying into her own class and the whole business need not be paraded in the press. Piers Devine could not grumble on that issue. Archie had heard how the girl's father was snobbish and could be quite cantankerous on the matter.

The next morning Archie sat in the library after breakfast watching the rain make tracks down the window. The wind was howling and blowing a gale. Winter was well on the way. He had been awake for much of the night thinking about his son's news. He wished to speak to his prospective daughter-in-law. He too was anxious that the child was born in wedlock male or female. He wanted a male child for obvious reasons but if it was healthy others would follow.

There was a knock at the library door.

'Enter,' he called.

Jane stood there puzzled by the summons to this man's presence. She was ready to justify her forthcoming nuptials.

'Come in, Jane, and sit yourself down,' he said. 'Don't look so frightened. I have no intention of eating you.' Then he smiled changing the contours of his face. Suddenly she relaxed and sat on the stiff backed hair sofa waiting for Archie to say what was on his mind.

'My son says he wishes to marry you,' the new Earl of Foray said, 'and as soon as possible.'

Jane stared him straight in the eye and said, 'Yes, my Lord. That is what we both want.'

'Is there a good reason for such haste?' Foray looked her up and down detecting the slight arc of her stomach. 'Tell me about it, Lady Jane,' he said using her title.

'I am three no nearly four months pregnant.' There was defiance in her eyes almost challenging him to deny that his house needed this possible heir.

'Are you sure that my son is the father?' Foray knew he was crossing the line here but he had to be certain that the child was a Severton for there was much at stake.

'I am not wanton, my Lord. I do believe that your son has been the only candidate for the honour.' Sarcasm was thick in her voice as she once more looked him in the eye. Foray believed her. He threw his head back and laughed uproariously.

'I admire your wit, young lady. So… you are Piers Devine's oldest daughter.'

'I am his oldest child. Would that make any difference in the marriage stakes, my Lord?'

'No, Jane, it would not. I have met your father at the House. I admire what he stands for. Does he know of your condition?'

'No. He would not be impressed by this for he already finds me difficult. However, he will know when Douglas and I are married.' Jane could not have been more honest in her reply.

Foray arched an eyebrow in question of this remark but Jane was not forthcoming on the details of her complicated relationship with her father. They were personal and she had sufficient loyalty to her family not to divulge such personal aspects of their life. Archie would have liked to know more but he respected Piers enough not to pry. However, there had been rumours in the House that the Earl of Westborough could at times be a difficult father. The Devines, though, closely guarded their private lives which remained a closed book not available for the public domain.

'Well, Jane, you might be carrying our heir so you have my blessing. I wish you and Dougie a happy life blessed with more children. However, like your father I don't want scandals or divorces to affect our house. I want you both to be sure that this marriage is for life.'

'I won't let you down, my lord. Douglas and I do love each other.'

Archie walked towards Jane and kissed her on both cheeks. 'Aye. Douglas says you love each other. Welcome to our family.' The smile on his face was one of sincerity hoping that the journey that the two young people were about to embark on would bring them true happiness.

Chapter 34

Following her return from London Scarlett had made up her mind to visit Westborough Hall to see her mother. This was totally against the plan she had made after the summer vacation but she had become intensely worried about Jane. She had telephoned Maudie to see if circumstances had changed but it had remained the same.

'I don't think that you should tell them. I promised Jane that I wouldn't,' Maudie was near to tears on two accounts. Firstly she did not want to be disloyal to Jane but there was the distinct possibility that her sister could be ill. There was also the fact that they could incur her father's wrath because she had lied to him by omission on their very successful time in London together.

'I don't think this has anything to do with promises,' Scarlett said pragmatically. 'What if she is ill or has tried to kill herself.'

'You don't think that she would try and do that do you?'

Scarlett thought about her words carefully. 'I don't know, but Jane can be rather a drama queen and has been known for doing stupid things.'

'I know but she is older now and hopefully wiser.'

'So…! I'm going home to see what my mother says. You can blame all this on me if Jane turns up. But it is better to be safe rather than sorry. Your father will have to know at some point.'

'Oh all right but let me know what happens.' With that the telephone went dead and Scarlett was left looking at the receiver in a perplexed way. The decision was made.

On Thursday evening Scarlett rang the Hall to speak to her mother. There was a pay phone in her hall of residence. This was a nuisance because she would have to keep feeding it with coins if it was answered by a member of staff at the Westborough end. They would have to go in search of Thea. But good fortune shone on her when Thea answered in person.

'Mummy.' Thea noted that she was not Mama again as the Devine children called her; sometimes the older ones called her Thea. It was just Scarlett trying to be different once more. Thea knew her daughter well.

'Hello, darling. This is a lovely surprise. How is everything?'

'That's why I am ringing,' Scarlett said.

Thea's heart tumbled wondering what was wrong. Scarlett's voice sounded different, not hostile like she had been for much of her summer vacation but more distracted.

'I'm coming home for the weekend. I shall be on the five o'clock train getting into Great Malvern. Could you pick me up? Oh and could you book a table for dinner. I have something to tell you.'

Thea's heart sank once more. 'Can't you tell me now, darling, for I shall only worry?'

'Tomorrow.' Scarlett said emphatically before she replaced the receiver.

Thea stood cogitating on the conversation, not that it had been much of one she thought ruefully. She would worry until she saw her daughter the following day. Piers entered the great hall with the dogs pattering behind him on the flag stoned floor. He saw his wife standing there in a reverie. Walking to her he put an arm around her shoulders. 'Penny for them,' he said planting a kiss on her cheek.

Smiling up at him affectionately she said, 'that was Scarlett on the telephone. She is coming home for the weekend and wants me to take her out for dinner.'

'Well, it is nice she is coming home.' Then he sounded serious when he said, 'I know when I'm not wanted, as there is no invitation for me.'

Thea regarded him quite sharply, 'Women's talk,' she said with a razor edge to her voice but then relaxed when she saw Piers laughing. He hugged her closer before kissing her.

'It will do you both good to have some quality time together,' he said light-heartedly. 'I shall have a tray on my knee in front of the television.'

Thea regarded him quizzically. It was unusual for the Earl of Westborough to even contemplate a television dinner. As far as she was concerned it had never happened before. But Piers was growing more relaxed in his attitude to life.

Thea kissed him. 'I'll tell cook,' she said walking towards the stairs which led down to the basement kitchen as Piers walked the dogs towards the boot room where they could dry off after their walk on the estate. She had never mentioned the fact that the dogs had made muddy footprints across the floor. Piers knew that they should have entered through the boot room but on this occasion Thea was dwelling on Scarlett's odd telephone call and for once he had got away with it.

Thea was waiting for Scarlett in her little red Morgan sports car, a present from her husband, which had been newly acquired, outside Great Malvern Station. After a stream of people had exited the station she spotted her daughter approaching. Scarlett stood looking around for a moment before

Thea tooted her horn. Thea noticed a smile curl her daughter's lips in response as she made her way to the vehicle. Opening the boot she placed her small weekend case inside before coming to join her mother in the front. The atmosphere between them was relaxed as they gave each other a kiss in welcome and Thea started the engine. Neither spoke at first; Thea was concentrating on negotiating the road and Scarlett was wondering how to approach the topic of Jane and her problems. This had haunted her throughout her journey from Oxford.

***

In the Scottish borders at Foray House, Archie Severton had left the young couple to their own devices to discuss their forthcoming matrimonial state but he had spoken privately to Douglas to warn him that whatever they decided Jane would require her father's consent as she was underage and it was normal procedure to ask a father for his daughter's hand in marriage. He knew enough of Piers and his legendary temper if things did not go his way. And Piers Devine like his father before him was as aristocratic as they came. Douglas had had an insight from Jane about her father and the difficult relationship which they had shared. Jane had been scrupulously honest about this from the beginning. It had not bothered Douglas for he had little inclination to visit Westborough Hall for his life was centred on his future inheritance and the life he led in London when some aspect of freedom summoned him. When they married Jane would become part of that life and if she needed to return to her ancestral home she could go alone. When all was said and done Douglas was his own person and was not going to live under the shadow of Piers Devine's wrath.

The answer to all this was obvious, waiting on their doorstep and Jane could write to her family when the deed was done. And so it was that Jane stayed at Foray House for the requisite three weeks to be married at Gretna Green placing her on a par with all those who ran away to get married which she was about to do. After their discussion Jane had a frisson of excitement about once more duping her parent and the consequences could take care of themselves. She would belong to her husband's family and in a few months would be making one of her own.

***

Thea had booked a corner table where she and Scarlett could talk privately and not be overheard. She was known in the area and it was always possible that there would be a member of the press around waiting for news of someone of such high celebrity status. However, strangely the little bistro was quiet for a Friday evening which allowed them to relax.

The two women sat opposite each other, Thea waiting expectantly for Scarlett to tell her what was on her mind. Neither of the women was anxious to order, the maître d' hovered around but they ignored him.

Scarlett cleared her throat and took a sip of white wine to give her fortitude. 'It's Jane. She went to see Maudie in London.'

'I know. Maudie told Piers.' She was nearly going to say your father but knowing how Scarlett had reacted over recent months it was wiser to adopt a more subtle approach. 'We were so relieved to know she was all right but she seems to have disappeared again. I don't know what she is up to.'

Scarlett sighed, 'The truth is that Maudie did not tell Piers the whole truth. You see…' She paused to think how she could explain this to her mother. Turning her head she noticed that the maître d' had moved to the other side of the restaurant. Gathering courage she knew there was only one way forward. 'She is pregnant, mummy. Maudie told her to get her life together and there was talk of an abortion, but not seriously apparently. Jane did not want Maudie to tell you. She is rather frightened of Piers' temper.'

Thea sat slumped in her seat before reaching for her glass of wine in need of its fortifying qualities. She was rendered speechless wondering what she would do next. This responsibility had passed from Scarlett's shoulders onto her own. It felt as if this had been her lot in life over the years and now she had to pass it on to Piers and wait for the storm to blow itself out for there would be a storm of great magnitude.

'I think I know who the father is,' Scarlett continued. Before her mother could ask the question she rambled on. 'I believe it to be that Douglas Severton who Jane had been seeing. Maudie said she saw them going into Jane's bedroom at the ball.'

Thea sighed wondering why Jane could be so thoughtless. The maître d' optimistically came to take their order. This time they obliged him knowing that they could not delay much longer.

Their appetites were small, and when the food came they pushed it round their plates but little was eaten. Thea felt somewhat relieved at the news that it might be Douglas, an aristocrat, to soften Piers' wrath and now all she wanted to do was to return to her mother. Now they could shoulder the burden of tracking Jane down. Maudie should be happy too she thought although she knew that her sister would avoid Piers for the moment.

Chapter 35

The days were short and the November gloom was upon them but this had not been enough to dampen the spirits of the young couple. They both wanted this marriage as much as the other. Archie had left them alone having travelled down to London on business. He had abandoned the Lords for the time being not wishing to bump into Piers in case any news had leaked out. He knew it was cowardly, but as soon as it was done then there was no going back.

It was during these weeks of waiting when Jane had to be a resident in the area that the young couple came to know each other better. They were constantly in each other's company and their feelings for one another began to intensify. They had convinced themselves that they were doing the right thing.

On the day of the wedding, Jane had dressed herself very simply in a red coat dress which hid the bump and on her head she wore a little pill box hat in red with a small lacy veil which resembled a Jackie Kennedy outfit she had seen in the Times only a few weeks previously. Douglas had driven them to Gretna Green where they were marrying in a small chapel. There were to be just two witnesses, Archie Severton who had returned home in time for the nuptials and the Estate manager Jamie Galbraith.

'We will be married over the anvil,' Douglas had joked to her. Jane had not laughed failing to understand the significance of the joke. If she was honest she was nervous and wished that some members of her family could be present. She suddenly felt alone although Douglas squeezed her hand to give her courage. She was taking a huge step into the unknown and it would be lovely to have people she loved cheering her on. Her hand caressed the place where the baby lay. This seemed to give her confidence for her child had every right to be legitimate with a title at stake if it was a boy.

Douglas had not noticed how nervous she was but continued to explain that in the past the local blacksmiths were legally allowed to marry people as long as there were two witnesses and they became known as anvil priests. Jane felt misgivings whether her family would accept the marriage but it would be binding under the law. It had been the only solution to the problem without incurring Piers' immediate wrath.

***

Thea was fraught with nerves at what she had to do. Piers had been pleased to see Scarlett home feeling that it would do Thea a lot of good to spend time with her daughter while the rest of the family was away. Even he had been aware of the coolness which had existed between mother and daughter over the summer months. Little Amelia took up much of Thea's time and was becoming quite a precocious child. A little bit of healthy neglect would do her good with his wife's attention focused on her eldest daughter. But as Scarlett's weekend at home unfolded he noticed a tension in Thea's demeanour and was rather puzzled by what might be going on little knowing that his future behaviour was the underlying cause of his wife's angst.

Thea's opportunity came on Sunday morning as they sat eating a leisurely breakfast in the little dining room. Scarlett had not surfaced and Thea had guessed that she would stay in her room until lunchtime or she was allowing her a moment alone with Piers. He was in an affable mood reading snippets of news to her from his newspaper. This habit never failed to annoy her but on this occasion she said nothing to maintain the status quo that was existing between them.

'Piers,' she said. He lowered his paper and smiled benignly at her.

'Yes.'

It was now or never before she lost her courage.

'Piers, there was a reason for Scarlett coming home this weekend.' She paused now knowing that she had his full attention.

'Oh yes,' he said his face clouding over just a little. 'She has not been sent down from university has she?'

'No don't be silly, but she wanted to tell me news that she has heard of Jane. We have all been rather worried by her prolonged silence.' She had Piers' full and undivided attention now. He had placed his newspaper, crisply folded back into its creases by the side of his empty breakfast plate.

'And?'

'It would rather appear that she is pregnant.' She had said it and now watched the clouds on Piers' face grow into a storm. He banged his fist hard on the table making crockery and cutlery bounce.

'How so?'

'Piers will you excuse me. I have something to attend to.'

Looking over his newspaper he smiled, 'Of course. I have nearly finished anyway.' He stretched his hand to clasp the handle of his teacup to drain the last of the cooling dregs before turning his attention to the Times once more.

Thea hurried to her sitting room and removed a letter from the pile. She had recognized the handwriting as belonging to Jane. The envelope was just addressed to herself which was strange. Picking up her paperknife she slit the envelope open and began to read:

Dear Thea,

I am writing to you hoping that you can tell Papa the news. I know that he will listen to you as you handle him so well.

I was married today at Gretna Green which is a village near where Douglas lives. His father is the Earl of Foray and we are living at Foray House for the time being. It will never be Westborough but it will be ours one day.

I expect you wonder at why the haste but it must be obvious to you. My baby will be born in the spring and we are all hopeful that it will be an heir. I know how you and Papa will understand about that. I must have been a disappointment to him then as I am now. Anyway I have chosen my destiny and have tried to make everything right.

I am a little homesick for Westborough for it will always be first and foremost my home. When the dust has settled I hope to bring Douglas to meet you all. I do feel that he is rather special so don't worry too much.

I write to you Thea for now I know that you have been the best mother to me even though you did not give birth to me. One last thing, I ask you to tell Papa for me and to ask for his forgiveness as I have been such a trial in my latter years but hope that now I will grow up to be a good wife and mother.

All my love
Jane.

Thea sat back in her armchair as the tears bubbled to the surface. She sobbed uncontrollably as she tried to reread the letter but the words danced in a blur on the page. Jane had finally grown up and had taken control of her life but the saddest part lay in the fact that her family had not been there to help her through the trials of this part of her life. She had had to deal with it by herself.

Piers knocked on the door and entered. He had heard her crying and wondered what was wrong. Thea said nothing but handed him the letter. Reading it Piers own eyes filled with tears, too.

Thea wanted to laugh all of a sudden. 'The usual w[...] desperately trying to keep her face straight.

'Thea please do not try and be facetious with me.' His ange[...] its zenith as he banged the table once more. 'How dare she? [...] I'll give her what for.'

'No you won't, Piers.' Thea suddenly felt released from the [...] had made her suffer so badly since Scarlett had dropped the b[...]

Piers now red in the face from temper looked at his w[...] thought had lost all reason. 'The aristocracy don't do such thi[...] us who we are.'

'Piers, that is so snobbish and ridiculous. May I remind y[...] pregnant with Harry before we married. If I remember correc[...] much later that I gave birth.'

The colour began to drain from his face as realization daw[...] was nothing that he could say. Thea had played her trump card[...] be peace in the family if she had anything to do with it. Pie[...] regarding his wife.

'We must support Jane. We need to find her and help he[...] she wants to do.'

Piers now a normal colour and suddenly more amenable c[...] 'Of course.' The storm had burnt itself out. But inside he felt d[...] his daughter had not come to him to confide her problem. H[...] was a reason for that and he was at the very heart of the mat[...] taken him long to work it out. Guilt played a part in his heart a[...] that Jane must be found and helped through a difficult time. [...] him as the jumbled emotions played out on his face and as [...] heart went out to him as he came to terms with another family[...]

Two days later Scarlett returned to Oxford rather relieved [...] that they had expected had come to nothing. Thea did not tell[...] all the details of her discussion with Piers. However, she had c[...] the fact that she had been pregnant with Harry at the time of t[...] They had laughed in private at this but the anxiety over Jane[...] absence left a dark cloud hanging there until she made contact[...]

Thea sat once more at breakfast on the day after Scarlett's d[...] first post of the day was delivered to the table by one of the ma[...] reading his newspaper as he did every morning but since the n[...] plight he had remained very quiet and a little remote. Thea shu[...] the envelopes as if they were a pack of playing cards and even[...] a pile to her husband. She had glanced at her own pile; somethi[...] eye which made her decide to open any correspondence in the [...] sitting room.

'I am proud of her,' he said.

Thea looked at him for just a moment and smiled. 'I think you should write and tell her that,' she said.

Piers having perched on the arm of her chair drew her close. 'I will, 'he said. 'It is about time I grew up, too. You have been a wonderful mother to all our children, Thea. What would we have all done without you?'

Tears again engulfed her but this time she kissed him tenderly and said absolutely nothing at all for she had often wondered that herself.

Part 2

Chapter 36

What a difference a few years made, Thea thought as she worked in the walled kitchen garden at the back of the Hall occasionally checking on her youngest child who had grown up so quickly. They loved to be out together in the spring sunshine planting and sowing. It was a day when the sun was warm and the world was full of joy after the dreariness of the winter. She straightened her back pushing a stray curl away from her face. Amelia who was nearly five was riding her red bicycle along the paths. Round and round she went, her stout little body feeling the heat from her exertion. Her cheeks were flushed giving her a healthy glow. Suddenly she stopped.

'Are you watching me, Mama?' She called to her mother, self-absorbed by her achievements like any child of a similar age.

Thea smiled and waved, 'Of course I can see you darling.'

'Watch me,' came the small, breathy voice again and once more she peddled off down the path looking behind her at one point to see if her mother was doing as she had been told. Her fair hair reminiscent of her father's in his youth flew in a cloud behind her as it caught the breeze. The lack of concentration had nearly made her tip the bicycle over but at the last minute she regained her balance and continued on her journey.

Thea observed these antics wishing to rush to her daughter but in her head she could hear Piers' voice urging caution.

'It is possible to smother her with too much love,' he said knowing how Thea was over protective of the little girl. She was like an only child now that the older Devines were away for most of the year. Thea watched as the child turned the bicycle and came peddling furiously back. It was difficult not to love the child too much but she knew that Piers was right to say that she had to have a measure of independence. But at the same time Piers loved the small girl as if he had never fathered others before her. Amelia was the child of their middle years Thea always thought affectionately and she could twist the whole family around her finger. Life was good Thea felt and constantly counted her blessings. But there were times when she felt lonely with Piers away a lot in London. She had enjoyed the camaraderie they had shared over the past few years when Piers had only visited the Lords when it was most expedient. Now, though, he was almost permanently in London with these scandals involving the politician John Profumo. She did not know much about it but it was in the newspapers daily and dominating news bulletins. Only bad news seemed to be filling the headlines. She wished it was otherwise.

Thea continued to dig and plant occasionally raising her head to check on her daughter's whereabouts but Amelia was content talking away to herself. Thea returned to her reverie. Family life was fragmented these days. Her sadness crept over her. Empty nest syndrome she thought but then smiled knowing that they still had Amelia for a few more years. But she must not spoil her; it was Thea's way to love the children too much even to the extent that they wounded her sometimes as they tried to shrug her off in their fight for independence. It was their right she knew but she could not quite help herself. She was a mother hen in every meaning of the word.

There were success stories that had rendered her proud. Scarlett and Maudie had graduated and had obtained firsts in their fields of study. She and Piers had attended their graduations, proud parents sitting amongst other proud parents. It had taken Piers a long time to reach this moment in time but he had won through showing the older girls that he was the father that they had always wanted him to be. It was probably Jane who had accomplished this for them all. Her antics over the years had focused him more than anything else into becoming a better father to his older daughters.

Thea remembered the letter which had changed their lives in many ways. Maudie had recently revealed how she had taken Jane to task to take her life in both hands and live it. Only she could move it forward and that was exactly what she had done. She had remained in Scotland until the baby had been born. By that time all the problems of having a baby out of wedlock had disappeared as both families had come to terms with the fact that the young couple did love each other and acceptance had to be the order of the day so that their lives could move on. Little Rose Severton was a momentary disappointment to her dynasty on account of her gender but her charm had won her a place in everybody's' hearts. A short time after the birth Jane had travelled south with her husband, despite his grumbling, and baby to spend quality time at Westborough Hall for a few weeks. Thea could see Piers in her mind's eye as the doting grandfather and on this score she was proved correct. As he had been a good father to his younger children, he shone as a good grandparent to little Rose. And Verity acting like a surrogate mother had spent her spare time with her new niece in the Nursery where Nanny was in her element with a new charge. Amelia had been jealous of the attention given to another small person when she believed it should be all her own.

But the news had been good on the last Christmas Eve when a second child had been born. This time Jane produced the heir, Alex, to the Severton family amongst much rejoicing. Her place had been secured and her marriage was flourishing. As a tender hearted person Thea could not help but shed a tear of joy that Jane had turned her life around and had found fulfilment in motherhood and a maturity which still belied her young age. The births of the two children had been celebrated in the society pages of the press. However, Thea could not quite understand how gossip had not spread about her elopement. That would always remain one of life's mysteries to her. Piers' regret remained that he had never been able to give his daughter away at a sumptuous wedding which he felt was her right. But Thea was of the firm belief that it was not possible to have everything in life. She was no snob, her feet were very firmly planted in terra firma but she could not say the same of her husband. But that was another story. Sometimes she worried about Harry and Charlie who had both inherited Piers' aristocratic bearing and philosophies. The genes had much to answer for.

She glanced up from her toil to observe her youngest child still riding along quite happily.

'Come on, Amelia, it is time for lunch,' Thea called glancing at her watch before collecting her tools and placing them in the basket she carried on such occasions. Together, after a protest, mother and daughter returned to the house along the gravel paths which crunched under their feet, the little bicycle dragging as Amelia pulled it behind her annoyed that she could no longer ride it. Amelia was to have a nursery lunch and had invited her mother to join her before taking her usual afternoon nap. A thought struck Thea as they entered the boot room of the Hall where she kept her few precious gardening tools. Tomorrow was Friday and her younger children would be home on an exeat weekend with a promise from Piers that he would be there to join them. Her face radiated joy as she took Amelia's hands to wash them before Nanny could grumble at their grubby state as they entered her domain in the nursery wing.

Chapter 37

Piers was glad to return to Westborough Hall on several accounts. The first was because of Thea. Several years previously he had made a promise to reduce his work load at the Palace of Westminster. She had carried so much responsibility for the Hall and estate that it was beginning to take its toll on her health but little by little in recent months it had all got out of hand once more. This he felt was not totally his fault for as a peer of the realm he had a responsibility to his country and he needed the stimulus of work although he loved being at home with Thea on the estate. This made him drawn between the two situations and guilt played a huge part in all of this. For several months now Thea had not travelled to London to stay in Belgravia to be with him and the root cause of this was Amelia. She felt that she could not leave the child for weeks on end to stay with Nanny and her staff. Although the child had stayed at the town house with them she was now older and could not be carted around like a sack of potatoes on a whim. This at first annoyed Piers who had enjoyed having his wife with him. She was still a beautiful woman even into her late forties and his love for her had never wavered. He had never been tempted to look elsewhere like men he knew in government who had affairs despite having a wife and family at home. But he had also learned from his father who had lived a lie dividing his time between his mistress and his legitimate family. He might not have been the best of fathers over the years but since his return from the POW camp he knew he had tried even if it was not good enough.

Also he had an insight into how torn a woman became with all the demands that were put upon her. He regarded himself as a rather modern man although he guessed that Thea might think otherwise. This he accepted with a wry sense of humour. And there was the fact that little Amelia was to begin the long road of her education and Thea was not a Victorian parent to wish to leave the child in the hands of a governess. Thea despite her role as a Countess had always been a hands on mother as much as her position would allow.

The second reason why he was happy to return home was to see his middle children as he regarded them. They were growing up swiftly and he had no wish to repeat the mistakes he had made with the older girls. These younger ones he found to be fun, not beset by the hang-ups that had afflicted his elder daughters. He rarely acknowledged the fact that he had been a major cause on that issue. He wanted the younger Devines to be happy. Verity was close to her mother but he loved this lively girl who teased him mercilessly while at home. She showed no signs of the difficulties and sulkiness of her older siblings but like them she was intelligent and he was sure that she would take the road of academia when the time came.

As for Harry and Charlie they were young men who would also take their place in the fullness of time within the realms of responsibility that life had thrown at them. Harry was more serious than his brother, but Piers felt some measure of responsibility on this account. Harry was very aware of the level of responsibility which would be placed on his shoulders in the future. He had begun his training as the heir. He was gradually drawn into all aspects of the running of the estate. Piers had decided upon this course of action from very early on having found his inheritance a great burden at the outset but this had also bonded him to his elder son for they had the future of Westborough Hall as their common denominator. As for Charlie, he was his own person who loved his home without the responsibilities that the future would place on his brother's shoulders.

Piers' mind was on several matters in the political arena. Although he was a conservative he was not a member of the current government led by the Prime Minister, Harold Macmillan. But for several months now he had been an adviser to the Ministry of Agriculture and Fisheries. He had had a private meeting with the Parliamentary Private Secretary, the twelfth Earl Geoffrey Waldegrave, on the issue and had readily accepted the position. As a huge landowner and hands on farmer his experience was valued by the department. His was not a unique experience among the landed classes but he had proved himself more than capable in the position he held. All this he took very seriously. Parliament had been a career as it had been for his father before him.

However, there were more deep-seated worries regarding the government for the Secretary of State for War, John Profumo, had caused a scandal which was of a sexual nature with the model Christine Keeler. In a statement to the House of Commons he had only recently denied any impropriety about what had happened two years previously. But in recent days he had been forced to tell the truth. Piers was apprehensive that the Government would be brought down by the actions of one selfish individual. The scandal had filled the headlines of the press but there were other issues as well. It was suspected that Christine Keeler may have been involved at the same time with a Soviet naval attaché called Captain Ivanov causing the possibility of a security risk. There were suggested other scandals as well; all these issues had made John Profumo resign. Piers was concerned about the Prime Minister whom he had met in the corridors of power. Having spoken to him at considerable length he felt that the man was losing his confidence and in private was talking about resigning over the affair. These conversations he was using as a sounding board with selected individuals before he made a final decision on the matter although he was advised to stay in office by the Members of Parliament he spoke to. All the hype of a possible resignation had saddened Piers because he respected the integrity of the man and felt that somebody else's irresponsibility had brought all this about.

All these issues had made Piers anxious to return to Westminster as soon as possible. He had spoken to Thea about these events. Of course she had read about it in the newspapers and had avidly listened to television reports and understood her husband's anxiety for the government that he supported so whole-heartedly. She had said little about Piers' constant absence not wishing to add to his anxiety of the moment but she fervently hoped that everything would be sorted soon.

Thea had sighed when Sunday afternoon came. She was not sure if it was from relief at the family departing or the sadness that she was left alone at the Hall with just Amelia. Minty, after all these years, was still in residence at the Dower House. They saw each other at times but there was no closeness in their relationship. There had been a truce called between the two women after Clarissa's will and Jane finishing her Season. Minty had admitted to Piers on one occasion when he had tackled her about the ongoing situation with his wife that it was an insecurity which had fuelled her hostility towards Thea; an insecurity which was brought about by her financial state and the husband who had left her for a much younger woman. Thea appeared to have everything that Minty had not. Jealousy was the root cause of the problem and Minty had tried to use Jane's Season to put between them. Piers had been less than happy about the situation; he delivered an ultimatum to Minty saying that either she behaved fairly towards Thea or she would have to leave the Dower to set up home elsewhere. He was not prepared to have friction between the people he loved most in the world. There had been enough animosity between his parents during their lifetime. History was not going to repeat itself.

Now everything was sorted for the divorce was over and money had been settled on her by her husband and Piers. It was strange what life did to people Piers had said to Thea in a profound way. Thea had agreed but had kept her distance from her sister-in-law for a considerable time not feeling that she could quite forgive her for such unfair treatment. But Thea's kind heart had melted as the months had passed eventually receiving Minty back into the fold. However, trust was a separate issue which always remained at the back of Thea's mind. Trust would have to be earned once more. Over time Minty filled a void in Thea's life when her family was absent allowing the two women to dine together on a regular basis. Time became a healer as the old adage said and Minty and Thea began to forge a similar bond which once had belonged to Clarissa. How the wisdom of the old woman was missed even after all this time.

***

Scarlett had decided that she wanted to take time to complete her investigations into her father's background. The desire to get to know him through his personal history still dogged her. She had not spoken to Thea about this for she did not want to upset her mother but had given the tale that she was worn out by her three years at university and required a break before deciding on her next course of action which was to become attached to a law firm in London when she was ready. She had done the foot work on this during the months leading up to the completion of her degree and there were several firms who were interested in her on account of her Oxford education and the fact that she had achieved a first class degree. All the girls had come into their inheritances so Scarlett felt that her independence had given her the right to pursue her dreams without obligations. Thea had not pressed her too deeply but her sixth sense told her that Scarlett was up to something, but she was going to watch and wait to see what was going to happen. None of this was mentioned to Piers for he was still engrossed in the Profumo scandal and was under enough pressure without the family's additional stress.

It had been Maudie's suggestion that now Scarlett was a free agent she should come and live with her in London. This suggestion had amazed Scarlett for Maudie was a free spirit. They both were if she was honest. On the other hand in some ways it made sense for Scarlett was going to be London based once her career took off. There was never going to be room for them living together in the apartment near the Conservatoire so there would be a hunt for a larger one. As it was Maudie had tired of being the penniless student that she had portrayed to her friends. She had never wanted to lord it over them, to appear spoilt and privileged, but now life was moving on and if she was honest she wanted her cake and to eat it as the saying went. She wanted luxury, but there was the underlying fact that she wanted to earn her own money as well as using her inheritance from her mother, Mary.

Neither of the girls wanted to live at the Belgravia Town House under Piers' regime. Thea had suggested the idea when Scarlett had told her mother what Maudie had proposed.

'I don't think that would be a good idea, Mummy,' Scarlett had said. 'I know you will understand that Maudie and I want our independence. We have lived our own lives now for several years.'

Thea did not understand as family was everything to her and she had never really lived an independent existence but she said nothing. However, she felt a little hurt on the issue. If she was honest she had thought the girls would want to return to their roots. She had not been to university and tasted the lure of independence. Her own life had always sometimes belonged to other people as in the war years and then marriage and subsequently children.

Scarlett had related to Maudie the conversation that she had shared with her mother.

'It would feel like being back at school,' Scarlett had said to Maudie when they were sitting eating a sandwich in the cramped flat which was now housing much of Scarlett's belongings.

'You can never go back in the same way except to visit,' Maudie said sagely.

'Quite right,' Scarlett said with her mouth rather full of sandwich.

'There is an apartment advertised for Kensington which is spacious,' Maudie said looking through the newspaper, the previous topic of conversation quite forgotten. 'We might as well go and see it tomorrow. I will telephone in the morning.'

By the following afternoon having viewed the apartment, they had agreed to rent it straight away. It had been as the advert said, spacious with very generous proportions to the rooms and high ceilings. It was time to give in notice for her flat but the intervening time would give them an opportunity to make a real home of their new place. Excitement abounded as they began their new adventure. But there was still a small tug at Maudie's heart when she remembered all the good times she had experienced in her little flat over the years. The best memory was where she had discovered the real father whom she loved without reservation. But life moved on chance what. New beginnings were on the horizon for herself and Scarlett.

Chapter 38

Scarlett had decided that she was going to indulge herself for the next year. She had secured her place at the Law Firm and they were happy to wait that long for her. She had been back to her father's London home on numerous occasions but the house was let out as before. Tenants came and went and new occupiers leased the property. It was not doing her any good going backwards and forwards for she learnt nothing new. Now she had to return to her mother's lawyer to find out more details about her unknown relatives. The last time she had seen Arbuthnot he had only meted out the barest of details giving her the impression that he was reluctant to tell her more. Her mother did not know any more about Jack Carson than she had divulged to her daughter and Scarlett did not doubt her mother's integrity.

Scarlett knew that she would have the apartment to herself for three months for Maudie had secured a contract to go on tour with an American orchestra where she would be playing classical violin in the States. This was her first love these days despite the fact that she still sang with jazz bands and folk groups. This time on her own would allow Scarlett to pursue her search for the family she did not know, without having to confide in anybody. The prospect excited her beyond measure.

Chapter 39

Alan Carson looked through his London office window regarding the central part of the city he knew and loved so well. The rain lashed out in the wind at anything in its path. People half ran huddled into their winter coats in their eagerness to seek shelter; umbrellas blew inside out and became abandoned for their uselessness in such inclement weather. Today Alan felt restless and began to wonder if he was beginning to tire of the life that had excited him for more than twenty years. It was the constant travelling which was becoming wearisome and the endless lies he had to tell to the people he loved best in the world. But on the converse side of it all when he was away there was the adrenalin rush which he experienced and made him suddenly feel alive, living on the edge until he returned safely home to Blighty and a normal existence. He was forty-seven years old, not old enough by modern standards to retire but he knew he was pushing the limits of returning safely to his wife and daughter as each year passed. His wife Jenny had been the love of his life since before the war. She had never grumbled at his regular absences and most of all had never asked questions knowing from the very beginning that it was not allowed. She must realize what he did but fortunately she did not know the half of it. Thank God he often thought when his mood was low or when there had been some very exacting times. Often he could be away months, perhaps weeks if he was lucky. On such occasions he could not communicate with his family but if anything went wrong his wife would be told but it would be only the bare facts and the world at large would hear a very different story.

Alan had sensed a restlessness in Jenny too just lately. He could not discuss with her anything that he did but he did not want to lose her. She was still a young looking and attractive woman. He knew for certain that she had never looked at another man but she was neglected through his constant absences although he tried to make it up to her when he returned. There was always the thought that even the best women in the world were human and needed the love and attention that most took for granted. Sometimes he did not return straight home after a prolonged absence. He would stay at a small safe house in London for debriefing and where he could unwind and allow the adrenalin to calm down in order to return home as normal as possible. He had heard of the young people taking drugs; getting a fix it seemed to be called. Somehow he could identify with that but he would never take drugs, as his brain had to stay alert at all times. But the adrenalin rush that he often felt with his job was addictive too.

He had met Jenny at university where they had both read French. Before the war they had both visited Paris and had fallen in love with the city of light and each other. They had married just before the onslaught of war and then Alan had been sent to the front. It had been a difficult time for them both but had it not been the same for every family in the kingdom.

It was after his return from the war that they had their daughter Joan. He had been fortunate that he knew his daughter from the start. Their only child was now seventeen and the apple of his eye. He hoped that she would gain a place at university too.

He was roused from his reverie by a knock on his office door. A head poked round and looked at him before grinning. 'The boss will see you now.'

He rose from his chair. Nobody kept the boss waiting. This was it then.

Chapter 40

Maudie had flown to New York to join the new Madison Orchestra which was trying to build its reputation in the music world. It was to tour many of the states in America before flying to Europe to spread its reputation. More established orchestras were snobbish about newly formed organizations feeling that they were inferior to those that had grown with their reputations. The cities they were anxious to play in Europe were London, Paris, Berlin and Rome. Maudie was hoping that the orchestra would make its mark and that eventually it would be acceptable to join the more renowned orchestras in Britain and the United States. Also when the Madison Orchestra arrived in London she hoped that it would have received good reviews in the press. She was anxious for her family to attend concerts which were to be held in the Royal Albert Hall. Home territory would make her name. She no longer wished to remain incognito. She used and even flaunted her title and dressed smartly in order to raise her profile. Some of her friends from the Conservatoire had been surprised at the change in her and even more so that she had a title which elevated her above them. Maudie had been sorry that she had done that in some ways but her father had told her to use anything that would get her noticed; but surely her talent was the greatest gift she had. For the first time ever Maudie wished her mother whom she could not remember could see the beginning of her success for had she not inherited her musical talent from Mary. This sensation had sobered her thoughts and for the first time Maudie understood Scarlett's obsession with her dead father. But as Maudie's world changed and grew in new challenges so her thoughts of Mary Devine flew to the furthest recesses of her mind for another time.

This could not be said for Scarlett. She was becoming more obsessive by the hour of her dead father, Jack Carson. Maudie's absence gave her time to concentrate her mind on what she wanted to do. In the silence of the apartment she made notes on what she remembered the solicitor Arbuthnot saying about Jack having a family. It was something about a twin brother as well as having a sister. There were grandparents in the equation too. However, they could be dead now she thought despondently. But if they were alive they would be able to tell her so much about her father who would have been in his forties had he lived. She tried to remember what Thea had said about her father. They had only been together for a short time. It sounded as if it had been an infatuation rather than true love particularly for her mother. Scarlett's conception had hurried Thea into marriage to make her child legitimate. Scarlett could not help but smile to herself for her mother seemed to make a habit of it. Her marriage to Piers had been in a hurry to legitimize Harry. One could not allow a potential heir to be born out of wedlock. At least her mother was honest, more than could be said for Piers whose memory had been short when he was critical of Jane. They had all laughed at Thea's outburst when the tale spread through the family.

Her thoughts returned to Jack. Why had he said that he had no family claiming that they were dead? Was there something to hide? Had there been a falling out? Of course she did not have the answers but now with time on her hands and the bit between her teeth she was determined to find out. Her poor mother had obviously believed everything that Jack had said. But Thea at times could be so gullible. She smiled to herself out of true affection for her mother. Despite their recent differences she loved Thea as did all the family. She was the one who could be spoken to in a moment of crisis and she knew just how to tackle Piers on issues. He could still be difficult although the older girls were in agreement that he was much better and it appeared that he loved all his children in his own way even herself. She knew what she was doing would hurt both Thea and Piers but if she did not try now it would all be too late in the future.

Lifting the telephone receiver she dialled the number of the solicitors and waited. After a few seconds a female voice came onto the line, 'Arbuthnot and associates.'

'Could I make an appointment to see Mr Arbuthnot?' Scarlett asked. There was a very audible rustling of paper coming down the line.

'Oh dear,' the plaintive voice said, 'we do not have one available until Wednesday of next week but we could fit you in with someone else.'

'I need to see Mr Arbuthnot. Next Wednesday will be fine.' Having given her details Scarlett knew that she had to be patient. It was not one of her greatest attributes but she was working hard to become a better person as she liked to think of it. She put the receiver back into its cradle and sighed.

***

Piers had insisted that Thea take a break in London. He wanted her with him for a while. Still having to spend much time in Westminster he was not finding it easy to return to Westborough Hall as often as he would like and then the Prime Minister had resigned over the Profumo scandal. Piers was deeply affected by the events of the past few months. The Conservative Party had not come out of these events easily and it did not bode well for the next general election either. Thea had missed her husband too but it was always Amelia who was foremost in her thoughts. It pulled at her heart strings to leave the child just with the nursery staff.

'Amelia must come as well,' Piers had been adamant. 'If you are worried about her education bring the staff with her.'

'But Piers…,' Thea had begun.

'There is plenty of room for the staff at the Town House. You of all people should know that Thea as you spent your childhood living there. You are just prevaricating.' Piers was now angry.

Thea was not sure whether he was angry at her or perhaps he was still trying to come to terms with what was happening in the political world. She decided to go to London but it was such an upheaval to take the whole entourage. However, she set the wheels in motion much to Nanny's annoyance. Cases were dragged down from the attics and the chaos seemed to reverberate through the house. The ageing nanny could be heard venting her anger on the nursery staff which made Thea cringe but for once Piers laughed.

'You're not frightened of the old goat are you?' He teased but more seriously, 'she is on our payroll and can leave if she's wants to.'

'Piers she has been with us for years. You can't do that because Amelia would be upset but she won't need a Nanny for too much longer.'

'We'll see,' he said noncommittally.

There had been many invitations to various important functions including formal dinners that autumn in London and Piers knew that the press would be there. A husband needed his wife on such occasions and there would be gossip if Thea did not attend. It was incredible that lies and false stories could be fabricated in such ways. Knowing how vicious the British press could be, there would be salacious comments about the state of his marriage if he was there alone. However, Thea had settled her little family quite comfortably into the Town House and witnessed Piers visibly relax. Suddenly she looked forward to the parties that would soon be upon them. Her depleted wardrobe would not offer anything spectacular to wear to these 'dos' as she called them so she spent time pampering herself visiting the big stores like Harrods to do her shopping. She had not had so much fun for years but it would have been even better if she could have spent time with Scarlett or any of the girls. She thought of Verity still a schoolgirl but it would not be long before the two of them would enjoy such a trip. A few days before the first event Thea took a long hard look at herself in the bedroom mirror. Piers was at the House and she was quite alone apart from the little group tucked up in the nursery quarters under the eaves. She turned the key in the door to her bedroom to keep young Amelia out just in case she escaped from Nanny's clutches and then proceeded to unpack the gowns she had bought in recent weeks. They were strewn over the bed; each was tried on in turn and she revelled in the thrill she felt when she looked in the mirror but it was all let down by her hair which was long and straggly just as Piers liked it. It was fine for country living when she was dressed in country attire for she spent so much time in the garden and on the estate but hearing Piers proclaim that the 'blasted press' were attending the events she was not going to have her photograph in the papers looking like a country bumpkin and aristocratic wives gossiping about her unkempt looks. She pulled the long, curly strands to their full length and pulled a face in the mirror. They were just going to have to go she decided. She was no longer going to be ruled by Piers' whims. If he wanted her to be in London he would have to put up with her decisions.

On the bedside table she picked up the extension receiver and dialled the number of the hairdresser that she had used before. Two days later she walked out of the Oxford Street salon feeling like a new woman. Her newly cropped style was reminiscent of the hairstyle she had had when she first met Piers. It curled naturally around her head like a luminous cap now that the grey strands had been bleached out. She was thrilled feeling ten years younger. Now she was ready to greet society and the press. Piers would be another matter.

Piers was taken aback with his wife's new look, but after they had attended the dinners and balls he felt wonderful with his beautiful wife on his arm. She looked glorious he felt and thoroughly approved of what she had done to transform herself back into the beautiful woman she was. He was reminded of the young Thea who had captured his heart all those years ago and even in his middle years his heart flipped at the sight of her. As the days passed they read the press coverage of the events. Thea had been proclaimed as the beautiful young wife of the Earl of Westborough. Thea, not vain by any means, was thrilled by the comments and had made up her mind that she would keep her new hairstyle even if it meant that she had to travel to London to have it styled every few weeks. She knew Piers would be pleased that he could see her more often until all this awful business with the Profumo affair died down.

Chapter 41

Scarlett had left for her appointment at the solicitors at the very last minute. It had seemed that public transport was working to rule and the taxis were overly full. However, she managed to enter the solicitors' chambers as the long case clock struck the hour. She had not noticed the clock on her last visit but today the chiming reminded her of her very near tardiness.

The receptionist looked over her glasses which fitted snugly on the bridge of her nose just as if she was a very stern schoolmistress.

'Mr Arbuthnot is waiting for you,' she said rather pompously leaving the implication unstated and indicating to the half open door of the solicitor's inner sanctum.

'Thank you,' she said to the woman without an apology and moved with dignity to the office door which she knocked out of politeness.

'Come in,' shouted Arbuthnot in an affable voice. Then the door opened wide and the solicitor put his hand out to be shaken. 'Good to see you again, Miss Devine.' His bonhomie gave no hint that she had nearly been late.

Scarlett did not correct him that she was currently using her father's surname. She sat in the seat indicated to her across the table from Antony Arbuthnot noting that he had appeared to have put on much weight since their last encounter. Looking around his office she decided nothing had changed since her last visit. But why should it have? It was a place of work not somebody's sitting room.

'What can I do for you today?' Arbuthnot came straight to the point but kept the benign expression fixed firmly on his face.

Scarlett looked straight at him thinking how pompous the man appeared.

'Well I have come to collect the information regarding my father's family. On my previous visit some time ago now you gave me some details but I would like to make notes today so that I can seek them out. I have finished my degree and before I commit myself to work this seems the ideal time to pursue my father's history.'

The expression on Arbuthnot's face had changed to bewilderment. He remembered Scarlett's previous visit with great clarity and had felt that he had succeeded in diverting her away from such an investigation. Regarding this young woman closely he could only guess at the intelligence behind the very attractive features. No doubt she was going to be a kind of Rottweiler who would not let go unless he gave her something.

'There is very little I can tell you,' he blustered. 'The Carsons are not my clients like your own family.'

'If I am not mistaken you had some kind of file that you referred to last time,' she said feeling unhappy about the secrecy which seemed to surround a very ordinary family. The obvious question was why but Scarlett had no answers to that.

'Did I really?' Arbuthnot feigned surprise. 'If you will excuse me a moment I will check my records.'

Scarlett's eyes had narrowed catlike as they followed him rise from his chair and cross the room to an overlarge filing cabinet which stood by the window partially concealed by the curtains.

'I will not be a lawyer for nothing,' she thought as she rose from her chair and on silent feet followed the very stout solicitor as he looked through files in one of the drawers of the filing cabinet.

Arbuthnot was not aware of Scarlett's presence initially and she took full advantage of the fact. The drawer was labelled as 'confidential' and she wondered why that should be. She had observed him opening the cabinet with a small key which was attached to a key ring holding much larger keys. Turning his head he became aware of somebody standing in close proximity to him.

'What are you doing?' He asked, his voice raised in anger.

Scarlett did not have an answer but she mumbled under her breath before returning to her seat feeling very perplexed. There seemed to be so much secrecy. Why would Jack Carson's family be regarded as 'confidential'? Arbuthnot had produced a file which he held very tightly against his plump body as he took his seat opposite her. He had regained his composure but his cheeks were still flushed from his flash of sudden anger.

'Let me see,' he said opening the file, turning the pages slowly as he skimmed each one. He glanced up at Scarlett with a thin-lipped smile. 'There is very little to go on, my dear. I think that I gave you the information on your last visit.'

'You gave me little information except to say that my father had a twin brother, also a sister. I would like their names and addresses please. I want to contact my family and get to know them.'

'I have no addresses for them but I have their names. The rest you must discover for yourself I'm afraid.'

Scarlett sat silently not believing a word he said but that information was better than nothing. She took a notepad and pen from the depths of her bag and waited for him to proceed.

'Ah, here we are,' he said adjusting his spectacles. 'Your uncle is Alan Carson and your aunt is Dorothy Maythwaite (nee Carson). There are no forwarding addresses I'm afraid. That is all I can tell you.' Removing his spectacles and rubbing the bridge of his nose he then closed the file with a snap emphasizing his point. 'Is there anything else I can help you with, Miss Devine? Also I was rather wondering why you wanted to get to know these people after all these years. Your mother never wanted to meet them.'

'My mother was told by my father that they were dead so never concerned herself with pursuing the matter. As for my reasons for wanting to meet them I must say that family history means that you can know yourself in a way but my father was a war hero and I am thinking of writing a book about him during this year that I have taken off. If I don't do it now when will I have time?'

'I think that is an admirable idea,' Arbuthnot said rising to his feet indicating that their meeting was at an end. His high colour had returned to normal now that he was no longer under the pressure of Scarlett's demands. He put out his hand to shake hers but she made a fuss of putting on her coat and picking up her handbag before turning towards the door.

'Goodbye, Mr Arbuthnot,' she said leaving his hand floating in mid-air as she made her departure but registering her displeasure at the same time.

Out in the street amongst the hustle and bustle of the traffic, Scarlett felt deflated at the negativity of what had transpired in the office. She decided to walk for a bit before taking the tube home. She had been full of expectation on her journey there believing there would be much information to solve some of the puzzles of her father's life as well as his family. She knew now that she was not going to receive any more information from the solicitor. There was some kind of mystery which she was not allowed to be a part of but it had made her more curious than ever. She was determined to discover what there was to hide but she was not sure how she would do it yet. It all had to be worked out but she would find a way through sheer tenacity; at least there was a name to go on, two in fact. She would go home and think about her next course of action. Suddenly she felt more upbeat as she walked briskly towards the tube station.

Chapter 42

Jane was feeling content with life on the Scottish borders at Foray House. It was her home now but there would always be that pull towards Westborough Hall and her family. She would return to her roots when she could or to the Severton House in London where she would indulge in meeting Scarlett or Maudie when she was in Town, which was not so often these days. She would take Nanny and the children with her on these visits for she did not want to be parted from them more than she had to. Jane believed that this was Thea's influence for her stepmother had been a hands on mother despite being a countess.

As she sat in the sitting room at Foray House, she watched the rain run down the windowpanes and the landscape beyond had taken on dark hues under an unrelenting sky. She was happy to be alone; it was an unusual event for there was always somebody who would disturb her solitude. There were a number of issues which engaged her mind presently. The uppermost one was the fact that she was pregnant again and she was now in the latter stages. She had not minded producing a third child, hoping that it would be another boy to ensure the future of the Severton family but now she hoped that it would be her last. She had no wish to emulate Thea who had given birth to five children. Her marriage to Douglas had proved to be a true love match, proving that she could get some things right in her life. Douglas stayed on the estate most of the time, running it successfully with a farm manager who had come to them just after the old Earl had died. This partnership with Alec Kilbride had proved successful. It had not happened overnight but the trust they shared in each other's ability had brought dividends to the prosperity of the estate and they reaped the financial rewards as the estate began to prosper.

This release of extra funds had found its way into Jane's hands. She was the woman of the house and, very slowly, she began to spend these profits on the furnishings of Foray House and its general upkeep. It was a gradual process; it was not possible to transform the whole house in one go, but slowly the main downstairs reception rooms changed beyond recognition bringing the old house to life but in subtle ways. It was no longer a man's house but a home with a woman's touch where they could all live comfortably together. Her next project after the birth of this child would be to transform some of the guest bedrooms, so that her family could be invited to visit. Thea had left huge hints since her marriage that she would like to visit, but the decline of Foray House under Douglas' grandfather's days had left Jane feeling like the poor relation and the last thing she wanted was to be pitied. This had prompted her to do something about the house as soon as she could. The House was then opened to the public like many of the great houses of the country. The public rooms that had received refurbishment had been a triumph leaving Douglas and Archie in awe of Jane's talents. The fortunes of the House and their dynasty were certainly beginning to turn round. However, Jane knew that the journey to complete success would be long and winding with pitfalls along the way.

Archie was impressed by the young woman who had come into their lives only a few years previously. She had made a difference to everything that was happening at Foray House. She ran the house well appointing extra staff and raising standards about meal times when they would dress for dinner as they had at Westborough. In fact many of the changes were based on Thea's way of handling everything. Dinner parties were arranged as had happened in the past making the old house come alive once more. At Christmas the servants and estate workers were invited to the house as a 'thank you' for their hard endeavours throughout the year. The New Year ball was revised having ended with the death of Douglas' grandmother many years before. Jane had done her homework thoroughly. She had spoken to people whose memories reached far back into the past or people who could recount the stories of previous generations. Jane had taken note of all that had been said and had put the ideas to Archie and Douglas. Archie had been reticent at first but hearing the enthusiasm of the young ones he had capitulated.

'Och go on then,' he had smiled at their enthusiasm. 'Just the once mind until we see how it goes.'

Jane felt euphoric at this change of events; so during the third Christmas of her rather successful marriage to Douglas the young couple had planned the event to the nth degree. It had cost the Severtons a fortune but it had been worth it as it had proved to be a resounding success in the local community and beyond. And as time moved on it became a fixture of the social calendar in the Border country.

Jane had certainly become the woman of the house standing alongside Archie and Douglas to receive their guests. As a result of all this revelry they were invited elsewhere allowing the border country to come alive once more.

Archie spent much time at Westminster taking his place in the upper house. Although he was not of the same political persuasion as Piers Devine, the two men had formed an alliance of some kind. They were related through the union of a son and daughter which brought them together to dine and discuss family issues.

'Och, Jane is a wonderful girl,' Archie would say in his Scottish tones when he was relaxed, at other times his accent was as cut glass as Piers' was.

Piers listened with pride hearing about his daughter's achievements. He wondered if this was the niche Jane had been hankering for most of her life. Was it security and her own little family that had brought her fulfilment? Although he knew that she loved Westborough and always would, Foray House was her home, the one place where she would eventually reign supreme alongside her husband. Piers took great pleasure at this thought. Perhaps it was time for a visit.

***

It was two weeks since Scarlett's visit to Antony Arbuthnot's office. She had been perplexed by what had gone on and was reading between the lines of their conversation but making no sense of it whatsoever. Not wishing to rush what she had to do she was still anxious to know the full facts about these unknown relatives. She had looked through The London telephone directory to find the names she had been given. There had been a handful of Alan Carsons listed but when she had dialled the numbers and spoken to the householders they were not related to her. There had been no good fortune with locating a Dorothy Maythwaite either. It was all very frustrating and she had no idea where to go next in her search. Then the thought occurred to her that she had to pay for the job to be done. She wondered why she had not thought of the idea before.

Purchasing many of the London papers she spent a dreary late November afternoon thumbing through the advertising sections until she found what she was looking for. She cut out several adverts leaving a paper trail across the sitting room floor. It was a good job that Maudie was away because she would have grumbled at Scarlett's untidiness.

Picking up the receiver she began to dial. After several attempts she had not managed to make contact with a private detective. This was not an avenue she wished to travel for her imagination conjured a vision of a little man in a dirty macintosh operating from seedy premises in a back street in London. Feeling depressed and thwarted she was about to give up to try another day but suddenly she thought she would try one last time and waited while the telephone rang and rang. As she was just about to return the telephone to its cradle a voice somewhat out of breath but very well heeled, came down the line.

'Banks and Littleton. Private Investigators. How may I help you?'

Scarlett, startled by having no previous response, paused for a moment but gathering her wits found herself saying, 'I need someone to investigate something for me.'

A voice with a smile in it said, 'Well that is what we do.'

Scarlett smiled too. 'I need someone to find information about my family. Shall I tell you about it?'

'No,' came the reply. 'We don't discuss matters over the telephone. I would need to see you in person.'

'Right,' Scarlett said. This was certainly a new experience.

Scarlett was surprised; 'Can you give me an address then and a time that I can come, please?'

'I have a free appointment tomorrow afternoon at two. Can you come then?'

Scarlett found herself agreeing. There was little pressing for her to do during the year she had put aside for just this purpose.

Having written down the address and time she replaced the receiver and sat back in her chair feeling that this next episode of her life was just beginning. She felt a frisson of excitement run through her body. She was now ready to discover her family.

Chapter 43

Maudie had landed at Heathrow in a flurry of excitement to be back in Blighty. Her time in the United States had been fulfilling; the orchestra had been a resounding success and as had been hoped, was to play a number of venues in several European cities and if that went well more dates might be added to the tour. It was all too magical for words. Everyone was exhausted. However, there was a month's vacation ahead of her and she wanted to go home to Westborough, not her flat in London. She wished to be pampered for a while and Westborough was the place for that. But she was not alone.

During the three months of her sojourn in the States she had become romantically linked with a member of the orchestra named Brad Susman, a Jewish New Yorker from quite a well to do family of lawyers. Brad was the black sheep of the family, who had not wanted, to his father's disappointment, to take up law like his two brothers. Instead he had followed his first love of music, studying in New York and hoping to find his niche in the music world. He had taken to Maudie immediately and having spent hours together during rehearsals they had grown close although neither of them had been looking for a relationship for the establishment of their careers had been what was uppermost in their lives.

Brad had taken Maudie to meet his family and she had been quite a hit. His parents had been impressed by her Englishness and her polish. At twenty eight, his parents were hoping to see Brad settled in a career and a relationship and Maudie was an answer to a prayer. Although, he had had relationships before, they had come to nothing while his brothers were settled in their careers and marriages which had produced a number of children. Maudie was like a breath of fresh air. They could see that their son was smitten and now hoped this beautiful English girl was the one.

On the other hand, Maudie during her infrequent letters or transatlantic telephone calls home had made no reference to any kind of relationship but only alluded to how well the tour was going and how much she was enjoying her time in the United States. She had not even acknowledged the relationship to Jane and Scarlett for she felt that this love affair could fall apart as quickly as it had happened but she had been wrong on that score.

Now that she was home in Blighty she wanted to rectify everything. But poor Brad was in for a surprise, too, for she had omitted to tell him that she was from a wealthy, titled family. She knew he was in for a shock.

Standing at the Carousel waiting for their luggage Brad stood with his arms wound round Maudie's shoulders.

'What happens now?' He asked in his American drawl. He liked to know what was happening. However, Maudie had maintained a sense of mystery.

'Well, Brad, I think that we will go and visit my folks now,' she smiled as she imitated his drawl and mode of language.

He smiled, having got used to her teasing, 'And where do they live?' He had never set foot in England before and only knew that it was a little island compared with the vastness of his own country.

'First of all I have to call them to say we are on our way and then we will have to travel into London to catch our train out.'

'Oh,' he said not fully understanding the geography of the place.

Their luggage arrived and was hefted through the 'Anything to Declare' channels until they were safely through the terminal. Maudie looked around at the activity and soon spied a telephone kiosk. 'Look after the cases Brad while I telephone home.' And she was gone leaving him to gaze at the activity around him.

'This is England, huh,' he murmured to himself. 'Little old England.'

The telephone rang and rang at Westborough before it was answered by Piers. He had waited for someone to answer it but the Hall seemed to be quiet despite the fact that he paid staff to do these jobs.

'Hello,' he said and waited. Maudie's heart had dropped at her father's voice. She had wanted to speak to Thea, but it would sound churlish if she asked for her stepmother when her relationship had turned a corner with her father.

'Papa,' she said, 'it's Maudie. I'm back in England, at Heathrow in fact—'

'Maudie?' Piers' voice boomed down the line. Maudie could hear the delight in his voice and her heart soared in response.

'Yes, it's me. I want to come home for a while. I have a month in which to do nothing.'

'Do you ever need to ask to come home?' Maudie could hear the smile and joy in his voice.

'No, of course not. I just thought it was the polite thing to do. You brought us up to do the right thing.' She said. She heard her father's infectious chuckle at the other end of the line. 'I have a friend with me, too,' she continued without elaborating on any more detail.

'The more the merrier.' Piers said. He was in a benevolent mood. 'Shall I send the car for you to Worcester?'

'No thank you, Papa. We will find our own way.' As she said that the pips sounded and the line went dead.

Maudie had not realized until now that she had felt so homesick during her time away. Wherever, she travelled in the world with her music, England would always be home near her family. She could not wait to get there.

***

'Where the devil are you when you are wanted?' Piers muttered under his breath, his frustration having flared after the bonhomie of the telephone call. And then he saw her. Thea was coming down the stairs holding the hand of Amelia who was chatting away to her mother, her face was earnest as she described something that she had done in the schoolroom. Thea's face was alight as she listened to her youngest daughter. Piers watched them and the contours of his face had changed from one of frustration to the love he felt for his wife and small daughter.

Thea glanced up. 'Piers,' she said, 'did I hear the telephone?'

Piers' faced clouded slightly but the frustration was only momentary. 'Let's go into your sitting room, shall we?'

Thea, still holding Amelia's hand as she continued her story, followed her husband into the room wondering if something was wrong as Piers had not volunteered what the telephone call had been about. 'Is anything wrong?' She asked as Amelia had reached the end of her story. She had released her mother's hand and wandered across the room to play with the few toys that lay scattered in the corner from a previous visit to her mother's inner sanctum.

'There is nothing wrong. Maudie was on the telephone. She was at Heathrow and wanted to know if it was all right to come home for a few weeks.'

Thea's brow puckered momentarily. 'What a strange question. This is her home and always will be.' Then her face changed bursting a bright smile like the sun coming out after the rain. 'Won't it be lovely to see her? It seems ages since she went to the United States.'

'She won't be alone. She is bringing a friend.'

'That will be nice,' Thea said now turning her attention once more to her youngest child.

Piers watched her still attractive face knowing how much she was an earth mother to his oldest children. He gave thanks that he had married her for his affection was stronger than ever for this woman whom had he had loved for more than two decades.

Chapter 44

Jane lay in her bed at Foray House with Douglas holding her hand. She looked tired and wan but triumphant. She had been safely delivered of her third child but more than that it had been a second son. Dougie was beside himself with pride that the Severton dynasty was safe. He kissed her on the cheek.

'I love you and thank you for our son.'

Although she was happy too, this pregnancy had been more difficult than the previous two and the attending doctor had advised that she should have a break before contemplating another baby. He had also passed that message on to Douglas who had been agreeable. It had been his idea to fill the house with children as he remembered his lonely and isolated childhood and the lack of a mother. But he had taken cognizance of the doctor's warning. Three at this moment in time was quite enough and Jane had done her duty. It had been useful to marry someone of his own class who understood the trauma of producing an heir but he also loved Jane and was not going to put her life in jeopardy.

Jane knew there would be no more little Severtons. Vividly she remembered Thea's tale of Mary, her own mother and the anguish that childbirth had brought her. There was to be nothing like that in Jane's world. She felt that she had done her duty. Archie had also been delighted at the news. Douglas had telephoned his father at their London house knowing how pleased he would be. He was; euphoric was the word but suddenly he felt lonely, bereft almost for there was nobody to share this good news with him. He suddenly had a longing for his long dead wife, Catriona. How foolish he felt because months went by when he did not give her a thought even though he had loved her dearly. Perhaps it was time to remarry, find a wife who would give him comfort in his advancing years. He could not continue to be a burden to Douglas and his family. They had their own lives. But after so long where would he look. Perhaps one of the Border events might be a good place to start. He would definitely give it some thought. He rang the bell in the drawing room. The maid promptly appeared.

'A bottle of the best champagne in the house,' he ordered knowing that the girl would not be confused for there was only one kind below stairs and it was certainly not a Moet and Chandon. Perhaps it was time to invest in a better champagne for the Severton fortune was like a phoenix rising from the ashes.

Laughing to himself he removed a champagne flute from the drinks cabinet not caring about drinking alone or even if he downed the whole bottle. Life was certainly improving.

'Cheers,' he said to nobody in particular, holding his overflowing glass in the air. Then he laughed from pure happiness.

***

Thea was in a buzz of excitement as she contemplated Maudie's homecoming. She had missed her stepdaughter considerably and three whole months had been a very long time without a visit. But then Thea missed all the children when they were away. She also wondered who the friend could be but it would be no bother for Thea made sure that the house was ready for the unexpected. She had high expectations of her staff but they loved her for the care she showed them and loyalty was their way of repaying her.

***

Maudie and Brad had crossed London in a taxi, to Paddington station to take the train westwards. Brad had been quiet just contemplating the sights he saw as the taxi sped on. The majestic old buildings he saw of the British capital had made him gasp with wonder. Although his family was wealthy he had not holidayed outside the vastness of his own country. Not that many Americans did. Each summer during his childhood they had fled the heat of New York to their second home in the Hamptons. He thought of his brothers who still followed such family traditions with their own wives and children. However, Brad was due to challenge this as new horizons opened up for him with the orchestra playing in so many of Europe's capital cities. His adventure was just about to start.

'Gee, look at that,' he said as he pointed to various buildings. Maudie just laughed.

On the train it was the same again. The train took them through spectacular scenery. 'This place is not so small after all,' he drawled.

Maudie did not have to answer but she laughed at his amazement. But she suddenly thought quite seriously that he was in for the biggest shock of his life once he reached Westborough.

The daylight was beginning to fade as a porter carried their luggage down the steps of Foregate Street station into the street below. A taxi rank was full across the busy road waiting for custom. 'I'll go and get us a taxi,' Maudie said leaving Brad with the luggage on the pavement.

Turning round and then pulling up in front of Brad, the driver stuck his head out of the window, a cigarette dangling from his mouth. He suddenly said in a disdainful voice, 'You'll never get that lot in 'ere.' He pointed with his finger to the back of the vehicle.

'It'll go in the trunk,' Brad said making his way to the back of the car. The driver opened the door and looked disgruntled. 'What are you playing at? What do you mean the trunk?' The man stood and scratched his head, puffing hard on his cigarette.

Maudie turned to the taxi driver with a disarming smile. 'It should fit in the boot. My friend means the boot.' The driver shrugged his shoulders in a manner of disbelief.

'Righto,' he said moving to the rear of the taxi to assist with the luggage.

'We will take the rest in the front with us.' Maudie continued. 'You don't mind driving us out to Westborough Hall do you? It is not far from Malvern.'

The driver was mollified that he had picked up a decent fare and did not fuss anymore over the huge amount of luggage that had crossed the Atlantic Ocean. He opened the cab door and got in. There was even a hint of a smile on his face as he started the engine.

When they reached Westborough Hall it was completely dark but the house was lit like a beacon to welcome them home like seamen viewing the lighthouse which brought them into calmer waters.

Chapter 45

Scarlett had found the address of the private investigator quite easily or if she was truthful the taxi driver had done so. The outer door of the set of offices had the name 'Marwell, Private Investigators' emblazoned across the glass and below were the words 'Please enter' which was exactly what Scarlett did. As she walked through into the outer office she saw a desk where a young woman was concentrating on some paperwork, a deeply engrossed look etched on her features. As she glanced up at the tinkling of the bell, she smiled suddenly, her eyes lighting up and Scarlett realized how attractive she was. The young woman rose to her feet and stretched her hand across the desk.

'Miss Devine, I presume. I am very pleased to meet you. I'm Josie Marwell.' Scarlett was back using the Devine name. She had felt that was for the best because she did not want the Carson relatives to know who she really was until she was ready to reveal her true identity. The Devine name also opened doors which as an independent young woman Scarlett was not always proud to use but it still held some sway on the few occasions when it might be required. Miss Marwell was doing a job and Scarlett was not going to reveal the reasons why she wanted these people followed. Josie Marwell did not care about the finer points as long as her client paid well and by the look of this one in her fine outfit and upper class accent that was the way it was going to be.

Scarlett took the proffered hand taking stock of the person in front of her wondering how a person so young could possibly be a private detective. The office looked spruce and perfectly clean unlike some of the down at heel places she had been imagining.

'Pleased to meet you,' Scarlett murmured wondering what might happen next. In her heart of hearts she wished that she had brought somebody with her for moral support but who would she have asked. Piers would have delved too far into the background of the private detective and Thea would have been too nervous to be there. Giving herself a mental shake up Scarlett adopted a business attitude and waited for the young woman's undivided attention.

Josie Marwell folded the paperwork that she had been working on into a tidy pile and placed it into the desk drawer before inviting her client through into an inner sanctum which sported well-polished furniture not unlike the offices of Arbuthnot and associates, solicitors.

'Please sit down, Miss Devine.' She indicated a chair opposite her own. 'Can I get you a cup of tea or even coffee? '

'No thank you.' Scarlett was anxious to get on with the business but she wondered at the lack of staff on hand. Josie witnessed the curiosity etched on Scarlett's features and felt duty bound to explain the rather odd circumstances. There was no way that she wished to lose this custom.

'I work here on my own, Miss Carson. That might be slightly strange but two months ago my father died rather suddenly leaving me to run the business single-handed. I had worked with my father for five years before his death. He taught me everything that he knew. At some point I shall be taking on more staff but with Christmas just round the corner I thought it could wait a few more weeks.'

Scarlett blushed, furious with herself that her face had given so much away.

'I'm sorry about your father, Miss Marwell. I hope you succeed in your business.'

Josie smiled tightly at her client and then said, 'now then how may I help you?'

Scarlett cleared her throat wondering where to start. 'Well, 'she began, 'my father died before I was born during the war. My mother knew very little about him but he did tell her that he had no living family. However, I have recently discovered that that was untrue. He had parents and a brother and sister still alive. Our family solicitor has told me that but is reluctant to give me any more information. I have done some investigating myself but have not managed to find anything out. That is why I have come to you.'

Scarlett watched the young woman scribbling diligently in a brand new notebook. She glanced up as Scarlett and smiled, 'and the names of these people.'

Scarlett supplied the last of the information. 'Will it be easy to trace them?' She asked.

'It may be, but sometimes people don't wish to be found which can make our search that much harder. Don't worry we can search as many openings as possible.'

'We?' Scarlett was puzzled.

Josie laughed. 'Yes. We. I might work on my own, but I have contacts that I can call on at times; they will help me out. Don't worry, they will be very discreet. With Christmas looming it might take a while to gather information but I will get back to you as soon as I have some news. So if there is a prolonged silence please don't worry we will be working as hard as we can. Now I'm afraid that I must raise the rather nasty question of fees.'

Scarlett wafted her hand in the air, 'don't worry about the cost I just want the information, that's all.'

Scarlett had the money. She knew that she could pay what was asked and she could do it without going cap in hand to Piers or her mother. A few more pieces of information were exchanged before Scarlett left bundling herself up against the elements which had taken a drastic turn for the worst on this blustery December day.

After Scarlett had departed, Josie leaned back in her chair to contemplate the interview that she had just had. She had wondered if the figures that she had been about to quote would have been too much for her client but had been surprised when Scarlett had not even listened to the quote. She thought about the young woman who had poise and elegance. She spoke with a cut glass voice but had given no clue to her background. Devine, the name she had heard somewhere before but for the moment nothing sprang to mind. Perhaps she should do a background check on Scarlett Devine which might also aid the investigation into these mysterious relatives. She knew just the people who could help her. Her father had used them many times in latter years. They were unobtrusive mixing in any circle without causing fuss. They were chameleon like blending into the background but tenacious enough to get hold of the vital information. She reached for the telephone feeling a frizzle of excitement run down her spine.

'Hello,' someone said at the other end of the telephone.

* * *

Breakfast had long been over but Piers and Thea sat drinking the remains of their tea which had turned cold in the pot but neither of them wished to send to the kitchen for more.

'Well, what do you make of Brad?' Thea was desperate to know what Piers felt. He had been particularly quiet on the matter ever since the young couple's arrival the week before. Thea already had an inkling about Piers' thoughts. Her husband was such a snob. Nobody was good enough for his children except members of the aristocracy. On this occasion Jane had made all the right decisions. The mere thought had made her smile.

Thea rather liked the young man who brought a breath of fresh air into the house. He was polite and effusive about everything English and could not quite get his head round the fact that Maudie had a title. But the fact that her father was an Earl and they lived in such splendour had tickled him pink.

'Oh my,' he repeated over and over as they explored the Hall and the grounds. The scenery with the Malvern Hills in the distance was breathtaking on a bright winter's day but he acknowledged that the summer would prove even better.

'Well what do you think of little Auld England,' Maudie had teased. But the reply was always the same.

Piers though did not know how to answer Thea's question. If he was honest he found the boy rather irritating with his fawning ways and always grovelling to Piers' title.

'I wish he would stop calling me Earl,' he eventually said. 'Damn it I told him to call me by my name.'

Thea giggled at his response. 'He is in awe of you, darling. The Americans don't have anything like us at home. They love all this about the aristocracy. Just let him get it out of his system. By the time he leaves he will be used to us. I do think that Maudie is rather fond of him though. I wonder if she has marriage on her mind.'

'Maudie is married to her music,' Piers said bucolically as he picked up his newspaper indicating that the discussion was at an end. Thea just laughed again before going to her husband to give him a kiss to which he responded with enthusiasm before his eyes rested on a piece of headline news which had taken his interest.

Chapter 46

Scarlett was disappointed that it would take a while to receive any information from Josie Marwell but she knew that patience had never been her greatest virtue and with Christmas rapidly approaching she had plenty to occupy her.

Foremostly, there was Christmas shopping to do. She had always been late with that but a quiver of excitement rushed through her as she thought of returning to Westborough. Although she was anxious to discover her Carson roots it would always be the Devines who would be her true family. It was as she matured that this thought had struck her almost like a blow to the chest. It was all right being a romantic as a teenager who imagined people in one light when in reality they could be something else. But there was still that urge to know, to give her peace of mind and mostly to see where she came from, where her roots lay and to define who she was. All the Devine children knew their heritage but she knew very little about her family's past. She thought of her own mother who had had a loving childhood but when the real truth emerged they were not her true parents. She had a side to her family through her father who was still a mystery. This, however, was where she differed from Thea; Thea was not anxious to know about her father. She did not wish to upset the applecart, nor did she need to for she had her happy marriage to Piers and the happy family they had created between them and that was enough.

***

The young Devines were due to return from school at any moment. Piers had volunteered to be the chauffeur knowing that Thea had more than enough to do for there was to be a festive season like no other seen at Westborough Hall for years. Jane had telephoned Thea only days before sounding anxious and depressed when she should have been buoyant from the recent birth of her new son. It reminded Thea of the days when Mary, Jane's mother, had been at her worst after the birth of her first child. This worried her beyond measure.

Thea had found Piers in the library, caught in the act of helping himself to a very large whisky before the appointed hour when it was regarded as the seemly time to have a drink. She could only remember Clarissa who had lacked self-control with the whisky decanter but Christmas was upon them. Perhaps that was enough of an excuse. There would have to be abstinence once the festive season was over.

'Would you like one, darling,' Piers said feeling rather guilty when he read the look on his wife's face.

'No thank you Piers,' she said a trifle frostily; then she remembered why she had come in search of her husband in the first place. She proceeded to tell Piers her fears about Jane and divulged her thoughts about inviting the Severtons to Westborough for Christmas. It had been a long time since Jane had been at Westborough at that time of year.

Piers sat down in front of the roaring log fire and took a huge gulp of his whisky as he contemplated Thea's words. 'Are you really serious about this?' He asked.

'Completely.' A silence ensued momentarily.

'You know that will mean inviting Archie as well,' he continued. 'Jane and family are the only family the poor man has. It is not a season to be left on one's own, is it? We forget how lucky we are to have such a large family.' This was a comment Piers would never have uttered at one point when he had felt that the older girls were beyond reason.

Thea smiled at Piers' generosity of spirit and the warmth he felt for having such a large brood. He had come a long way since those early days.

'I will go and telephone her back. It will be lovely to have the whole family together including Jane's little ones.' Thea said before he could change his mind and remember what it was like to have small children running rampant pulling Christmas decorations down while a baby yelled non-stop in the nursery. Even such a thought made her shudder. She expected Jane would bring their own nanny along but there was no knowing what their own nanny would say at such a change in circumstances. They always seemed to be very territorial by nature and as for Amelia…. She gathered her imagination together before it ran away with her any longer. Amelia could be a tyrant if she was not held in check.

With these thoughts still racing in her head, she had left Piers in a benign and sentimental mood with the thought of the approaching season which he loved without reservation and just a little help from the whisky that he was about to top up, hopefully before Thea's return.

And so the Christmas preparations began. Brad had been delighted to help; and was anxious to see how an English Christmas compared with his family one in New York. His love of England was growing and to be in the bosom of a grand English family at this time of year was a double blessing. The great hall was alight with the Christmas tree and decorative lights but great shadows were cast in the corners of the old historic room. He could only stand there and say 'wow' over and over again much to the amusement of the younger Devines who mimicked him beyond reason outside of his hearing. However, they were not malicious for they had found him different. In response he just loved to listen to their English accents. Even Scarlett was amused by him. But when Archie and the other Severtons arrived Brad was in seventh heaven knowing that there was another Earl in their midst. Was this how all of England behaved?

'It is the best Christmas ever,' Verity continued to proclaim throughout the whole period.

Nobody could dispute her claim for everything had gone so well and the unexpected guests had only contributed to the party atmosphere. Archie and Piers had become genuine friends over the five days of their stay and could often be found in the realm of Piers' study discussing politics quite amicably although they were of a different political persuasion. Their amicable disputes were often lubricated by a number of whisky bottles which Piers had brought from his cellar near the basement kitchen. However, Archie, after a tour of the Westborough Estate was keen to question his host on the running of Foray House's smaller estate. Now that the fortunes of the Severtons were rising he was open to as much advice as he could muster. During these long, protracted conversations Archie could not sing Jane's praises enough which made Piers mellow towards his eldest daughter who had caused him so much angst in years gone by.

Thea need not have worried either because Jane had her small family under control and nanny so well trained. Thea loved the little ones but most of all she saw the transformation of Jane who had appeared wan and low in spirits on her arrival but had suddenly blossomed during her time at Westborough.

Finding Jane in the library one dreary morning she had her to herself for the first time.

'You're looking much better, Jane, since your arrival. Have you missed Westborough so much in the last few years?'

Jane looked taken aback by Thea's words. She did not know how to respond to her rather observant stepmother.

'Yes, I have rather, more than I thought I would. This after all has always been my home.'

'You will get used to Foray House,' Thea continued kindly.

'I love Foray House; don't get me wrong and one day I shall be Countess. It is also my children's inheritance.'

'Yes, it is and it will be different when you are at the helm. Is everything all right with you, Dougie and Archie?'

Jane smiled, 'Everything is fine Thea. I just get a little bit homesick.'

'Well we must put that right straight away. You must come more often to Westborough to give you something to look forward to. We would love to have you and the children here regularly. The place is so empty these days when everybody is away. Promise me that you will come.'

'Yes, of course I will and thank you, Thea.' Jane rose from her chair and came to Thea, throwing her arms around her in gratitude.

It seemed to Thea that at last Jane had properly returned to the bosom of her family and it gave her an inner glow that only family and the people you love most can achieve.

***

As the Christmas season drew to a close members of the family began to depart to their different lives including Piers who had to be at the House for an important debate. For once Thea did not react badly to the peace and quiet that was left in their wake. She was tired and wanted some normality in her life which was also to give more attention to her small daughter who had not been neglected during the festivities and was quite capable of looking after her own interests but Thea knew that she felt guilty just as she often did.

The Severtons had been the first to depart, followed by Brad and Maudie who had to meet with the rest of the orchestra in order to practice and finalize arrangements for the continuation of the tour which was to start in Paris towards the end of January. The Devines were to return to school imminently which left Scarlett who felt at a loose end until she received the information that she was expecting.

London did not seem as exciting in January although the sales lingered but Scarlett was not an ardent shopper. Thea was pleased to have Scarlett to herself for a few more days. She was not sure what her daughter was going to do in London on her return but experience taught her not to question too deeply about the lives of her older children.

Chapter 47

Dorothy Maythwaite pulled her Ford Anglia to a halt outside her house in a pleasant part of Richmond in the North Riding. She sat and looked through her rear mirror trying to find evidence of why she felt so frightened. She had locked the car doors as she did every time she drove, as her husband instructed. She was not sure why he was so insistent on such matters but it made her feel rather foolish because not all women locked their cars driving around such a quiet, rural backwater. She was sure that it would be different living in the towns, but where she lived people did not even lock their front doors. They went out shopping and left their houses unlocked. It was just the way it was. There were tourists of course but they did not wander into the residential areas; they just wanted to look at the magnificent Norman castle, explore the lovely market square and take in the scenery.

Dorothy was not normally a frightened woman and would travel long distances on her own, but just recently she had felt that she was being followed. If she said this to her husband he would say she was being delusionary despite his insistence on locking the doors. Not normally prone to be fanciful Dorothy had convinced herself of the fact that everything was different just lately. There always seemed to be a silver car in the distance when she glanced in her mirror and she was convinced that there were not that many silver cars on the road. And there was yesterday when she met her friend for lunch; she had the strangest feeling that she was being followed. Looking behind her, there were people going about their business and there was nobody she could claim to be suspicious looking hovering around. She had ducked into several shops where she had loitered by the window to watch the world go by but there was nobody there.

She sat still watching for the silver car to pass but nothing happened. Then she thought that she would drive off again taking a more circuitous route before returning home. If she saw the car again she would be convinced that she was being followed and have to do something about it but the last person she would tell would be her husband, Ralph. He would not let her out of the house by herself and the last thing she wanted was to become a prisoner in her own home. She would have to tell somebody about this or she would go mad. Alan would be the best person to tell if he was at home. He spent a lot of time away working but he never said what he did. It all seemed rather peculiar to her although his wife, Jenny, never complained; perhaps she was just used to the routine. She would go and spend a few days with them in London. It was a long time since she had been to visit so Ralph could not stop her going. She knew that Ralph would not want to go for he disliked leaving the dales.

'I was away too long in the war to want to see anywhere else,' he would say regularly as if such thoughts had never been uttered before.

'Old stick in the mud,' she would murmur sotto voce when he carried on about such things.

There were times when she wondered why she had married him. 'Love is blind' was another of her sayings. It had been her greatest regret that they could not have children. It would have made life more bearable. They had had all the tests and there was no explanation why it had never happened but life carried on and they had learned to live with it. She had filled her life with friends and her niece, Joan, helped to fill the void. It was stupid, she felt, to fill your life with regret and negativity.

Dorothy sat in the car with her thoughts whirling in circles through her troubled mind. Suddenly she looked up only to see a silver car pass by. She squealed believing that some harm was to come to her but it drove slowly past without stopping. She had tried to take a look at the driver's face as he glanced towards her car. But his face was partially concealed by a hat which was pulled low over his brow. It was not possible to tell if it was a man or a woman. This all seemed curious to Dorothy but Ralph always said that her imagination ran away with her. Then, there was the number plate which seemed to be concealed by dirty smudges, almost as if they had been put there on purpose. She could not quite make out the registration number before the vehicle speeded up and was disappearing around the bend in the road and was lost to sight. Indeed, it was all very curious. Why would people want to follow her? She was too boring to the world at large; this was a conclusion that she had come to long ago.

Dorothy clambered out of her car in a hurry before the silver car had chance to return. She wanted to be in the security of the house with the doors locked. Now in her haste her keys fell to the ground making her fumble to rescue them. The contents of her handbag spilled out. Everything just seemed worse the more she hurried. Now with the key in the lock the door yielded in submission. Inside the house and now locked in she let out a long breath and a cry of pent up emotion before entering her small kitchen to make a restorative cup of tea before thinking about her next move. She would telephone Alan before Ralph came home.

***

It was the end of January and Christmas was a distant memory. The weather had been wet and miserable for weeks which had literally dampened Scarlett's mood; she was bored and anxious waiting for the results of the investigation. In some ways she wished that she had not taken this year off but had started work to keep her mind occupied. She still did not have enough friends in London. However, she knew that would change once she mixed in new circles. With Maudie away with the orchestra, she had felt lonely. Such feelings were alien to her for had she not had Jane and Maudie to grow up with and then at Oxford she had made friends easily being gregarious by nature.

She could return to her mother at Westborough. The idea was tempting but Thea would wonder what the matter was and ask awkward questions to which Scarlett would have to give evasive answers. The last thing she wanted was to lie to her mother. Eventually she wished to deliver the story of Jack Carson's family as a fait accompli. The underlying problem was the fact that she had not heard from her private detective. She knew the matter would take time but Scarlett wanted to do everything yesterday as Thea always said.

Scarlett had tried telephoning Josie Marwell several times but there had been no reply. Of course she seemed to work alone which meant that she would not be sitting by the telephone waiting for it to ring.

She tried again, as she watched the snow whirl in the bitter cold wind that seemed to howl around the buildings.

'Josie Marwell,' she said. Her voice sounded quite curt.

'It's Scarlett Carson here. I wondered if there was any news concerning—'

'I don't discuss cases on the telephone,' Josie said matter of factly. 'However, all I can say is that we have gathered a lot of information for you but we need more time to finalize our investigation. I trust in your patience. We will notify you as soon as our enquiry is complete.'

The telephone clicked as the receiver was replaced on the other end of the line. It was still a waiting game Scarlett had to acknowledge irritably.

Chapter 48

Thea had found this January of 1965 a trial but it was nothing new; she did every year. Christmas had been wonderful with all the family together and she missed each and every one of them when they had gone. Jane had been a little tearful when the time came to depart but Thea had made up her mind to travel to the Scottish borders, with or without Piers, to give Jane some moral support so that she did not feel so isolated from her own family. As the relationship on both sides had improved over the years it was important to feel a sense of togetherness Thea thought. She realized that here she was juggling the family yet again but Jane was a special case. She had been stalwart in every sense of the word since her marriage to Douglas but deep down there was a touch of her mother about her, a kind of vulnerability that would rise too much before she was ready and she had been so very young to marry and have so many babies in quick succession. She blamed Archie for putting on Jane so quickly after the wedding before she had managed to get her feet under the table to gain experience at running a big house. Thea thought about herself. She understood what it was like to run a large household but in her case she had had Clarissa as a sounding board until recent years. The old woman had been so supportive but if Thea was to support Jane it had to be insidiously done so that she did not look as if she was interfering. She did not want to interfere but someone had to keep Jane afloat until she regained her strength mentally and physically after the birth of her last child.

Thea had decided that she would take Amelia to Scotland because the little girl had so enjoyed having other children in the nursery. Even nanny had not complained for she was glad of the company and help of the Severton nanny. The two women had bonded despite the considerable difference in their ages. When Jane had learnt that Thea would venture forth in the early spring she had been placated. There had also been talk of the Severtons' return in the summer even if Douglas could not accompany his family. He had been pleased about the meeting of the clans and had been concerned about Jane's well-being; this had been the first time he had witnessed Jane's downward spiral into a depression which they were now referring to as the baby blues. She needed to have as much fun as she could to raise her spirits. Thea had witnessed this side to Douglas' character and had warmed to him immediately. One night in bed she had explained the situation to Piers who felt heartened that Jane had chosen a husband who cared about her so much. He felt that Archie liked Jane too and much appreciated what she had done for the Severton family. But everything took its toll if it was to land on fragile shoulders.

'I am just so grateful that Jane and I have settled our differences over the years. What if we had not been able to do so?'

'This is not a time for regrets, Piers. Your mother would be proud of you; she managed to move on from your father's neglect but it was long after his death. You have done it in your lifetime.'

Piers had looked at Thea quite stunned by her perception of the circumstances and her words of wisdom. 'My darling, you astound me with your sagacity and confidence in our family and people in general.'

Piers had kissed her deeply. Thea blushed at his words and revealed nothing of her innermost thoughts. Life experience had taught her much.

* * *

Piers was once more in London. For some reason he had not wanted to return to the capital because he had enjoyed Christmas and the festive time at the Hall but then the family had returned to their respective lives but duty called beckoning him once more to London. However, he had promised Thea that he would be home again as quickly as possible. And then the unthinkable happened. Thea had watched the nine o'clock news on the BBC with Richard Dimbleby's face particularly solemn. At the end of the broadcast she turned the television set off waiting for the telephone to ring as she knew it would. She was proved correct. She jumped up from her seat by the library fire and ran into the great hall to pick up the receiver.

'Hello,' she said.

'Thea, have you heard the news?' Piers asked his voice full of emotion.

'Yes. What a great pity,' she said, 'but he was over ninety.'

'Yes, but it is still a shock when a great statesman passes away.'

'Yes,' Thea reiterated as she remembered the one and only time she had met Winston Churchill when she had gone to meet Piers at Westminster. He was in the Lobby and Piers had introduced her. He had been charming and his distinctive voice had resonated with her from years ago when the British had listened to his stirring speeches on the wireless giving the people hope that the war would be eventually won.

'Thea, are you still there?'

'Yes, sorry. I was just thinking about his speeches during the war. He gave us all so much hope.'

'Yes. Thea, I want you to come to London for the funeral. All Parliamentarians will be there and I want you with me.' Piers' voice sounded sentimental again. 'He will be lying in state at Westminster Hall. It will be the first time a commoner will have done so since the first war. It will be a state funeral.'

'Must I come? You know I don't like such big occasions and then there is Amelia…'

'Thea, you will come,' Piers said emphatically. 'Amelia will be fine. You will not be away from her for long. I will telephone again when I know more.'

The line went dead and Thea stood looking forlornly into the receiver which was still in her hand.

True to his word Piers rang two nights later.

'The funeral is on the thirtieth. Can you be here in a couple of days?'

His voice was almost pleading instead of being dictatorial.

'I will be there, Piers.' Thea knew that her place was by her husband's side as his Countess. She had already gathered her funeral wardrobe together the previous day. It had not seen the light of day since Clarissa's funeral but one did not necessarily wear a fashion statement on such an occasion. She was too well aware that there were too many people who would be present at the funeral who were far more important than herself or even her husband.

'I'll see you at the Town House tomorrow.'

'Thank you,' Piers said before he ended the call. He knew that he wanted Thea by his side at such a moment.

Winston Churchill was old but he had seemed invincible over the years and had yet again been Prime Minister in the previous decade lending fatherly advice to a very young Queen. Piers felt emotional about the death of a great man whom he had hero worshipped for such a very long time and had met regularly in the corridors of power but now he was to see him rightfully applauded by the nation at large as he went to his final resting place.

Chapter 49

Josie Marwell was becoming increasingly more and more frustrated with the Carson case; in many ways she wished that she had not taken it on but in truth she needed the money badly. She had found Dorothy Maythwaite quite easily or her deceased father's old chum, Harald, had. She had used him on occasions before and had found him solid and reliable. A little bit of knowledge said to be a dangerous thing also could be very useful if used wisely. Maythwaite as a name could be found anywhere in the country but it also sounded very Yorkshire and that had led him to look at that county but it was a big county and his investigation had been slow but thorough and eventually it had all paid off, everything falling into place. He had followed the woman around the area and now knew that she suspected she was being followed either on foot or by car. However, the woman was not aware that there were two vehicles that followed her. Harald used a very old car that belonged to his father when he needed to be more circumspect and somebody else was following her on foot. This tactic although not subtle sometimes triggered the person under surveillance to do something rather stupid which in this case might lead Dorothy to go straight to her brother.

However, at present, there was no trace of Alan Carson. It was a common enough name but his whereabouts had not been identified. Harald had scoured the North Yorkshire area engaging more and more assistance but nothing had been revealed. The mystery was strange for it appeared that the man did not want to be found. Many people had secrets but eventually something turned up which was the final piece in the jigsaw puzzle. However, it was not the case this time. The only way they would find him would be for this Maythwaite woman to lead him to her.

Josie Marwell was becoming annoyed for she was harassing Harold to get to the crux of the matter. Josie was frustrated about the lack of progress on two accounts. The first was the fact that Scarlett wanted results and Josie did not blame her for there was a lot of money being paid out. She had the feeling that Scarlett as a young woman was well off although she did not know the full circumstances of her client. During their first interview Scarlett had alluded to being well enough off to be able to pursue the case to its conclusion and she had paid out a lot of money for expenses and had implied that she expected results.

The second reason for Josie's concern was that the money was running out and she would have to press for more funds. It was a complete vicious circle and the side of the job that Josie detested. But there was no rushing this and Scarlett just had to understand that.

The telephone rang in Scarlett's apartment just before she was due to walk out. 'Hello,' she said.

'Miss Carsen, it is Josie Marwell here.'

Scarlett sank down onto the sofa, her breath held tightly in her chest as she awaited news.

'Are you still there, Miss Carson,' Josie said wondering if the line had gone dead.

'Yes, I'm still here. Have you found them?'

'I can't discuss this on the telephone as you know but I do need to see you as soon as possible. Can you manage today?'

'Yes,' Scarlett said. She had been going to go shopping but that was unimportant now. 'Shall I come to you?'

'There will be no need for that as I'm in your area later on today if you would not mind waiting.'

'No that would be fine.'

The line went dead.

Scarlett did not know what to feel, but a frisson of excitement was beginning to bubble inside her; there was an equal measure of uncertainty too. Only time would give her the answers.

***

Thea had done as she had promised catching the nine thirty train from Worcester. Reaching the Town house by lunchtime, she knew that she had the whole afternoon to herself before Piers arrived home. She had whole days to herself before the funeral. This was such a rarity that she planned to go shopping to the West End and arrange to have her hair done, a luxury when one lived out in the wilds of the countryside. I must try not to be such a country bumpkin she chastised herself but knew that she would never change. She loved living in the country but her childhood had been spent in the city. It was the War years that had made the transformation for her and now she would not have it any other way. On the second day she would visit Scarlett in the new apartment which she had not yet seen. But it suddenly came to her that she could not do that because that would be the day of the funeral and she was unsure about the length of time it would take. And then there was travelling through the city. There would be hours when roads would be closed off. She sighed deeply wondering whether she could stay another day but she had promised Amelia who had stood on the front steps of Westborough Hall holding tightly to Nanny's hand while she sobbed her heart out. Thea remembered the early childhood of all the Devine children. The eldest three had each other to distract themselves and so did the next three but Amelia was like an only child which tore at her heart. It would have been wonderful to have had another child near Amelia in age but they had a lot of children as it was but time had not been on their side when Amelia was conceived.

Thea was surprised to find Piers at home on this rather dismal January afternoon. He was drinking a cup of tea in the sitting room and there were the remnants of a half-eaten sandwich on a plate by his cup and saucer.

'Hello,' Thea said as she put her head around the sitting room door.

Piers looked up from the handful of papers that he had been perusing and smiled his lop sided smile. 'What a wonderful surprise. I thought you weren't arriving until tomorrow.'

'I thought that I would surprise you darling and there are a few things that I want to do before the funeral.'

'Well you have some time to do that,' he said without wondering what she was about to do.

'Would you like to go out for dinner? I have already told the staff not to make anything for me.'

'That would be such a treat, Piers. We can catch up on what's been happening.'

***

The funeral was to be held at St Paul's Cathedral which Churchill had attended during the long years of the War. The old statesman was immensely impressed by Wren's feat in the architecture of the iconic building which had replaced the original cathedral, having been burned down in the great fire. On the day of the funeral the coffin stood on a catafalque with six candlesticks of gigantic proportions surrounding it. Thea and Piers had taken their seats surrounded by members of the government and leaders from around the world. Winston's family was there talking in muted tones. Thea was in awe of what she was experiencing. Looking from right to left and back again, she glimpsed faces that she had only seen on television. The members of the Royal family sat looking straight ahead, used to such sombre occasions, their faces inscrutable. But Piers' thoughts were in a dark place as he contemplated the man himself and his achievements.

The Royal family had attended the ceremony of a commoner which was unprecedented but he had been Prime Minister during the war years when King George was on the throne and then he had been there in the same role to greet the young Queen and to be a mentor in the early years of her reign. On this very day although still young she had poise and experience which had stood her in good stead for the nation she reigned over. But it was also important to pay her respects to the man who had led the country that he loved when times were difficult and had supported her father, George VI and his Queen. It was all that the leaders of the nation could do to pay homage in the most fitting of ways to the man who had become an icon to the country he lead during its darkest hours.

As the service drew to a close the coffin left the cathedral through the great west doors and to continue its journey to Tower Bridge Pier on its way to the final resting place at Bladon in Oxfordshire. It was a solemn moment to think that the great man was mortal and was taking his last journey.

Piers and Thea stood for a while talking to other dignitaries in hushed tones before moving towards the doors to return to normal life a little sober in their thoughts. For Thea it was an experience that she would never forget and for Piers it was a grief that it would take some time to recover from.

Chapter 50

Dorothy Maythwaite had packed her rather ancient and battered brown leather suitcase which had been purchased well before the war. She did not need many clothes because she had promised her husband that she would not be away very long. She just wanted a few nights to catch up with her family. Alan had not been there Jenny had said but he would be back quite soon and she was welcome to come whenever she wanted. And so she had left on one of the local buses in the market place in Richmond which would take her to Darlington from where she could catch the train on the east line for London. She wished that she was confident to drive that far but Ralph always seemed to undermine her confidence. He always wanted her safely at home he would say but Dorothy knew better. He was controlling and a bully and she wished that she could stand up to him more but she never did. And so life carried on in much the same way.

***

Scarlett had waited and waited and now the twilight of a dreary February afternoon was beginning to descend on the apartment. The lights in the street had just been lit but she sat in the semi darkness waiting for her visitor. Thea had telephoned for a chat. She had sounded lonely and depressed after the funeral and leaving Scarlett feeling guilty at neglecting her mother. Piers had remained in London for there was much for him to do and Thea had dutifully returned to Westborough Hall to be with Amelia as she had promised.

'Would you like to come home for a weekend, darling? You can't be that busy. You are not working. I don't know how you fill your days,' Thea had said during their conversation.

Scarlett's heart had dropped knowing that her mother sounded needy. It was so unlike Thea to be like that. The thought of returning to Westborough was attractive for it was home after all but she wanted to be in London in case there was news. She could pass the Westborough telephone number onto Josie but she was still reluctant to divulge her activities until there was significant news.

'I would like to come, Mama.' Thea's emotions took wing when she heard those words but nosedived when Scarlett said, 'but I'm a bit tied up for the next couple of weeks.'

'I could come and see you and stay at the town house. I won't be a nuisance to you, darling. Possibly I could bring Amelia this time.'

'Just let me consult my diary and I will get back to you.'

Scarlett heard the sigh at the other end of the line and felt guilt flood right through her once more. She disliked treating her mother like this but she was so close to finding out about her father's family that she wished to accomplish something before she shared her information. There was a knock on the front door disturbing Scarlett's conversation.

'Mama, there is somebody at the door. I will ring you back.'

Scarlett heard another sigh before Thea put down the telephone severing the call.

'Coming,' she shouted hoping that her visitor was Josie Marwell.

As she led Josie into her sitting room she offered to take the young woman's outer garments.

'I'm fine Miss Devine,' she said. 'I have another engagement when I leave here.' But she did unbutton her coat for the room was rather warm after the cold outside.

'Have you news?' Scarlett felt beside herself with curiosity and nerves that she had not realized that she possessed now that she was about to learn possible secrets of her family.

Josie smiled, 'I have but it is not as good as you will believe. We have found Dorothy Maythwaite who lives in Yorkshire but there is no news of her brother. This means that we will have to wait until she leads us to him. As it is she knows that she is being followed.'

'How so?' Scarlett sounded rather annoyed and disappointed at such a transgression.

Josie laughed. 'Don't sound so alarmed for it is a tactic we use occasionally to make someone panic into making rather rash decisions and on this occasion it is to take us straight to someone else.'

'Oh,' said Scarlett rather taken aback.

'However,' Josie continued giving a little embarrassed cough, 'we are running out of funds for the case and wondered if we could agree on a top up.'

'Oh,' Scarlett said again trying to remember how much she had paid in expenses already. 'Will my aunt recognize the person following her?' She wanted to know more details before she signed another cheque. In many ways she wished that she could discuss the whole affair with somebody like Piers but she had got herself into this mess so she must see it through.'

Josie watched the emotions dance across her client's face and she felt some sympathy for her.

'We will use a different person to follow your aunt this time and we will get our man. Now she will not know that she is being followed and I can guarantee that. And it is quite normal to ask for more in the way of expenses when it takes such a time to find our man.'

Scarlett had been studying Josie's face at length and suddenly she felt that she could trust her.

'All right,' she said reaching for her chequebook. As she began to scribble the amount she suddenly looked at Josie with curiosity. 'Tell me something about my aunt, Dorothy whatever.'

'Dorothy Maythwaite,' Josie smiled at her client. 'We don't know a lot but she lives in North Yorkshire in Richmond. She is in her late forties, a little mouse of a woman. She seems frightened of her own shadow. Yesterday she caught the train to King's Cross and now is being followed. We hope that she is going to her brother. That would save a lot of time and expense.'

Scarlett digested this information with a sense of excitement. Perhaps this was nearly at an end and she could meet these siblings of her father. Her heart was pounding in her chest.

Signing the cheque with a flourish she passed it to Josie with gratitude. Before rising to go, Josie buttoned up her coat against the elements and placed the cheque in her handbag. Turning once more to Scarlett she smiled. 'We will find him. You must be sure of that.'

After her visitor had departed, Scarlett sat staring into the flames of the fire. It was her dearest wish to be in touch with this other family but she also knew that there was no way that she could be disloyal to the Devines. The fact that she had wanted to discuss everything with Piers made her realize how far their relationship had come in recent years and now he was the father that she had never known.

She continued to sit by the fire mulling over the day's happenings. She still had to talk to Thea and find a way to keep her at Westborough until everything was settled. The sound of a key being turned in the front door, followed by a familiar voice shouting, 'Is anybody at home?' made Scarlett return to her senses. The sitting room door opened and there stood Maudie smiling broadly and close behind stood Brad.

'Maudie, how wonderful to see you.' Scarlett threw her arms around her sister and hugged her tightly. 'Why didn't you say you were coming? Has the tour finished?'

'Stop! Stop! One question at a time,' Maudie laughed. 'No the tour has not finished but we have time off so that we could take a break. We have a week and then we are off again. We are tired but we will stay here tonight and then go on to Westborough for a few days. I can't wait.'

Brad stood behind Maudie, a look of expectation on his face and then Maudie delivered the Bombshell.

'Brad and I are engaged.' She flashed a large solitaire diamond in front of a speechless Scarlett.

'Wow,' was all Scarlett could say. 'What about Papa? Are you going to ask his permission? You know what a stickler he can be on matters of etiquette. By the way I am very pleased for you.'

'Thank you. We will go down to Westborough tomorrow to ask Papa, won't we Brad.'

'Yes, of course,' Brad said looking very unsure of the whole affair. He was a little in awe of Piers and his title although his American upbringing would have dictated the same standard of behaviour.

Scarlett did not know if Piers would be at Westborough but it had been the answer to a prayer. As Maudie went to show Brad around the apartment Scarlett went to telephone Thea knowing that any distraction for her mother was better than nothing. She was off the hook for the time being.

Chapter 51

Dorothy had reached King's Cross Station. She had been paranoid about being followed on the journey south and although she had been vigilant she had not seen anybody acting suspiciously. Consequently, she had relaxed into reading her book and glancing up occasionally to smile at other passengers before returning to her Agatha Christie novel which she hoped would give her more in-depth knowledge on the world of the criminal mind. Ralph had always said that she had an over active imagination which was fuelled by the books she devoured. But here she was safely in the capital as the train steamed in drawing to a halt with much commotion. She stood up in the rather stuffy carriage as everybody else did to retrieve their luggage in readiness for their onward journey. A rather fresh faced young man looked at Dorothy thoughtfully.

'Would you like me to lift your case down for you?' He asked in a very polite way.

'That would be so good of you,' she said as she indicated the battered, brown suitcase. The young man impressively dressed in a smart suit over which he wore an unbuttoned grey overcoat and a trilby hat topping off the ensemble, looked rather pompous Dorothy thought as she took a more in-depth look at him. But he was kind to help her. He hefted down the case and looked at the label for what seemed a long moment.

'You're nearly at journey's end,' he said in a jocular way smiling and raising his hat in a gesture of farewell. Before Dorothy had time to thank him he had disappeared into the melee of bodies leaving the train and was lost to sight. Dorothy thought nothing more about it as she circumnavigated her way towards the taxi rank to pay for a luxury that she could not really afford. The young man who had followed his target concealing himself from her vision scrutinized the activities of the middle-aged woman as she climbed into the taxi giving the driver instructions of her onward destination. She did not see a silver car pull up in front of the young man who climbed into the front passenger seat as the car glided away following the taxi at a safe distance.

***

Thea had been distracted from her loneliness by Scarlett's telephone call. To have Maudie and Brad arriving for a short visit was the answer to a prayer and then Piers had added to her delight by announcing that he was taking a break from the House for a short while and would be home the next day. He had had to smile as he listened to the joy in Thea's voice as she had told him about the impending visit. Piers had been pleased, too, but was a little puzzled that they had flown all the way back to Blighty just for a few days, but young people led a very different life from the time when he had been young. He had forgotten what it had been like to be young. The War years had robbed him of some of his youth as it had a whole generation of young people. He had been a little maudlin of late dwelling on the death of the great man even though he had been so advanced in years. Returning to Westborough and Thea would gladden his heart as it always did.

Thea sat in her sitting room with Amelia on her lap looking at some picture books which had just enough words underneath to help her read. She had just started in the schoolroom earlier than would have been the case for Thea was trying to occupy the child who seemed advanced for her years and it would fill some of the time in her lonely little world.

Outside Thea heard a car pull up, followed by doors banging. Amelia cocked her head to one side. 'Who is that, Mummy?' She lisped looking at her mother for an answer.

Thea smiled, 'I think that must be Maudie.' She gently pushed Amelia onto her feet before taking her hand to go and welcome her stepdaughter. However, the great front door of the Hall was flung wide open and Mollie the newest maid was helping to bring luggage indoors, wondering why people needed so much.

Thea and Amelia walked into the cold February air to greet the newcomers but to her surprise she saw Piers as well as Maudie and Brad. She opened her mouth to say something but Piers grinned at her,' we were all on the same train from King's Cross and it made sense to travel with them. I don't know how long they are staying but there is enough luggage for a month's stay.'

Piers transferred his attention to his youngest daughter. Stepping forward he picked her up and twirled her around as she giggled before shouting, 'Stop it, Papa, I'm dizzy.'

Maudie stood watching this display of affection with her little sister. The look on her face had become masked but an intuitive Thea watched her stepdaughter who would remember being a similar age to Amelia when Piers had remained a distant father to his oldest children. How times had changed. But the look had gone as quickly as it had arrived with Maudie giggling and joining in the fun. Thea, though, had not taken her eyes from her stepdaughter. She noted the sophisticated black trouser suit, with Maudie's hair swept high in an elaborate chignon. Gone were the bohemian clothes of student days to be replaced by a truly professional ensemble which made her look a million dollars. The thought made Thea laugh as she turned her attention to Brad whose face remained sombre, as he appeared to be deep in thought.

Thea's mind was in overdrive once more wondering why the young couple had returned to Westborough with just a short window of time before they must return to their musical journey of many great European cities. Piers was still clutching at Amelia's hand as they headed for the house. Maudie had stopped to plant a kiss on Thea's face.

'Hello, darling,' Thea greeted her stepdaughter with the great affection she held for all the Devine children.

Brad held back as he looked like an interloper amongst all the family greetings but nobody could accuse Thea of not giving her full attention to anyone who was a guest within her four walls.

'Hello, Brad. Lovely to see you again.' She flashed her generous smile at him and held her cheek out to be kissed.

'Lovely to see you again, Lady De—'

'Thea. Always call me Thea,' she said as she followed the retreating backs into the welcome warmth of the building. The light of the February afternoon was swiftly fading as Thea thought that she must see cook to order a welcome home dinner.

Chapter 52

Dorothy Maythwaite had reached the end of her journey and she was relieved for the day had been long and protracted. She looked in her purse to find her fare. Having done so, she climbed out from the rear of the taxi and leaned into the front driver's side to pay the man.

'I need my suitcase,' she said rather abruptly.

'Sorry, love. I was miles away. My missus has gone into hospital to have our little 'un and I cannot afford to be with her because I will lose money. It is nearly the end of my shift though.'

Dorothy stood back allowing the taxi driver to open the door. She had never had children and did not warm to the fact that the poor man was under pressure to earn a living but give support to his poor wife. She took her suitcase but did not press a tip into his hand after his tale of woe. Turning towards the terraced house she looked up at it before going to knock the brass knocker and wait for entry. The driver removed his cap to scratch his red thatch of hair wondering at the meanness of the human race.

Down the street a silver car moved discreetly into a parking space and waited. In the interior two men watched Dorothy admitted to the house before they discreetly moved forward to take note of the number of the premises and drove slowly away to pass the information on to their boss.

***

The first night of Maudie's return home had been blissful. The family had sat around the table in the small dining room enjoying a delicious meal and the best red wine from the Devine cellar which Piers refreshed every few months. The Devine wine cellar had been legendary in the days of Piers' father and Piers had continued the same tradition except for his absence from the hall during the war years. He had suspicions that his mother had reduced the stock for her personal consumption and her habits of enjoying a generous tipple were well known in the local area. These days the best cognac was cased and sent from France whenever the stocks became diminished. But the black market had flourished during the war and Piers would not have put it beyond Clarissa to have had connections in that direction. Nothing seemed impossible with his mother's influence in the local community. These ideas swirled in Piers' mind as he savoured the best Bordeaux his cellars could muster and he smiled affectionately at the memories of his mother, regret at her absence; a sentimental lump formed in his throat as it nearly always did when he thought of her. How he would have loved her to see the flourishing relationship that he now shared with the older girls. He could almost hear her say, 'and about time too.' His face twisted into a wry smile at the very thought.

But there was also a sense of gratitude that his large rumbustious family partly filled the void in his life that her absence had left. Then as he surveyed the dinner table he saw Maudie and his beloved wife, Thea, deep in conversation, a warmth there that any onlooker would believe to belong to that of mother and daughter, the bond between them so obviously close. His eyes slid across the table to the young American who looked down at his plate, obviously ill at ease with the situation as his hand fiddled with the tightness of his collar and tie. And suddenly Piers knew why Maudie and Brad had made the long trip back from Eastern Europe instead of taking a quiet break before continuing their arduous tour.

Brad, unaware of being under such close scrutiny, had been nervous throughout the meal knowing that he could not put off his conversation with Piers. He saw how the Earl was mellow in his thinking as he poured his fourth glass of wine. Thea giggled at the conversation, her cheeks pink from the warmth of the room combined with her own generous consumption of the wine, having imbibed more than usual. Maudie wondered when Brad would make his move to speak to Piers but she recognized how ill at ease he was and flashed encouraging smiles across the table. Piers, rising from the table looked at Brad with interest.

'Would you like to join me for a brandy in the library, Brad?' He asked. 'We will leave the women to their conversation.'

Maudie stopped mid-sentence in her conversation with Thea and regarded her father wondering if he was intuitive. Brad looked at Maudie who mouthed something unintelligible but her smile gave him courage and a little backbone. He followed Piers from the room like a lamb to the slaughter.

Piers had poured two ample measures of the best cognac into two brandy blooms before handing one to Brad as he took a seat beside the library fire which roared and spat in turn. Standing before the fire Piers turned his attention to the young man who was already half way down his brandy desperately trying to find Dutch courage to speak to this rather stern aristocrat. Maudie had relayed the story of Jane's runaway marriage and Brad wondered if that might be the solution in the long run. Piers regarded the young man intently waiting for him to begin but silence ensued and the silence continued except for the sonorous ticking of the long cased clock.

Piers, taking pity on the young man suddenly coughed causing Brad to look up at Maudie's father whose benign look, fortified by good wine and cognac enabled him to find the right words to ask the question which was uppermost in his thoughts.

Chapter 53

Dorothy Maythwaite sat in her brother's sitting room sipping at a glass of sherry. She loved this house belonging to her brother for it had a feeling of grace and luxury about it but it was also homely. It reflected the money that her brother obviously earned although she was never quite sure what he did for a living. He and his wife Jenny seemed quite vague when she asked questions about his frequent absences on business. But her visits here were a world away from her own life in the north and her life with Ralph. Here she basked in the luxury of her brother's success but the rest of the time she was a northern housewife attached to the kitchen sink, waiting on Ralph hand and foot. She felt trapped, wondering why she had married the man in the first place but her quarrels with her parents in her youth had led her to marry the first man who had proposed to her in order to escape one prison only to have found another. But she and Alan had managed to remain close despite everything that had happened over the years. However, Jack had been her favourite brother and his death during the war had upset her deeply and if she was honest more than twenty years on it still did.

'Are you all right, dear?' Jenny asked looking with concern at her sister-in-law. The two women had never been close over the years but Jenny possessed a kind heart and did what she could to ease the path of Dorothy's troublesome existence.

'I am now,' Dorothy said feeling mellower after the sherry had done its job.

'Alan will be down in a few minutes. He has just been having a nap after his flight home. He got home in the early hours. I never seem to know when he will turn up.' Jenny pulled a half smile for she was used to her husband's strange schedule. She had perched on the arm of the sofa trying to soothe Dorothy's rather strange mood. She had not divulged the purpose of her visit but had said that she needed to speak to Alan rather urgently. Jenny was used to Dorothy's odd behaviour and fussiness and was only too pleased that the visits were infrequent.

'Hell and damnation,' both women heard Alan Carson swear as he had nearly tripped over his sister's luggage which had been carelessly abandoned at the bottom of the staircase.

He entered the sitting room, his face red with annoyance at the prospect of his sister's appearance so soon after his return from a particularly difficult assignment. All he had wanted was time alone with his wife whom he had not seen for nearly two months. They deserved some precious time together. Was it not time to give up his line of work he had often wondered but while he was embroiled in the excitement of it he had an adrenalin rush of living on the edge but one could not live like that forever. Dutifully he calmed down before going to kiss his sister on the cheek.

'Nice to see you, Dorothy. It's been a while.'

'I'll go and make some tea,' Jenny said diplomatically, hurrying from the room.

'Well, Dorothy, what is this all about? Jenny says that you are rather anxious at the moment.'

Dorothy, her cheeks flushed, placed her empty sherry schooner on the occasional table in front of her before turning to her brother.

'Oh, Alan, I am so worried.' He could see the anxiety in her eyes and felt a feeling of disquiet wondering what she was about to disclose. But she was always worried. He thought that she might have left her domineering husband and wanted a roof over her head. That would be a disaster but he had to hear her out before he thought the worst.

***

Thea sat up in bed waiting for Piers to finish his conversation with Brad. She knew what it was about for Maudie had told her. Both women were excited but also anxious about what Piers would say on the matter. Thea, though, had a fair idea but was not prepared to disclose what was in her mind. Maudie had to wait to find out. The bedroom door opened and Piers appeared in his night attire having used the connecting dressing room. He walked across the room and climbed into bed, his face was inscrutable.

'Did you have a good conversation with Brad?' Thea asked innocently but Piers was not fooled. Suddenly he smiled his lop sided smile which had always made her heart flip. 'He is such a nice young man.'

Piers chuckled, 'You've known all along what this was about.' He was slurring his words slightly for the contents of the decanter of brandy had been reduced considerably by both men.

Thea remained tight-lipped knowing that Piers would divulge everything in his own time.

'He was asking for Maudie's hand in marriage. At least he had the good manners to do so unlike Dougie.' It still annoyed him that Jane and Douglas had married in Scotland. It was not the done thing in aristocratic circles to elope, but he had to admit it had been better than Jane walking down the aisle the size of a hippopotamus.

Thea remained silent on the matter of Jane's marriage knowing that despite everything it was a very successful union. 'I asked about his prospects for I did not want a gold digger after Maudie's inheritance. But it would seem he is from a wealthy New York family. He does not need to work but loves his music as much as Maudie.'

Thea sighed but continued her silence waiting for the final part of the story.

'I told him straight that I had hoped that my daughter would marry an English aristocrat….'

'Oh Piers, you didn't. What a thing to say.' Thea shuffled in bed to sit up straighter. 'Did you tell him that you did not give your permission?'

'How could I do that? They would have eloped like Jane.'

Thea visibly relaxed. 'I gave our blessing. I know you often think that I am a stuffy old Earl, Thea, but I am not going to lose my children now that we have made our peace.'

Thea's eyes moistened with unshed tears as she turned to give her husband a kiss. 'You're an old softie underneath that crustiness,' she said.

'Glad you think so,' he said as he kissed her again before turning out the bedside light leaving them both to their private thoughts.

***

'You say that your sister said she was being followed,' the boss said writing a note down on a piece of paper. His face was inscrutable to someone who did not know the man but Alan could tell that was not the case.

'She could be being fanciful,' Carson said not sure whether that was the case. But by the sheer nature of his job they could not take risks. On her own merits, Dorothy Maythwaite was of no interest to anybody in particular. Carson knew that his sister led an innocuous life but due to her close kinship to himself it all told a very different story. He was the target of this investigation and they had to know who was behind it all and why.

'Go about your ordinary business now that you are on leave and we will have you watched and then discover who the culprits are.'

Carson was not happy with this but there was nothing he could do about it. He could be a target for a hit man and that was one of the risks you knew about when one was embroiled in espionage. Everything was explained before you signed on the dotted line but he was not prepared to put his wife at risk.

'My wife…,' he began but the boss wafted the implication away.

'Your wife will be protected at all costs, you have my word but your sister must go home. Your wife, we know, will keep her mouth shut. She has proved that time and again. She never asks questions but your sister is an unknown quantity. You have to deal with her firmly and send her on her way.'

Carson looked at his boss knowing that the man was correct but he did not know his sister. The woman enjoyed her visits to London where she enjoyed the attention that they lavished upon her. Now she had to return rather quickly to her boorish husband believing that she was not being followed but it had all been a figment of her rather overactive imagination. But one thing he knew about his sister was the fact that she was far from stupid and if she thought she was being followed she undoubtedly was.

Chapter 54

Thea was happy. Maudie's world was settled and she was wearing the expensive engagement ring that Brad had bought. It was a solitaire and she showed it around with a flourish of enthusiasm. The swift appearance of the ring made Piers believe that the engagement had been a fait accompli just as he had expected. But, his sense of humour was intact as the visit came to its conclusion and Maudie and Brad decided to stay in London for a few days before returning to meet the orchestra in Europe for the final part of the tour after which they were flying to New York to spend time with Brad's family. There was no wedding date settled but the two young people were happy to present to the world the fact that they were an item and content in their lives together.

Thea had transferred her attention to Jane and the promised visit to the Scottish borders. The March days were spring like bringing a new joy as the world opened up after the dreariness of a long winter. Thea had forgotten about her loneliness and the pressure she had placed upon Scarlett to return home for a visit. Scarlett wanted more time to sort out the Carson business but she intended to return to Westborough for the Easter weekend. She was anxious to see her family and explain her recent activities should the outcome of the investigation have been made known to her. The silence from her Private Investigator was unnerving, Josie Marwell had always been so good at informing her at every step of the way and now that Dorothy Maythwaite had been discovered it seemed only a matter of time before her uncle was found as well. Should she tackle Josie again on the issue, after all she had paid a small fortune for the right outcome.

***

Josie Marwell had replaced the telephone receiver in its cradle with a rather shaky hand. She sat gazing into space not knowing what to do or think. Deliberately avoiding Scarlett Devine for the last few weeks, had made her apprehensive as she did not know what to say to the young woman; and now she had been on the telephone demanding what was going on. She wanted results after spending so much money. She had sounded very aristocratic in her manner and had quoted some aspects of the law at her. She was obviously someone to be reckoned with. The investigation had been called off by another source telling her quite categorically that if she did not do so she would be in serious trouble with the authorities. Josie, not a coward by nature, had taken this warning to heart. She still shivered as she thought about what had happened.

    She had been the one who was doing the surveillance outside the Carson home. She did not always use her contacts but wanted to keep her skills honed. There was something exciting to know that she could remain invisible while following somebody; it kept one on the edge, made you feel alive. On this particular day she had parked her vehicle further down the street from the Carson house watching the comings and goings of the members of the household. A taxi had drawn up one day to take a middle-aged woman to the station for she had luggage a plenty. A man and a woman waved her off looking rather relieved at her departure. That must have been the Maythwaite woman from the description she had been given. There was much coming and going but the man she assumed was Alan Carson did not keep regular hours so it was obvious that he was not working and his wife did not appear to leave the house; and then the unexpected happened far too quickly. Now that she reflected on the events of those few hours she wondered about her own skills as a private detective. She was slumped low in the driving seat of her car when a large black vehicle with darkened windows suddenly pulled in in front of her and four doors opened simultaneously, the engine left running. At first she was unaware that she was the victim of a mafia type kidnap as she was bundled out of her car into the limousine but fear overtook her as she was driven off at high speed. There was little to be seen through the darkened windows but the vehicle eventually turned into an underground carpark. Everything suddenly calmed down now that they had turned off the main thoroughfare as the doors opened allowing her to alight from the vehicle and be escorted in a more civilized manner to a nearby staircase which took them upwards into a plush interior displaying offices and an aura of normality. Now as she reflected on the events she realized that nobody had spoken. It was like an event that had been rehearsed many times before. But what these dark suited men with grim expressions etched on their faces wanted with the likes of herself left much to the imagination and her fears only intensified.

    She could hear typewriters clacking in what must have been a typing pool. One brawny man opened the door into an office and she was more gently escorted inside where a man with a benign smile on his face pointed to a chair opposite him. His attention then returned to the stack of papers on the desk.

Josie sat on the chair and began to visibly shake. For all she knew she could have been on a film set of one of the James Bond films which she had watched a couple of years back. What was it called? She was struggling to think and then it flashed through her mind, *From Russia with love*. How she had enjoyed it and for a time had romanticized about being a spy but instead she was working as a private detective finding herself in seedy places which did not resemble anything to do with the movie. Hearing the office door shut with a click she returned to her present situation and the man in the chair coughed making Josie look up to meet his eyes. This time his face was serious.

'Can I have your name please?' he had asked politely enough.

But Josie was beginning to recover. 'Where am I?' She asked.

'I ask the questions. Name please?' He asked again.

'Josie Marwell, Private Investigator.'

The man arched an eyebrow. 'And you have some identification on your person?'

Josie had decided that she wanted to get out of this place. It was too frightening for words. Perhaps she had never had the stomach after all to be a spy. Confusing fact with fiction was not on her agenda now. She delved into her pocket and brought out her card before handing it over.

The man looked at it turning it round in his chubby hands before placing it on the desk in front of him.

'Who is your client?'

'I have lots of clients and there is such a thing as client confidentiality.' This comment had nearly made her smile but not for long.

The man banged his fist on the desk making papers bounce; his face had turned the colour of puce as he struggled to control his anger. Josie's eyes widened in fear.

'I want the name of your client. This is a matter of national security. I demand the name.'

Josie wondered why she was a PI. This was getting her into deep trouble. This was no game. She wanted to be out of here. These people were not to be messed with.

'Can I go if I tell you?' She asked. Her demeanour was pleading and her interviewer not known for his sensitivity felt a little sorry for the young woman. Although she did a risky job there was also a vulnerable quality about her.

The man nodded to answer her question but the expression on his face did not alter as he waited. He was determined to get to the bottom of the mystery.

'Scarlett Devine is her name.'

'Who is she?' He asked.

'Nobody special; I haven't looked into her background. She pays so I do the job. That's it.'

The man lifted his head as his brain assimilated the piece of information. It was a mere woman who wanted the information about Alan Carson. But why? Who did she work for? He could find no answers to his own questions. He knew nobody by that name, but Devine was a name he had heard of but could not quite place. He walked to the door, opened it and nodded to one of the men who sat in the corridor.

'Take her back to her office and bring me the file on this Scarlett Devine.'

Turning to Josie he said, 'I take it you have kept a file.'

She nodded, 'Course I have. I'm a professional.'

The man allowed the comment to pass. He had almost finished with this woman for the moment.

Josie Marwell half rose from her chair, impatient to be gone, only too relieved that the ordeal was not as bad as she feared but the man had not quite finished; there was one last comment to make. 'You will finish this investigation forthwith. Tell your client that you cannot continue. Do you understand?'

She understood all right. There was no way that she was going to mess with these people. 'Righto,' she said standing and straightening her dress.

She was escorted from the building in a more civilized fashion. This time she sat in the passenger seat of a rather ordinary saloon vehicle and was driven more sedately away from the underground car park. As they reached road level she breathed a sigh of relief but could not identify the area of London when they joined the flow of traffic. She did not care as long as they fulfilled their promise to return her to her office where she hoped that she could think straight about events. All this had been a shock to her system.

***

The man was already sending out far reaching fingers to discover more about Scarlett Devine and why she was so interested in Alan Carson. He did not like this at all.

He picked up the internal telephone. 'Send him in.'

Alan Carson knocked and entered the room. He had been awaiting the outcome of all this.

'Sit down, Alan,' his boss indicated the chair that the girl had vacated.

'Do you know a Scarlett Devine from all your travails?' The Boss waited for an answer wishing to clear this mystery as soon as possible.

Carson thought but then shook his head. 'Don't know the name but it could be false.'

'Hmm. Well, we will get to the bottom of it.'

Carson left the room mystified that a woman was trailing him while his boss picked up the telephone once more to put his own investigation in motion.

Chapter 55

Thea had packed her suitcase for a short stay with Jane taking young Amelia with her while Piers had returned to London and the House for the run up to the holiday when Parliament would be in recess. Amelia was excited about the visit but she was also tired by the long, tedious journey which kept her high spirits curtailed in a railway carriage where ageing matrons looked on disapprovingly when the child became too exuberant. But by the time of arriving at their destination Amelia had fallen asleep leaving Thea with the problem of the sleeping child and juggling the luggage. However, a kind young man lifted the suitcase onto the platform while Thea carried her sleeping daughter from the train. There on the platform stood a smiling Jane whose melancholia had dissipated as the months since Christmas had passed. The baby blues seemed well and truly behind her. A porter was hailed to transport the luggage out to the awaiting car. Still carrying her daughter, she managed to negotiate the curves of the back seat to settle the child but to no avail. Amelia woke not knowing what was going on but seeing her mother there she settled once more into a slumber that only a child can achieve.

***

Several days into her visit Thea felt ready to return home. If she was honest she was a little homesick for Westborough and wanted to see Piers. The Scottish spring had turned chilly and Foray House was cold unlike the luxury of Westborough. 'I have grown soft in my old age,' she thought as she wrapped extra layers around her slim body.

Sitting on the edge of her bed her mind wandered over the events of her visit. She had much to tell Piers on her return. Jane was happy with her little family. Dougie was an attentive husband and Archie was obviously very fond of his daughter-in-law.

'She has made so much difference to our lives here,' Archie told Thea one evening after dinner. 'It has been a long time since there was a woman about the hoose.' His Scottish accent was broader as he drank his second dram of malt. Thea had declined anything alcoholic knowing how much the aristocrats could consume of the hard stuff.

She smiled broadly basking in the joy that Jane's presence had brought to this home. How she had grown up in the past few years and turned herself into a wonderful wife and mother. Piers would be very proud of her. Jane had shown Thea around Foray House indicating the improvements that had been made and describing what was to be done next. Her enthusiasm was contagious as Thea sat and listened. Many of the days had been balmy for the time of year allowing for days out and time spent in the great gardens where the children explored and hid from each other. There were outbursts of laughter indicating their delight after being kept indoors during the cold days of winter. But suddenly it turned colder as if the weather was telling them that winter had not quite lost its hold. They were forced back inside and the children became sullen having to be confined to the house once more.

Amelia had also enjoyed her stay. She lived in the nursery quarters at the top of the house with her little Severton relatives. As the oldest child she had been in her element directing proceedings. This was a far cry from home where she lived her solitary life. Leaving Foray House was going to be a wrench for the child. Thea knew that she would have to do something about Amelia's solitary state when they returned to Westborough Hall even if it was to invite local children to come and play. Before too long Thea worried that she would have lost this child to the world of preparatory school and the mere thought filled her with foreboding as it had on all the occasions when her children went away to school. It was a mother's lot but the youngest child's departure would be the hardest of all to endure. But Amelia had been sent to them as a bonus and Thea knew that every moment with this precious child was to be enjoyed to the full.

Chapter 56

Thea had returned home full of joie de vivre. Piers was amused at her happy state of mind, knowing that their time apart had renewed their desire to be together. Thea talked endlessly of her days spent with Jane and her children. Piers felt at peace knowing that Jane was happy with her lot and that everything was improving.

Easter had arrived and with it the arrival of the young Devines and Scarlett. Thea was amazed at how adult the young ones appeared all of a sudden but most particularly Harry. He was facing his final term at Eton before going up to Oxford in the autumn. He appeared serious and studious knowing that he must achieve his grades. He had come home armed with textbooks and notes for revision purposes and only made an appearance at meal times.

'He appears rather worried,' Thea had said to Piers as they sat one evening in her sitting room enjoying a glass of good claret.

Piers laughed. 'He knows that it is serious now. He will pass his examinations with flying colours. He is intelligent like all the rest of our brood. He wants a law career like Scarlett and that will only come with working. By the way is Scarlett all right? I have found her rather quiet, almost brooding at times.'

Thea's brow had puckered at her husband's words. She had felt the same way and had been tempted to take her aside to ask if anything was the matter but as usual when the family was at home she became distracted by their needs and different demands on her time. Verity had wanted time with her mother. She had demanded shopping trips and required new school uniform. This daughter had grown considerably in recent months and her interests were becoming those of an older teenager. Thea thought that Scarlett might have shown more interest in her younger sister this holiday but that was not the case. It was all very disturbing. Although she was the mother and stepmother of numerous children, Thea found it quite strange how different in character they appeared. There never seemed a time when she could sit back and sigh with relief that her world was calm and untroubled.

Scarlett was brooding. Piers had been quite correct. She had hoped that she could return to Westborough Hall with news about her natural father. She so much wished to reveal what had been uppermost in her mind but all her efforts had turned to nothing. Josie Marwell had suddenly faded from the scene saying that her investigation into her father's family had proved futile. She had offered to pay Scarlett back for some of the fees. She did not wish to gain the reputation of extracting money by false pretences. Some of her work came from word of mouth from clients who had found her efficient and gained results from her efforts. But Scarlett Devine was another kettle of fish. There was something going on there that had unnerved her. She did not wish to become entangled with those kind of people whoever they were. Josie's overactive imagination could guess but she was not going to try and find out any more. Since her release from their clutches she had been looking over her shoulder wondering if she was being followed. Their skills in that direction were far superior to her own. As the days had turned into weeks and nothing had happened she began to relax and look for a more mundane type of assignment that would pay the bills and would be over quickly. The wealthy like Scarlett Devine would be a thing of the past she thought. She had no desire to serve them again.

***

The Easter weekend had been unexciting. Every member of the family appeared to have their own agenda, only coming together for meals and then there seemed little joie de vivre. Thea had retreated to the kitchen garden to begin the chore of preparing it for planting. This had always been an escape for her over time. Amelia spent much of her time with her mother and a puppy which had been given to the family, chasing it around the network of paths that divided the little vegetable areas. She was in her element particularly when she knew her mother seemed preoccupied. They did not need to constantly talk but it was companionship and comforting to know the other was there.

Piers was enjoying time out on the land, walking and overseeing what urgent jobs needed doing before summer. Scarlett was finding it hard to occupy herself. She was missing Jane and Maudie who were engrossed in their own lives and with their menfolk. Scarlett's lack of a romantic interlude did not worry her. She was not ready for such distractions but she knew that she required some mental occupation to fill her days to prevent the frustration she felt over the lack of information about Alan Carson. The idea of going to see Dorothy Maythwaite had begun to creep into her head but she had to formulate a plan before taking action. Her thoughts had taken her to the law firm who was employing her from the autumn. Perhaps she would investigate whether she could begin sooner. They could only say no. She would return to London after the holiday and see what would happen. But was she truly ready for work with so many distractions commanding her attention.

Before the younger Devines were to return to school there was a sudden change to events that seemed to throw the family into freefall. Piers enjoying the change in the spring weather sat under a tree at the front of the hall drinking a cup of coffee. His attire was casual making him look more of an estate worker than the owner of the estate. He was enjoying a moment's solitude before his return to the House after the Easter recess. If he was honest he wanted to remain at Westborough with Thea. Politics and its demands were becoming a trial. He never believed that he would ever think this way but perhaps he was ready for retirement. His health had given him a few worries of late. He could not quite pinpoint what it was except for feelings of weariness. He had not visited the doctor feeling that he would appear foolish nor had he told Thea who would have fussed making him in some ways feel worse although her intentions were of the very best. He smiled when he thought of Thea. They deserved more time together. She had been stalwart in their marriage. She was the glue that kept the family together. He tilted his face upwards enjoying the intensity of the sun's rays, suddenly feeling a moment of peace and contentment. Then, he heard the sound of a vehicle approaching, wending its way along the long drive.

Curiosity had aroused him. There were no visitors expected but he stood up and leaned on the shovel that he had been using earlier watching as the car drew nearer. It was a black limousine with darkened windows obliterating any chance to see inside and who the visitor might be. The vehicle drew to a halt near him. Now Piers was totally intrigued. He lifted his flat cap from his head and scratched his head as he had seen some of the elderly gardeners do over the years. There was mud on his face from his efforts on the land. He scratched it away self-consciously.

A back passenger door opened and a rather tall man with greying, thick hair alighted. He was dressed in a dark suit which had been sharply cut, possibly from a Saville Row tailor. The other passenger door opened and another man disembarked. He was younger than his colleague but equally smartly dressed. Piers was bemused by the whole proceedings.

'Could you point me in the direction of the Earl of Westborough; that's assuming that he is at home,' the older man asked, his voice clear with a note of authority.

Piers smiled, amused that his dress code did not give away his true identity. He could play along with this but curiosity had engulfed him.

'I'm Piers Devine;' he smiled affably and immediately noticed the change in demeanour on the part of the two men. 'I like to get involved with the estate whenever I can.' He did not need to explain but something had prompted him to do so.

'May we go inside, sir? We have something of importance to discuss with you,' the older of the two men said.

'Can you tell me who you are first?' Piers was puzzled by the formality of the two men. He detected something serious here. His mind fled to thoughts of Maudie and Brad. Jane was in the country and the Severtons would have telephoned if something had been wrong.

The two men took out documents from the inside pockets of their jackets and handed them over for Piers' perusal. He frowned before handing them back.

The chauffeur slowly manoeuvred the vehicle into a more appropriate parking space while Piers led the men towards the house allowing his spade to lean against the ancient walls of the Hall. He wondered what all this was about but it was official from what he detected.

Chapter 57

Piers led the two visitors across the impressive entrance hall towards the library. There was nobody about but the library door was closed. He turned the handle hoping that there was nobody inside. Harry had taken to doing some of his revision there for the space offered him opportunity to spread his books about on the grand table. However, on this occasion there was nobody there. A fire had recently been stoked up making the interior warm and inviting. Although the spring day was warm the library felt cold until the full blast of summer had arrived allowing the mullioned windows to be thrown wide. Ushering the visitors inside Piers closed the heavy panelled door and indicated a seat.

'Could I get you anything? Tea, coffee or something stronger.'

The tray of decanters occupied a side table. Piers went to pour himself a finger of whisky. It was not the time of day when he would normally drink. He had not had to resort to that just yet. He held up his tumbler to the men.

'Yes that would be fine, sir,' the older man spoke for both of them.

Piers took a sip of his whisky suddenly feeling rather nervous for the first time. He handed each man a generous measure before taking a seat at the great table.

'How can I help you, gentlemen?' He asked. 'This seems rather formal.'

'It may be or it might not,' the older man still answered. The taciturn one sat and allowed his whisky to swirl around in his glass as he looked around the impressive room. The words 'how the other half live' had drifted through his mind but to the onlooker his face remained impassive, a habit he had been at great pains to cultivate over time.

'Well, sir, I might as well get to the point. You are a member of Her Majesty's government or rather have been. I have been given permission to tell you that we are MI6 agents.'

Piers gripped his glass so hard that he wondered if it would splinter. 'And why do you need to see me?'

'I have been followed just recently by a private detective who was employed by a woman by the name of Scarlett Devine. My department is a little nervous about the reasoning behind it. The woman we have been told is a relative of yours.'

Piers put the glass of whisky down on the table before it broke in his grip, wondering what Scarlett had been up to. 'She is my daughter, or to be correct my stepdaughter. I have no knowledge of why she would have you followed. Who did you say you were?'

The older man pulled out his identity papers once more and slid them across the table. His colleague did the same. Piers picked up the first, perusing it carefully. He wondered why his brain had not fully computed the names the first time round. He also saw that both men were members of MI6 just as they had said. It was no wonder that there was such furore about being followed.

'Alan Carson,' he had read and suddenly a light seemed to flash in his brain. 'Are you Jack Carson's brother?'

'Yes, I am. We have never met before have we, sir?'

'No,' Piers said but he suddenly laughed now realizing what Scarlett had been up to in recent months and why her mood had been so bleak since her return home for the Easter vacation. 'Let me tell you that you have nothing to worry about. Scarlett is really Scarlett Carson, Jack's only child. She was very young, just a baby, when her father died in North Africa.'

Alan Carson sat in his chair trying to absorb all that he had been told. He had never known that Jack had been married and had a child. There were questions on his lips but Piers forestalled him as he continued. 'Scarlett's mother, Thea, was married to Jack very briefly. She has been my wife since the end of the War. Scarlett has been very interested in her father's side of the family for quite some time, but I did not realize that she had gone to such lengths to find you. She has been staying with us over Easter and has said not a word.'

'Is she still here, sir?' Alan Carson asked.

'Yes she is still here. I suspect for a few more days.' Piers rose from his seat having finished his malt. He wondered about having a top up but decided against it. Now that he knew what this was about he did not require the support of the amber liquid. He needed to keep his wits about him.

'If you will excuse me I will go and find out where my wife is. She should be able to tell you more.'

Piers left the room closing the door behind him with a small click. The two men still drinking their rather fine malt looked at each other and then broke into laughter.

'I bet you are relieved, boss,' the younger man said matter of factly.

'Too true; it is a surprise that Jack had a family. He kept that close to his chest but I hadn't seen him for a while before his death. I don't think that he told our parents. He was always a bit like that. A bit of a loner but then the war came along and changed everything.'

The younger man mulled over the piece of information, wondering what Jack Carson had been really like.

***

Piers had found Thea coming out of the boot room. Her cheeks were flushed by the warmth of the spring day and her exertions. She looked particularly beautiful he thought. But this was not the moment to be thinking of such things as he turned his mind back to the real purpose of why he wanted to see her.

'There you are. I have been looking for you. There are some people here you should meet,' he said.

'Who?' She asked brushing a smudge of soil from her cheek.

'You will see,' he said mysteriously.

'Piers, I can't greet people like this. I look a fright. My hair is…' She did not complete her sentence.

'Thea, stop it. You look particularly beautiful. I must warn you that one of the visitors is going to be a shock to you. A case of déjà vu. '

Now totally intrigued she followed Piers across the great hall, first of all stopping in her little sitting room to make herself more presentable as she looked into the mirror which stood on top of the mantlepiece. Eventually satisfied that she had done as much as she could to rectify the damage that the spring day had done she followed her husband to the library, taking note that both their attires made them look like the estate workers rather than the owners.

Chapter 58

Alan Carson rose from his chair as the Earl and his Countess entered the room. He regarded the woman who had been his brother's wife and could instantly see what his brother had seen in her all those years ago. Time had not withered her beauty and he felt drawn to her for some reason.

Stretching out his hand for Thea to shake, he said, 'Alan Carson.'

Thea shook his hand but looked at him blankly, trying to place him but failing badly. Piers had not informed her of the situation so now he had to rectify the situation. 'I'm Jack's brother,' he said.

Alan watched as the cogs turned slowly in Thea's brain. Eventually, she said 'Jack did not have a brother.'

Alan smiled, amused at Thea's disbelief. 'I'm afraid he did and a sister as well as parents.'

'Why did he lie to me? He said that he had no family.'

Piers said nothing but watched as the story began to unfold.

'I was in the SOE at its first outset in the War and it was better that nobody knew. My parents never knew nor my sister. But Jack found out by some means but we tacitly agreed that it was easier to say that he had no family. We did not speak again and never knew that he had married or had a child. He never told the rest of the family either.'

Thea sat down on one of the library chairs, suddenly seeing Jack's face vividly in her mind's eye. He was laughing as he was prone to do, living every day to the full. Thea had felt that she could not conjure up his face as the years had passed but here he was as large as life. She felt that she had been married to Piers for a lifetime and Jack had ceased to exist except that of course Scarlett was a constant living reminder of their coupling but Thea these days thought of her daughter as a Devine. Piers looked concerned for Thea's face had turned pale despite the exertion of her time in the kitchen garden. She remained silent as the images whirled through her mind. All three men watched her intently.

'Thea, are you all right?' Piers asked, concern etching his features.

'Yes,' she said, 'just a bit shocked, that's all.'

'I'm sorry to do this to you, but we had to know who was following me. The agency had to find out for obvious reasons.'

'What do you mean who was following you?' Thea asked not fully up to speed about what had been happening.

'Scarlett has been having me followed,' Carson said.

'Oh.' Thea flopped down onto one of the library chairs. So that was what her daughter had been up to. She fully understood what it was all about now. Scarlett used whichever surname that suited her whim of the moment.

Piers said, 'I think that we fully understand what has been happening but we need to tell Scarlett the whole story so that she becomes used to the idea. Have you a telephone number where she can reach you once she is used to the idea. She lives in London for most of the year. Perhaps you could arrange to meet her on neutral territory.'

'I had hoped to meet her on this occasion,' Carson said, his voice sounding heavy with disappointment.

'Well, you can see what it has done to my wife so I would like Scarlett to be forewarned despite the fact that she has initiated all of this.'

Carson detected the note of authority in Piers' voice for after all he was a peer of the realm. They had that je ne sais quoi about them. Knowing that he would not make any headway if he argued his corner, he capitulated before handing a telephone number to the Earl who took it and then placed it in the pocket of his trousers.

'I'll walk you to your vehicle,' Piers said, 'and Scarlett will be in touch as soon as possible.'

Piers glanced with concern at his wife and was happy to see the colour returning to her face. She smiled at the men and held out her hand to be shaken as they made their goodbyes. As soon as she heard the front door shut, she left the library and walked slowly to the boot room door making her way out into the gardens. She needed to be alone for a while to think about what had happened and how she was going to explain to Scarlett the story which had unfolded. For the moment she still could not get Jack out of her mind. He was like a ghost who had returned to haunt her. It was all too disturbing for words. She could not face Piers yet either. It was as if her two husbands were facing each other for the first time. Thea knew she was being fanciful but that was exactly how it seemed.

Chapter 59

Scarlett had returned to London in a state of euphoria. She had never wished to upset her mother or Piers but she needed to know about her father and his family. She had the telephone number safely in her handbag and was going to make contact with the Carsons as soon as she was home in her apartment. However, she felt slightly nervous as well as wondering if she was going to open a Pandora's Box by what she had started. But she had begun this investigation and now had to see it through.

Piers had left it to Thea to tell Scarlett about the visit. He had felt that this was out of his domain; Jack was Scarlett's father after all and Thea had been his wife. At these thoughts, Piers knew that he was jealous despite the fact that Jack had been dead for over twenty years. It was part of Thea's life that he could not share and over time they had been honest and open with each other. But he had witnessed Thea's reactions almost as if her dead husband had walked into the room. Piers knew he was being foolish about the whole business and just as Thea had disappeared into the garden to gather her thoughts, so Piers had found sanctuary in his study to try and come to terms with it all. He had also reneged on his promise to himself and made a detour to the library to find the whisky decanter, pouring a large glass to drown the emotions he felt to be ridiculous. Thea was his wife but the past appeared to have a way of haunting the present. He could not confess his feelings of jealousy but he remembered with great clarity how Thea had had to cope with Mary all those years ago.

Thea, once she had gathered her wits had found Scarlett in her bedroom reading. This had been her passion over the Easter vacation, partly because it would prevent her brooding upon events of the previous few weeks. She glanced up when she heard her bedroom door open and her mother stood there regarding her. It was so unlike Thea to walk straight into a room without knocking for she was a stickler for etiquette as she liked to have time and space away from the family and was one to respect that the others might feel the same.

'May I come in?' She eventually asked closing the door without waiting for a reply. She sat down on the edge of the bed as close as she could to her daughter, taking her hand in her own.

'Why didn't you tell us that you had been looking for Jack's family?' She asked without prevarication.

Scarlett looked surprised. 'How did you find out?'

'Did you not hear the visitors this afternoon?'

'Yes, but I did not know who they were. I just heard voices and then they stopped when a door banged shut.'

'I don't like it when you keep secrets, Scarlett. I have always said that you can talk to me about anything. You know I say that to all the children.'

'I know, Mama. But this was something that I wanted to do. I thought it had ended a few weeks ago without success. And now suddenly....'

Thea continued to regard her daughter wondering if she knew her at all. But suddenly she smiled. Nothing was going to come between herself and her oldest child. Scarlett returned the smile and squeezed her mother's hand. Thea recounted the events of the afternoon while Scarlett listened intently.

'Was Alan Carson like my father to look at?' She asked eventually when Thea had finished the story.

Thea thought for a moment. Jack's face seemed to have receded from her mind's eye almost as suddenly as it had appeared.

'I do believe there is a look of Jack about him, but a much older version. Jack possibly would have looked more like his brother if he had been here today. Remember I only knew the young Jack. I did not know him very well for we had such little time together but this new uncle should bring him into focus for you. He should have photos of him from their childhood. That should make everything more alive for you. It does seem strange to think that we never had a photograph taken together. But that was the War for you. Everything happened so quickly. Life moved at a pace but we lived in the moment. There was never a future for we did not know what would happen tomorrow. We lived life to the full and never allowed ourselves to look forward for it would be like looking into an abyss.' Thea said.

Scarlett watched her mother's face as she reflected on the past. She had never really heard her mother talk much about the war and her own memories were dim, almost non-existent. They had been times which had caused much heartache she thought. Scarlett remained totally unaware of the guilt which had reared its head in her mother's heart. The fact that Jack had not meant that much to her was a hidden memory, a fact that she could never reveal to her daughter ever.

Chapter 60

Scarlett picked up the telephone receiver in her apartment and looked at the number on the piece of paper Thea had given her. Her heart appeared to miss a beat. The receiver returned to its cradle with a thud. Rising from her chair she walked to the mantelpiece to look at her reflection in the mirror noting the paleness of her skin. She had wanted to make this contact for years but was afraid that it would change her life for good. What if her father did not live up to the expectations that she had imagined of him? And then she remembered his posthumous medal for bravery which she kept with pride in her bedroom at Westborough Hall. That was enough to tell her about her father.

She could remember Piers saying once that it was circumstances like the war which brought out the courage and the measure of a person. If they had not experienced such events they would not know their own capabilities. Scarlett now understood what he had meant.

Returning to the telephone with a measure of courage she dialled the number and waited. A male voice answered. She listened to the timbre of his voice as he enunciated his words. Somehow she could not place the accent but it was definitely a regional accent tinged with received pronunciation. It was a little odd she felt.

'Is that Mr Carson?' She asked realizing that no name had been given.

There was a smile in his voice as he answered with a question. 'Scarlett?'

'Yes,' she answered then laughed now feeling more relaxed.

'I am glad that you have telephoned. It is good to hear from you. Would you like to come and meet us for dinner?' Her uncle asked, his voice light with relief that at last she had rung.

'Yes, I would. When and where?'

'Tonight here. My wife, Jenny, says she will cook. She is an excellent cook. Our daughter, Joan, will be home too. We are looking forward to meeting you.'

It felt silly to be so surprised that Alan Carson had a family. Why should he not? It also felt strange to suddenly find so many new relatives.

'Thank you,' she said, 'I would love to come.'

She wrote down the address and when the telephone receiver was replaced in its cradle, she suddenly felt elated that a whole new life beckoned.

Chapter 61

Scarlett dressed carefully to meet this new family. It was going to be difficult to know if her ensemble was going to feel right but she decided that a dress in pastel shades under a red jacket was the right choice. Her high heeled shoes and clutch bag were also red. Surveying herself in the mirror she was pleased with her reflection feeling stylish but not too overcooked as her mother would sometimes say. She had left her reddish hair loose having softly curled it but it framed her face prettily making her look younger than her years.

The taxi transported her through the still busy early evening London streets into North London and then into unfamiliar territory before pulling up outside a large terraced house. She sat gazing around to drink in everything. This was definitely not Devine affluence she thought before chiding herself for her snobbishness but this could have been a life she could have lived if it had taken her down a different path. There was nothing wrong in being middle class but Scarlett knew that she was a pampered spoilt girl and wealth was always going to play a major part in her life.

The driver turned in his seat puzzled by the delay in his passenger disembarking. Scarlett, noticing his movement, was aroused from her reverie and dug deeply into her bag to find the money for her fare.

'Here you are. Keep the change,' she said leaning forward towards the internal window of the cab thrusting several notes at the driver.

As she climbed out of the vehicle the driver touched his peaked cap as a thank you and was ready to drive to his next fare. Almost at that moment, as Scarlett stood on the pavement clutching her handbag tightly to her, the front door opened and a kindly face greeted her. So this was Alan Carson she thought taking a long, hard look at her father's twin brother; she saw a middle-aged man and made an assessment of him taking note of the tall athletic figure. His hair was greying at the temples making him appear rather distinguished and undeniably handsome. Would her father have been the double of this man had he lived, she wondered but life's journey tended to treat even siblings differently whether kindly or badly. But her father had died long ago so these thoughts were pointless.

'Come in, come in,' Alan said hospitably opening the door wider. Although time played tricks on memories he saw a family resemblance in Scarlett and could not wait to get to know her. It still seemed impossible to have a niece after all this time. Before she was hardly over the threshold he had leaned forward to kiss her cheek. She had flushed with embarrassment not quite knowing how to react but from nowhere two female figures greeted her and guided her into the sitting room. It was all happening too quickly, Scarlett felt suddenly full of apprehension at meeting with these strangers. But this had been what she had wanted for so long now.

A glass of sherry had been thrust into her hand as she sat in a wing backed chair in the spacious sitting room. Opposite sat Alan feasting on the sight of her, drinking in every facet of her sophistication. She felt bemused and tongue tied, feelings that were alien to her normal self. The two women, obviously her aunt and cousin, disappeared diplomatically to make tea, leaving Scarlett to face Alan Carson alone.

'Well I never expected to find that I had a niece after all these years,' he smiled at her.

'I never knew I had a family other than the Devines or my mother's family. 'She returned the smile. Continuing she said, 'could you tell me something about my father?'

Alan was silent for a moment gathering his thoughts. It was only in recent weeks that he had thought about Jack. It had been a long time since he had thought about his brother. He coughed before continuing looking Scarlett straight in the eye.

'Your father and I were close as boys. We were twins,' he began.' We did a lot together, getting into trouble with the local village bobby and our parents, teasing our sister Dorothy. The adults would give us a stern warning and that would be the end of it. We grew up in Devon but the war parted us. I speak fluent French and was drafted into the SOE at the outset of War. I couldn't tell anyone, not even my closest family but somehow Jack found out and I had to swear him to secrecy. He took it a bit to heart so when he joined up we saw little of each other. It was a shame but the War did things like that to people. He never told us that he had married and had a child. I suppose we all thought that the War would end one day and if we came through unscathed we would all be reunited. The motto, though, was live for now. But one can never take such things for granted.' His face showed signs of sadness and Scarlett felt his pain. Her generation did not really understand how their parents had suffered. Life was good all these years on.

Scarlett who had been listening intently suddenly said, 'but my father told my mother that he had no family. What was that about?'

Alan frowned as he thought. This interlude in the conversation gave Scarlett a moment to look at her surroundings again noticing for the first time the antiques which were set around the room indicating that there was no lack of money or taste but it was a kind of faded glory. Again she felt guilt at her first perceptions of this new family. Not many people lived like the Devines at Westborough. The long case clock chimed the hour making her realize just how hungry she felt.

She was instantly brought back to the present when she heard Alan say, 'Jack fell out with our parents before the war but kept in touch with our sister Dorothy. She did not see much of him particularly after he joined up. That must have been the reason. I can't think of another.'

'Did you know that he had died a hero?'

Alan saw the immense pride on her face which made him smile. Thea had told him that Scarlett held a torch for her courageous father in her heart.

'Sadly, not until the end of the war. I had wanted to find Jack but my investigations told me what had happened. I had wanted to mend the rift between us all but my parents had died during the early part of the War. It was all so immensely sad. They would have been so proud of him had they known.'

Again Scarlett detected the sadness in his voice but he made light of it all showing that time could be a healer and it was best not to dwell too long on the past. As time went on there would be many questions to ask but for now it was to take these new relationships slowly. Her aunt and cousin Joan returned with trays laden with afternoon tea and this was the excuse to turn the tide in the conversation.

***

When Scarlett returned to her apartment she could not sleep. She had left the Carson's home at quite a late hour returning by taxi through the lively London streets. She knew that New York was meant to be the city that never slept but at that moment she felt that could apply to the British capital. She had let herself into her apartment and for once was glad that Maudie was still away. Her mind needed to assimilate all she had been told. She wanted to begin to draw a picture of her father in her head adding to it as she learned more about him. He was at last becoming real to her. She had poured herself a very large glass of wine before curling up on the sofa to think. The room was in darkness except for the headlights of passing traffic illuminating the walls briefly before everything returned to the comfort of the dark. Thea had asked her to telephone to let her know how the visit had gone but that would be tomorrow for tonight was her own to reflect on what she had discovered.

She pondered first of all on Alan Carson. She felt it was too soon to call him Uncle Alan. Perhaps she never would. Only time would tell on that score. But as for the man she had warmed to him as he had spoken affectionately about her father. Jack had obviously been a bit of a lad in his youth but he had fallen out with his parents. As there had been so much to talk about Scarlett had lacked the presence of mind to discover the true reasons behind that but there was the next time for she had agreed to visit them again soon. Alan had said that he would telephone her with a date. But what had taken Scarlett's breath away was the Carson photograph album. There were childhood photos of the whole family. Her grandparents had looked stern as they posed for the camera with their three children. Dorothy as the only girl had taken centre stage but there was Jack to the left smiling broadly, mischief gleaming in his eyes while Alan stood more erect, his demeanour serious. But it was Jack who had fascinated her. It was his humour which shone out, endorsed by Alan and her mother but most of all it was the first time that she had seen him in the flesh so to speak. The two brothers were identical and as Scarlett looked at Alan she could almost believe that she was looking at her father. As the pages were turned there were other photographs of Jack as he grew up until they reached the final one which must have been taken at the onset of war. This was the man whom her mother had seen and married. Scarlett had known for a long time that Piers had been the love of Thea's life for so long but she must have seen something in Jack to marry him. That was another story which she would pursue in the future but now she had to be content with what she had found out. Reaching for the lamp on the small table, she turned it on to look at the small photograph that had remained in her hand since she had left the Carsons' home behind. Alan had taken it out of the album knowing that Scarlett was entitled to it more than any of them. Now she regarded Jack, a roguish smile on his face as he drew on a cigarette and looked directly down the camera lens into her eyes. Her eyes filled with tears as she regarded the man she had never known. There was no way that the clock could be turned back and she placed the snapshot on to the coffee table before turning off the light as she headed for bed.

Chapter 62

Thea, if she was perfectly honest with herself, had to admit to a feeling of intense jealousy. She had not discussed her emotions with anybody feeling rather foolish but Piers who knew his wife better than anyone had found her very insecure over a period of some weeks. He had discovered it by little questions that Thea asked and little comments that she made. What it boiled down to was the fact that Scarlett's time was being claimed by this new family. She had visited them frequently over several weeks, making her comments very favourable when she spoke of the Carsons. 'Jenny's wonderful. She makes me feel so welcome,' she would enthuse down the telephone to her mother. There were comments that they had visited the West End shopping several times. She had enjoyed her cousin, Joan's company and they had talked about university where she was going in the autumn if she had the right grades. She so desperately wanted to go to Cambridge to read languages. She had a natural flair for them like her parents.

'When are you coming home for a weekend?' Thea would ask despondently but the answer was always the same.

'Soon, Mama but I have to go and see the Carsons over the weekend,' she would say and so it went on.

Thea had never had to share Scarlett with anybody before. The girl had a dead father and if she was honest her relationship with Piers, although on a much better footing, had never been close. The bond between mother and daughter had always been close except for the rare occasions when they did fall out. Piers had worked out what was the matter and felt Thea's negativity could not go on forever.

On Sunday night as they sat down for dinner in the small dining room, Piers had opened a bottle of white wine, one of the best in the Westborough cellar and poured Thea the biggest glass that he could find. She did not usually drink much alcohol but after some protest she capitulated and drank thirstily. Piers topped up her glass and for the first time in weeks he could see her visibly relax. This was his moment to have words.

'This will not last forever you know, darling.'

Thea looked up and stared at her husband. 'What won't last forever?'

'This with Scarlett. The Carsons are new to her. They will never replace you in her heart.'

Thea looked at her husband, seeing the lopsided smile on his face that she had always loved. She knew there was no point in denying how she felt. She could bluster all she liked but there were times when Piers could be very intuitive. Tears filled her eyes and she blushed. Her husband stretched his hand across the table in a gesture of the love they still shared and took her hand. He noticed that she had hardly eaten a thing. Releasing her hand, he stood up.

'Come upstairs,' he said smiling sweetly at her as if they were in the first flush of a love affair. Suddenly she giggled like the girl she had once been and the tension which had been building for weeks was at last broken. The detritus of their meal was left behind for cook to cluck over but they would never know. Entering the bedroom, Piers took Thea in his arms and kissed her. They sat side by side on the bed but there was one thing that Piers had to say to her.

'You know, Thea, you have to be aware that one day Scarlett will probably marry and you won't be the most important person in her life any more. You will be one of them.'

'I know,' she said, 'I have accepted it with Jane and Maudie, haven't I.'

'I know that you love Jane and Maudie but you did not give birth to them. You and Scarlett were joined at the hip for many years before the younger Devines came along. There is some bond other than natural motherhood which binds you together.'

Thea did not bother to argue with Piers for she knew that he was correct. He had said what he wanted to and now he took her in his arms and began to kiss her as if that was all that mattered in the world and it was.

***

Scarlett had enjoyed her time with the Carsons. They were a close family and enjoyed each other's company. By being with them she felt closer to her father. Over those weeks Alan would tell anecdotes about his childhood and these would invariably include her father. She was building a mental image of Jack. He had been devil may care, not allowing life to get him down. All these reminiscences began to knit together with her mother's picture of him and the brief love affair that they had shared. The war had kept life on the edge, there was a sharpness about not wanting to miss anything as if there was no tomorrow. Scarlett was beginning to see what life had been like all those years ago. And like a drug she wanted more of it; it was like an addiction. She saw how the year was advancing and her freedom was being eroded. Before she knew it she would be starting work and then the real world would beckon. She did not know what she wanted but she could not defer the inevitable. Piers and her mother would lecture her just as they had done during the years when she, Maudie and Jane had been teenagers, tearaways wasting their time at school.

Summer had arrived. It was hot; London streets were dry and dusty. Scarlett had decided to spring clean the apartment. The windows were flung wide but the rooms seemed no cooler and the relentless noise from the streets rose and filled the air. The air was still and stuffy, not like the fragrant breeze that often blew through the gardens and land of Westborough Hall. It brought back a feeling of nostalgia, of childhood and her other family and if she was honest the family that meant the most to her. This new family would never quite compensate for the one she had known all her life. New relationships were not built in a moment. They had to be nurtured and that took a long time. She never thought to utter these thoughts to her mother.

Into these thoughts that had filled her mind as she scrubbed and washed stepped Piers. He was dressed in a suit, carrying a brief case and the times as he habitually did. He sat tentatively on the edge of her sofa looking hot and bothered and out of place amongst her detritus. It was all she could do not to giggle but the look on his features forbade it. It was the look of her childhood when the children knew that they were going to be told off.

'Can I get you a drink, papa? Hot or cold?'

'No thank you,' he said curtly.

Scarlett waited for him to continue but she had noticed a slight softening of his expression when she had used the familial 'papa.'

'I have come,' he began pompously using his aristocratic bearing, 'to tell you about your mother.' His voice trailed off. Scarlett rose from her chair and stood facing him.

'You don't have to tell me. I have been rather a pig lately. I have worked it all out while I have been doing this.' She flung her arms wide as if her stepfather had not taken cognizance of the mess. She had noticed him blanch at her use of language. He had paid for a good education for her and wished that she showed it in a more ladylike fashion.

'I take it that you will go to Westborough soon to see you mother.'

'Yes, next week. Can I ask you something, Papa?'

Piers had thought that the battle would be more difficult but suddenly the fight had gone out of him.

'Yes,' he said in a more conciliatory tone.

'Alan Carson wants me to travel to North Africa with him to see Jack's grave. He feels that it will put some of the ghosts to rest for me. What should I do?'

'Piers looked at her for a long moment. 'What do you want to do?' he asked.

'I think Alan is right. I do want to go.'

'Then go. I think Carson could be right, but first of all for goodness sake go and see your mother. She is so worried about all this.'

Piers bent to kiss her cheek. His mood had changed and his humour fully restored. She had returned to the fold where she rightly belonged. The fact, that she had addressed him as 'papa,' had filled his heart to overflowing but he had no intention of telling her. That was the one area where he still failed; it was a lesson he was still learning.

Scarlett watched him depart through the open windows, about to hail a taxi to make his return to the Devine Town house. As she watched him go a lump rose in her throat and a feeling of true affection flooded through her. He was a funny old thing she thought. It was no wonder her mother loved him to distraction.

Chapter 63

It had all happened so quickly. As she had promised Piers she had returned to Westborough Hall to see her mother. Guilt had consumed her about the neglect of Thea, the only true parent she had known. She had put her small suitcase down on the great hall floor and looked around her. She had never told her mother that she was coming, wanting to surprise her. She walked straight across the hall to her mother's sitting room and opened the door. As usual Thea was catching up with her correspondence. Glancing up to see who had intruded on her peace, her spectacles sliding down her nose giving her a stern expression, she dropped her pen on the table in her excitement, stumbling towards her daughter to give her a huge hug. Piers had never told her about his visit to Scarlett in London. He had every confidence that Scarlett would visit her mother.

'You should have said you were coming,' Thea gently admonished her daughter but a smile hovered on her lips. The two women hugged without reservation and the unhappiness of past days had disappeared into the ether.

***

Now as she sat beside Alan Carson in the British Airways aeroplane on the flight to Cairo she could hardly believe what was happening. Just five days after returning to London from Westborough, her uncle had arrived unannounced at her apartment waving the flight tickets. They were leaving in three days to visit her father's grave in the Commonwealth Cemetery at El Alamein.

During the flight Alan told Scarlett about his first visit to the war graves several years before. 'Having worked for the SOE during the War I thought I had seen everything but there is nothing that will prepare you for the emotions that surface when you see the rows of white head stones, the graves so immaculately kept. It was the flower of youth that had died for their homeland, many as young as eighteen or nineteen. They had never experienced life as such and then there is the grave of a loved one and that tears you apart. I want you to be prepared, Scarlett.'

She nodded taken aback by the emotion in his voice. He was once more reliving that time very vividly in his mind.

'I will be,' she promised but felt nervous at the prospect.

They both remained silent for a while lost in thought.

This was the first time Scarlett had flown. It was never that the Devines could not afford to travel abroad anywhere they wanted but the fault lay with Piers. Thea had often suggested that they could go to the South of France or the United States but he had steadfastly refused. It was by chance that the reasoning had been revealed. It lay with the war when he had been abroad for five years without the chance of leave with his incarceration in the POW camp. Thea had told Scarlett one day during her visit to Westborough. Having discovered where her daughter was heading in just a short time. They had been sitting in a sheltered part of the garden sipping at a morning coffee. Then Thea had revealed Piers' revelation.

'Come with us,' Scarlett had said.

Thea had shaken her head sadly. 'Jack is too far back in my life now. I have to look forward. Piers would find it strange and there is Amelia too.' A whole string of excuses were found but Scarlett had no argument with her mother's reasons. She understood that her father had not filled her mother's life owing to their short time together. Time had made her grow up and she knew that the candle she had held for her dead father would one day be quenched but this was the last act that she would do on that journey to solve the mystery of Jack. She had learned much from the Carsons about the man, the young Jack. Of course there would never be an older Jack so now she was about to turn the last page of his life's story and then he could rest in peace as he so deserved.

Scarlett's experience of driving through Cairo had left her spellbound. It was a colourful city with its busyness, noises and smells of spices and there were street markets where business went on at a frantic pace. The people flocked everywhere in eastern style clothes and some western too. Alan had told her that many British had spent time here during the war, just as he had too. Perhaps her father had driven through these streets as well but she did not know for sure. She drank in every sight and every sound until they reached the hotel where they would stay the night before travelling on by taxi for a few hours until they reached their destination.

The hotel was fairly basic but it was clean and the food was reputed to be quite good. Scarlett was fascinated by everything but she was tired and the heat was becoming too much to endure. Above them in the hotel lobby a fan whirred trying to do its best to keep the interior of the building cool. Scarlett longed to sleep but her mind was a whirr of emotions and the sights that she had seen. Tomorrow would be the first time that she would meet her father. The mere thought made her smile. At least it was the nearest she would ever get to him. The thought also gave her a pain right in her chest. It was all too emotional for words.

***

The next day they set out on their journey to El Alamein. Alan knew that he had to organize the visit as well as he could for this was not England. The locals took their time over things especially in these temperatures. Also Scarlett did not quite understand what awaited her however much he had tried to explain. The journey was tinged with long silences as each was wrapped up in their own thoughts. Alan had never thought he would travel here again. He had said his 'goodbyes' to his brother long ago but now he knew it was his duty to take Jack's daughter to do the same before allowing his brother to rest in peace in such a well-cared for place.

Scarlett watched the passing scenery, dusty and dry, mile upon mile of sand dunes with little greenery but her thoughts were active, as she felt nervous to be this near to her father. This was the culmination of all those years wanting to know him ever since her mother had placed the DSO into her hands at five years old, when the questions had first started forming. Her mother had not had all the answers, not because she wished to hide anything but simply because Jack had been an enigma to her too. Occasionally she glanced across at Alan and they exchanged smiles before returning to their own thoughts. The driver drove erratically lifting his hands from the steering wheel in exasperation at the incompetence of other drivers and filling his passengers with apprehension wondering if they would reach journey's end in one piece. But somehow they did.

As Scarlett and Alan read the statistics about the battle it moved them deeply seeing how many soldiers had given their lives from Britain and the Commonwealth and beyond. It had been an incredible sacrifice they had made for a free world. As they followed the paths through the line of graves so beautifully kept by the war graves commission Scarlett began to weep for the lost lives of these young men who would never see their homeland again. And it was now that she had real understanding for Piers and others like him who did not want to set foot outside their native country again. They had given of themselves thoroughly and were empty inside not wishing to tell their loved ones what they had seen or experienced. Suddenly there he was, Private Jack Carson, posthumously awarded the DSO for gallantry above and beyond…. Scarlett could not read any more for her eyes were thick with tears. Alan Carson took her hand and held it tightly in his as his emotions stirred within him as they had done the first time he had stood in the same spot. Scarlett did not want to leave him there but he had lain there for more than twenty years surrounded by his brothers in arms. It was a peaceful, a much loved place to lie for eternity. She lifted her eyes and saw other visitors doing the same, looking for their dead family and her heart went out to them. Suddenly she put her hand into her handbag bringing out a photograph attached to a small stick. Alan watched her but said nothing, just touched at what she was about to do. It was a photograph of herself and her mother. On the reverse side she had written the words, 'For you, Daddy, with as much love as we can give. With our love Scarlett and Thea.'

Scarlett had not mentioned this to Thea, but she had been his wife, however short the time they had spent together. She had no feelings of guilt. She bent down and stuck the stick into the dusty ground. Standing back she observed her own handiwork, watching her image waft in the gentle breeze alleviating just a little of the heat of the day.

Looking at Alan she said, 'Can you take me back now?'

'Sure?' He asked observing her red eyes and wobbling chin.

'Sure,' she said as she moved away allowing herself one more glance behind her.

'Good bye, Daddy,' she said to herself, 'sleep tight.' She blew him a kiss and walked bravely on. Alan Carson noted all this, fervently wishing that Jack had known his daughter and how very proud he would have been of her indeed. The last few hours had taken him on an emotional journey that he thought he would never make again. Catching up with Scarlett he tucked her arm under his before they walked on, never glancing back as it was all too painful to contemplate.

***

When Scarlett and Alan returned to the hotel in Cairo it was dusk. They were emotionally weary from their experiences and bone tired from the travelling on a hot day. Scarlett had declared that she was not hungry and just wanted to go and rest. Alan understood how the girl felt and made no comment. He was used to eating alone in the places he had travelled to over time and he said nothing other than to wish her a good rest and he would see her early at breakfast before they were due to fly back to Blighty. He kissed her temple, a rush of true affection passing through him. She smiled at him tiredly and then turning to pass the reception desk on her way to her bedroom she heard a voice call her in broken English.

Glancing up she saw a man shaking a piece of paper wildly at her.

'Telex, missy,' he said showing a mouth full of gleaming white teeth.

She took it from him showing no curiosity in its contents. Weariness was etched across her face as she climbed the stairs to her room.

Chapter 64

Thea was inconsolable. She had reached London as soon as she could after hearing the news. She had thrown clothes into a suitcase haphazardly and made plans for the nursery staff to look after Amelia until her return. She was to be found at the Town house if anyone needed to make contact. Amelia was bewildered as she watched her mother's sudden departure. She had never before witnessed her mother in a heightened state of anxiety but despite her six years she kept her own feelings to herself until her mother was out of sight but then the waterfall fell as nanny tried to placate her.

'Mummy, will be back before too long. You will see.'

'Where's my daddy then?' Amelia shouted at the staff. They remained mutely silent on that question as they glanced at each other.

'Let's go and see Miss Dorkings in the school room, shall we,' Nanny said taking her firmly by the hand and leading her back up the stairs to the nursery part of the house. Distraction was always the best tactic Nanny felt in a time of crisis and it was certainly one of those times. Her heart had gone out to the countess. She was somebody the whole staff cared for deeply.

A local taxi had taken Thea to Worcester and from there she caught the London train. Later, when she thought back on that journey, she wondered how she had kept herself together but somehow she had. A black London cab drove her to the hospital. The cabbie had tried to make conversation but gave it up as futile when he saw how tense his passenger looked, her teeth clenched together and her eyes looking red raw as she continued to maintain the stiff upper lip. At the hospital she almost ran up the steps to find her husband. She wondered if he was still alive. Her thoughts drifted to James Devine, the man she had believed to be her father but turned out to be Piers.' He had died of a heart attack. Did it run in the family?

As she followed the signs she turned into the private wing where she saw a reception desk and stopped. The nurse looking up from perusing papers, smiled and observing the agitation on the woman's face said kindly, 'Can I help you?'

'Thea Devine,' she said, her words coming out in a whisper, 'Is he…?'

The voice in the nurse's head supplied the missing word 'dead' but brightly she said, 'The doctor is with him now, Lady Devine. If you just wait here I will see if the doctor will see you.'

Thea sank down onto the bench, only too relieved to take the weight from her legs. He was still alive then. All the way to London she had wondered if he would survive, if she would see him again. Surely, they deserved more time together. They were not old. Please God and the thoughts travelled round in her head like a carousel. Somehow she could not put her foot down to stop the merry-go-round in her head. She heard a door open and close and she stood up in expectation but it was just a nurse scuttling by on her daily routine. She offered Thea a sympathetic look but disappeared through glass doors. Thea slid down onto the seat, heart pounding ready to wait again.

This time the door opened again and a man in a white coat walked towards her. He stretched out his hand but his face remained impassive. 'Lady Devine....'

'How is he?' She asked thinking the worst.

'Stable for the moment but it has been touch and go. He is not out of the woods yet. He won't be for quite some time I'm afraid.'

For a moment Thea allowed herself to draw breath and hope. While there was hope.... Her thoughts stopped as she heard the Doctor continue, 'He is in an induced coma so don't be too alarmed. There are a lot of tubes and drips attached to him. It looks worse than it actually is. The coma will give him time to rest and heal. Sit with him and even talk to him but he does need quiet and rest.'

Thea followed the doctor into the private ward where Piers lay looking pale and frail, far from the robust man she knew striding around Westborough, a picture of health and energy. She sat on the chair next to him holding his limp hand in her own. For the first time ever she did not know what to say to him. Some of the machinery bleeped at intervals. Nurses were in and out checking on him and then would scuttle away without a word. What was there to say and they saw such happenings as a regular event.

Her thoughts lingered on the string of events which had led her here. The telephone had gone during the early hours when Thea was sound asleep. She had been woken by the bedside telephone ringing. Sleep was forgotten as she picked up the receiver. Her mind was all over the place wondering if it was Scarlett out in Cairo. She had worried about her going. It seemed so far away.

But a voice that Thea knew but could not place spoke to her.

'Lady Devine, it's Selma from the Town House.' Thea knew immediately that it was Piers for he was staying there. The House had had late night sittings and he had felt that he should be there.

'What is it?' She could feel her throat constrict with emotion.

'His lordship has been taken to hospital with a suspected heart attack. I am so sorry, Lady Devine.'

'I will get there as soon as I can,' she said sounding more in control than she felt. 'Is he...?'

'He seems to be holding his own. I will make the place ready for you.' The line went dead but Thea stood and held the telephone in her hand for what seemed minutes before she galvanized herself into action.

There was no sleep to be had now. There were things to organize, the family to be told. Telegrams were sent to the three oldest girls. Telephone calls were put through to the younger Devines' schools. It was a whirlwind of activity which kept her in control of her own emotions. Once the girls were home she could transfer family responsibility to them and be able to concentrate on Piers. Not particularly religious, Thea prayed harder than she had done for years and she still found that she was doing it now as she looked into her husband's ghostly face. Tightening the grip on his hand, she gently chided him for not looking after himself.

The door opened and the same doctor entered. He checked Piers and nodded at Thea.

'No change,' he mouthed and he was gone before Thea had the presence of mind to ask the questions that were beginning to formulate in her mind.

She felt deeply afraid and wished that her children were here. She thought about Clarissa and how stoic the old woman would have been. That gave her a modicum of courage as she tightened her grip on Piers' hand and bent over him to kiss him.

'I love you,' she whispered, 'don't leave me. Ever.'

The door opened but she hardly noticed. She had no idea what time of day it was but suddenly looking up she saw that darkness had closed in on them. How had that happened?

'Mama,' a voice whispered and there stood Scarlett. I came as soon as I could.'

They embraced tears flooding their eyes. Now Thea felt that she could let go as the sobs engulfed her shaking her slight body as Scarlett held her.

'I'll stay with Papa. You go and find something to eat. You look done in.'

But she shook her head, 'I can't leave him.'

'You must eat. You have got to stay strong.'

Thea did as she was told as Scarlett sat in the vacated chair talking to Piers in soft tones, tempting him to get well for all their sakes. It struck her deeply that she had wept at her own father's grave, only hours ago, a man she had never known in the flesh but this was the man who had cared for her through most of her childhood into her adulthood as if he had been her natural father. She knew that he was a complex man who had found it hard to relate to these older children but time had healed and love had been at the forefront of their relationship in latter years. She looked at the shell of a man and her heart twisted in the fear of losing him. He was her father in every way but name and that showed no disrespect to the man lying in a faraway grave. She wept holding his hand as she urged him to return to them from that faraway place that he was inhabiting.

***

The situation was endless. There appeared little change. All the children had arrived and were all living at the Town House. Maudie had flown in from the United States, this time without Brad. He had protested but she wanted to be on her own with her family. This was not a time when she needed him but her family needed her. Jane had taken charge travelling to London with the young Devines. They appeared bemused by the situation for their parents had always been there for them. After seeing their father they thought he was going to die. In a moment alone with Thea Harry had cried bitterly and she had to be strong for them all.

'I don't feel ready to become an Earl,' he said, his eyes red from crying.

Thea stroked his hair as she had done as a young child. 'Ssh,' she soothed but he was only echoing her own thoughts. She did not know how she would cope if anything happened to Piers but Clarissa seemed to sit on her shoulder like a guardian angel and whisper in her ear.

'Remember how you coped in the war. You can do it again.'

The days dragged by without change. The doctors would not predict what would happen. It all seemed in the hands of the gods. Thea was tired but she had resisted the pressure to go home to rest. A bed was set up in Piers' room where she slept fitfully. When she could Scarlett made her mother go home telling her that they all needed her as well as Piers. Reluctantly she took the advice sleeping like the dead until she rose to return to Piers' side and begin the whole process once more.

But one morning she returned to the hospital.

The young nurse on the desk waylaid her. 'Please don't go in. The doctor is with your husband.'

Thea sank down onto the seat in the corridor and her heart sank with her.

'What was happening?' She did not want to think. Then the doctor walked towards her, his face was impassive. She wondered why she could not read what was in her mind.

'You can go in now', he said and then turned away.

She ran. She had to know. And when she pushed open the door she saw him. There he was awake, weak but he had returned to the land of the living. His eyes had been focused on the door and when he saw her he smiled his lopsided smile which she had loved for so long. Walking up to him, she smiled and took his hand, covering it with kisses.

'Hello,' she said, 'I have missed you.' She did not talk for long because he was beginning to fall asleep again but suddenly there was hope in her heart.

The door of the room opened and a nurse said sotto voce, 'The doctor is waiting outside for you.'

This time the doctor smiled at her. 'I think that he will make it now, but there must be changes to his way of life. We will discuss that when he is ready to leave hospital but that won't be for a while yet.'

Tears of happiness filled her eyes. 'Thank you, Doctor, for everything', she said before returning to his room, her heart lighter than it had been in a very long time.

Epilogue
Six Months Later

Thea sat at her desk in her sitting room writing Christmas cards. It was that time of year again. She looked up and noticed that the light was fading outside. Abandoning her task for the day, she walked to the fire and noticed that it had burnt low. Throwing logs on, she sat in her favourite chair watching the flames curl, flicker and nibble until the fire roared into life bringing warmth to the room. The peace and solitude was welcome before Christmas came with a vengeance. This Christmas was going to be one of thanksgiving for the whole family. There were to be no guests, just themselves.

She reflected on past months. They had taken their toll but somehow they had pulled through, all of them, gathering an inner strength they had not believed possible. Piers had survived his ordeal but it had been touch and go for a few weeks. Thea had remained in London during his hospitalization but eventually he was brought home in a private ambulance to recuperate. The doctors, pleased with his progress, had stipulated a change of lifestyle. They had not fully known what had caused it. Perhaps it was genetic or it could have been stress or even a combination of things. But whatever, things had to change and change they had. Thea had seen to that.

The greatest change had been his retirement from politics. He had made that decision himself and as he made a full recovery he pottered on the estate becoming physically fitter and mentally more relaxed but was wise enough to call it a day when he grew too tired. The time at home with Thea and Amelia without pressure had been cathartic. Thea, his nurse and gaoler as he would refer to her, had also been his salvation and their relationship had grown ever closer if that had been at all possible. Even Amelia had flourished by spending more time with her father. She had felt abandoned by her parents during Thea's time in London and had become clingy in the weeks following their return to Westborough. But now it was back to normal for an excited six year old with only Christmas on her mind.

When Piers was in hospital, the family had rallied, a supportive group, who had been united in their grief. The three oldest girls, who remembered the darker side of life when they had felt unloved by the father whose affection they had craved more than anything had spent time alone with Piers when Thea needed to rest. These had become the best times. They had laughed with him about those days when they had misbehaved and driven him to distraction. They talked more seriously about their adult lives and their successes and desires for the future but most of all it was about the affection they felt for him and the rest of the family which had brought tears to his eyes. They all treasured the bond that they never felt would be there. They held his hand and talked while Piers relished every moment, just thankful that he had made it through.

Scarlett was the one who surprised them the most. Her journey to find Jack had been cathartic. She had stayed in touch with her new family, was grateful to them for accepting her into their lives but it was Piers' flirtation with near death, which had grounded her more than anything. Jack had been dead for a long time and Piers was a constant in her life and would continue to be. She had told Piers the story of her journey to Egypt and the emotional and rocky road she had travelled. But now she had been duty bound to tell him how she felt about him as her father and the constant in her life.

'You will always be my daughter, Scarlett, as much as the others,' he had said. They had both cried together. Tears came easily these days, tears of happiness. Emotions were always near the surface but only good ones. The fear for his health had receded just a little.

In the past few months Scarlett had moved forward with her life. She had taken up her job at the lawyers' firm in London and was learning her craft and loving it. And for the first time she had someone special in her life but it was early days. There was no hurry in the marriage stakes.

But life was moving on for all of them. Next year would see the marriage of Maudie and Brad, in an interlude from their hectic musical careers. These days they were based in New York but they would make it home for Christmas. In the Spring Piers, Thea and Amelia would travel to New York to meet Brad's family before the wedding in the summer at Westborough.

Jane was the only one not to make it home for Christmas. She had informed them crossly that she was pregnant again but Thea felt that she was secretly pleased. Jane had found her own niche in life as a wife, mother and future Countess. Thea secretly thought that there was no better life than being a wife and mother despite all the highs and lows that went with it.

And as for the young Devines they were progressing with their academic lives on the way to independence. Despite all the upset of the summer, Harry had acquired the grades that had taken him up to Cambridge to read politics and law. He had a new maturity about him and was anxious to learn about his future inheritance. But Thea still offered up a prayer to the Almighty that it would not be too soon.

The door opened into her sitting room revealing Piers trailing Amelia by the hand in his wake. He smiled at her before closing the door. Thea had noticed their brightly coloured cheeks from their walk but now that it was dark they came to find her as they did most days.

'Mama,' shouted Amelia and ran to her mother to cuddle close.

'I will go and order tea,' Piers said smiling at his wife. He looked at her for a short moment counting his blessings for the woman he had loved for more than thirty years.

He closed the door quietly to shouts of 'Yummy.'

Smiling again he thanked God for his new life. Clarrisa in her wisdom had often said there was a reason for everything and had she not been the wisest woman on the planet? With that thought in his mind he went in search of the tea and cakes before it went completely out of his mind.